GENERATION 8

GENERATION 8

HEATHER COMINA

Matador
Unit E2 Airfield Business Park,
Harrison Road, Market Harborough,
Leicestershire. LE16 7UL
Tel: 0116 2792299
Email: books@troubador.co.uk
Web: www.troubador.co.uk/matador
Twitter: @matadorbooks

ISBN 978 1803136 998

British Library Cataloguing in Publication Data.
A catalogue record for this book is available from the British Library.

Printed and bound in Great Britain by 4edge Limited
Typeset in 11pt Minion Pro by Troubador Publishing Ltd, Leicester, UK

Matador is an imprint of Troubador Publishing Ltd

For Katherine & Lauren

PART 1
FALLING APART

In the corner of a field stands a tree. It is nearing the close of its time gracing the verge of the meadow, where it has hosted many generations of short-lived things. It is a thing of haphazard beauty, of riven bark and broken branches. Twisting roots delve into the banks of what was once a tumbling brook. Now, just a trickle running dry each summer. Soon it will share one last winter with us before, with rotten trunk, it succumbs to the roaring gusts of an easterly storm.

CHAPTER 1
THE DAY

"Ladies and gentlemen, the captain is about to switch on the seatbelt signs, please return to your seats and prepare for landing."

Lilly stood up and stretched, releasing the tension in her back from crouching down, counting the remaining cans of drink in the trolley.

"Haven't you finished that yet? We'll be landing in 20 minutes, and you know Karen will have your hide if the paperwork's not ready," chided Paul, the assistant purser.

Lilly pulled a tight-lipped smile to acknowledge his encouragement and rummaged in her pocket to fish out a pen before sitting down to check the logs. Just 20 minutes, and they would be on the ground and a step closer to a weekend of kicking back and relaxing. She loved her job, but after back-to-back long-haul flights between London and Shanghai she was ready for a break.

"Cabin crew seats for landing."

She strapped in, grinning at Megan in the seat opposite.

"Almost party time," enthused Megan.

"Yeah, I can't wait! Karen is such a slave driver; I've hardly stopped all flight."

"Tell me about it! So, are you on turn around or do you get a proper break?"

"Flying out to Hong Kong on Monday, so just a short one but should be able to get in a club or two tomorrow night. What about you?"

"Same, heading out to Singapore."

"Ooh you lucky thing, I've not been there yet."

A jolt and sideways lurch followed by the roar of engines throttling into reverse.

"Ladies and gentlemen, welcome to London. Please remain seated…"

"Right here we go how long until someone gets up?"

"I'll give it twenty seconds…"

"…eighteen, wow close, first drinks are on you!" Lilly grinned.

"Doors to manual and cross check."

"That's my cue, see you on the other side," said Megan as she unclipped and moved forward to adjust the doors to the accompaniment of hundreds of beeps and pings as everyone re-connected with the outside world.

Lilly's phone buzzed but she didn't have time to look at it before Paul was back demanding the log files and checking all the stowage in the galley area.

"Hmm, not bad Lilly. Might even pass inspection this time."

Faint praise indeed! She pulled a face as he turned to go and winked at the little girl standing in the aisle making her giggle. The aircraft slowly emptied, leaving the crew to retrieve their bags and coats before stepping out into the cool drizzle of a Thursday evening at Heathrow. Lilly grimaced, why did she always seem to get the short straw and end up on a remote stand? Her pocket started to vibrate, and she juggled with her bags to reach her phone as she stepped onto the bus.

"Hi Fi," she sighed.

"Do you ever read your messages?"

"Sorry, you know how it is, can't possibly be late with the logfiles!"

"Enough said. Listen, are you heading straight home tonight?"

"Probably, to be honest I'm totally knackered."

"Me too, I thought we might share a cab?"

"Okay, I'll meet you at the usual place then."

"Great! Love you babes," replied Fi hanging up and leaving Lilly to contemplate the dimly lit, oil-slicked tarmac as she waited for the bus to pull away.

Half an hour later, their taxi was battling through the evening traffic vying for a place on the A4, as they crawled towards Hammersmith.

"Why I thought it was a good idea to get a flat near Shepherd's Bush I'll never know," muttered Lilly.

"You know why. It's a cool place to live, and sooo close to all the action," teased Fi. "Lills is it okay if I crash at yours tonight? I don't think I can face slogging across London on the tube."

"Sure, so long as you promise not to snore!"

"Wow, cheeky! For that I think you will be buying the drinks tomorrow evening."

Lilly groaned, she always ended up buying the drinks on a night out with Fi. A great friend, who never seemed to have any money, but made up for it with witty jokes and crazy dancing.

"Okay, I'm off now. I'll see you at eight outside Maggie's bar. We can grab a bite before we dance!" shouted Fi through the bathroom door.

"Okay," Lilly replied settling back into the luxurious foam bath and juggling the rubber duck with her toes. She closed her eyes. "Peace at last," she whispered to herself. Except it only lasted about thirty seconds before Fi was banging on the door and shouting.

"Lills you need to come and see this… I don't believe it. I don't fucking believe it! The bastards, the utter bastards!"

Wow thought Lilly. This had to be important, Fi didn't usually use such colourful language. Soapy and dripping she emerged from the bathroom wrapped in a towel to find Fi sitting on the edge of the bed in tears. She looked up from her phone, agony in her eyes.

"They're suspending all flights. We have to go into HQ. We, we might not have a job anymore," she wailed.

"What? Slow down! What on earth are you talking about?"

Fi just looked at her and broke down into tears again. Lilly wrestled the phone out of her hand and read the message.

To all airline employees,

With immediate effect, all flights in Asia have been grounded. Government restrictions are now in place to limit the spread of the Covid-19 virus. It is important that you attend a staff briefing this afternoon to discuss the future of your employment...

Lilly's eyes began to blur with tears as she set the phone down. She and Fi sat together, sobbing, and staring at the wall. Suddenly life felt like it was coming apart at the seams.

"Come on! We are going to be late. I don't know why you never wear sensible shoes!" moaned Lilly as she and Fi bustled their way through the busy foyer at airline HQ.

"Hold the lift!" she shouted.

"I'm coming, I'm coming! Bloody security guard, I am sure he does that deliberately," complained Fi as she struggled to stuff things back in her bag whilst simultaneously wrestling her way back into her coat. The lift was crowded with other airline employees all looking long-faced. No one said a word.

The meeting room was already packed full, they had to stand in the aisle.

"Totally against fire regs I'm sure but who gives a shit anyway!" muttered the man wedged in next to Lilly.

"Shh! They're about to start," she hissed.

The head of HR stood up and shuffled his crumpled papers. He was visibly shaking, and his voice quavered as he started to speak.

"Th, thank you all for coming...

...I, I wish we could be getting together under better circumstances. As, as you are aware, we are in the throes of a global pandemic and, and urgent measures have had to be taken to safeguard us, us all..." he stammered.

"Get on with it!" shouted someone from the back.

"No need to be rude! I'll skip to the crux of it then..." he responded, his face colouring.

"All flights to Asia have been grounded for the foreseeable future. It is likely that flights to other regions will also be affected but we do not yet know to what extent. As a result, we have been forced to make some difficult decisions. To ensure the continuity of the airline we have no choice but to let some of you go..."

Lilly gasped and looked round at Fi. The room had erupted into such a commotion she could barely hear what was being said.

"If we can please stay calm! The news is not all bad. Some of you, those with more than two years of service, will be transferred to other roles. The rest, I am afraid, we will have to let you go with one months' pay. These changes will take effect as of Monday; you will each receive an email with further details..."

Lilly slumped to the floor. She had not yet completed her second year of service; she was out of a job. Looking round she saw Fi pumping the air with her fist and high fiving her neighbour; she had worked for the airline for three years and would keep her job, for now at least.

"Oh, don't look so glum Lills baby! You will find something else, talented girl like you. Let's go to the pub and get totally pissed. You never know we might even pull!"

"Jesus Fi is that all you ever think about?" spat Lilly in

reply. Her chest felt tight and constricted; this had to be absolutely the worst day of her life. Maybe even worse than the day she lost her Mum. *No perhaps not that bad*, she thought.

Feeling utterly dejected, she looked up at Fi. "Okay then, it's not like I have anything better to do!" Hopefully a few drinks would help to dull the pain.

CHAPTER 2

ABANDONED

A long with half the airline's workforce they had descended on the nearest bar in Soho. After a considerable number of drinks Lilly was feeling none too steady on her feet. She propped herself on a barstool and watched Fi doing her usual crazy dance routine with a guy called Ralf.

"Come on and dance!" shouted Fi but Lilly just shook her head. If she did anything more than sit, she would probably be sick. Forcing back tears and trying to smile convincingly she waved Fi off.

"It's OK. You go and have fun," she slurred.

"Oh, don't be like that. Come on, leave worrying until tomorrow, things will work out!" said Fi grabbing her arm and trying to drag her onto the dance floor.

"No really, I'm OK here thanks," shouted Lilly. She was

becoming increasingly frustrated. How typical of Fi, carrying on having a good time, not caring about anyone else.

Half an hour later Fi and Ralf were busy groping each other in a corner and Lilly was tired of staring at the chaos around her; of being a spectator at somebody else's show. She ordered another scotch.

"Are you sure you haven't had enough love?" asked the barman. He was right she probably had. She turned and noticed Fi and Ralf slinking past with their coats.

"Oh, are we off then?" she asked.

"Well Ralf and I are heading back to his place; you know…" said Fi pulling the face she always pulled when she knew that she was letting Lilly down but was going to do it anyway.

Lilly was left to stare at their backs as they shuffled through the crowd on their way to the door. She could barely face the idea of getting a cab home, but it was raining and walking to the nearest tube station was even less appealing.

Slowly, Lilly emerged through layers of fog which clouded her senses. A droning noise continued unabated. Confused, she pushed wisps of auburn hair from her eyes, the room steadily came into focus. She was not on a plane; she was lying fully clothed on her bed with one remaining shoe dangling precariously from the tip of her toe. Much to her relief the droning noise ceased but was followed shortly by a ping; it was her phone ringing not the sound of aircraft engines as she had originally thought. But where was her phone? Cautiously she propped herself up on one elbow, her head started to spin, and the feeling was not improved by closing her eyes. Slowly she drew herself into a sitting position; she had the mother of all hangovers. Easing herself up she took a few tentative steps towards the bathroom. Just as she reached the door the droning noise started up again; she ignored it and focused all her attention on not being sick before she reached the toilet.

Half an hour later she was starting to feel a little more human. The glass of water and some pain killers were beginning to have a positive effect. Her memories from last night were still a little vague; the last thing she remembered was watching Fi and the guy she had pulled leave the bar. Oh, what was his name? Not that it mattered, she was pretty sure she wouldn't be seeing him again, not with Fi's track record. Feeling quite wretched she flopped down on the bed and was just contemplating going back to sleep when the droning started again; someone really wanted to get hold of her. The sound seemed to be coming from beneath the pile of bedding which had slipped onto the floor. Just as she was rummaging in her coat pocket it stopped again and was followed by another angry ping as the caller left a message. Looking at the screen she realised she had missed six calls, all from the same person: Simon, the airline colleague who owned the flat which she was subletting whilst he was based in the US. What could he want? He was meant to be in Boston. Selecting "play" she listened.

> *Lilly my love, I wish you would just pick up the bloody phone! I really need to speak to you, it's urgent. Call me back when you get this darling!*

Despite the "love" and "darling" Simon sounded totally pissed off. She hit the "call back" option. After a long delay the phone started to purr.

"Finally, I have been trying to get hold of you for hours!" barked Simon. But before she could say anything he pressed on. "Listen my love, I am on my way home. They are shutting down the American routes and I need to fly back before they lock down everything. I don't want to be stranded over here. So, the thing is, Lilly my love, I am going to need you to find somewhere else to live. I have been told I will need to quarantine when I get back and well the flat just isn't big enough for the two of us."

"Hold on a minute! You want me to move out?" spluttered Lilly, she couldn't believe her ears.

"Yes darling, I know it puts you in a bit of a bind but well there it is, can't be helped."

"But I have paid up until the end of next month, you can't just kick me out."

"I know it seems harsh darling; I'll pay you back the rent of course."

Lilly knew she didn't have a leg to stand on. She was only subletting from Simon on a casual month by month basis. He had every right to want his flat back.

"OK, so when are you going to need me out by?"

"Well now there is the rub my darling. It's going to be rather short notice I'm afraid as I expect to be back on Sunday evening."

"What! But that's tomorrow; you have to be kidding!" suddenly she felt flushed and very angry. There was no way she could find somewhere else to live that quickly.

"Calm down darling; you'll think of something, resourceful lass like you."

"Oh, don't be such a patronising shit!" spat Lilly. Boiling with rage she cut the call and threw her phone across the room. She sank to the floor sobbing. Feeling abandoned last night was nothing compared to this. She cried for so long that her bed clothes became sodden with tears, she turned and stared at the ceiling, her mind as blank as the paintwork.

After a while, her little inner voice of resilience told her that it would be okay. She couldn't just sit there she had to get up and get on with it. With her hangover slowly receding she felt a little better. A feeling which was improved further by strong coffee and toast with jam. Having showered and dressed she felt almost human again.

So, who to call first? She thought to herself. The obvious answer was Fi. Hitting speed dial, she called Fi's mobile. It went straight to voicemail.

"Hi Fi, can you call me back as soon as you get this, please." Lilly didn't like leaving messages, it always made her feel unimportant. Hopefully Fi would get back to her soon. She glanced at the clock; it was three in the afternoon. Surely Fi couldn't still be asleep!

The next two hours were filled with a mixture of clock watching and packing. Most of the stuff in the flat belonged to Simon; Lilly just had her clothes, toiletries, make-up, and a few odds and ends. She didn't really own a lot, being always on the move she had never felt the need to accumulate much. Looking round she spotted her iPad sticking out from between two sofa cushions. "Shit, I almost forgot that," she said to herself starting to feel a little flustered. "Now where is the charger? Oh, and my phone charger." She could feel the little voice of judgement creeping in. *You never have been terribly organised, have you? I don't know how you can be an airline steward. Surely, they have to be much more meticulous...* The voice sounded just like her stepmother.

Five thirty and still no call back from Fi. Lilly was starting to feel anxious. She tried her number again and again it went straight to voicemail. "Arghh!" she breathed, her frustration building. She made a start with sorting the kitchen although she couldn't really be bothered. *Sod Simon!* She thought. *He can sort the food out himself, he'll be glad of something to eat anyway.* Although she wasn't entirely sure that would include the mouldy lump of cheese and the half-eaten can of beans in the fridge. Just as she was contemplating whether to empty the bin, her phone rang.

"Lills baby! Sorry I only just got your message. My phone had run out of charge, and I was a bit too busy with Ralf to notice until now," sniggered Fi. "So, what's so urgent?"

"Simon called me, he needs the flat back, I need to move out right away, I'm almost packed, I was wondering if I could crash at yours for a few days until I can sort something out..." Lilly gabbled, barely pausing for breath.

"Slow down babes, what are you talking about? Isn't Simon in Boston?"

"Yes, he is, but he is coming home. He wants to beat the lockdown and will need to quarantine so I have to be out by Sunday evening."

"Wow, talk about short notice!"

"So, I need somewhere to go. Can I come over to yours?" Lilly asked in a pleading tone. She knew Fi wouldn't be thrilled as Lilly was bound to "cramp her style" as she would put it.

"Oh, I am sorry babe but no can do. You know I've only got one room."

"But what about the couch?"

"Look, I'm sorry babes but with lockdown coming and as we are meant to be quarantining it just won't work."

"But Fi, please. I don't have anyone else I can ask."

"What about your dad? He has that fancy place in Croydon, I'm sure he would have room."

Lilly was just about to answer when she heard a man's voice in the background.

"Who is that?" she demanded.

"Oh, just Ralf. He has such manly urges, wants me to come back to bed," giggled Fi.

"How can you be so unfeeling? I thought we were friends Fi. Clearly I am less important to you than your precious love life!"

"Oh, don't get snippy, just because you didn't pull last night."

Lilly put the phone down. She would give Fi a few minutes to get her priorities straight and then call her again. Deep down she hoped Fi would call her back first.

Thirty minutes later Lilly gave in and dialled Fi's number. When it went straight to voicemail, she realised that it wasn't worth leaving a message.

"Leave it dear, we are in the middle of dinner. Whoever it is will leave a message. You can call back later."

Lilly's father settled back into his seat. There was no point in antagonising his wife, she was already in a crabby mood because the Spanish nanny had handed in her notice that morning. It was not until nearly nine o'clock that he was able to sneak into the study and retrieve his phone. The message was from his daughter Lilly. Before he had a chance to listen his wife was at his shoulder.

"Well, who was it then?" she griped.

"Lilly."

"Hmm, wonder what she wants, can't be good. She is always looking for handouts and you are far too soft on her."

"Shh! Let me listen…"

Hi Dad, its Lilly. I know I'm probably interrupting Sunday dinner, but I need your help. Could you please ring me back as soon as you get this? He hit the "dial back" option.

"I told you she wants something…"

"Shh! It's ringing…"

"Oh Dad, thank goodness. I was beginning to wonder if you had got my message…"

"Put it on speaker, I can't hear what she is saying," interrupted his wife.

"Just putting you on speaker, hang on…"

Oh great! thought Lilly to herself, *the she-wolf is on the line; this will be fun…*

"There we are, so what seems to be the trouble love?"

"I need to ask you a favour Dad. I have to move out of my flat at short notice and I was wondering if I could stay with you until I can find something else?" said Lilly, her fingers tightly crossed.

"Well, I'm not sure love, when would you need to move? We don't have much space what with the twins and nanny…" he said, trying to stall for time.

"Hmm, well that's just it. I have to be out by tomorrow evening; I know that is really short notice but…"

"Short notice!" shrieked her stepmother. "It's bloody ridiculous if you ask me. Out of the question totally out of the question!" she carried on.

"Can I please speak to my father!" shouted Lilly exasperated by the rudeness of her stepmother but not at all surprised.

"I think I'm going to have to call you back love," he said and put the phone down before his wife could say anything further.

He turned to her balefully, knowing full well that this was an argument that he was not going to win. His second wife hated Lilly and he knew that Lilly was aware of it; she must have been really desperate to have asked.

"Look before you get into a complete funk can we please discuss this rationally?" he said sternly. "I realise she won't be able to stay here but perhaps we can help find her somewhere."

"Well, what about a hotel? Surely that would be an option."

"Hmm, we could suggest it but I'm not sure Lilly would be able to afford it for long, you know she never seems to have much money."

"Yes, well we are not offering to pay, if that's what you are thinking!" she retorted. "I know, what about those two grandparents of hers? They haven't lifted a finger since Caroline died."

"Well, I guess I could suggest that, although I am not sure how they are getting on these days."

"Nonsense, they have got plenty of room on that farm of theirs. Bit of country air will do Lilly good."

"OK, OK, I'll call her back then," he hit the re-dial button and the phone barely rang before Lilly picked up.

"Hi Dad, so what do you think? Can I come?" she said hopefully but expecting the worst.

"I'm sorry love but we really don't have the room. Don't worry though, we had an idea. What about your grandparents? They have plenty of room and you always got on well with them…"

Lilly was speechless. She hadn't seen her grandparents since her mother's funeral when she was twelve, that was nearly ten years ago. Why on earth would she want to stay with them on their farm in the middle of nowhere.

"Lilly, are you still there?"

"Yes, yes Dad, I'm still here," she muttered with a resigned tone. "Can you give me their number then?"

"Hmm, yes, I think I have it somewhere. I'll have to call you back in a minute."

"Oh, just text it to me Dad, I don't want to put you to any more trouble," she hung up. Ten minutes later she received a text with a number for her grandparents. She sat on the end of the bed staring out of the rain-streaked window at the lights over Shepherd's Bush feeling utterly numb and totally abandoned. It was getting late; she would have to muster the courage to call them soon.

CHAPTER 3
LAST RESORT

"Who was it dear? Must have been urgent calling this late."

"It was Lilly, she was in a terrible state poor love."

"Gosh, she must be in a fix if she is calling us. I can't think of the last time we spoke to her, and we didn't even get a card last Christmas."

"Oh now, don't be unkind dear. You know how that dreadful woman filled her head with silly ideas about us after Caroline passed away. It's no wonder we lost touch."

"Anyway, what was it that she wanted?"

"Well, she wanted to know if she can come to stay with us for a while. I couldn't understand everything she said she was sobbing too much. Something about having lost her job with the airline and being kicked out of her flat all because of this Covid business."

"Hmm, yes I had wondered about Lilly when I heard they were stopping the flights from Asia. So, when does she need to move?"

"Well, that's just it dear, she said she needs to come tomorrow. Oh, and something about having to quarantine from us for the first two weeks in case she's got it."

"Tomorrow! Where on earth are we going to put her?"

"Well, I wondered about the attic. There's plenty of room up there and she will have her own bathroom."

"I expect that will work. It's a bit cluttered though."

"You'll have plenty of time to clear it up before you go and fetch her from the station tomorrow."

"Oh, I will, will I?" grumbled Gramps as he settled down into bed and turned out the lamp.

"Don't be such a grouchy old thing. I am quite looking forward to getting to know our granddaughter again after all these years," said Oma snuggling up and kissing his cheek.

"Goodnight, dear," he sighed. If Lilly was anything like her mother had been, he was in for a whole load of extra trouble. He had never been able to resist those pleading eyes.

Sunday morning had passed in a blur. She had finished packing and found a courier service that would be able to take her boxes as long as she could get them to a drop-off point by midday. That was in half an hour, and she was already in the taxi heading to the station.

"Could you stop here and wait for me?" she said to the driver as they neared the courier depot. She managed to pull the first box off the back seat but the second caught on the door and she almost dropped it.

"Shit!" she hissed through gritted teeth, holding back tears of frustration.

"Let me help you with those Miss," said the kindly cabbie, and he carried them over to the counter for her.

"Thank you, you are very kind."

"Now, Paddington, wasn't it?" he said as they pulled out again into a steady stream of traffic.

"Yes please," she sighed, she wasn't at all sure that going to stay with her grandparents was a good idea but then she didn't really have much choice.

The station was heaving. The first two automatic ticket machines she found were out of order and the queue at the counter wound back along the concourse so far that she couldn't see the end. Looking up at the departure board she realised she had just missed a train that would get her to Didcot, and she would have to wait an hour for the next one.

"At least I've got plenty of time then," she muttered to herself.

Fifty minutes later, ticket in one hand and coffee in the other she stood waiting at the platform. Looking around at the crowds of fellow passengers it was clear that the train was going to be very full, she would be lucky to get a seat.

"The train now arriving at platform nine is the delayed ten fifty-four for Birmingham New Street..." Lilly was confused, this wasn't her train she wanted the Bristol service.

"Passengers requiring the Bristol service please be advised of a platform change. This train will now depart from platform twelve."

"Shit!" said Lilly loudly. Just what she needed on top of everything else she now had to navigate through a sea of other passengers and with only five minutes until her train was due to leave. Could things get any more difficult?

Sweating and out of breath she clambered aboard the First-class carriage just as the doors were closing. Spying an empty seat, she flopped down. If the ticket inspector came, she would just have to think up an excuse, she really wasn't in the mood to force her way through the standard class coaches looking for that elusive empty seat which probably didn't exist.

As the train pulled away, she was filled with a sense of grief. Everything that was familiar to her was being stripped away. She felt like a child again; like the twelve-year-old Lilly being driven away from her home on the day of her mother's funeral. She had spent years clothing herself in new memories, creating a new identity for herself as a means of shutting out her loss. Now that she was being forced to go back, she felt raw with the pain. Her little voice of resilience, her mother's voice, straining to be heard. *It will be okay, you'll see.* But she wasn't sure she believed it.

The train jolted as it crossed the points and lined up to its new destination. As she gazed out of the window at row upon row of blackened terraced houses Lilly mused to herself; her life had been one long list of destinations. Ever since her mother was taken ill, she had been on the move. First to live with Oma and Gramps on their farm in Oxfordshire whilst her mum was having treatment. Dad hadn't been able to cope and had spent more and more time at his flat in London rather than at home with Lilly. He claimed it was due to pressures of work, but it was probably more than that. The *she-wolf* appeared far too quickly on the scene after Mum had passed away. Lilly remembered it so clearly, being wrenched from the farm after the funeral, driven away to the flat in London and then just a couple of weeks later being introduced to *her*, just a friend from the office who was going to help out for a while. Well, *she* had certainly helped Dad out.

When the summer had come to an end they'd had to decide on a school for Lilly and she was shipped off to a minor boarding school in Kent. By Christmas the *she-wolf* had moved in, and they were not going to see *those awful country people* again. Lilly recalled the terrible rages she got into when Oma and Gramps were referred to in that way as though they were uncouth heathens. Over the ensuing years Lilly's mind had been slowly poisoned against them; she was led to believe that they never wrote or called, that they didn't want to know her anymore. Now she was beginning to suspect that she had been horribly misled.

She became surrounded by wealthy, privileged people at home and at school. She so desperately wanted to fit in, to be popular. She was pretty and athletic. She had a lovely smile and engaging way about her. She learned to project an air of confidence and turn on the charm. It seemed a perfectly natural choice when she decided to enrol as a trainee airline steward; several of her friends had signed up too. She remembered thinking it was going to be so much fun, that she would get to meet so many people, see so many new places. It was her chance to escape and live her own life. Of course, it had not turned out to be as glamorous as she had imagined; the hours were long and often dull, most of the people superficial and demanding. But that was something she had been too busy to really notice and now it was all gone anyway. She had come full circle; she was heading back to the place where it had all begun. This was not a new destination, and it was the one place she was not sure she could face returning to.

"Next stop Didcot Parkway, passengers are kindly reminded…" Lilly was shaken from her reverie, Didcot was her stop. *No use dwelling on the past anyway* came the whisper of the little voice in her head. "Easy for you to say," she muttered audibly which earned her a strange look from the lady in the seat opposite that Lilly returned with a thin smile. Peering out of the window into the gloomy countryside she felt so far from the glamour of the lifestyle she had up until so recently enjoyed. How could her life have fallen apart so quickly?

Gramps shook the rain from his umbrella as he entered the ticket hall. Lilly had phoned to say she had arrived about half an hour ago, but he couldn't see anyone waiting.

"Gramps is that you?" he heard a gentle voice enquire from behind him. As he turned his heart skipped a beat. Lilly was the image of her mother, for a moment he was taken back in time.

"Lilly my love," he said as he went to hug her. But she backed away before he could.

"Best not Gramps, don't want you catching anything," she said cautiously.

"Oh, right, well, err... Well, we had best get you home then. Car's this way..." and he led her out into the pouring rain.

Welcome to Didcot she mouthed to herself. It was as grotty as she had remembered.

"Oma is looking forward to seeing you, she's baked some of her special cakes for you," he said looking over his shoulder as she slid into the back seat.

"That's very kind Gramps, I am looking forward to seeing her too." Although she wasn't entirely sure about that, everything was getting to be a little too difficult. She felt stretched thin, as though at any moment she would simply just melt away. The last time she had seen Oma, she had been given one of those special cakes too. She could still taste the warm tingle of ginger on her tongue. Tears started to trickle down her cheeks as they made their way along the country lanes towards the farm.

"Here we are then, home sweet home!" said Gramps enthusiastically as though she was still twelve years old.

Standing on the doorstep in the glow of the porch light was Oma. She hadn't changed a bit.

"Come on in dear, your Gramps will get the bags. You must be exhausted love, come in and have some tea, I made your favourite cakes." She bustled Lilly over the threshold and into the cosy sitting room.

"Thanks Oma," she said shrugging off her coat and stepping out of her sodden shoes.

"I want more than anything to give you a hug, but I probably shouldn't. Don't want to give you any germs."

"It's okay dear, I understand. We have got everything ready for you in the attic. You will have your own bathroom and I've made up the old bed. Have you got everything you need love?" she gabbled as she poured Lilly a cup of tea and forced some cake into her hand.

"Thank you, yes I think so. Maybe if you could tell me the WiFi password that would be helpful, I expect I will be spending a lot of time online as there won't be much else to do during two weeks of quarantine," replied Lilly, taking a sip of tea.

"WiFi, oh we don't have WiFi," snorted Gramps as he shuffled past with her bags. "Never needed any of that new-fangled stuff, nothing wrong with a good book in my opinion."

Lilly was shocked, surely everywhere had WiFi these days!

"Sorry love, but you'll have to make do. There are quite a few books in the attic and Gramps managed to dig out the old telly for you, although the signal might not be great. I'm sure you'll be able to get some channels," said Oma, hopefully. "Let me show you where things are."

Lilly followed Oma up to the attic and half listened as she was shown *the facilities* as Oma called them.

"Well, I'll leave you to unpack then. Dinner will be ready at seven thirty, I'll bring it up on a tray, shall I?"

"What… Oh yes, thanks," said Lilly distractedly. *This is going to be hell*, she thought as she flopped down on the bed and buried her head in the pillows. After what seemed like five minutes there was a tentative knock at the door.

"Lilly dear, are you awake? I've brought your dinner. I wanted to check that you are warm enough, are you okay? Got everything you need?" while Oma paused for breath Lilly took the chance to interject.

"I think I'm okay although I must have dropped off. It

is a bit cold; do you maybe have a heater or something?" Actually, she was frozen but that may have had something to do with falling asleep in wet clothes.

"I'll just leave your dinner here and go and see if Gramps can dig out a heater for you."

Lilly felt a little awkward, Oma was trying her best and all she had done so far was complain. The food smelled amazing, and she realised she hadn't eaten since leaving London. Toad in the hole with mash and loads of gravy, good hearty English food. She had to stop herself from shovelling it into her mouth.

"I'll just plug this in for you." Gramps had appeared from nowhere and made her jump; she turned to him a little embarrassed with gravy running down her chin.

"Fanksh," she mumbled through a mouthful of food. Gramps grinned at her and laughed.

"Nothing like a bit of Oma's cooking to cheer you up!"

"Thank you, Gramps, and say thank you to Oma too. I am really grateful to you both."

"Our pleasure my dear. Now get that down you and get out of those wet things. The fire is on so you should start to feel warmer," he said and turned to go.

"Sleep well and I'll bring you up some tea in the morning."

Replete and warm after dinner and a shower, Lilly was starting to feel a tiny bit more relaxed. Maybe this was not going to be quite so bad after all. She contemplated her bags at the end of the bed but gave in to her fatigue; unpacking could wait until the morning.

Lilly wakes to a crack! It is semi-dark, and all is confusion around her. The sky is roaring, booming, swirling with a whipping, rustling, whooshing. She is drenched, her hair is matted to her forehead. The world is swaying violently with no rhythm, lurching up, down, back and forth like riding a wild horse. Snapping, crashing noises all around her, a blinding light, a boom and a violent crash. She is falling, falling, and with a sudden burst of pain she feels like she has been hit by a train.

Gasping she found herself awake in a silent room; her heart was pounding, and she could hear the blood rushing in her ears. Bathed in sweat with the bed clothes knotted round her legs, slowly she realised she had fallen out of bed. Tentatively she sat up, a pale moon visible through the attic window, all was calm and quiet. *Just a crazy dream* she thought to herself. Dragging the bedding back onto the bed, she crawled under and tried to get warm again. Slowly the lurching sensation from the dream subsided and she drifted back to sleep.

For the rest of the night Lilly tossed and turned in a state of half sleep. Her mind a confusion of disjointed thoughts bubbling up from the past two days mixing with a weird sense of otherness creating a tangled narrative in her head. As the dawn light seeped through the faded curtains, she woke feeling cold and exhausted. The sound of birds scrabbling in the rafters above her head did nothing to help calm her nerves. Yet, in spite of this, fatigue won out and she dozed for an hour or so until there was a gentle knock at the door.

"Morning Lilly, I've brought you some tea. I'll leave it on the table by the door. Did you sleep OK?" It was Gramps sounding far too bright and cheery.

"Thanks," Lilly managed to say feeling groggy and a little disorientated.

"What would you like for breakfast? Oma is just making something before she heads off to work."

Lilly wasn't feeling at all hungry but knew from experience that food always helped when you are feeling tired and hungover. Not that she'd had anything to drink but the poor night's sleep had left her with that same fuzzy headed feeling.

"Oh, don't go to any trouble Gramps, just some toast will be fine." Toast, she could manage toast.

"Right oh, if, you're sure. I'll bring it up in a few minutes then." He was gone before she could say anything in reply.

CHAPTER 4

QUARANTINE

D ay one of quarantine. Tea and another shower helped to ease the aching behind her eyes and gave her the strength to contemplate getting dressed. Lilly had never been one for lying around in her night clothes. Thirty minutes later she was dressed and had started un-packing when she was interrupted by another knock at the door.

"Toast delivery!" said Gramps, cheerily. She opened the door to find him grinning, she had forgotten how lovably playful he could be. His grin quickly transformed into a look of concern.

"Are you okay dear?"

"Oh, I didn't sleep too well," she said, wondering just how awful she must look without her make-up on.

"Was the bed, okay? The last person to sleep on it was your uncle James when he was here for Christmas a few years back. One of the struts gave way, bit of woodworm had got to it. I ended up replacing half the frame with some of the poplar wood I had lying around in the workshop. Solid wood poplar and nice and flexible too." Gramps had been a talented carpenter in his day and still liked to potter about, fixing things.

"Oh, the bed was fine. I just had a really weird dream which woke me up and then I couldn't get back to sleep," cut in Lilly before Gramps got too carried away with his story.

"Well, I'm sure it's just being somewhere new. You'll be right as rain in a day or two. I'd best leave you to your toast. I brought you some tea things and a kettle so you can make your own. I'll be going out to the workshop now so hopefully you've got everything you need." He shuffled off before Lilly had a chance to thank him. It was going to take a while to get used to being isolated in the attic.

Having finished her toast and un-packed the rest of her clothes she decided to experiment with the television. She was used to having cable and access to Simon's Sky plus account, she knew that the set-top Freeview box was not going to match that, but she was not prepared for the ensuing disappointment. After re-tuning the system three times she could only pick up a handful of channels well. Flicking through she found a film channel which seemed okay and settled down to watch with her freshly made cup of tea. Five minutes later she gave up, the image and sound were so glitchy it was impossible to watch. The only other channels that seemed stable were cluttered with dreadful daytime TV shows which were aimed at stay-at-home mums or old-aged pensioners, or the news channel. She threw the remote down in disgust.

By force of habit, she picked up her phone and checked for messages, nothing new. She tried to access her email, but the network connection was not great and after watching the *wheel of death* spin on the screen for over a minute she gave up.

"Fuck, fuck, fucking fuck!" she shouted as she threw her phone at the wall. Being isolated was bad enough but now she had absolutely nothing to do. How on earth was she going to manage two weeks of this? Tears of frustration threatened to overwhelm her. She was so tired, if only she could get some decent sleep maybe things would feel better. As she flopped down onto the end of the bed, she noticed her remaining bag which she had somehow forgotten to un-pack. It was the one which contained all the last-minute odds and ends she had hurriedly gathered up before leaving the flat on Sunday morning. A smile crept across her face; there was a half-full bottle of brandy in the side pocket. She looked up at the clock on the bedside table; was ten thirty too early to have a drink?

"Sod it, it's not like I have to be anywhere any time soon," she said to herself as she grabbed the bottle and took a large swig. The brandy burned the back of her throat and she revelled in the glowing warm sensation as it slowly filled her stomach. She settled down on the pillows and quickly dosed off to sleep.

Lilly wakes to a crack! It is semi-dark, and all is confusion around her. The sky is roaring, booming, swirling with a whipping, rustling, whooshing. She is drenched, her hair is matted to her forehead. The world is swaying violently with no rhythm, lurching up, down, back and forth like riding a wild horse. Snapping, crashing noises all around her, a blinding light, a boom and a violent crash. She is falling, falling, and with a sudden burst of pain she feels like she has been hit by a train.

Gasping she woke to a silent room. As her thumping heart returned to normal, she looked round; she was on the bed fully clothed. The sun was streaming in through the attic window; the bedside clock said eleven twenty. She had slept for maybe half an hour, but it felt like a lifetime, and it was the same awful dream. Exactly the same. She rubbed her shoulder where a bruise was slowly forming; at least she hadn't fallen out of bed again.

"Maybe brandy wasn't such a good idea," she mused to herself. "But how can I have had that same dream again? What on earth can it mean?" she was feeling quite rattled, it was a long time since she'd had such dreadful dreams. During the period after her mother died, she was plagued by them but nothing quite as haunting as this and never the same one twice. *What's happening to me Mum?* she thought, feeling once more like the confused twelve-year-old girl she thought she had left behind.

The first week of quarantine was filled by days of lethargy and nights of confusion. The dream repeated again and again, always the same with the abrupt ending. She hadn't fallen out of bed but frequently woke up soaked in sweat and tangled in her bedclothes. In desperation on the seventh night Lilly drank the remaining brandy in the hope that this would block out the dream. She emerged from a deep sleep feeling groggy from drink but elated. "I didn't have the dream again!" she exclaimed to herself sitting up excited. She quickly sank back onto the pillows; it would take a while for the effect of the hang-over to wear off.

She spent a quiet day nursing a headache and then browsing through the magazines that Oma had bought her. So far, she hadn't felt much like tackling the novels on the bookshelf; she had never been much of a reader and Jane Austen and Thomas Hardy were not really her thing. The only other option would be the TV, but she had found the continual catalogue of Covid-19 statistics so depressing that she couldn't face watching it. By dinner time she was feeling quite a bit better, and the lovely roast dinner followed by jam roly-poly pudding had helped to revive her spirits. It still felt quite odd having to eat alone in her room but then at least she didn't have to engage in small talk. After a week she felt like she had pretty much run out of things to say to Gramps, and Oma never seemed to be around.

As she looked around after tidying her dishes, she spotted the empty brandy bottle on the shelf. She sniffed it and tipped it up to see if there was even a drop left. *Maybe Oma has some; I shall have to ask when she comes up to collect the tray*, she thought to herself. About half an hour later there was a gentle knock on the door.

"Are you all done dear?" asked Oma from the landing.

"Yes, thank you. It was really lovely; you are such a good cook," replied Lilly brightly.

"Oh, I'm glad you enjoyed it. Roly-poly was always your favourite when you were little," she beamed.

Just as she was turning to go Lilly remembered the brandy. "Oma, I don't suppose you have any brandy?" she asked hopefully.

"Oh, sorry dear. No, we don't have any spirits in the house. I only get brandy at Christmas for the cake, and we have used that up. Perhaps you would like some peppermint tea instead? I always find that good for the digestion," she offered.

"No, it's okay. Thanks anyway," replied Lilly with a hint of disappointment.

"Well, good night then dear. I hope you sleep well." Oma gathered up the tray again and headed down the stairs.

"Chance will be a fine thing," muttered Lilly under her breath as she smiled at Oma before shutting the door. She was not at all sure that she would be able to get any sleep without the aid of some alcohol to knock her out again.

It is cool and bright, there is a gentle breeze playing on her face. She is swaying to and fro, a soothing feeling like being in a hammock. There is a bird singing nearby and an odd tickly sensation on her arm as though something is hopping up and down along it. She feels an inner strength as her arms and legs flex in rhythm with the breeze. A swooshing, rustling sound and a low groaning like the sound of a rocking chair moving back and forth. The light is dancing on her face, she can't really see it but feels a sensation more like her eyes are closed and she is sensing shadows of leaves rustling and patches of brightness in between. A sighing in the background like a whispered voice but she can't make out the words. She drifts off again. Suddenly the sky is roaring, booming and the familiar dream repeats itself again.

Lilly woke in a sweat after the same sensation of falling followed by a sharp pain.

There was a knock at the door. "Lilly dear, are you okay?"

"Yes," she murmured "I'm okay".

"I heard you shouting love, are you sure everything is alright?"

"Yes Oma, just a bad dream. I didn't realise I was shouting, sorry, I didn't mean to wake you."

"Oh, you poor love, can I get you anything dear?"

"No, I'm okay, really, I'm fine now."

"Alright then dear if, you're sure. I'll bring you a nice cup of tea in the morning then."

"Thank you," Lilly sighed. *Why do people always think tea is the cure for everything?* she asked herself. Looking at the clock she realised it was only two thirty, the morning couldn't come quickly enough.

As the day dawned with a grey mist shrouding the fields, Lilly could barely face getting out of bed. *I can't take much more of this,* she thought. The strange dream seemed to have transformed in some way; at first it had felt quite nice and comforting like she was being hushed to sleep but then it got all violent and angry like before. She had never put much stock in the interpretation of dreams; her mother always held that such things were nonsense. Now she was not so sure. Hopefully things would get better once she had finished this tortuous period of quarantine and could get out of the house. *It's just cabin fever* she told herself, trying to be optimistic, *just two more days to go, yay*!

Finally, the last day of quarantine arrived. It was a mixed blessing; according to the news the nation was about to enter a period of lockdown so she wouldn't be able to experience the kind of freedom that she had been longing for but at least she could get out of the attic. Never before had she found herself longing so much to be outside in the fresh air and to be able to have some physical contact. Finally, she would be able to give Gramps and Oma a hug. Tears pricked her eyes at the thought of that; it had been more than ten years since their last embrace. Right now, she was so very desperate for some sleep; attempts to doze during the day had proven unsuccessful. Whilst reading she found herself losing focus and almost drifting off but as soon as she set her magazine aside sleep became elusive. She spent hours studying the attic ceiling with its spider's webs and dust motes, counting the nails in the beams above her head. Her thoughts oscillating between trying to understand the strange dreams and berating herself for thinking about them.

In the late afternoon Lilly realised that for once she was alone in the house. Oma was at work or out delivering food parcels and Gramps had taken a last chance to collect some items from the DIY store. She was overtaken by a sudden craving to find something to drink, anything which could anaesthetise her and help her to sleep. Having spent half an hour meticulously searching the dining room cabinets, the kitchen, the pantry she realised that Oma was telling the truth, there really were no spirits in the house. All she could find was an out of date can of barley wine which must have been left over from Christmas. *Oh well beggars can't be choosers*, she thought and was about to open the can when she heard the gravel churning on the drive outside. "Shit!"

she exclaimed stubbing her toe on the door as she scrambled into the hall and up the stairs. Placing the can on her bedside table she perched on the windowsill to see who had just returned home. Oma's car was in the drive which meant she would have about an hour to kill before dinner. She eyed the can of drink longingly, her heart racing.

What has become of me? she thought and swept the can into the bin. *Barley wine, what even is that*?

Twenty minutes later the little voice in her head telling her that if she drinks the wine, she will be able to sleep started to wear her down. "Maybe a little bit before dinner won't hurt," she told herself. She didn't have a clean glass, so she decided to drink it straight from the can; this she instantly regretted as she realised that barley wine was a bit like stout, not a wine at all and, it tasted totally disgusting! Feeling quite revolted and ashamed of herself she tipped the rest of the drink down the sink and buried the can in her bin. "What was I thinking? Hopefully some dinner will help to get rid of the manky taste," she muttered as she took up her seat by the window and waited for dinner time.

Hours later Lilly was lying awake in bed. The ghastly taste of the barley wine had been replaced by a persistent garlic flavour which even two rounds of teeth cleaning could not dissipate. Oma had always been a little heavy handed with herbs and spices in her cooking. Wishing desperately that she had found something stronger to drink Lilly resigned herself to another night of tedium, waiting for the dawn to come. In the early hours she drifted into a doze and the dream came again; it felt soothing and peaceful like the last time. The sighing in the background that she heard before seemed to be a little more distinct. It was like a mellow voice trying to say something "ooh, haah, ool, haah, oold haah, oold haahaa, oold hakka…" Just as she thought she was able to make out some of the words the dream lurched into a repeat of the first one; the sky was roaring booming…

She woke to the sensation of falling, her head was spinning, she slowly calmed her breathing and turned to see the first hint of the grey light spilling round the edges of the curtains. The last night of quarantine was nearly over. As she pulled on her dressing gown the words from the dream drifted back into her mind, "oold hakka", it didn't mean a thing to her.

Lilly spent her first day out of quarantine feeling quite restless. The novelty of being allowed out of the attic wore off rather quickly. Because of the strict lockdown which had come into effect over the weekend she was only able to go for a walk around the garden. Oma was out working at the veg shop; it seemed that food shops were about the only places that people were allowed to visit.

Sitting in the garden she looked up at the clear blue sky. Suddenly it occurred to her that the sky was too clear; normally you would see the wisps of jet trails crisscrossing everywhere. The trails left by the multitude of travellers on their journeys to foreign lands, exotic destinations. Now nothing; it was as if the world had hit the pause button. Lilly felt suddenly overwhelmed by grief. It was a harsh reminder of her loss; just three weeks ago she would have been on board one of those shiny craft tracing arcs across the firmament. Feeling her chest constrict she wiped hot tears from her eyes and turned away. That life was gone now, she was cast adrift, floating, listless. In an attempt to distract herself she headed to the workshop to see what Gramps was up to.

Gramps had spent most of the morning in his workshop pottering about. Lilly spent a little while watching him and trying to strike up a conversation, but he was immersed in whatever he was doing and that made him difficult to talk to. She soon got bored; "I think I'll go in for a bite to eat and then try to have a nap," she said, trying to get his attention.

"What's that? Oh, a nap, yes sounds like a good idea. You do look a bit peaky," he said not even looking up.

"Great!" she thought as she wandered back inside, "not sure why I bothered coming out of the attic," she muttered, feeling disgruntled and lonely.

After a light lunch she settled down on her bed hoping to snooze. The warmth of the sun on the bedclothes had made the room feel quite cosy and sleep was not long in coming, she soon found herself enveloped in the embrace of a luxurious and relaxing dream.

Swaying gently back and forth as if she is floating on a warm current of air, she feels happy for the first time in weeks. A little bird chirrups softly, and she feels a tickly sensation and gentle nibbling on her cheek. There is a background sighing, soothing and gentle like that of a childhood nurse singing a lullaby "oold haa, oold ma hakka, oold haa, oold ma hakka."

She snoozed on but before the usual jolt when the, now familiar, dream became violent she was woken by Gramps calling her, asking if she wanted some tea.

As she stretched and shuffled her feet into her slippers, she found herself humming the words from the dream, "oold hakka, ooold ma hakka…"

"Did you have a good snooze love?"

"Mmm, yes thanks Gramps," she answered, stifling a yawn. She started humming again.

"What's that you say?" asked Gramps.

"Oh, nothing really. Just a rhyme from a dream I keep having. Something like oold hakka, oold ma hakka. I can't quite make it out and I certainly don't think I remember it from anywhere."

"Old ma hakka, interesting. I don't know a rhyme about it but there is an ancient brook called *Hakka's Brook* which runs through the village and down past the bottom field."

"Oh, I don't know Gramps, how would I know about that?" responded Lilly a little tersely. She was sure she had never heard that name before. The kettle started to whistle, and Gramps went to finish preparing the tea. Lilly was left gazing out of the window humming softly to herself. She couldn't get the rhyme out of her head.

CHAPTER 5

FINAL DESCENT

For the first time since arriving at the farm, Lilly joined Oma and Gramps in the dining room for dinner.

"Mmm, thanks Oma. That was lovely," she said brightly.

"Oh, I don't know. Not my best, I would say. We seem to be running short of things; I didn't have everything I usually like to put in. I'll have to plan to go shopping."

"Well, I like pasta and your sauces are always tasty," reassured Gramps. Oma had been feeling a little worn down after a tricky day at the veg shop.

"Not that I really want to go shopping," she continued, seeming to ignore Gramps completely.

"Why's that Oma?"

"Oh, people are behaving rather strangely at the moment. What with this lockdown and things. No-one seems to trust each other. We had a couple of really rude customers today, not wanting to wear face masks or keep their distance, and Agnes was telling me that she'd heard people have been stock piling things, so some shops were running out."

"Running out of loo roll, I heard on the radio. I mean loo roll for goodness' sake!" chipped in Gramps. Then changing the subject completely, he asked "What's for pudding?"

"Stewed apples and custard. At least we have plenty of jars of stewed apples left, last year was a good apple year. Would you mind clearing the dishes while I make the custard?"

Yum! thought Lilly to herself as she cleared away the dirty plates, she had never really liked the baby food consistency of stewed apples. She forced herself to smile enthusiastically, she didn't want to hurt Oma's feelings.

"Lilly dear," said Oma as she returned with the jug of custard. "I was thinking, now that you are out of quarantine it would be good for you to be busy and maybe get out of the house. You must be so bored of being cooped up."

Hmm, I know where this is going, thought Lilly, *she'll want me to help out in that grotty veg shop*. Before Oma could say anything further an idea popped into her head.

"I'll be more than happy to do the shopping if you like. If you'll let me borrow the car that is."

"Ooh, that is a good idea!" said Gramps, chipping in before Oma had a chance to object. He knew what Oma had in mind but had a sense that Lilly would need to be brought round to the idea of helping in the shop a little more slowly. Oma had never been one for being subtle.

"Well, OK. I'll have to write you a list and you'll have to drop me at work on your way into town," replied Oma somewhat reluctantly.

Lilly was pleased, she was itching to get out to somewhere a bit more civilised; somewhere with a decent phone signal or maybe even WiFi! She hadn't been able to check email or social media for over two weeks, everyone must think she was being really rude.

"Great!" she grinned, "do you want me to help with writing the list?" Even the apple stew and custard somehow tasted better now that she had something to look forward to. Another thought crept into her head, maybe she would be able to get hold of a bottle of brandy too. Her eyes lit up as she smiled to herself.

"It's good to see you looking happier love," said Oma misinterpreting the reason behind the smile. "I have been so worried about you," she hugged Lilly fiercely.

After dinner they had all settled down to watch the news. It seemed to be devoted entirely to Covid-19, how many new cases, how many people had died that day. Gramps kept muttering and making scathing comments for which Oma admonished him repeatedly, but it didn't seem to make any difference. After a few minutes Lilly had seen as much as she could stomach and had headed for bed.

She did not sleep well. The familiar Hakka dream had plagued her and now, as she sat at the breakfast table contemplating tea and toast, she felt utterly exhausted.

"Are you almost done there, dear? We need to get a move on. Here is the shopping list and the bags are in the boot of the car already. I'll just go and see to Gramps and then we need to go," gabbled Oma, barely pausing for breath. It felt like being back at school. Lilly was more than a little nervous, she hadn't driven for several months and with Oma in a grumpy mood she felt sure things were bound to turn out badly.

Fortunately, Oma's car was an automatic, the only thing that Lilly had to get the hang of was the size, it felt like driving a tank. Having dropped Oma at the veg shop and promised to call in on her way back from the shops Lilly took the route into town. *Freedom at last!* she thought to herself as she switched on the radio and cruised along enjoying the morning sunshine. As she pulled into the supermarket carpark it slowly dawned on her that this was not going to be the exciting trip that she had imagined. There were hardly any cars, it was like a ghost town. A long snake of people all standing two metres apart wound its way around the side of the shop. There were signs everywhere asking people to *Stay safe and protect the NHS.*

As she entered the shop and reluctantly donned a face mask she was assailed by a constant stream of information repeating over the public address. "Customers are reminded to please keep two metres apart. Customers are reminded to please be patient at the checkout and do as the staff direct. Customers are reminded that due to shortages the purchase of some items is restricted…" It felt like being in some kind of police state like you saw in the movies. Lilly found it very un-nerving. Clutching the list that Oma had given her she made her way slowly around the complex one-way system that had been hurriedly devised to help people socially distance. Half the customers were studiously obeying the rules and the other half seemed oblivious or just didn't care. Although some of the produce section seemed a little depleted it was not until Lilly reached the dry goods aisle that she realised what Oma had meant by *shortages*. There was nothing there save one lonely bag of dried kidney beans which had been split open and discarded. No tins of beans, no pasta, no rice, nothing! She looked down at the shopping list and quickly realised that she was not going to be able to get half the items that Oma wanted. As she passed the end of the aisle, she almost stumbled over a palette of goods still wrapped in thick plastic and waiting to be unloaded. She spotted some of the items on her list. Heart racing and feeling like a petty thief she started to pull at the plastic in an attempt to get at some tinned tomatoes.

"Anyone would think you work here," came a voice from behind her. Turning frantically and desperately trying to think of something to say by way of an excuse she realised that it was a young shelf stacker. He was grinning.

"It's OK, love. Here be my guest; less for me to put out." He cut some of the plastic away and handed her a tin. "Is there anything else you need?"

"Oh, er well thank you," stammered Lilly "yes, have you got any sweetcorn?"

"Indeed, I do," he bent down with a flourish and tugged out a large tin for her.

"Oh, thank you so much. Gosh I have to say I was a bit shocked when I saw the empty aisle."

"Yeah, tell me about it. Been like this for two days now. As soon as something arrives, we put it out and it's gone again in half an hour. People panic buying is what started it. I mean who needs twenty cans of chickpeas?" he shrugged looking thoroughly dejected. Lilly was about to say more but was interrupted by another frustrated customer.

She was nearly at the checkout queue when she realised, she had forgotten about the brandy. "Shit!" she muttered under her breath, she was going to have to navigate the one-way system round half the shop to get back to the spirit aisle, she hoped that it would be worth it. Five minutes later she was relieved to find that people had not yet thought to stockpile bottles of spirits. She put two large bottles of brandy in the trolley and then decided to grab a third, just in case.

After what seemed like an eternity of queueing and chatting politely to the man on the checkout Lilly finally made it out of the shop. She took a moment to get her breath, it was only then that she realised how anxious she had been. Normally after packing everything away in the car, she would have found somewhere for a relaxing coffee but nowhere was open. Spying a bench next to a barren looking raised flower bed she flopped down to look at her phone. *Please, if there is a god, let there be a decent signal*, she thought. "Result!" she punched the air with delight, three bars of 4G signal and a local WiFi hotspot.

Scrolling through her emails she quickly realised that most of it was junk. There was one from the airline, several from her bank but none at all from any of her friends. She was not too deterred, most of her friends preferred to use social media. She had a couple of messages from airline acquaintances but nothing from Fi or any of her other friends. Scrolling through Instagram it seemed no one had been sharing much apart from pictures of their room or the view out of their window. She resorted to Facebook but again no messages. Some of her friends had been posting things but she wasn't mentioned in any of them; not that they were about anything particularly interesting. *Who wants to know what you had on your pancakes for breakfast anyway*? Lilly reflected frowning. It slowly dawned on her that the busy exciting life she had led in London had been empty of any real interest. *Fuck em*! she thought to herself and tossed her phone back into her bag in disgust. All those hours she had spent worrying about what she was missing, and how worried everyone would be about her. She now realised that it had all been a superficial illusion, she had just been another one in the crowd, another mate who wouldn't mind paying for the drinks or the cab home. She felt used.

The drive back home was a sombre affair. She quickly turned off the radio, the chipper chit chat of the presenter grated on her nerves. Having got stuck behind a bus and then a tractor she felt like she wanted to scream by the time she got to the veg shop. Even then things didn't improve; the sullen young girl on the till informed her that Oma had gone out for a delivery and wasn't sure when she would be back.

"Oh, well can you tell her I dropped by then please? I can't wait as I have frozen stuff in the car." Lilly wasn't sure why she had felt the need to offer an explanation. Even so, when she got back to the car, she couldn't resist taking her phone out and checking to see if she still had a signal. Not much of a phone signal but surprisingly the shop did seem to have WiFi which she could access. She went through the ritual of checking email and social media in the hope that by some miracle something new had appeared in the half hour since she last checked. Of course, there was nothing, well unless you counted two emails from PayPal and a couple of photos of someone's coffee cup. "Might as well send Fi a quick message just to check she is OK," Lilly said to herself, although she didn't hold out much hope that she would get a reply. "I don't really know why I am bothering," she muttered, suddenly feeling disgusted with herself for being so needy. Even so she couldn't stop herself from thinking that it was good to know the shop had WiFi and that she would need to find an excuse to go there again soon. Pulling out of the carpark she had to swerve to avoid a cyclist who had seemed to appear out of nowhere. She was barely able to hold back tears of pent-up frustration before she got back to the farm. Switching off the engine she just sat there sobbing until Gramps appeared. He whisked her into the kitchen and sat her down with a cup of tea insisting that she just sit there while he unpacked everything.

"Sorry, Gramps," she snivelled, blowing her nose and trying to regain her composure. "I don't think I was quite prepared for how ghastly it was going to be."

"It's OK dear, I saw some of the shops on the news. I guess it's much harder to deal with when you see it for real. I'll just pop these out in the freezer, back in a mo," he said shuffling out to the pantry.

Just then Lilly spied the bottles of brandy in the one remaining bag. Thankfully, Gramps hadn't spotted them. She wasn't in the mood to try to explain them away. She slipped them under her coat and made her way upstairs. "I'll be back down in a moment, just need to freshen up," she called as she hurried to hide the bottles in her room. She was looking forward to a good stiff drink later, just to calm her nerves.

After a couple of days of *calming her nerves* and enjoying the oblivion of dream free, brandy induced sleep, Lilly decided that she could face the world again. The lure of internet access enticed her into agreeing to help Oma out at the veg shop.

"Oh, you are an angel!" Oma exclaimed in relief. She had half expected Lilly to turn down her request which would have put her in quite a bind as they were now two staff members down due to suspected Covid cases.

"I don't want you to rush your breakfast but if we can be ready to go in ten minutes that would be good."

"That's OK Oma, I don't really feel hungry anyway. I'll just do my teeth and grab my shoes," replied Lilly as she headed for the stairs. She was sure that minty toothpaste would hide the smell of alcohol on her breath.

The morning at the veg shop passed quickly enough. Lilly had been set to work unpacking deliveries and re-stocking shelves. It was simple work, but Lilly found it therapeutic, a bit like re-stocking the galley trolleys before a flight, it was strangely familiar. This led her to thinking about the internet and by the time she got a chance to have a short coffee break she was quite anxious to get online and check her email and Facebook. It had been nearly three days since she last checked. *Surely Fi will have replied by now*, she thought to herself. She held her breath as the little wheel whirled round on her screen, her email took forever to load. Her momentary excitement at seeing fifteen new items in her in-box was soon lost as she scrolled through and realised it was all spam. Undeterred she opened Facebook and found herself hoping that Fi would have decided to reply to her message there instead of via email. There had been a fair bit of activity and even a few posts from Fi, but she wasn't tagged in any of them.

"Lilly love, if you have finished with your coffee could you come and help me with the tomatoes?"

"Coming!" groaned Lilly as she stuffed her phone back in her pocket and downed the last quarter of her now cold cup of coffee. The gentle rhythm of restocking shelves had lost its appeal entirely. She spent the rest of the day dwelling on the fact that Fi had not thought about her at all. Her mood became blacker by the hour, and she started to make lots of mistakes.

"Oh, Lilly. The carrots don't go there, the label says broccoli. Can you refill the potatoes we have customers waiting and I've asked you twice already? I don't know what's up with you, you seem very distracted. I can hardly believe you used to work as an air stewardess, you don't seem to be able to follow the most basic of instructions!" The string of complaints uttered by Agnes, the other shop assistant, kept growing and growing.

By the end of the afternoon Lilly was in a foul mood and quite relieved when Oma finally suggested they head home for some dinner. As they arrived back at the farm Lilly found herself starting to sweat a little and her hands were shaking.

"Are you OK, Lilly love?" Oma was quite concerned at how pale she looked.

"Yes fine!" snapped Lilly. "I just need a bit of a lie down that's all," she said as she kicked her shoes into the corner of the hall and made her way upstairs. *All I need is a nip of brandy and a lie down*, she thought to herself.

The sound of Gramps calling her for dinner came as a jolt. Surely, she had only just closed her eyes. Looking round her room Lilly realised it was almost dark and she must have been passed out for over an hour. She eyed the empty brandy bottle on her bedside table warily, it had been a quarter full yesterday. "Hmm, that's not good," she muttered as she pulled on a clean top and headed down the stairs a little unsteadily.

Oma and Gramps were both sitting at the table waiting for her quietly. She flopped into her chair and looked across the table with a blank stare.

"Are you okay Lilly?" asked Gramps, a frown of concern creasing his brow.

"She's drunk is what she is. You can smell it on her breath!" spat Oma, the colour rising in her cheeks.

"So, what if I am. I'm not twelve anymore and I can do what I like!"

"Lilly! Don't speak to Oma like that!"

"You're just as bad Gramps! Since I've got here you have done nothing but smother me and talk to me like I was a child!"

"Now hang on a minute..."

"No, I won't hang on. You don't get it do you, neither of you. You abandoned me when Mum died, I never heard from you. You didn't write, you didn't call. And now it's happening all over again. I lost my job, I lost my flat, I lost my friends, no one answers my calls, no one replies to my messages, I'm invisible! I might as well be dead!" Lilly slumped onto the table sobbing uncontrollably.

Oma and Gramps looked at each other in stunned silence. Neither of them was quite sure what to do. Oma had been about to launch into a great long rebuttal, the accusations made by Lilly had been hurtful and untrue. After Caroline had died, she had tried many times to contact Lilly but was always refused access by her stepmother. It was clear that Lilly was not aware of that, but this was probably not the moment to share such information. Regrettably Oma had a lot of experience in dealing with irrational drunks; her father had given her plenty of practice. Taking a tissue out of her pocket she put her arm around Lilly and comforted her.

"It's okay Lilly. You just let it all out," she said in a calm voice, her own heart feeling like it was about to break. Life could be so cruel.

CHAPTER 6
A HELPING HAND

Having cried herself to the point of exhaustion, Lilly felt thin and her heart empty. Oma had helped her to the sofa where she fell instantly into a deep and dreamless sleep. It was nearly noon the next day when she awakened. The soft shuffling step of Gramps moving about the kitchen slowly filtered through to her along with the clinking of cutlery and a murmur of voices. She opened her eyes to find the curtains still drawn, the faint glow of sunshine peeking through the gaps, dust motes drifting in a warm current of air. Lilly's head was sore and her throat dry, but she felt more rested than she had done for weeks. Gingerly she sat up, the room whirled a little and slowly settled into place, she was going to have to take her time. As if by some sixth sense Oma suddenly appeared at the door.

"Ah, I thought I heard you stir. How are you feeling? Do you want something to drink?"

"Err, yes please. Some water would be nice," croaked Lilly.

"Here you go. Now just take sips to start with," fussed Oma. Although Lilly didn't mind, she was past being angry with Oma.

"Shouldn't you be at work Oma?"

"Oh no Lilly dear. I didn't want to leave you, not after last night. Besides you are far more important to me than a silly old veg shop! I wish I had realised that before," Oma swallowed and fought back the urge to cry.

"Thank you, Oma." Lilly put her arm around Oma, and they sat quietly as she sipped her water. There was no need to share words; just being close was enough.

When Oma stirred beside her, Lilly realised that they had both drifted off to sleep. It must have been some hours later as the sun had moved round, and the room was in shade. The clock on the mantelpiece chimed three.

"How about a cup of tea and something to eat? Maybe we could sit outside now the sun has gone round."

"That sounds lovely Oma," said Lilly as she slowly rose to her feet. Her head felt clearer, and she felt ready for some food. Oma walked with her out to the veranda and made sure she was comfortable before returning to the kitchen. Gramps was trimming the edges of the lawn and raised a hand in greeting.

"I had forgotten how peaceful it is in your garden," commented Lilly when Oma returned with a pot of tea and some toast.

"It is isn't it. I would say it's even quieter at the moment with less traffic about," mused Oma pulling up a chair and pouring the tea.

"You know I have been so out of it these past few weeks I don't think I know what date it is. Must be mid-April or there abouts?" said Lilly quizzically.

"It's nearly May dear. I find it hard to keep track myself, all the days seem to be the same."

Lilly was shocked, she couldn't have been here for over a month already surely.

"Have they said when lockdown will end, and things can get back to normal?"

"No not really. I don't think anyone knows for sure, but I expect it will be a few more weeks yet. Don't worry love, right now we should focus on getting you well again. You've had quite a shock and it will take time; but trust me it will get better."

"Thanks Oma." Lilly gave a thin smile and felt a little reassured although it was hard to believe, she still felt completely numb inside.

"I'll leave you to your tea and toast." Oma got up and made her way over to where Gramps was just finishing putting his tools away.

Lilly just sat and watched the birds hopping between the path and the hedge hunting for insects that Gramps had disturbed. Slowly she drifted off to sleep again. It was nearly dark when Gramps shook her gently and told her it was time to come in for dinner.

Sitting up to the smell of lamb stew wafting across the table, Lilly suddenly felt ravenous. They said little during dinner, each of them just enjoying their food and the chance to sit and relax. When it came time to clear the table Gramps insisted on doing it, suggesting that Lilly and Oma retire to the lounge to put their feet up. Lilly didn't complain, she was still feeling strangely weary. She flopped down on the sofa and yawned.

"Oh, you are a sleepy head. Still, I'm not surprised with all the emotional trauma you've been through. Maybe you should head off to bed dear," suggested Oma.

Suddenly Lilly was gripped with a cold fear in the pit of her stomach, what if the dreams came back?

"Are you okay? You've gone very pale all of a sudden," said Oma, placing a hand on her brow to check whether she had a fever.

"You look like you've seen a ghost," said Gramps from the doorway as he brought in some peppermint tea for Oma.

Lilly wasn't sure what to say, she didn't want Oma and Gramps to think she was crazy.

"You know that funny dream I told you about the other day Gramps. The one about old Hakka or whatever you said the name of that brook was."

"Oh, vaguely dear. You said it was like a sort of nursery rhyme, you kept humming it."

"Well, nearly every night since I have been here, I have had some form of that dream. I feel like I am going crazy or something. The only thing which seemed to help was getting really drunk. I don't want to keep drowning myself in drink and I don't know what to do. I'm terrified every time I go to bed that I will have the dream again…" her words trailed off and she started sobbing, her whole body trembling.

"Shhh, my love," soothed Oma as she wrapped her arms around Lilly and rocked her gently to calm her. "Finally, we are getting to the bottom of things," sighed Oma, relieved that Lilly had decided to be open. She had not been looking forward to having to drag things out of her.

"What if you sleep down here again?" suggested Gramps. "You didn't have a bad dream last night, did you?"

"No but then I was still drunk and exhausted," countered Lilly. "But I suppose it's as good an idea as any," she conceded suddenly feeling very tired.

"Thank you for being open with me dear. We can talk more about it tomorrow when you've had a chance to rest." With that Oma bustled off to get a pillow and blanket. By the time she came back Lilly was already fast asleep.

Oma had decided to take the rest of the week off to help Lilly onto the path of recovery. She knew from her own experience that it would be a long journey with many twists and turns. It was going to be essential that Lilly felt she had someone she could turn to, someone that she could trust.

"How are you feeling?" asked Oma as she set down a steaming cup of coffee and a bowl of muesli on the table next to Lilly.

"Huuaahh," yawned Lilly, as she sat up and rubbed her eyes. "What time is it?"

"Nearly ten o'clock, I thought I would leave you to rest, you looked so peaceful," Oma smiled down at her and then headed towards the door. "I'll give you a few minutes to wake up, don't let your coffee go cold."

Lilly stretched, she hadn't had such a good sleep in, well she couldn't recall how long. *No dreams either*, she thought to herself, or maybe she just didn't remember. Either way it was good. She indulged in the coffee and muesli that Oma had left for her, savouring every last mouthful. She spent the next half hour just gazing out the window, raindrops streaking the glass and wind buffeting the trees. It was going to be an indoor kind of day today, she mused.

"All done there dear?" Oma seemed to have appeared from nowhere.

"Oh, yes. Thank you, it was lovely. Just what I needed," smiled Lilly. Her first genuine smile in quite some time. Oma settled down onto the sofa next to her.

"What were you watching?"

"Oh, just the rain and the trees. It's amazing how different the garden looks compared to yesterday. I think it's going to be a slow day today."

"Slow is good sometimes," sighed Oma. She reached for a tissue to blow her nose. Lilly noticed that she was crying.

"Are you okay Oma?"

"Yes dear, sorry. It's just you look so much like your mum, and I guess I just miss her sometimes. It took me a long time to get over losing the both of you, but the pain passes with time. I am so glad you have come back to us dear and that I can be here for you now when you need me. I wish I could have been there for you then too…" she croaked a little and struggled to finish her words. Lilly just sat silently watching her, tears rolling down her cheeks.

"Loss is a terrible thing. It feels like the end and that there is no point in going on. Time is a great healer, I learned that from the grief counsellor. We can be so impatient to move on that we often bury our feelings deep and grasp at the first new thing that comes along. We think we have found a new sense of purpose, but we are usually wrong, and it comes back to find us eventually. I think maybe that is what has happened to you dear; did anyone ever help you to process your grief and move on?"

Lilly felt stunned. It was like the last ten years had been someone else's life, not hers but a fantasy of who she felt she had to be. A way of coping with her loss without dealing with it properly; a complete disconnection from her former self.

"No, I don't think they did," was all she managed to get out before the tears of relief overwhelmed her.

"It's okay dear. Take it slowly, you have a lot to process. There is no point in dragging it all up and causing yourself more pain. You can't change the past; let yourself be and the path forward will slowly become clear," Oma said gently in that soothing voice that was like rich golden honey, calm and comforting. They sat side by side on the sofa, watching the rain as it ran slowly down the windowpanes, taking their time to just be.

It had rained for the past couple of days but now the sun had returned, and a warm gentle breeze was slowly drying the paths and lawn. Oma and Lilly had just finished feeding the chickens and searching for eggs amongst the apple trees.

"Four eggs, that will make a lovely omelette lunch for the three of us," enthused Oma as they returned to the kitchen. "Could you pop them in the basket while I fill the kettle?" Oma had something of an addiction to tea, or so it seemed to Lilly.

"We can have a quick cup and then get on with picking some of the early salad leaves. I love it when we start to get our own things; so much fresher than the stuff we sell in the shop at this time of year."

Lilly was curious, she remembered Oma having a kitchen garden when she was young but not that she worked at a veg shop.

"Oma, maybe I'm not remembering but weren't you a teacher before you had to look after Mum?"

"That's right dear, I was," Oma paused and contemplated the ceiling; a habit she had developed as a way of ordering her thoughts before saying something difficult. "When we lost your mum, well I fell apart I suppose. It took me a good few months to come to terms with it. I was tempted to go back to teaching and try to pick things up again as though nothing had happened, but my counsellor gave me some really good advice," she paused and looked Lilly in the eyes.

"What was that, Oma?" Lilly sensed that Oma was struggling to control her emotions.

"Well, it was really simple. He asked me what I loved doing most in the world. He didn't want an answer right then, he told me to think about it for a while. The next time we met I had an answer for him. I liked to grow vegetables. It was something I had done as a child with my Oma when we lived in the Netherlands. She was from Suriname and had learned to grow things and trade them in the local market so that the family would have enough to eat; they were very poor. I used to help her with the sowing and the harvest; she would take me to our village market to trade and buy some exotic things which we would have as a treat. I realised that losing your mum had provided me with a gateway, an opportunity to do something different, something that brought me much more joy than teaching had ever done. It all started from that simple question; what do you love doing most in the world?" Her eyes were shining, and she reached out and touched Lilly just above her heart.

Lilly was feeling choked up and lost for words. Her heart ached so much; Oma's gentle touch sent a warm and soothing feeling right through her chest. It helped, it really helped.

"It's okay Lilly. It will take time; you need to let go of so much before you can start the forward journey. My counsellor gave me a really good book which helped to explain it all to me; how to make that transition. I'll dig it out for you if you like." Oma looked hesitant; she wasn't sure how Lilly would react to her being so direct.

Lilly managed a smile. Maybe she should take Oma's advice for a change. "Thanks, yes, I think that might help. Trying to do it my way hasn't got me very far has it," she half chuckled.

"Having a good natter, I see," chipped in Gramps as he slipped off his clogs and looked wistfully at the kettle. "Any chance of a brew?"

"We were having a good heart to heart, until we were so rudely interrupted," chided Oma with a grin on her face. Gramps had a knack of appearing just when conversations ran the risk of getting awkward. Lilly went outside again; she needed a bit of time to herself.

The weeks of May passed gently by. Oma and Gramps kept Lilly busy during the day helping out in the garden and around the house. She had been content to spend time on simple menial tasks giving her overactive mind a chance to switch off for once. She spent the evenings delving into the book Oma lent her, doing the exercises it suggested and finally being honest with herself about who she really wanted to be. Thoughts about email, Facebook and what her former friends were doing crept into her mind less and less.

She no longer dreaded going to sleep. The dream came from time to time, but it felt less threatening somehow and she often found herself humming the gentle Old Hakka lullaby as she went about her daily tasks. By the end of the month, she had almost forgotten that they were in lockdown, she had been living in her own little world, content to roam the garden and share the company of Oma and Gramps at mealtimes.

"You are looking so much better dear," noted Oma as she laid the table for supper. "I was thinking, maybe you would like to join me at the shop tomorrow. You must be getting bored stuck here on the farm all the time. I bet Gramps hardly says two words to you all day."

Lilly looked up at her; a frown of concern crossing her brow. She wasn't at all sure she was ready to face the world again.

"It's alright dear," reassured Oma. "You don't have to do anything with customers. Maybe you would like to help in the greenhouses; we have plenty of seedlings to pot up."

"Err, well that sounds alright. So long as you show me what to do," replied Lilly somewhat hesitantly but also relieved. Plants seemed a safer bet than people right now.

"Of course, I can," smiled Oma warmly. "Right, now, let's see to that gravy before it boils over, shall we?"

As it turned out Lilly was quite adept at repotting seedlings. She had slender nimble fingers and a good level of patience. In the space of three days, she had made her way through all the seed trays and moved on to sowing more seeds. Oma had taken great delight in telling her all about successional sowing and how to keep a steady supply of lettuce and other salad leaves coming throughout the summer. Lilly enjoyed the chance to get out and do something different and was beginning to get her confidence back; so much so that she agreed to help in the shop for the rest of the week. *How hard can it be?* she thought to herself.

Thursday went smoothly; she was kept busy helping to unload pallets and re-stock shelves like she had before. She actually enjoyed chatting to a couple of the young lads when they dropped off deliveries and was flattered that one of them kept flirting with her even though he was really not her type, it was nice to have the attention. It was all harmless fun and helped her to feel just a bit more normal.

On Friday morning, Oma received a call from one of the till staff saying they were not feeling well and couldn't make it in. Lilly had made such good progress over the past couple of days that she thought nothing of asking her to help on the shop floor and take a shift on the till.

"I guess I can do that," responded Lilly as they got into the car and headed off to the village. As they drew closer and closer to the shop, she felt her palms begin to prickle with sweat and realised she was breathing a little faster than normal. *You can do this*, she told herself, although her little voice of doubt was whispering otherwise. The morning whizzed past; she was so busy re-stocking shelves that she barely had time to get anxious. After a short lunch break Oma asked her if she could take over on the till.

"I have to nip out for a few minutes; Agnes will show you what to do," she said in a rush and before Lilly could say anything she was gone.

Great! thought Lilly. She was not a fan of Agnes; she found her bossy and impatient tone quite grating. Agnes was none too thrilled at the prospect of showing Lilly the ropes and she took no pains to hide it.

"Come on then, let's go through how the till works. It's pretty simple, even you should be able to do it."

Thanks for the encouragement, thought Lilly, smiling politely through tight lips.

"Although why Brenda couldn't have gone through it with you at lunch time I don't know."

"Sorry who?" asked Lilly.

"Brenda, oh you probably call her Nan or something," replied Agnes gruffly.

Actually, it's Breda not Brenda, thought Lilly but decided correcting Agnes wouldn't help the situation. Lots of people seemed to struggle with her Oma's Dutch name.

Agnes whizzed through things at such a rate Lilly struggled to keep up. After asking a couple of questions which were met with rather stern and somewhat sarcastic responses Lilly decided it was best to keep her mouth shut. *How hard can it be anyway?* she thought to herself optimistically although she was starting to feel less than calm. The added Covid measures did nothing to reassure her; sitting behind a plastic screen with a face mask on made her feel quite claustrophobic.

The situation went from bad to worse. The queue of customers, all standing two metres apart seemed endless; she had no time to rest, and her legs were starting to ache. As her thirst grew, she realised it had been a mistake not to bring a bottle of water. Just when she thought she would get a chance to step away, Agnes decided to disappear and leave her with a rather surly customer. Lilly's head was beginning to swim, but she was determined to soldier on. *Just one more and then*

I'll excuse myself, she told herself. This customer turned out to be particularly tricky to deal with, the sort that she used to hate when she worked at the airline, impatiently tutting and looking at their watch. She could have just about coped had they not decided to purchase some of the more obscure items which Lilly struggled to identify and inadvertently mischarged for. Most customers would probably not have even noticed the extra fifty pence on the bill, not this one. Having previously seemed impatient to get on they now proceeded to insist on having a fully itemised receipt and spent an age scrutinising every line.

"You've made a mistake here you silly girl!" she barked. "I bought Sharon fruit not pomegranates; you've overcharged me!"

Lilly was flummoxed, Agnes hadn't shown her how to do refunds. She felt suddenly very hot and started to breath rapidly, her panic rising. All she wanted to do was run and hide yet she felt frozen to the spot. She was suddenly really conscious that she badly needed the loo and was terrified that she would wet herself. *What is happening to me?* she thought; she had never experienced a panic attack before. Luckily the next customer in the queue was a kindly old gent who helped to diffuse the situation.

"I'm sure it's a genuine mistake Doris; don't give the lass such a hard time."

Having earned a few seconds reprieve Lilly managed to gather her wits enough to say that she would have to go and ask and then made a dash for the back of the shop. Agnes was standing there chatting on the phone and was none too pleased to be interrupted. Lilly rushed past her in a mad dash to the toilet.

"Can you help the lady at the till please; I really need to pee." Lilly locked herself in the toilet and sat there shaking her breathing so rapid that she was beginning to feel dizzy. It was a good twenty minutes before she managed to calm down. *Get a grip*! she told herself feeling mightily frustrated. She had always managed to cope before. Right now, the temptation to find that last bottle of brandy which she had banished to the back of her cupboard was very great indeed.

There was a gentle tap on the door. "Are you alright in there?" It was Oma. Lilly felt relieved that it wasn't Agnes but still she expected some harsh words. Reluctantly she opened the door.

"I'm sorry, I guess I panicked. I didn't mean to make a mistake with the bill. I didn't know how to give a refund and I couldn't find Agnes. You must be really cross. I'm so stupid. I didn't mean to let you down," Lilly blurted before starting to sob; she felt completely pathetic.

Oma thoroughly regretted having left Lilly alone with Agnes; she should have known better, and Lilly's mental state was clearly not as good as she had hoped. "Let's get you home; it's nearly teatime anyway." She put her arm around Lilly and steered her towards the car. *Maybe some counselling would be a good idea*? she thought to herself. Perhaps it was coincidence that she had bumped into the pastor's wife that afternoon or maybe fate. Apparently, the group counselling sessions that she ran were going to be starting up again now that some lockdown measures were easing. *Now all I need to do is persuade Lilly to go*, she mused.

In the end convincing Lilly to join the counselling group had proven surprisingly easy. That night Oma had woken to the sound of a thud followed by Lilly sobbing. She pulled on her dressing gown and ascended the stairs to the attic room. Pushing open the door, she caught sight of Lilly sitting on the edge of her bed staring blankly at a bottle of brandy, next to it, a half full glass on the window ledge. She was shaking.

"I can't stand it anymore Oma," she sobbed. "Why won't the dreams stop Oma? Please make them stop."

Oma took Lilly in her arms and gently stroked her hair. She whispered softly that everything was going to be okay. "I'm going to help you dear; we will find a way to make things better."

PART 2

DREAMING

In the corner of a field stands a tree. It is a Signal Tree standing watch over this place. Like the generations of long-decayed ancestors before it, holding testament to the transforming landscape. Casting shadows into memories, imprinting patterns in the very tissues of their wood.

CHAPTER 7

MEETING MARGARET

The first group counselling session that Lilly attended was in a somewhat unusual location. Lockdown restrictions meant that groups were not allowed to meet indoors. Janet, the pastor's wife, had been quite resourceful and had set up an outdoor meeting space in the grounds of the old rectory. It was bedecked with a canopy strung between the trees to keep out the elements and had a set of chairs arranged in a semicircle all two metres apart. Propping her bicycle against the fence and puffing slightly from the unaccustomed exercise Lilly made her way towards the last remaining seat. Janet was just about to speak.

"Welcome everyone! It is good to see some familiar faces and one or two new ones."

Lilly looked around wondering who else was new, she caught the eye of a couple of others who were doing the same. A wave of relief washed over her; she was not the only new person.

"As it's been a while since we last met it is probably worth everyone saying a few words by way of introduction." Janet looked around smiling, waiting. After a long pause one of the older men gave a slight cough.

"Huhumm, my name is Jacob, I lost my wife last year and have been struggling to cope," he sighed and looked at his shoes, clearly a little upset.

"My name is Susan, I went through a messy divorce a few months ago and I am slowly working on putting my life back together," chipped in the mousy little woman sitting next to Lilly.

They gradually worked their way through the group, each person introducing themselves and sharing a little about their current situation. *It's exactly like you see on the telly, surreal!* thought Lilly to herself. She was so caught up in her reverie that she didn't hear Janet prompt her to say something.

"She means you!" whispered Susan.

"Ahh" croaked Lilly, her mouth suddenly dry and her heart racing.

"My, my name is Lilly and…" her mind went blank, she hesitated, "…erm, basically I feel like my life is falling apart, I've lost all sense of my place in the world I guess," she stammered, her cheeks burning.

"Thank you, Lilly," said Janet smiling warmly.

"Now, I am sure that you have all been finding things hard over the past few months. The Covid pandemic and lockdown has taken its toll on all of us. Even though most of us have been fortunate not to get the virus we have all been faced with mental health challenges, that is why I thought it was so important to re-start these sessions as soon as possible. Please remember that although we meet as a group every week you can talk to me at any time. You all have my number; don't be afraid to use it."

Looking round, Lilly saw everyone nodding and a few were murmuring to their neighbours. Lilly had spoken to Janet a couple of times already and knew that she was a great calming influence.

"I would like to invite you now to share what is on your mind, tell us anything that has been troubling you. For those of you who are new to the group you may feel reluctant to do this but be assured that you will feel better for just sharing something."

Over the next half hour several people shared how they had been feeling and what they had been struggling with. Lilly listened with interest, initially she was a little sceptical that this could make a difference, but the supportive atmosphere generated by the group and the lack of judgement expressed by others was clearly making the volunteers who'd spoken up feel a little better.

"Now we have time for one more person. Does anyone else want to share?" enquired Janet as she scanned round the group.

"Erm, I will give it a try," Lilly found herself saying as she got to her feet. "I'm not quite sure where to begin…" she tailed off, her courage wavering.

"It's okay, say as much or as little as you feel comfortable with Lilly."

"Before all this I worked as an airline steward. Because of Covid I lost my job and had to move out of my flat in London. I struggled to find anywhere to go, luckily my grandparents were able to offer me an attic room in their farmhouse. I had to quarantine for two weeks as I had just flown back from China. I started to have this strange dream about someone called Old Ma Hakka. Every night it was the same and I would wake up terrified; I became too anxious to sleep and found that the only thing which helped was to get really drunk, too drunk to remember the dream. That was when my life seemed to completely unravel, I couldn't seem to cope with even the simplest of things…" Lilly's voice faded, and she felt hot tears wetting her cheeks. She sat down, too emotional to say any more.

"Thank you, Lilly," said Janet softly. "Thank you for sharing, you have been very brave. It will become easier."

"Now let us all join in a moment of quiet reflection. Let us be grateful to each other for the opportunity to share and for the love and trust that we bestow on one another in these moments of anguish."

Lilly closed her eyes, she felt surprisingly relieved. Janet's gentle voice leading them through a quiet mindfulness exercise was very soothing. She felt better than she had in a very long time.

As the group dispersed and she was preparing to leave a voice called out to her.

"Lilly, isn't it? I don't want to keep you. I was just wondering if you had a moment; what you said reminded me of something." It was the lady called Margaret.

"Erm, okay," replied Lilly a little uncertain.

"You mentioned Old Ma Hakka."

"Yes, or at least that is what I think the voice in my dream is saying."

"Well, I find it very interesting you see, because a friend of mine also had some dreams about an Old Ma Hakka. It was a few years ago now..."

"Really, you're kidding!" said Lilly, suddenly feeling a surge of excitement.

"Yes, I'm pretty sure. She asked me to do some research on it for her; I'm a history professor you see, or at least I was before I retired. Anyway, if you're interested, I can take a look at my old notes, I don't think I found out much, but you might find it useful."

"Oh yes please. Do you want to swap phone numbers and maybe you can call me..." Lilly trailed off. The mobile reception at the farm was so poor that Margaret might not be able to get through to her. "Actually, I should probably give you the number for the farm as well just in case."

"Excellent!" replied Margaret. "Well, I'll be in touch then."

Lilly found the cycle home surprisingly easy; it was as though she had been carrying around a huge weight these past few weeks and it had suddenly been lifted. *I can't wait to tell Oma*, she thought as she pedalled up the driveway.

"Hmm, now where did I put that box of notes from 2005?" Margaret was starting to get impatient. She had been through all the filing boxes which she had brought home from the college when she retired. The one from 2005, the one which would have the notes from her Hakka dream research, seemed to be missing. "Typical!" she muttered to herself. Then she remembered, she had shifted one box into the library to use as a footstool so she could reach the upper shelves. *I bet it's that one*, she thought to herself as she shuffled across the passageway. "Damn this arthritis!" she exclaimed; every joint seemed to be on fire after her exertions in the study.

She spied the box in the corner by the window, the 2005 label partially obscured by a curtain. The contents were just as she had remembered, and she found the notebook she wanted near the top. "At least my memory still works, unlike the rest of me," she said easing herself onto the window ledge. Thumbing through she quickly found the section on the Hakka dreams which her friend Hannah had told her about. She hadn't seen much of Hannah these past few years; now that their children were grown up and had moved away, she only rarely heard from her. Just the usual exchange of birthday and Christmas cards. It seemed like only yesterday that they would meet up for a chat outside the school gates. *Tempus fugit* she thought to herself. They had been quite close friends despite their very different backgrounds. Margaret an aspiring history professor at Oxford, Hannah a nurse at a local hospice. Yet they were so similar in many ways, both passionate about their children and endowed with a similar love of music and theatre.

The Hakka dreams episode had been something of a crossroads for Hannah. On looking through her notes Margaret was reminded that the whole experience had proven too much for her. She had been struggling to cope with the pressures of being a hospice nurse, helping all those patients through their last few days. She had suffered a breakdown and quit nursing for a while. When she recovered, she had retrained as a midwife which she seemed to enjoy much more and as far as Margaret knew, she was still doing. Hannah, being a few years younger than Margaret, was not yet ready for the *scrap heap* as Margaret called retirement.

As she had suspected, Margaret had not been able to find out very much about Old Ma Hakka. She had found a reference to a local stream called "Hakka's brook" the name of which had its origins in Saxon times but nothing else of note; certainly nothing about dreams. *Hmm, not much there,* she thought. *Maybe Hannah would be willing to talk to Lilly. I don't expect it will help to solve the mystery but talking about it might help.* Margaret was pretty sure she still had Hannah's number; *Perhaps I should give her a call?* Looking at her watch she realised it was gone four. *No time like the present,* she thought to herself and with some difficulty managed to heave herself off the window ledge and set off on a hunt for her phone which she was pretty sure she had left in the kitchen.

"Hello, Hannah speaking."

"Hannah! I'm glad I caught you. It's Margaret. I know it's been an age, but I wondered if you have a few moments for a chat?"

"Margaret! Oh, wow. It has been a long time. Is everything all right?"

"Oh, yes dear. No need to worry, I'm well and so are the family. Nothing to worry about, are you all okay too?"

"Yes, we're fine. I've been super busy as we've been quite short staffed. They have diverted quite a few of us onto other wards to help with Covid patients. I have to say I am relieved they didn't need me; I don't think I could cope with that."

Suddenly Margaret felt a little unsure that it was a good idea to bring up the topic of the Hakka dreams as they had upset Hannah so much. She decided to push on anyway, Hannah could always say no if she didn't want to talk about it.

"Are you still there?"

"Yes, yes sorry. Just getting a little distracted in my old age," joked Margaret.

"Come now, you're not old!" replied Hannah chuckling.

"Feels like it some days. Anyway, I didn't call you to have a moan. No, something came up in a conversation the other day and it made me think of you."

"Oh really, what was that?"

"Well, I was at one of my group therapy meetings and…"

"I didn't think they would be running those during lockdown," interrupted Hannah.

"Well Janet, the lady who runs them, is very resourceful. She has set up an outdoor meeting space. Anyway, during the meeting a young lady mentioned that she had been having these weird recurrent dreams…" Margaret paused.

"Go on," said Hannah, interested but suddenly sounding a little nervous.

"She mentioned Old Ma Hakka."

"Really!" gasped Hannah.

"Yes, well I thought of you. I found my old notes from the research we did together but there isn't much to go on."

"No, I remember being a little frustrated at the time. But that was all years ago, I haven't really thought about it for ages."

"I know, and I don't want to upset you, my love. Gosh, that's the last thing I would want. I was just wondering if you would be willing to have a chat with her. I think it would really help her. She seemed quite excited to know that she's not alone." Margaret crossed her fingers, desperately hoping that Hannah would agree.

"Hmm, well I'm not too sure. Tell me a bit more about this young woman and what she told you about her dream."

It was a beautiful morning; Lilly was basking in the late summer sun enjoying the remains of her breakfast and hoping that Oma had forgotten that she had agreed to help with the laundry. She and Oma had quite different priorities on days like this. Just as she was drifting off into a reverie about Spanish villas and holidays long past, she was interrupted by Oma calling her from the kitchen.

"Lilly dear, there is a phone call for you; says her name is Margaret."

Lilly jumped up, upsetting the crockery on the table and spilling her coffee. Not that she noticed, she was too excited. She had been wondering when Margaret would call. It had been almost a week since the group meeting.

"Margaret, so lovely to hear from you."

"I have good news! I managed to get in touch with my old friend that I told you about, Hannah."

"Yes…" replied Lilly expectantly.

"Well, it turns out she does remember the dreams about Old Ma Hakka and after a little persuading she has agreed to talk to you."

"Oh Margaret, thank you! That will be amazing, I can't wait…"

"Now don't get too carried away. I must tell you that she was very shaken up by the experience and was not overly keen to rake over the past. She is not sure if she will be able to tell you anything that you don't already know."

"Of course, I quite understand. It will be good just to share with someone who has had a similar experience. Until last week I thought I was going completely bonkers."

"Hannah wasn't too keen for me to share her phone number, but she has agreed to meet with you. She works as a midwife at the local medical practice and said she will be free tomorrow afternoon after her shift finishes. There is a park next door to the surgery where you will be able to sit and talk; she will meet you there at four o'clock."

"It all sounds a bit clandestine, like a spy movie," said Lilly excited but instantly regretting her flippant remark. "Sorry didn't mean to sound so trivial, I am really grateful that Hannah is willing to talk to me at all. Four o'clock will be fine, I'll be there."

"Great, I will let her know. Oh, and Lilly maybe you should wear something to help her recognise you; something like a red carnation." Margaret had thought the spy reference was actually quite amusing. Hannah was being a little paranoid, she thought.

"Great idea, a carnation it is!" chuckled Lilly feeling slightly relieved. She was beginning to like Margaret.

"OK then, do let me know how it goes." Margaret hung up.

Lilly did a little skip as she crossed the hall to place the phone back on its charger.

"You look mighty pleased with yourself," said Oma. "Now, how about you help me hang this washing up; don't want to waste a good drying day."

CHAPTER 8

HANNAH

Lilly woke to the sound of rain lashing against her window. She was bemused, the previous day had been such glorious sunshine. *No wonder Oma had been so keen to get the laundry done*, she thought and turned over to look at the clock. It was seven thirty, she could hear Oma moving about downstairs, she was always an early riser. Pulling on her dressing gown, Lilly decided that she wasn't going to get any more sleep either, she was too excited.

After breakfast she persuaded Oma to show her the map again, she wanted to go over the route to the medical practice just one more time before she headed out for the day. Lilly was terrified of getting lost especially as she would be going by bicycle and was not at all used to the complex network of paths and tracks which criss-crossed the fields between the village and the outskirts of Didcot.

"Now, I'm sure you will be fine. Gramps has checked your bike for you; all in good working order."

"But what if it's still raining, I'll get soaked," Lilly looked up from the map a little disgruntled. She was trying to find an excuse to get a lift so she didn't have to go on her own, her anxiety beginning to creep in and take hold.

"The forecast says it will be drying up by lunch time, so don't worry," Oma smiled, trying not to show her growing impatience. If she didn't leave soon, she was going to be late. "Gramps said he wanted you to help him with sorting some of the stuff in the old barn," she added escaping through the back door before Lilly could ask her anything else.

Great! thought Lilly, it never ceased to amaze her the number of ways that Gramps could contrive to keep her busy. The latest project was sorting through all the junk he had stored in the outbuildings. On reflection Lilly was actually quite pleased to have something to keep her occupied; four o'clock was going to come round very slowly.

As it turned out the ride into town had been remarkably straightforward and Lilly arrived a few minutes early. She propped her bike next to the bench by the entrance and sat down in the shade to wait. Oma had been right; the sunshine had returned, and Lilly was actually feeling uncomfortably warm after her exertion. It was a surprisingly quiet spot given the location near to the centre of town. The summer flowers were still fragrant, and the small fountain sparkled in the late afternoon sunshine. She noticed a small group of people doing Tai Chi practice in a space normally set aside for cricket. She smiled, Tai Chi was something she had watched routinely on her trips to China, she found it very calming.

"Hello, you must be Lilly," said a kindly voice. Lilly turned to see a lady in a midwife's uniform settling down at the other end of the bench.

"Er yes, sorry, you must be Hannah," she stammered, unsure how long Hannah had been waiting.

"No need to apologise, it's a lovely place, this. I come here often after work to relax."

"Yes, I was watching the group practicing Tai Chi. I didn't know anyone did that in England."

"Hmm, yes. They started coming here during lockdown; It's amazing how creative people have been at keeping up their hobbies these past few months," mused Hannah.

"Well anyway, I'm afraid I don't have long. Margaret told me you have been having strange dreams about Old Ma Hakka," said Hannah, getting straight to the point.

"Yes, indeed. I have to say when she mentioned your dream, I was very relieved. Up until then I thought I was going mad."

"I can quite understand. I found the whole experience quite unsettling. I can tell you a little about it, but I don't want to go into too much detail. I don't want to go back to having nightmares about it."

For a moment it looked like Hannah was going to stall. Her eyes took on a slightly vacant look and she started to look a bit pale.

"Sorry, just give me a moment," she said and took a couple of deep breaths before continuing.

"At the time I was working as a hospice nurse. I was staying in the Old Manor House at Upton helping the lady who lived there through her last few days. I stayed for five nights in total, sleeping in the room next to the master bedroom. Each night I experienced the same dream. I felt quite haunted by it and thought there must be a ghost, even though I told myself that I didn't believe in ghosts. I'm ashamed to say that I was relieved when the old lady passed away and I didn't need to go there again. I never had the dream again, thankfully. I don't remember the exact details, but I did write it down in my diary."

Hannah took an envelope from her bag and passed it to Lilly. "I made copies of the relevant pages. I hope you can read my writing."

"Oh, thank you. That is really kind of you," said Lilly, taking the crumpled package and trying not to look too impatient to open it.

Hannah continued with her account. "I did a bit of research at the time, with Margaret's help. All we found was a story about the origin of the name "Hakka" in relation to Hakka's Brook. No reference at all to an Old Ma Hakka."

"That is similar to what I found too," replied Lilly. She had hoped that Hannah could tell her something new and clearly her disappointment showed.

"I'm sorry, you were probably hoping for more…" Hannah paused. "…there was one thing which I do remember about the place. The furniture in the room I slept in was really ornate, it was like being in a stately home, it felt a little unreal. There was this peculiar old chest at the foot of the bed. I remember it because of the countless bruises I obtained when I bumped into it in the night and also because it was quite rare. When the estate was auctioned off after the lady of the Manor passed away it was bought by a local museum. I expect it's still there. Anyway, it's probably not relevant; I don't remember whether Margaret found out anything about it…" she broke off again and started to look a little distracted, fidgeting and looking at her watch.

"Do you remember the name of the museum?" asked Lilly, anxious not to miss any details.

"I think it was something like the Oxford Furniture Museum, although I'm not totally sure. Anyway, I am sorry, but I need to head off now. I hope this has helped; I am sure Margaret can answer any other questions you have," Hannah got up and hurried off leaving Lilly with no chance to say any more.

"Thank you!" she called out as Hannah scurried quickly away. Lilly felt a little selfish, it had clearly taken a lot for Hannah to come and talk to her. She also felt excited, hungrily she tore open the envelope which was still resting in her lap and started to read.

Excerpt from Hannah's Diary

6th Mar 2005 – I have had this strange dream for the past two nights now. It is the most vivid dream I think I have ever experienced, and it has left me quite shaken up. I read somewhere that it's useful to write down such dreams as soon as you wake up, so if I have it again, I will try to do that.

7th Mar 2005 – I have just woken up from the dream; now that my heart has stopped racing, I will try to write down as much of it as I can remember.

It starts off with a sensation of sinking softly into a gentle swaying motion, feeling warm and bright. I can't really see anything clearly just a vague sense of green all around. My other senses feel like they are on overload. I can taste this amazing, sweet taste of fresh water as though it's come straight from a cool spring. The air smells rich with the sickly scent of flowers and is so fresh it's like being on a mountainside. There is so much sound, like layer upon layer of notes from a wide range of instruments but like none I have ever heard before. Buzzes, whirring, tick-ticks, whistling and chirring, knocking and thudding all on top of a background whooshing and moaning. My skin feels tingles and prickles all over, sometimes punctuated with a tickling sensation as though something is scampering over it. It's all quite unnerving. As the dream goes on the low moaning becomes stronger, an "ooh haa, ooh haa" kind of like a giant sleeping and the sound of their breath but mellow and soothing. It becomes gentle like a lullaby "ool haa, ool hakka, ool ma, ool ma hakka" on and on. I get the sense of being lulled to sleep even though I am already dreaming. Then there is a sudden change; it's hard to describe. There is a jolting, thudding, jarring sensation a bit like when you hammer a tent peg with a wooden mallet. Then an awful cracking sound followed by a lurching, falling feeling finishing with a jolt and nothing more. All of the sensations from before are gone, everything is quiet and there is this overwhelming sense of loss. At this point I wake up with the words "oold ma hakka" whispering over and over in the back of my mind.

The cycle ride home had passed in a blur. She kept thinking about Hannah's dream, it was so similar to her own and yet subtly different, somehow richer and more vibrant. The link to "Old Ma Hakka" was unmistakable though. As Lilly wheeled her bicycle into the shed, she was interrupted from her thoughts.

"Did you have a good trip?" asked Gramps as he wiped his hands on an old rag.

"Yes, thank you and I didn't get lost," she replied, rather proud of herself. The meeting with Hannah had put her in a really good mood.

"Oh good, I look forward to hearing all about it over dinner. I just need to tidy these tools away and then I'll be in."

Lilly always found it rather odd that Gramps kept up a running commentary of what he was going to do next. It was quite endearing but could also be quite irritating at times. As she entered the kitchen, she was greeted by the heady smell of chicken pie. "Mmmm!" she thought, Oma always did a really good pie.

"Make sure you wash your grubby mitts in the cloak room and not my kitchen sink! Oh, sorry dear. I thought you were Gramps," said Oma appearing from the pantry with her hands full of runner beans. "Dinner will be about twenty minutes, love. Oh, and you had a good trip I take it. You can tell me all about it at dinner." She bustled off to talk to Gramps before Lilly had a chance to utter a word.

"Twenty minutes, that will give me just enough time to make some notes about my conversation with Hannah," said Lilly to herself as she kicked off her shoes and trotted upstairs.

An hour later as they sat around the dining table having

just polished off some lovely pears in custard, Lilly was finally able to share her news.

"So, I had a good meeting this afternoon. Margaret had put me in touch with Hannah who…"

"Sorry love, who is Margaret?" asked Gramps.

"Oh, yes. I had probably best start at the beginning. At the first group therapy meeting I went to I talked about the Hakka dreams that I have been having. One of the group members, a retired history professor called Margaret, said that a friend of hers had mentioned having a similar dream some years ago. So, she arranged for me to have a meeting with her, Hannah, and that is who I went to speak to today."

"Right, so what did she have to tell you?" asked Oma, a little impatiently. Lilly had told her about Margaret before.

"Well, she didn't tell me much that I didn't know already. She and Margaret had not been able to find any references to Old Ma Hakka, just a story about how Hakka's brook got its name."

"Yes, as I thought, that's where I had heard of it before too," commented Gramps.

"Anyway, she gave me a copy of her diary which includes a description of her dream. It's similar to mine but not quite the same. She said she thought it was a ghost or something as she had no other way to explain it. She told me that she had the dream when she was staying at the Old Manor in Upton."

"Oh yes, I know the Old Manor. Keith and I did some repairs for them the other year when the roof was damaged in a storm…"

"Stop interrupting dear, let Lilly finish," chastised Oma who was still impatient to hear the rest of the story.

"She also mentioned something about an unusual piece of furniture in the room she slept in. Some sort of old chest. I thought it was a bit odd that she would mention it, but she must have felt it was important somehow."

"Did she say anything about the chest?" asked Gramps, looking sheepishly at Oma and realising that he had interrupted again.

"She did actually. Apparently, it was quite rare and was subsequently sold to a local museum. Hannah thought it was the Oxford Furniture Museum or something like that."

"Hmm, can't say I've heard of it," murmured Gramps.

"So, Oma, I thought maybe if I come into the veg shop tomorrow, I could use the computer in the office to have a look for the museum on the internet. I can help out in the shop as well if you like." Lilly grinned at Oma, hopefully.

"Well, I expect so dear, maybe at lunch time or after closing. I could do with an extra pair of hands in the storeroom as we need to do a stock check," replied Oma with surprising enthusiasm.

"Great!" said Lilly jumping up. "Shall I do the dishes?" she asked as she cleared the table and headed off to the kitchen.

Oma and Gramps smiled at each other a little bemused. They were not used to this energetic version of Lilly.

It wasn't until after closing time the next afternoon that Lilly had a chance to use the computer in the office. Oma had offered to wait but Lilly thought it best if she didn't have someone looking over her shoulder, so she had agreed to walk home; it was a lovely evening, and she was starting to enjoy being out in the countryside after so many weeks cooped up indoors.

"Now let's see," she murmured to herself as she entered the name of the museum that Hannah had given her into the web browser. She found herself holding her breath in anticipation as the computer whirred and the progress wheel span round and round on the screen. The internet connection was slower than she was used to.

The first hit on the list was for "The Oxford Museum of Furniture" which was roughly as Hannah had remembered. Lilly clicked on the link and a web page slowly loaded. Initially she was a little disappointed; the museum was currently closed due to Covid. She sighed; she couldn't bear the idea of having to wait weeks to find out if the chest was of any relevance. She clicked through the various menus and found a heading which said, "on-line tour". *Hmm* she wondered, would it be worth a look or a wild goose chase? "What the hell," she said to herself and clicked on the link.

It took her to a series of images of notable exhibits in the museum. One of them was an old chest. Her pulse quickened, was this the chest that Hannah had mentioned? There didn't seem to be any information about it but as she hovered over the image, she realised she could click on it. Another window opened with more images of the chest and a picture of a house, the Old Manor at Upton. "Bingo!" she exclaimed. Beneath the pictures of the chest was a brief description; it was thought to date from the late Tudor or early Stuart period and the lid was unusual as it was carved from a single branch of Poplar wood. Lilly wasn't sure whether the information was relevant but she decided to print the pages anyway so she could show it to Margaret along with the copy of Hannah's diary entry.

Gramps will probably be interested too, she thought to herself chuckling; she could imagine him getting very excited and explaining at great length the craftsmanship that would have gone into making such an item. She was becoming very fond of Gramps.

She packed up her things and headed out into the warm evening, a faint scent of freshly mown hay drifted through the air and the evening chorus of bird song swelled around her. Initially she had been relieved to find that someone else had shared a similar dream, but now other questions started to nag at her. What could be causing these dreams, why her and Hannah, were there others?

CHAPTER 9
MICHAEL

In the two years since Margaret had retired, she had developed an intermittent relationship with alcohol. It was not because she felt lonely, indeed she actually quite enjoyed the peace and quiet. Both her girls had long since left home and her ex-husband, well he was just that, an ex. No, it was the sudden lack of any sense of purpose which had hit her quite hard. She no longer had a reason to get up in the morning; no lectures to give, no essays to mark. Although she rather liked being alone in her thoughts she did miss her students and the excitement of joining them on their journeys of discovery, their shared treasure troves through the historical archives.

This unexpected bereavement, for that is how she saw it, this loss of purpose, had led her to turn to drink. The days seemed to pass quicker that way. So what if she didn't get up until lunch time, there was no-one to get dressed for, nowhere she had to be. After a couple of months of Margaret missing phone calls and not turning up for Sunday lunches, her eldest daughter had decided to intervene and had sent Janet round to see her. Janet was a really exceptional therapist; she had a knack for seeing just what a person needed to help them climb out of the mental pit they had fallen into. She had persuaded Margaret to take an interest in local history, getting her to contribute regular articles to the Parish magazine. She had even suggested that Margaret write a book but, so far, her heart had not been in it; she couldn't find a topic she felt worthy of her effort and after one or two false starts had given up on it.

Her drinking had improved, with only the occasional lapse, usually around family gatherings or college functions when the temptation was too great for her to resist. The regular group therapy meetings served to keep her pretty much in line; she knew that if she missed one then she could expect a visit from Janet which was always rather embarrassing. Janet was kindly but firm with an ability to make you feel like a scolded child just by looking at you in a particular way.

Lockdown had been tough on Margaret but she had managed pretty well thanks to regular phone calls from Janet and a couple of her fellow group members. She had surprised herself by feeling quite excited about going back to the group meetings; the chance to meet people face to face and have a proper conversation felt like a real treat. When Lilly had mentioned her Hakka dreams, Margaret had to stop herself from jumping out of her seat with excitement. All of her pent-up zeal for historical research came flooding back. Her brain began to buzz, and she found herself almost salivating in anticipation of solving an intriguing mystery. "The Hakka Dreams", she could almost picture the words emblazoned in gold script on the cover of a book, her book. This indeed would be a reason to get up in the morning.

Having put Lilly in touch with Hannah, she set about a new task. *What if there are other examples of the Hakka dreams and I just wasn't looking in the right place before?* she asked herself. The online archives had grown exponentially in the last ten years. So much more had been scanned and analysed, keywords and metadata added. Every man, woman and their dog seemed to have diaries and letters which someone had found in their attic and donated to historical collections; all of it was now available at the click of a mouse. *I just need to get access to the university databases,* she thought. That was not going to be trivial; although she had a computer at home she couldn't get onto the archives from there, she didn't have access to the servers. The system was a little old fashioned in that respect, nobody had quite got round to making it available via a web portal, quite frustrating really. She would have to go into college; something she was perfectly entitled to do as an Emeritus professor. The tricky part would be logging in; her account would have expired by now. She was going to have to find someone who would be willing to help her.

Fortunately for Margaret she had been much liked by her research staff and one of her former postdocs still worked in the history department. Andrew had a soft spot for her so when he got a call quite out of the blue, he had been more than happy to help. After a further two, frustrating, weeks waiting for the lockdown restrictions to be eased Margaret finally returned to the college library for the first time since she had retired. It felt like coming home.

"Hello Prof, how are you?" Andrew smiled and just managed to stop himself from stepping forward to give Margaret a hug; physical contact was not allowed, and he would have to remember to keep two metres away. It was good to see people face to face, but the Covid restrictions made things feel a little weird when you did; even after a few months he was still not used to it.

"Not too bad, all things considered," she replied with a grin. It had always been something of a running joke between them; how could you possibly consider all things?

"Good to see that you haven't changed," he chuckled. "Now let's get you settled in." He set off down the corridor.

"Slow down dear!" puffed Margaret, she was a little out of shape having been cooped up for the past few months. Not that she had been exactly fit before then, more of a bookworm than an outdoor person.

As they entered the library, she paused for a moment to take in the atmosphere of the place. The layout may have changed with new, fancy desks and computers everywhere, but it still smelled the same. That complex aroma of old books and photocopiers mixed with an undernote of slightly unwashed students. She never thought she would have missed it so much.

Andrew was waiting for her at the end of an aisle. "You can use this desk; I have already sanitised it for you."

She shrugged off her jacket. She wasn't quite sure why she had put it on as it was a bright sunny day. Just another of her old habits, having to be dressed for the occasion. As she sat down, she noticed that Andrew had already logged onto the archives for her using a guest account.

"You should be all set. If you need to print anything it

will go to the central printer over by the entrance, I can help you with that if you need me to."

"I'm sure I can work it out, I may be old but I'm not senile," she snipped and then realised she was being a little unfair on Andrew. "Sorry, you know me. Never one to accept help lightly, too proud," she raised her eyebrows and smiled.

"Same old Prof," he said before turning to go. "I'll be in the office if you need me."

Half an hour later Margaret was feeling quite pleased with herself. Her initial search of the database using the term "Hakka and dream" had turned up a couple of results. They seemed to be related to one another, an article from a Journal of Psychiatric Medicine and a diary entry. Both of them were authored by a Dr Hurleyman, a former Oxford professor. The database entries had hyperlinks next to the citations.

It's my lucky day, thought Margaret, *the youth of today don't know how easy they have it*. In her early days as a historian, she would have had to fill out a paper request for each of the articles and take them down to the archive librarian. If she was lucky, she would get to see them the next day. Now all she had to do was click on the link and another window would magically open containing a copy of the article.

"Voilà!" she said as the first article popped up. It was a full paper in which the esteemed Dr Hurleyman expounded on his theory about schizophrenia and the link between delusions and dream states. It was quite a hefty piece, thirty pages in length, all in quite technical language. *Oh boy, this is going to be fun*, thought Margaret. Undeterred she scrolled through the pages. Sometimes articles like this had little sections which contained direct evidence interspersed with the bulk of the text. She spotted just such an excerpt on page fifteen. It was entitled "Michael's Dream". She felt her pulse quicken and her palms prickle with sweat, she realised she was holding her breath in anticipation. She read on.

- Michael's Dream -

"In his apparently more lucid moments, Michael was able to describe the content of these dreams he has been having about "old ma Hakka" as he calls her. At first, they are like a soothing lullaby where old ma Hakka is singing to him but then they get hard and angry with banging and shrieking, and they end with a sudden lurch and falling sensation. At this point I believe he wakes up although it is hard to be sure as Michael usually gets very agitated and starts crying. He rambles on about how old ma Hakka is angry and he must have done something wrong, he needs to fix it. "I must fix it, I must fix it," he whimpers with shining bright, terrified eyes gazing at me in a plea for help. This is typical of the kind of delusions experienced by schizophrenics; they hear voices of others telling them to do things; in Michael's case he seems to only hear the voices in his dreams which leads me to think that it has something to do with his REM sleep function."

Bingo! she thought and started to scribble frantically in her notebook. She was meticulous about keeping track of her sources and the key pieces of information that they provided.

Over the years she had filled hundreds of notebooks just like it; all of them now filed neatly away in the archive boxes that were crammed into her study. Eagerly she returned to the search results and clicked on the other link which revealed a scanned image of a diary entry. It was written in a tight, spidery script which she was going to find difficult to decipher. Feeling a little disheartened she let out a sigh. "This is going to take a while," she said to herself as she took off her glasses and rubbed her eyes. She was quite unused to staring at computer screens.

"How are you getting on?"

"Oh, you made me jump!" she gasped.

"Sorry, I heard you sigh and thought I would pop over. Need any help?" asked Andrew with his head on one side looking over her shoulder. It was tricky to read the screen from two metres away.

"Well, I found a couple of things but this second one is in a difficult hand which will take me some time to figure out."

"Scroll down a minute, right to the bottom," suggested Andrew. As she did so a line of typed script at the bottom of the page was revealed. "Click here for an annotated transcript," it read.

"Oh, you are a star!" exclaimed Margaret brightly. "I quite forgot we aren't in the dark ages anymore and these things have been done for us by computers," she said with a hint of irony. "The dark ages" was how Andrew had always referred to the paper indexing methods that Margaret had grown up with, when everything had to be done laboriously by hand.

"I'll leave you to it," he said as she clicked on the link. He knew full well that Margaret would get quite huffy with him if he stood behind her while she was trying to read.

- Excerpt from Dr Hurleyman's diary -

Mar 2ⁿᵈ 1970 – Today I had the occasion to visit my current patient, Michael, at his home. He rents an attic room in a cottage called "The Old Croft" at the edge of Upton. Michael was having one of his brighter, more lucid days and was happy to show me his room. He explained in much detail the depiction of old ma Hakka in the multitude of sketches he had plastering the gable end wall. To an untrained eye the images would seem most disturbing, but I found them to be a fascinating rendering of what Michael has described to me in previous consultations. The sunken, dark eyes and pitted, riven skin which had a curious texture almost like that of tree bark and dark fissures giving the mouth a heavy set and quite ominous appearance. I can understand why Michael finds her frightening.

I was quite relieved to descend into the dining room and continue our conversation over tea and cake which Michael's landlady had so kindly provided. After a few minutes Michael complained of feeling tired and left me to finish my tea in the company of the lovely Helena. She was quite worried about Michael and commented that when he had first come to lodge with her, he had seemed to be in much better health. He began complaining that he couldn't sleep; she hadn't thought anything of it until he was sent home from work after some kind of accident. Shortly afterwards was when the episodes of raving about this "old ma Hakka" started. She had been forced to call the doctor who had to sedate him.

Helena was not shy about telling me a great deal concerning her current situation. The fact that her husband had passed away recently and that with the recession she had been forced to take in lodgers even renting out the attic for the first time. Apparently, she'd had no trouble finding lodgers, with the new power station opening up there was hardly enough accommodation to go round. Michael was very sweet but now that he had become ill, he was starting to upset the other lodgers and she was thinking she would have to give him his notice. She wondered if there was anything I could do to help.

"Well now that is interesting," commented Margaret to herself as she clicked print, sending copies of the publication and diary excerpt to the printer down the corridor. Slowly she eased herself up out of her chair and hobbled off to fetch them before she forgot all about them; she had a terrible habit of leaving unclaimed articles on the printer. "It would be much simpler if we all had our own printers," she muttered to herself, forgetting for a moment that she wouldn't have her own one anyway as she was formally retired and didn't have an office.

"Now we have three cases of "Hakka dreams" and all localised around the same set of local villages. Lilly will be pleased," she mused to herself as she progressed steadily along the hallway.

On her way back from the printer Margaret was so engrossed in reading the printed copy of the diary transcript that she almost tripped over a wastepaper basket. "Steady Neddy," she muttered to herself as she faltered and put her hand on a desk to recover her balance. "I wonder if I should sanitise that?" she said to herself, her train of thought completely broken. By the time she got back to her desk she had forgotten about sanitising and flopped back down into her seat with a huff.

Now, where was I? Ah yes, the Old Croft at Upton, she jotted a note to remind herself to carry out a follow-up search on that. "Ooh, and I should probably check out Dr Hurleyman too. You never know where these little threads might lead," muttering to herself she made further notes; it had always been a habit she had tried to instil in her students. "Leave no stone unturned," she used to say. She was just thinking that Andrew had been one of her better students who actually followed that advice when he popped into view again.

"Sorry Prof but I'm afraid you'll have to finish up now. It's my turn to home-school the kids this afternoon and I can't leave you on your own. Who knows what mischief you might get up to," he said with a cheery smile.

"Okay, I guess I will have to come back tomorrow then, if that's possible." She made as if she was a bit put out, but Andrew could tell that she was rather pleased at the prospect of coming back again; he got the impression that she had rather enjoyed herself.

"Yes of course, tomorrow will be fine. Now could you wipe down your desk and keyboard before you go? I'll meet you by the main doors in a couple of minutes." He dashed off before she could say anything else.

"So, what's on the home-school syllabus this afternoon then?" she asked as they made their way out to the carpark.

"Well, I thought I might introduce my six-year-old to a spot of ancient Greek," he replied with a wink.

She chuckled; Andrew had always been pretty dreadful at Greek.

The following morning Margaret was excited to get going again. She had decided not to share anything with Lilly until she had been able to complete the extra searches on "The Old Croft" and Dr Hurleyman just in case there was something significant that she had missed. She settled back into her "new spot" as she thought of it and started to type.

The first search for further information about Dr Hurleyman pulled back a few hits which she spent a while trawling through. There didn't seem to be much of any significance; he had passed away in 2018 and his personal diaries had been donated to a local museum of science and medicine by his widow Mrs Helena Hurleyman. *I wonder if that is the same Helena who was Michael's landlady? Sly old dog,* she thought to herself. Most of the other hits related to his medical career, papers he had published, lectures he had given, prizes he had been awarded, but nothing which seemed relevant to the Hakka dreams. She saved the hit list just in case she wanted to go back to it and then moved on to her next topic.

Searching for "The Old Croft, Upton" gave her three hits. One was the reference to Dr Hurleyman's diary that she had already but the second one was something quite different. It was a reference to an article in an architectural journal with a curious title "On the use of pollarded wood from poplar trees in the construction of buildings from the Tudor and Stuart period." She clicked on the link to the original article. At the bottom of the second page was a photo of a cottage; the legend underneath read "Photo of The Old Croft at Upton, Oxfordshire in which the use of a pollarded branch from a poplar tree can be clearly seen on the gable end wall of the attic." Margaret hit the print button thinking that this may be something interesting to look at in more detail later. *I wonder if the cottage is still there?* she thought.

The final hit answered that question for her. It was a reference to a newspaper article entitled "Fire ravages cottages in Upton"; it seemed that "The Old Croft" had been the victim of a careless fire in which two period cottages had been badly damaged. The photograph showed the remains of a chimney stack still standing amid piles of smouldering rubble. "Oh, that is a pity," she muttered, then decided to print a copy anyway just for completeness.

She sat back and stretched. All this sitting down and peering at computer screens was playing havoc with her joints. Rubbing the back of her neck, she had a familiar feeling of an impending headache. *I must get my glasses checked*, she thought to herself although she couldn't quite recall whether the opticians were allowed to open at the moment. She found the ever-changing lockdown rules quite confusing. Heaving herself out of her seat she started the slow plod towards the printer. "I think I will call it a day after this," she mumbled to herself.

Just as she got back to her desk her mobile began to ring. After a minute of frantic rummaging in her bag she managed to find it just as the caller rang off. "Oh bother!" she exclaimed. Looking at the screen she realised it was a missed call from Lilly. She decided to call her back.

"Hello Margaret, thanks for calling back so quickly."

"Ah yes, sorry about that Lilly dear. I took an age to find my phone. What was it you wanted?"

"Well, I wanted to update you on the Hakka dreams. I had a very interesting meeting with Hannah a few days ago and she gave me some stuff. I was wondering if maybe we could meet to discuss it."

"Very interesting. Actually, I have some news on that front as well. I have been doing a bit of sleuthing in the historical archives and I have found something which I think you will find quite exciting."

"Ooh really, do tell!"

"Well, I think I have found another example of a Hakka dream. I still need to tie up a few loose ends, but it seems quite relevant; what is more the person concerned was living in Upton so there seems to be a geographical link."

"Gosh! That is amazing Margaret. Wow! I can't wait to hear more about it."

"Yes indeed, it's probably best if we meet in person so I can show you some things. How about we have a little catch up after the next group therapy meeting on Wednesday?"

"Oh yes, that sounds like a great idea."

"Well, I'll see you on Wednesday then."

"Okay, bye."

Lilly hung up. Wednesday would give Margaret plenty of time to get all her notes in a coherent order. She was feeling rather pleased with herself.

"All going well?" asked Andrew, appearing next to her as if from nowhere.

"Oh, I wish you would stop doing that!" said Margaret.

"Sorry, it's this carpet, it seems to mask my footsteps."

"To answer your question. Yes, things are going very well. I think I have everything I need for the moment so I will probably call it a day. I feel like I have one of my ghastly headaches coming on and would rather get back home before it really hits."

"Oh, that is a shame. I was thinking we could enjoy a picnic lunch together. Never mind, maybe another time. I am right in assuming there will be another time?"

"Yes, I am sure there will be. Oh, and thank you Andrew. I really appreciate you helping me out. It's given the old bird a reason to get up in the mornings."

"My pleasure Prof. Shall I see you out to your car?"

Lilly's mind was racing, she was so excited to be seeing Margaret. She kept rehearsing over and over in her head all the things she wanted to say and ask. She was desperate not to forget anything. She had been quite distracted all afternoon and hardly said a thing at dinner. Now she was arriving at the group meeting all hot and bothered and five minutes late. She nodded briefly at Margaret as she took her seat; under the watchful eye of Janet, she dared not risk saying anything. It was supposed to be a moment of quiet reflection for the group before they got started.

"Now close your eyes and relax into your seat. Feel your feet touching the ground. Lengthen your spine. Imagine the top of your head pushing up to the heavens. Slow your breathing, breathe into your abdomen and slowly out through your nose; let your in breath be soft and your out breath be long and smooth," Janet intoned softly.

Lilly found it remarkably effective at helping her to relax. Her mind cleared and she was able to focus on the meeting. She was quite proud of the fact that she had not had a relapse; not a drop of alcohol had crossed her lips for weeks. In fact, she couldn't recall even thinking about needing a drink. Her dreams were still there but she felt more in control; they were always pretty much the same and although the ending was abrupt, she kind of knew to expect it.

Margaret too had experienced her best few weeks for a long time. The Hakka dreams project seemed to have given her a new lease of life; so much so that Janet came over to her at the end of the meeting wanting to reflect on her progress. Margaret answered her questions politely, she was desperate to get away and talk to Lilly who she could see looking frustratedly at her from over Janet's shoulder. Fortunately, one of the other group members was hovering nearby anxious to speak to Janet so she was able to make her excuses and extricate herself without feeling rude.

"Sorry about that. It seems I have been a good girl for a change," said Margaret with a grin.

"Oh, that's OK. Janet means well and you do seem to have more of a spring in your step," replied Lilly. "Shall we find a bench to sit on?" she continued, looking about for somewhere to sit.

They found a comfortable spot, perching at either end of a bench by the church; not quite two metres apart but it would have to do. Margaret took great delight in revealing the notes she had made, drawing them out of her bag with a theatrical flourish.

"As I mentioned on the phone, I have found another example of a Hakka dream. A young chap called Michael who experienced a psychotic episode involving some strange dreams. A psychology professor wrote a research paper about it and there was also an excerpt from his diary which had been deposited in the archives."

"Wow, that is amazing. And it specifically mentions old ma Hakka, does it?" asked Lilly.

"Yes, it does. He was lodging at a cottage in Upton during 1970, just after starting a new job at the Didcot Power Station which I believe had just opened."

"Ooh, do you think the cottage is still there?"

"Afraid not. It seems it burned down a few years ago. I found a newspaper article about that too," said Margaret and then keeping up her sense of drama she continued. "All is not lost, my dear. I also found a reference to the cottage in an article from an architectural journal. Something about timber used in constructing buildings from the early Tudor period. I forget the details; there is a copy in the notes I have made," she said and passed an envelope to Lilly.

"The Tudor period, now that was fifteen-hundreds, wasn't it? So quite old then."

"Well early Tudor dates from around 1480, so it could be even older," said Margaret with a hint of surprise. She had not expected Lilly to be as knowledgeable, most of her university students didn't seem to know their dates, she had rather low expectations of the younger generation.

"Anyway, you said you had a meeting with Hannah. Did it go okay? I had the feeling she was reluctant to drag things up again."

"Yes, I did thank you. Although you are right, she did seem quite disturbed by it. I felt a little awkward to be honest." Lilly produced a sheaf of paper from her bag to show

Margaret. "She gave me these. They are copies of some pages from her diary which describe her dream. It is a lot like mine but also different in some ways. Did the notes you found on Michael describe any of his dreams?"

"I think there was something yes. It's probably best if you take a look for yourself. If you write down what your dream is like maybe we can compare them, now that we have three examples there might be some patterns," suggested Margaret. "Did Hannah tell you anything else?"

"Not much, she said that neither of you were able to find out anything significant at the time. Although thinking about it she did mention something which seemed a bit odd. She talked about a chest which was at the end of the bed in the room where she had the dreams. She told me it was now in a local museum; it's closed at the moment, but I looked it up online and did find a reference to it. In fact, I have just realised, it mentioned that the chest was thought to be from the early Tudor period; now surely that's not a coincidence. I think I printed out the page from the website," she added as she shuffled through her notes. "Yes, here it is," she said proudly showing it to Margaret.

"Very interesting," replied Margaret as she tried to read it in the failing light. "Well, I think we have plenty to digest. I shall have a good look at everything and maybe we can talk some more over the phone in a few days' time," she suggested.

"Thank you, Margaret, that sounds like a great plan." Lilly stuffed the notes in her bag and rummaged around for her bike lights. It was getting quite dark now and she didn't want to get caught out on her way back home. "Speak to you soon!" She waved to Margaret as she turned to go. Thoughts were already starting to whir in her mind. She couldn't wait to read about Michael's dream and the Tudor cottage, surely there must be some kind of link to her and Hannah.

CHAPTER 10

ALBERT

Lilly woke to a thumping sound. She was emerging from a confusing dream in which she was chopping at a piece of wood which had fallen from a tree into the back garden. Initially she thought the thumping was a part of the dream but as it persisted, she realised it was Gramps knocking on her door.

"Lilly dear, are you awake? Its seven thirty and time for breakfast."

"Just getting up," she fibbed as she buried her head under her pillow. She was still fuzzy from her dream and tired from all the excitement of the previous evening. She had stayed up late reading the notes that Margaret had given her and jotting down ideas. It was all very intriguing but so far, she had not managed to make much sense of it. *No time for that now*, she thought to herself as she threw back the covers and started pulling on some clothes. Woe betides her if she was late for breakfast; Oma ran to a strict schedule and Lilly was now expected to help out at the veg shop on weekdays.

She flew down the stairs and raced into the kitchen just as Oma was setting down some toast and coffee. "Mmm, that smells amazing," she said grinning at Gramps and trying to avoid Oma's glare.

"We'll be leaving at eight. Hopefully, you can eat that without getting indigestion," said Oma softening a little. She was starting to get used to Lilly's cheeky ways, infuriating, and endearing all at the same time; she wasn't quite sure how that was possible. "Make sure you bring your boots; I need some help with harvesting cabbages and it's probably going to be muddy."

They left at eight on the dot. Oma realised she hadn't really asked Lilly how things had gone at the group therapy meeting. She had assumed, given Lilly's bright mood, that all was well.

"How was the meeting last night? You seem to be full of beans, so I am guessing it was good. You do seem to be so much happier these days and Janet mentioned that your sessions with her are going well." Seeing Lilly nod Oma didn't wait for an answer, she barely paused for breath and launched into another topic. Oma was always on overdrive in the mornings, verbalising what was running through her head as she planned the day. Usually, Lilly found it quite exhausting to listen to but today her mind was elsewhere.

Just a couple of days until the weekend and I can get stuck into the Hakka dreams, she thought to herself. Then an idea popped into her head.

"Oma, can I use the computer at the veg shop on Saturday afternoon?" she asked.

"Oh, well yes, I suppose so. I didn't think you were going to work on Saturday?" replied Oma, a little confused.

"I wasn't planning to, but I can help out if you need me. I was just wanting to do some internet searches, following up on some things for the project that Margaret and I are working on."

"Oh, yes of course. No, I probably don't need you in the shop on Saturday, but you are welcome to use the computer."

"Great!" said Lilly and planted a big kiss on Oma's cheek.

Now that the autumn was drawing in the days were becoming colder and wetter. Saturday morning arrived accompanied by a howling gale and rain lashing at the windows. Lilly had hoped to cycle to the veg shop so she could avoid an early start. Looking at the clock she realised that if she hurried, she would be able to catch a lift with Oma as she headed in for the morning shift.

Oma was just donning her wet weather gear as Lilly plunged down the stairs. "Can I catch a lift with you?" she gasped as she hurried to the kitchen to grab a cereal bar.

"Oh, Lilly! I wish you wouldn't rush so; you nearly bowled me over," admonished Oma.

"Sorry, I didn't want to miss you," Lilly replied sheepishly as she turned to give Oma a hug.

"OK, I'll be waiting in the car. Don't be long."

As they arrived at the veg shop there seemed to be some sort of drama playing out. A delivery driver was shouting and gesticulating at one of the staff.

"Oh my, what can this all be about?" uttered Oma her brow furrowing in concern as she pulled up into her parking space and got out.

"What do you mean there is no one to help me unload!" the delivery man was shouting.

"Is there some sort of problem here?" said Oma adopting an air of authority. She had no time for overbearing behaviour especially when it was directed at her staff.

"Oh, thank goodness you have arrived," replied Agnes. "Clive hasn't turned up and I'm not strong enough to help with these pallets."

Oma looked about perplexed; she and Lilly were probably not strong enough either. Just as the driver was about to continue with his rant one of the waiting customers stepped forward.

"I can help out if you like, if it's just a few pallets to shift that shouldn't be a problem."

"Oh, thank you Robbie! You are a godsend, yes please. I'll make sure you are well rewarded for your kindness," replied Oma looking much relieved.

Lilly watched as Robbie set about manoeuvring a trolley; she hadn't seen him around before. He wasn't particularly handsome but had that strong rugged look and big hands that she found quite attractive. Oma coughed to get her attention. "You can help Robbie with his shopping later," she said raising one of her eyebrows in a wry smile. Lilly blushed.

"I may need you in the shop after all since Clive isn't here," sighed Oma. It was hard to get reliable staff at the best of times; the Covid pandemic made things even more complicated with staff often having to self-isolate at very short notice.

"That's okay Oma. I can do the stuff I wanted to do on the computer after lunch. Now what is it you need me to do?" replied Lilly still watching Robbie out of the corner of her eye. Most of the people who came to the shop were middle aged or older; it was nice to meet someone nearer her own age for a change. Not that she had met him yet, strictly speaking, but she was looking forward to being properly introduced later.

Lilly spent the morning helping on the till. Oma had given her instructions to let Robbie have his shopping for free and to offer him some of the last of the season's honey if he wanted it. Luckily when he finally arrived at the counter the shop was quiet, and she was able to chat without feeling spied on; she felt her pulse quicken slightly as he stepped forward. He looked completely different with a face mask on, warm brown eyes crinkling slightly as he smiled.

"Hi, you must be Robbie. I'm Lilly, Oma's granddaughter," she said in her best air steward voice; warm and cheerful. She looked radiant despite the veg shop overall and baggy sweatshirt. Robbie blushed and looked at his feet.

"Er, yes, er that's right," he stammered not knowing where to look. Attractive women like Lilly terrified him.

"Oma, oh sorry you probably know her as Breda. Breda wanted to thank you for helping with the delivery so you can have your shopping for free. Oh, and if you want a jar of honey as well then I can get one for you."

"Oh, well, er thank you. That is so kind. Er yes, I would like some honey; just like Breda to remember that it's my favourite."

Lilly stepped over to the shelves to grab a jar. "What size would you like?" she asked and then realised that was probably a silly question. She picked up the largest jar and turned back to the till in time to see Robbie had been watching her with curiosity, head tilted to one side. He looked away quickly and blushed.

"Thank you," he said as he stuffed the honey into his bag and rushed off.

Lilly stood there watching him go. He had a free and easy gait which suggested a level of self-confidence that he had not displayed a moment ago.

"I think he likes you," said Oma who had crept up behind her.

"Oh, stop it!" said Lilly blushing. Oma laughed. "Is he a regular? I haven't seen him before."

"Yes, comes in pretty much every Saturday morning. I think he works as an arborist for a woodland charity, and yes, he lives on his own, before you ask."

"I was going to ask what an arborist is actually!" responded Lilly indignantly, although she had been wondering that too.

"Oh, something to do with planting and looking after trees. Gramps knows him quite well; Robbie supplies him with wood for his carpentry from time to time."

"I shall have to help out on Saturdays more often," said Lilly grinning. "Is it time for lunch?"

Margaret had slept little on Wednesday night. Her mind was awash with thoughts about the Hakka dreams. She kept circling back to the comment that Lilly had made about finding patterns in the dreams and was frustrated that there was so little to go on. Two transcripts and some comments from Lilly were not enough; she needed more, there had to be more. Try as she might, she couldn't shake these thoughts. One o'clock then two o'clock ticked by and still no real sleep. Her joints were troubling her more than usual which only made matters worse. "Must be due for a change in the weather" she mused to herself as she turned over and tried to get comfortable. It was the kind of pain she experienced a few days before a big storm but surely it was too early in the year for one of those. At four o'clock, having managed to doze lightly she finally gave up on sleep and dragged herself out of bed. She had resolved to call Andrew as soon as it was socially acceptable to do so. "There must be more examples of these dreams, I am missing something," she said to the kettle as she started to make her first tea of the day.

Margaret waited and waited as the clock hands made their inexorable journey around the dial slowly ticking off the hours. Finally, by eight o'clock she figured it was not too early to call; after all he had small children, so he was bound to be awake already.

"Hello?" came a muffled voice.

"Hello Andrew, its Margaret. I hope it's not too early. I wanted to catch you before you head off for work."

"No, it's not too early Prof," sighed Andrew. "How can I help?"

"I was wondering if you had some time today for me to pick your brains. I have been following up on those searches I did the other week, and I'm a bit stuck. Thought maybe a fresh pair of eyes would help to see a way through it."

"Sounds interesting, let me think," Andrew paused to mentally review his plan for the day ahead. "I can't do today but I should have some time tomorrow afternoon. I tell you what, why don't you come up for that picnic lunch we were going to have, and you can talk me through it."

"Oh, Andrew thank you. Yes, that will be perfect. I shall bring some nibbles."

"Okay then, meet me outside the department tomorrow at twelve thirty and we can find a nice spot in the park."

"Twelve thirty it is," said Margaret just as Andrew hung up.

She smiled and almost did a little skip before remembering that would probably not be a good idea; her knees were already complaining. "Now time to take my medication," she mumbled to herself as she struggled up the stairs to get dressed.

The weather on Friday morning was mild and sunny with only a gentle breeze. *Maybe I was wrong about that storm coming*, she thought to herself as she got out of the car, although her joints thought differently.

"Right on time as always," beamed Andrew as he joined her. "I've got your favourite pasty from the local shop."

"Oh, you do spoil me. Now where shall we sit?"

"There's a nice bench in the shade by the pond. I thought we might try there."

"Good, lead on Macduff," replied Margaret. She had never been one for lunch time picnics during her time at the college, always too much work to do in the office for that. Now thinking back, she regretted it, sitting outside was actually rather stimulating and could help to get the creative juices flowing.

As they sat down at either end of the bench, Andrew produced some hand sanitizer from his pocket and offered it to her. She grimaced. "Ghastly stuff this, I really don't know why they have to add such cloying scents to it. I mean who wants to eat their lunch with hands smelling of cucumber and aloe?" she huffed but rubbed some onto her hands anyway. "Better safe than sorry I suppose."

Together they laid out their contributions for the picnic, it was quite a feast. Pasties, some vegetable crisps, scotch eggs, cherry tomatoes, sticks of cucumber, some blueberry muffins. Margaret picked up a stick of cucumber and sniffed it. "Doesn't smell at all like that ghastly stuff," she griped. Then looking up at Andrew she realised she was spoiling the mood. "Sorry," she said a little sheepishly.

Andrew decided to ignore her comments, usually best in his experience. "So, tell me all about this project of yours. What have you found? It must be something really complex to have you stumped; or maybe you're losing your touch." He winked at her, a wry smile on his face.

"Now don't be cheeky young man," she replied, grinning. Andrew always knew how to lighten the mood.

She spent the next half hour taking him through the information she and Lilly had gathered about the Hakka dreams. Between mouthfuls of food, she laid out the details of each case, the sources of information, the apparent geographical link between them. She showed Andrew some of the key documents and answered his questions patiently.

"Hmm, interesting. I think we need some tea," he said jumping up and heading over to the nearby café which still offered hot drinks to take away.

Margaret watched him go. She knew that he was using it as an opportunity to buy some thinking time; to let the information percolate through his brain. She crossed her fingers, hoping that he would come up with something.

Andrew had a way of seeing things which was different to other people. It was as though he could navigate a complex web of interrelationships just by closing his eyes and seeing the patterns emerge before him, a rare talent.

"You say you found the Michael example from the archive search that you did last time," he said as he returned with two steaming cups of tea. He handed one to Margaret before sitting back down and making a start on one of the muffins.

"That's right," replied Margaret. She couldn't quite see where this was going.

"Hmm," mumbled Andrew through a mouthful of muffin. Nodding to himself he paused to take a sip of tea. Margaret fidgeted; she was starting to get impatient. She could tell that Andrew had thought of something and now he just seemed to be dragging things out for effect. She frowned at him.

"Oh, sorry. Yes, you are probably wondering what I'm thinking." Before Margaret could reply he moved quickly on. "What search term did you use?"

Margaret consulted her notebook. "Hakka and dream" she said, she turned the book so he could read it.

"And you used that specific spelling of "Hakka", interesting. Why did you choose that?"

"Hmm, I'm not sure," she replied suddenly realising that something had biased her thinking. "Yes, I know. It's because when I looked into this before with Hannah, a few years ago, the only reference I could find was to "Hakka's Brook", with that spelling."

"Ah, so local knowledge influenced your thinking," Andrew grinned at her. It was something that Margaret had taken pains to coach him on during his earlier years as a researcher; she had fallen into a common trap.

"I must be losing my touch after all," she said, a little dejected.

"Oh, now don't be so hard on yourself. Now, let's rethink it. If someone told you a story about a dream in which some being like "old ma Hakka" featured, how might you spell the word Hakka?"

"Probably H A C K E R, the normal spelling of hacker, I suppose," replied Margaret with a sudden surge of excitement, as far as she was concerned lunch time was over now. "Shall we go into the library and see if you can teach the old dog some new tricks?" she beamed, eager to get going and see what they would find.

Having got comfortable at her now familiar desk in the library, Margaret entered a new search term into the data base. "Hacker and dream" she typed. She found herself holding her breath in anticipation as the computer whirred. Search results began streaming down the screen; there were hundreds of them.

"Oh boy!" she sighed. This was going to take forever to sift through. For once she was glad that Andrew was hovering around behind her back. Turning to him she asked, "Any suggestions maestro?"

"Let me take a closer look," he replied and she pushed her chair away so that he could get to the desk. It was difficult to work together and socially distance at the same time.

"Hmm, we could try a filter. A lot of these hits look to be about an author who writes horror stories." He mused, chuckling to himself and miming a stabbing action "eee, eee, eee," he said looking at Margaret and then realising that the horror film reference was completely lost on her. He selected the "non-fiction" option from a drop-down list and hit return. A much smaller set of fifteen hits appeared.

"Ooh, that's much better," said Margaret, itching to get back into the driving seat. "I think I can manage from here."

"Of course, here you go. If you need me for anything else just shout, I'll be in my office." With that Andrew made a swift retreat, leaving Margaret to peruse the list at her leisure. He hoped she would find something useful; he was starting to feel quite intrigued himself.

Margaret skimmed through the keywords and short abstracts from each of the hits looking for anything that would stand out. She would do a more thorough review later. One hit, in the middle of the list seemed interesting; it related to D-Day preparations and the railway line at Upton. She flagged it and continued with the other hits; she didn't want to miss anything by getting distracted.

"Hmm, not bad for a first pass," she said returning to the one hit she had flagged. It seemed to relate to a letter written by an officer in charge of the improvements to the Didcot to Newbury line which took place in 1942-1943 as part of the preparations for the D-Day invasions. Whilst he was encamped at Upton Manor some sort of incident had occurred which he had deemed interesting enough to write about in a letter to a fellow officer.

"It's amazing what pops up in the military archives," she thought to herself. The volume of material which has been scanned and indexed was quite phenomenal. No document was considered to be too trivial. One of the officers concerned must have been someone of influence for them to have kept his letters. Clicking on the link she found both an image of the original letter and a transcript of the text. She started to read.

Excerpt from letter by Capt. John (Jonny) Coates to a friend – From historical archive relating to D-Day preparations

Upton, 12th October 1942

Dear Bunny,

I still can't believe my rotten luck. This latest posting to the Berkshire Downs is turning out to be really rather dull. I don't quite know why they feel the need to double track the stretch of railway line between Didcot and Newbury, but I'm told it is of strategic importance. All a bit hush hush I think, certainly the Major doesn't seem to be in the know any more than yours truly. At least the digs are okay and the tucker that the land lady provides is a lot better than we were getting in Essex. Even some fresh veg from the village thanks to the Dig for Victory folks. They seem to be growing the stuff everywhere, even the lawn of the Old Manor House here in Upton has been dug up to grow cabbages or something.

Anyway, having said it's dull, there was one recent episode which caused quite a stir and I thought, as a medical man, you might be interested. We had a couple of new recruits join us the other week and one of the lads got himself into quite a pickle, went quite off the rails, so to speak. Private Albert Noakes was his name. Big brute of a lad with not much going on upstairs if you know what I mean. Said he was eighteen but behaved like he was still tied to his mother's apron strings. Seemed to expect to be looked after, fat chance of that, we are all run off our feet. I had to billet him in the old barn, and he came to me complaining that the Sergeant had made him sleep on the floor as we'd run out of cots. What he thought I could do about it I don't know. Anyway, I told him to use his initiative and sent him off with a flea in his ear.

A couple of days later I bumped into him in the yard, he came dashing over to me pleased as punch. Insisted on showing me the cot he had made himself from the frame of an old cart he'd found at the back of the barn. I'll say this for him, he might have been none too bright, but he was a dab hand at carpentry. It was shortly after that things started to go wrong for the lad. The Sergeant came to see me saying that Private Noakes was causing all sorts of trouble, upsetting the men in the barn at night, creating such a hullabaloo that no one could get any sleep. The Sergeant was quite indignant about it, said it was as if the lad had suddenly lost his marbles and he couldn't get him to make any sense. He told me he'd had to lock Noakes up in the stable for his own safety, the others were that fed up with him. Asked me if I could come and try to talk some sense into him.

Reluctantly I paid a visit to the stable and asked Noakes what all the to do was about. He was quite calm, morose even. Wouldn't look me in the eye, just stared at my feet. He said he'd been having strange dreams, thought it was his grandmother trying to reach him, to call him back home. "She's sick you see, sick and missing me," he said. I asked him what he meant, and he described what he feels in the dream. "It starts with her singing to me, old ma, old ma, old ma hacker," she sings and it's all light and warm and swaying, nice like being in a hammock. Then she starts to get sick, the song gets all wheezy and raspy, and I feel like I can't breathe, like this tightness in my chest and a smell of smoke and taste of soot in my mouth. I start to feel this terrible loneliness, I can't explain it, like I'm the only one left in the world. The hammock starts to rock and sway violently and with a massive cracking sound it shakes me awake. It's my Nan, I tell you, she's sick and lonely and I have to go to her." At this point he started to cry all tears and snot. Seeing a grown man reduced to that filled me with disgust. Goodness knows how he would have coped if he was out at the front line.

I couldn't get any more sense out of him, the Sergeant and I agreed we should keep him away from the others, it would be bad for morale. As it was, the problem took care of itself. That night, Noakes escaped from the stables and went AWOL. He didn't get far, the MP's picked him up on the outskirts of Didcot. The last I heard he was in Reading jail awaiting court martial. I must confess I was glad to be rid of him, he was having such a bad effect on the others. I struggle to see how anyone could become delusional so quickly, maybe the weak minded are more susceptible to such things. Perhaps you can offer me your medical opinion when we catch up at the end of the month. I have to say I am gagging for a decent drink; I hope the wine cellar at your place hasn't been ransacked.

Yours,
Johnny

Trying to stay calm, Margaret forced herself to read it through again. She couldn't believe it; another example of a "Hakka or Hacker dream" and in Upton of all places. There certainly seemed to be a pattern emerging. She quickly saved the search results and hit print; she wanted a copy of this article and the other abstracts as well. Reading things through on screen was just not the same as good old-fashioned paper in her opinion. She was just about to summon up the will power to journey over to the printer when Andrew appeared.

"You must have a sixth sense," she said turning to him.

"Not really, I heard the printer start up and assumed you must have found something," he replied with a grin. "Do you want me to go and grab the printouts for you?" he offered, seeing that she seemed to be struggling to get out of her seat.

"Oh, would you, thanks. My joints seem to be really playing up today for some reason."

Margaret watched impatiently as Andrew dawdled back from the printer skim reading the documents as he went.

"That does look interesting. Another piece in your puzzle, I think." He placed the printouts on the desk.

"Indeed, it is," she huffed, snatching up the papers. A familiar glimmer in her eyes, giving away the fact that she was getting really quite excited about this project. "I shall have plenty to follow up on from this one," she commented, her mind already processing ideas for additional searches on *D-Day* and *Dig for Victory* to provide more context and maybe offer more clues.

Andrew interrupted her thoughts. "I wonder," he paused as she looked up. "I wonder if there is another term you should search for."

"Oh, and what would that be?" replied Margaret, a little annoyed at being interrupted.

"Well, the letter mentions *old ma hacker*. Didn't that phrase come up in some of your other hits as well?"

"Possibly," she said, a little dismissively.

"Just a thought," said Andrew, realising that he might be treading on Margaret's toes. He had forgotten that she could get a bit possessive over her projects and didn't like to be rushed. He turned to go.

Margaret blushed a little. "I'm sorry. It's a good suggestion. I'll make a note to follow it up. All this excitement has made me quite tired. In fact, I think I might call it a day. Perhaps I can come back next week?" she asked as she started to gather her things.

"Of course. I will be happy to help. Just give me a call and we can arrange something."

"Thank you, Andrew."

"My pleasure Prof," he smiled. "Now let me help you with your things and don't go wearing yourself out over the weekend will you," he admonished, knowing full well that she would push herself to the point of exhaustion now that she had the scent of something.

She frowned at him, not liking to be fussed but then conceded that maybe it would be a good idea if he helped her to her car; her joints were really beginning to burn.

CHAPTER 11

WILLIAM

The wind was still howling and the rain whipped sideways into her path as she made a mad dash from the car to the front porch. Lilly was soaked through and feeling quite dejected; her latest internet searches had turned up nothing new.

"Is that you Lilly?" called Gramps as she was stripping off her wet layers. "Oh my, you look like a drowned rat. Here take this," he said handing her a towel. "Oh, before I forget, there was a call while you were out. A lady called Margaret, asked if you could call her back."

"Okay, thanks Gramps." Making her way upstairs Lilly started vigorously towelling her hair. *I wonder what Margaret can want.*

Having changed into dry clothes she settled down in the living room with a cup of tea kindly provided by Gramps. She could hear Oma clattering around in the kitchen making a start with the supper preparations. *I wonder what's for dinner*, she thought, her stomach starting to growl. She decided now would be an ideal opportunity to call Margaret. On the second try, the phone was answered with a lot of puffing and panting.

"Phew, Hello? Huff."

"Hello, Margaret, it's Lilly. Are you okay?"

"Ah yes, yes I'm fine," came the reply. Although Lilly was not at all convinced.

"Let me catch my breath dear. My arthritis is playing up terribly at the moment, it's the damp weather. I never do well in damp weather." Margaret sounded like she was really struggling.

"I can call back another time if now is not convenient," suggested Lilly.

"No, no. Now is good. I am glad you called. I have some exciting news," she continued before Lilly had a chance to respond. "I went through our findings with a former colleague of mine, and he suggested doing some different searches in the database. Using some alternative key words. He helped me do that yesterday afternoon and we found another example of a Hakka dream. It's silly really, I should have thought of it before. I just had to use a different spelling for Hakka…"

"Sorry, what, slow down a bit. You say you found another example?" interrupted Lilly excitedly.

"Yes, yes, I have. I had made a classic mistake, just sticking to one spelling of the word Hakka based on what we had found before. A bit embarrassing really for me to make such an elementary mistake, must be losing my touch. Anyway, I found a reference to a letter written by an army Captain during the war. It was about a soldier who had a dream about old ma hacker, spelt H A C K E R."

"Oh, I see…" replied Lilly finally realising the point Margaret was trying to make.

"Yes, and you'll never guess where the soldier had his dream," continued Margaret not pausing to give Lilly a chance to answer. "In Upton, a barn near Upton Manor."

"Now that is exciting, it looks like there is definitely something to do with Upton and the dreams, although of course I don't live in Upton, but our farm is not far from there," Lilly tailed off, hesitating to make a definitive link at this stage.

"I need to follow up with some further searches. I rather ran out of steam on Friday. Andrew, that's my colleague, he suggested a further search for *old ma hacker*. At the time I didn't think much of it but looking back at all my notes, every dream so far refers to *old ma hakka*."

"Yes, that's right, that's what I hear in my dream too," responded Lilly. "I wrote out my dream for you as you suggested so we can make comparisons. I can let you have a copy next time we get together."

"Marvellous! I am hoping to go back into college early next week so I might have even more to tell you about."

"Sounds good. What about after our meeting on Wednesday again? No wait, I'm not sure. Didn't Janet say something about having to miss this week as she needs to find a different location now that the weather is getting colder?"

"Hmm, yes, I think you're right. Well perhaps you could come over to my place for a socially distanced cup of tea. I have a large conservatory which we could use, that sort of counts as being outside."

"Great. I am working during the week. What about Saturday afternoon? You live near to the veg shop don't you; maybe I could come over after my shift?"

"Excellent! Let's make it after lunch at around two o'clock then," replied Margaret.

Lilly agreed and they confirmed the details of Margaret's address. Hanging up, Lilly could hardly contain her excitement. Thanks to Margaret their project was flying along; they now had four solid examples of Hakka dreams and all of them emanated from Upton and the surrounding area. It really couldn't be a coincidence, there had to be some kind of link. Then another thought crept into her mind; she had engineered a reason to be at the veg shop next Saturday too. *I wonder if Robbie will be there again,* she thought, humming quietly to herself as she wandered into the kitchen to tell Oma all about the latest news.

"You're in a good mood. Still thinking about Robbie by any chance?" teased Oma.

"No, actually! I was just on the phone to Margaret. She has found another example of a Hakka dream," replied Lilly, indignantly.

"Oh, that is interesting. You can tell me all about it while you peel those carrots if you like." Oma thrust an apron into her hand and made room for her on the worktop. Lilly ran through the latest news that Margaret had shared including the observation about the use of different spellings for Hakka.

"So, we have agreed to meet up next Saturday afternoon and discuss the new information in more detail. It turns out Margaret lives quite near to the veg shop so I can drop in there after my shift."

"Ah so you want to work Saturday mornings more regularly now do you. I wonder why that might be?" Oma chuckled and Lilly blushed.

"What's for dinner?" asked Gramps, poking his head

around the kitchen door and once again unwittingly rescuing Lilly from an awkward conversation.

"Stew and dumplings with vegetables. Assuming Lilly gets round to preparing the vegetables," replied Oma looking at the unpeeled carrot in Lilly's hand.

The storm raged right through the night and well into Sunday morning. Lilly was woken several times by small pieces of tree debris being flung against her windows and the rattle of roof slates tumbling off into the gutter. When she finally surfaced it was nearly ten o'clock. Pulling her curtains, she half expected the garden to be a scene of devastation. Everything turned out to be remarkably normal, just a few small tree branches on the lawn and an upturned garden chair teetering at the edge of the pond. It was still raining steadily but the wind had dropped significantly. She could see Gramps craning his neck, trying to survey the damage to the roof.

As she flopped down into one of the kitchen chairs Gramps came in from the garden. He looked a little put out.

"Is everything okay?" asked Lilly.

"Bit of bother with the roof. A few tiles were blown off in the wind."

"Yes, I think I heard that happen, it made a terrible racket."

"I'm not surprised it woke you," he replied placing the remnants of several tiles on the table in front of her. "I shall have a devil of a job getting to the spot, they came right off the ridge by the chimney. I don't think I've got a ladder long enough," he grumbled as he shuffled off to wash his hands.

Lilly made some fresh coffee and noticed that Oma

had left her a plate of breakfast on the warmer. She was just tucking into the juicy bacon and scrambled eggs when Oma appeared. She placed a book down next to Lilly.

"Something you told me yesterday sparked a memory. It took until this morning for me to realise," she said somewhat cryptically. Lilly looked up, a wave of confusion crossing her brow.

"Oh sorry. The new Hakka dream example that Margaret had found. You said she used a different spelling of Hakka."

"Yes, that's right. Not H A K K A but H A C K E R."

"Well, I realised I had seen another spelling of it somewhere, but I couldn't think where. Then it came to me this morning. In this book on local history there is a discussion of the origins of the name Hakka, and it seems that *kk* was often replaced by *cc*. In some of the sources, particularly the older ones, the spelling is *Hacca* rather than *Hakka*," she said pointing to the page in front of Lilly.

Lilly swallowed hard on her mouthful of food. With eyes watering she skimmed over the text. She coughed slightly "Huhum, now that is curious. I'm not sure whether Margaret has considered that spelling. She certainly didn't mention it. I shall have to add that to the list of things to go through when we next meet up. Thanks Oma!" she beamed and reached over to give her a hug.

Oma smiled, pleased that she could be of some use. It seemed that the Hakka dreams project was really helping Lilly to recover; she appeared much less anxious and more engaged with the world around her. Lilly watched as Oma tidied up the breakfast things, humming gently to herself. She was glad that Oma was taking an interest in her project, it gave them something to talk about other than cabbages.

It wasn't until Tuesday that Margaret had recovered enough to make the trip into Oxford to conduct her further research. The poor weather had played havoc with her joints, so much so that she had been barely able to get out of bed. After a brief foray into town to collect her prescription, she decided she felt well enough to make the trip, that and the fact that she didn't think she could face another day stuck at home with little else to do.

It turned out that Andrew had been right; a new search using the term "old and ma and hacker" resulted in a further hit. This time it was for some medical archives from the Berkshire Asylum in Moulsford; some case notes written by a Dr Malcolm about one of his patients. *Hmm, Moulsford, that's only a few miles from Didcot*, thought Margaret as she clicked on the link to reveal a copy of the record.

Excerpt from Medical Case Notes written by Dr Malcolm, Berkshire Asylum, Moulsford
Patient – Mr. William Tomlin
Dr. Malcolm attending

Date – December 10th 1918

The young man seemed bright and alert at first, relating to me the circumstances which had brought him here. It seems that on returning from Flanders, where he served as a Private with the Princess Charlotte of Wales Regiment, he found himself destitute with no home to go to. His mother had passed away last winter and his place as an apprentice wheelwright had been given up to another younger and more gifted lad. The village wheelwright, having felt sorry for William had allowed him to sleep under an old cart in the workshop until he could find something better. I really felt for him; this seems to have happened to so many of those returning from the trenches. They had given everything they had to King and Country and come back to nothing, those that did come back, that is. My brother served alongside William and was less lucky if you can call him lucky now. He was admitted to the asylum three days ago having been detained by local constables who had found him raving outside the Hagbourne village shop and lashing out at passers-by.

I asked William to tell me how he came to be arrested. At this point he became quite agitated, started rocking back and forth, wringing his hands, and clutching at his hair. I recognised the common traits of shell shock; I have seen them all too often these past few months. "It aint fair, it aint fair, I wasn't doin no harm. They wouldn't listen, no one would listen. I was only lookin for her and askin if they'd seen er." When I asked him who he meant, thinking he must have been referring to his poor deceased mother, he started to sob violently, tears and slobber running down his chin. "Old ma, Old ma Hacker" he said gulping. "I couldn't find her, she wasn't there. Last night my cart had gone so I had nowhere to sleep and now I can't sleep no more, I've lost old ma Hacker." I asked him who "old ma Hacker" was and where she lived. He kept ranting "I've lost her! She was under my cart, but it's gone and now I've lost her!" His eyes were bright, pleading, from *a place of pure agony as though his whole reason for being had been erased. After that I couldn't get him to say anything at all. He just sat rocking, clutching his knees, and whimpering like a child.*

William seems to have deteriorated significantly over the past two days. His eyes are dark and sunken, his skin grey with a fine sheen of sweat on his brow. As before he adopted a hunched posture, clutching his knees, rocking back and forth, not making eye contact. I asked him if he had been sleeping. "Can't sleep, can't sleep, she's gone. No one to sing me a lullaby." I asked him who he meant, and he referred to "old ma Hacker" again although he still wouldn't say who she was or how he knew her. After that he said nothing. I walked him to his bed, and he lay down and curled up like a child just staring at the wall and whimpering softly. The nurse told me that he does little else now.

William was not able to leave his bed today such has been his decline over the past twenty-four hours. He has a high fever like so many others on this ward and I fear he has succumbed to the Spanish flu. He looked at me with pleading eyes and whispered something. I drew closer and asked him to repeat it. "Old ma

Hacker, she was trying to tell me something, it's all too loud, I can't hear her. Shh Shh, listen, I can't hear her." Sadly, that was the last thing that he said. I sat with him for a while as his breathing slowly grew softer and less regular, until it stopped.

Time of death – 3.15 pm

Margaret was not generally the sort to feel sentimental, but this tale of woe left her feeling a little breathless. "Oh, my goodness," she croaked hoarsely trying to supress the tears which were welling up in her eyes. It was unusual for a medical account to contain such a degree of emotion; Dr Malcolm must have felt a real connection with young Will, maybe because of his own brother. After a couple of deep breaths, she felt composed enough to read the account again. There were definite similarities with the other Hakka Dream examples and the geographic link was there too, this was the second example of a Hagbourne dreamer. "Lilly will be excited," she whispered half to herself as she hit the print button.

Struggling to get out of her seat she looked around wistfully hoping that she could get Andrew's attention and ask him to retrieve the copies from the printer. His office was empty, and he was nowhere to be seen. "Bother!" she muttered to herself. Deciding that she didn't have the strength for a return trip to the printer she reluctantly packed up her things and made her way to the exit which was just past the printer station. Just as she was leaving the building, she saw Andrew coming the other way. He was carrying a cup of tea and what looked like a bag of muffins.

"Oh, are you off already Prof? I had bought these as a treat for us to have at teatime."

"I wondered where you had got to. I'm not feeling the best so I thought I should call it a day. I found what I had been looking for, your suggestion was spot on as usual," she replied a little tersely. The disappointment with her own frailty spoiling the excitement and masking the gratitude she should have felt.

"Good," he said and then quickly added "I mean, good that you found something, not good that you are going. Would you like one of the muffins anyway? They are blueberry your favourite."

Margaret accepted the proffered bag. "Thank you, Andrew. You are always so kind, I'm sure I don't deserve it." She smiled weakly.

"Now you make sure you rest when you get home. If there is any more information you need just give me a call. I can always do the searches for you and send the results by email," he offered.

"I might just take you up on that," she replied and turned towards her car. She was already imagining putting her feet up and tucking into one of the muffins with a nice hot cup of tea. "Maybe I am getting too old for this," she muttered to herself.

As Lilly pedalled through the village, she tried to put out of her mind the disappointment she felt at not having seen Robbie at the veg shop that morning. For the tenth time she found herself wondering if it was because she had been late arriving, maybe she had missed him. She cursed the fact that one of her tyres had been flat and it had taken her an age to find the bike pump.

Oh stop it! she thought to herself angrily. She felt like a silly schoolgirl with a crush. At least she had remembered to bring all her stuff for her meeting with Margaret. She glanced at her watch, she was running a couple of minutes late and she was not completely sure that she was going the right way. As she turned what she thought should be the final corner she came to a very grand looking house. She checked the map on her phone again. *Well this should be it*, she said to herself, trying to be optimistic as she churned her way through the deep gravel driveway. Slithering and sliding she sincerely hoped that no one was watching, she was not at all sure she wasn't about to make a very ungraceful entrance.

The house had a very large front door, painted black, with a traditional Victorian style bell pull at the side, it jangled loudly. *At least I know it works*, she thought to herself. It was very quiet, after a minute or so she was beginning to think she was in the wrong place after all. Just as she was fishing about in her bag for her phone Margaret appeared at the corner of the house.

"Hello there. I thought it best if you came round the side. You can prop your bicycle against the wall," she said and then disappeared again. Lilly almost tripped over a pedal as she hurried to follow her.

The rear of the house gave onto a sweeping lawn leading down to an apple orchard. Margaret was waiting for her at the entrance to a grand looking conservatory which overlooked an extensive kitchen garden. "This place is beautiful!" Lilly commented as Margaret ushered her inside.

"Oh, it's not what it was. I have someone come in once a week to keep it tidy but sadly I don't have the energy these days to grow much myself."

Margaret had set out a table with chairs at either end. "I guess it's not technically outside but with all the doors and windows open it is probably good enough. There is a blanket on your seat in case you get cold," she said as she thrust some hand sanitiser in Lilly's direction. "Ghastly stuff this but probably best to use it if we are going to be passing things between us."

Lilly took a generous squirt and started rubbing it into her hands. "Do you want me to wear a facemask?" she asked, suddenly realising that Margaret was probably feeling a little vulnerable.

"Oh no, that shouldn't be necessary. Now, what can I get you to drink?"

"Tea would be nice, if that's not too much trouble. Oh, and maybe a glass of water as well," she added, suddenly realising that the bike ride had made her feel quite thirsty.

"Righty oh," replied Margaret and shuffled off inside.

Lilly sat down and searched in her bag for her notebook. She flicked to the latest page and reviewed the list of things she wanted to discuss. "Oh bother!" she muttered. She had quite forgotten about the suggestion that Oma had made about an alternative spelling for *Hacca*. She had intended to phone Margaret earlier in the week to tell her about it, but it had completely slipped her mind. The days at the veg shop had passed in a blur. With the number of Covid cases on the rise again there were an increasing number of customers requesting home delivery. Lilly had proved herself to be particularly adept at managing the online orders and logistics of preparing the deliveries, so Oma had delegated that side of the business to her. She had been completely run off her feet all week. The Saturday morning shift behind the till had felt like a holiday in comparison.

She was just trying to decide at what point it would be best to bring Oma's suggestion into the conversation when Margaret returned with a tray of tea and cookies. "Oh, good. I see you have come prepared. Shall we go over our list of topics that we want to cover before we get stuck into the details?" she asked eyeing Lilly's notebook, hungry with curiosity.

"Er yes, if you like. I have a copy of my dream that I wrote down for you," she replied patting a sheet of paper that she had laid out next to her notebook. "I also have a further suggestion of a search you could try." She pulled the copy of the local history book out of her bag and started thumbing through the pages to the one she wanted. "Yes, here it is. My Oma found it actually."

"Yes, and…" said Margaret, through barely disguised impatience.

"An alternative spelling of Hakka with *cc* in place of *kk*. Apparently, this was a common spelling in older texts," said Lilly turning the book so Margaret could read it.

"*Hacca*, yes, I see. Well, we can certainly try that as well. Andrew said he could do some searches for me so I can ask him." Margaret scribbled a note down to remind herself. Lilly was pleased, she had worried that Margaret might get frustrated about having to do yet more research; it was clear that all the toing and froing to Oxford was having quite an impact on her health. She thought it best not to tell her that Oma had made the suggestion nearly a week ago and quickly moved the conversation on.

"So, you mentioned this new example of a *Hacker dream*," she prompted.

"Ah, well now that is where it gets interesting. I think I told you I was going to do a further search for *old ma hacker*, yes?" Margaret replied and then continued not waiting for a response from Lilly. "I found another example with the spelling *hacker*. This time in the medical records of a young veteran soldier, William Tomlin, who had been admitted to the Berkshire asylum."

"Oh, so not so local as the others then," stated Lilly.

"Actually no, he was from Hagbourne village and was admitted to the local asylum after having a psychotic episode outside the village shop."

"But Hagbourne is in Oxfordshire. Is there a second village called Hagbourne?" asked Lilly, a little confused.

"Hagbourne was in Berkshire until quite recently. It was only when they changed the county boundaries in the nineteen seventies that the area south of the Thames was redesignated as South Oxfordshire."

Margaret paused to take a sip of tea. Lilly could hardly bear the suspense but decided it would be impolite to rush her.

"This new example concerning Will bears some remarkable similarities to the one about Albert that I told you about on the phone. In both cases an old cart seems to be involved and their dreams seem to be quite similar; they refer to *old ma hacker* singing to them. Although Albert's dream also talks about old ma being sick and lonely which is new," continued Margaret and she passed the transcripts across to Lilly to read.

Nibbling on a biscuit, Lilly quickly skimmed through the documents. Margaret was right they did seem quite similar. "Do you think it could be the same cart or would that be too much of a coincidence?" she asked.

"Hard to say. Either that or there could be something which is common to carts from this area. Or it could just be a coincidence. Maybe something else to look into further," said Margaret as she made another note to herself.

Lilly read the account about Will again. "This is awful though. Poor Will, fancy returning from the First World War only to find you are homeless and then dying of Spanish flu in an asylum all alone." She felt quite choked just as Margaret had. "Can I keep these?" she asked pointing to the printouts.

"Yes, of course. I made them for you. If we both go over these as well as the others, then maybe we will see some patterns. At the moment it feels like there is something there, but I can't quite put my finger on it."

"Okay that sounds like a good idea. I can ask my Gramps about the carts; he knows quite a lot about carpentry and being a farmer, he may know something about their construction. It's the sort of thing he would be interested in. When do you think your friend Andrew will be able to do the further searches?"

"Hopefully this coming week. He said he would be happy to help, and he can email me the results. I can give you a call if he finds anything and we can arrange to meet up again. I have to say it's nice having someone round for tea. Did you want another cup before you go?"

Lilly eyed the grey clouds outside and wondered if it might be about to start raining but she thought it would be rude to refuse another cup of tea. Margaret was clearly enjoying the company. "Thank you, that would be nice."

The ride home felt much easier than the journey to Margaret's house. The late afternoon was surprisingly warm for the time of year, and the wind was at her back. Lilly enjoyed the rush of the breeze as she free wheeled down the hill and cruised up to the turning by the farmhouse. Her head was buzzing full of the new information that Margaret had shared. It was as if she was on autopilot, hardly aware of her surroundings. Her reverie was abruptly broken as she entered the drive and narrowly missed the Land Rover that was parked up in front of the barn. She could hear voices, Gramps was in conversation with someone, they were discussing the roof repairs. As she headed to the back door Gramps appeared followed closely by Robbie. *What on earth is he doing here?* she thought to herself, quickly scuttling inside to avoid being seen.

Oma looked up from her baking in surprise. "Are you okay Lilly?"

"Er, yes. Fine. I'm fine. What is Robbie doing here?" she enquired her face colouring as a broad grin spread across Oma's face.

"He has come to look at the roof. He has a big ladder which should be long enough to reach the place where the ridge tiles have come away," she replied with a wry smile and a cheeky wink.

Lilly blushed even more deeply and stifled a giggle. *A big ladder*, she thought to herself.

"I was going to offer him some tea, there is some in the pot. You can take it out if you like."

Lilly hesitated. She wanted to go out and talk to Robbie but suddenly she felt like a love-struck teenager, all tongue tied. She had no idea what she should say to him. Gramps saved her the trouble of deciding. "Lilly love. Would you be a dear and pass out a couple of teas for the thirsty workers."

Get a grip, she told herself as she poured the tea. Taking a couple of deep breaths, she headed out to the garden. Gramps and Robbie were standing by the patio table. She set the tray down. "Here you go," she said smiling. She was about to turn away when Gramps stopped her.

"Have you met my granddaughter, Lilly?" he asked Robbie.

"Yes, I believe we met at the veg shop the other week," he grinned a little sheepishly. "I didn't see you this morning though but then I guess you don't always work on Saturdays," he continued with a wistful look in his eyes before staring at his shoes as though his confidence had suddenly deserted him.

Lilly tried not to blush. "I was a bit late getting there this morning. I had some trouble with my bike," she replied.

"Robbie is going to help me repair the roof," chipped in Gramps.

"Well, I think its best if I go up the ladder, William. I wouldn't want you getting into any mischief up there," said Robbie in a mock stern voice. "I should have some time next weekend if that suits you."

Robbie gulped down his tea. "I had best be off anyway," he said and hurriedly turned to go. "Say hello to Breda for me."

Gramps turned to Lilly with a big grin on his face. "I think he likes you," he teased.

"Oh, shut up and drink your tea," replied Lilly blushing as she headed back inside.

CHAPTER 12

AGNES

A s she watched Lilly cycle away Margaret mulled over their conversation. *Hacca*, she thought to herself, *how could I have missed that*. She knew she had a copy of the book that Lilly had showed her; it was written by an acquaintance of hers from her college days. She scanned the shelves in the library, impatiently she started pulling out larger volumes in case the smaller book, more of a pamphlet, had got lost behind them. Finally, she found it lying sideways across the top of some books on Roman architecture. *How did you get there?* she mused.

She quickly found the page which referred to the alternative spelling of *Hacca*. It seemed that documents from the late 1800s onwards started to use a mix of spellings with the spelling *Hakka* becoming more common in later texts.

The book did not offer a satisfactory explanation of why this had occurred. *Hmm, another thing for me to look into*, she grumbled. She found the lack of rigour applied by some of her fellow historians quite irritating. She looked at the biography on the back cover with some disdain. "Distinguished scholar, my aunt Nelly!" she snorted. She had never had much time for this particular gentleman.

Pulling her thoughts back to the present, she reminded herself that it did not do to dwell on past events. She looked at the clock. It was nearly supper time; maybe if she called Andrew now, she could catch him before he sat down to eat. She was anxious to know whether this new spelling of *Hacca* would unlock any further information; hopefully he would be able to run the searches for her early the following week.

On Sunday afternoon, just as Lilly was clearing away the remains of their lunch, the phone started to ring. Frantically drying her hands, she rushed into the lounge. Oma had beaten her to it and started chatting, it clearly wasn't Margaret. *Don't be silly*, she thought to herself as she returned to the kitchen, *there is no way that she could have the new search results back already*.

"Lilly, it's Janet on the phone. She was wondering if you were free for a chat," called Oma.

"Okay, just coming!" *What could Janet want?* she wondered.

"Hello Lilly. How are you?"

"Pretty good thank you," replied Lilly a little hesitantly,

she wasn't sure she liked being checked up on. She knew the subtext to the question was more to do with how she was sleeping and managing her anxiety.

"Good, I'm glad to hear it. You are probably wondering why I have called."

Maybe thought Lilly sarcastically.

"I expect you have heard that we will be moving into a further lockdown next week. That means I will have to suspend the group meetings again. I'm really sorry about that. I know you were enjoying them, and you seemed to be getting to know Margaret quite well. I think you are quite good for one another."

Lilly wondered where all this was leading. "Er, yes…" she replied.

"Good, good. Well, I thought that it might be helpful if we picked up again with our one-to-one calls. I know you found them useful before."

"Okay, if you think it will help then I am happy to give it a try." Lilly didn't really feel the need for more *therapy* right now, but she knew Oma would start to worry about her if she refused.

"Excellent. Perhaps we can arrange a weekly call for Thursday evenings, would that work?"

"Yes, that should be good."

"Right, I will pencil you in for seven thirty on Thursday. Just one question before I go; are you still having the dreams you mentioned?"

"Sometimes," replied Lilly. In fact, recently they didn't seem to bother her quite so much as before; it was just when she had been feeling anxious that she tended to notice them a bit more.

"Okay, well I have a suggestion I would like you to try. It might help if you start keeping a dream diary. If you can note down when you have them, how they make you feel, what you were doing the day before, that will help us to see if there are any patterns," said Janet hopefully.

"Uh huh, I can give it a try. I'm not sure there is much of a pattern, the dream is always the same but, okay then," replied Lilly reluctantly.

"Super, well I'll let you get on then. I look forward to talking again on Thursday." Janet hung up leaving Lilly a little bemused, she hadn't been anywhere near as disturbed by her dream in recent weeks. She still felt tired a lot of the time but the utter exhaustion and anxiety that she had experienced before seemed to have passed. Wondering if Oma was still worrying about her, Lilly headed back into the kitchen where she could hear her clattering about.

It had been a busy week for Andrew as he made preparations to work from home again during the coming lockdown. He hated working from home, there were too many distractions and he always found that whatever book he wanted was not one that he had remembered to bring back with him. Finally, on Thursday afternoon, during his weekly two hour visit to the college, he had found the time to carry out the further research that Margaret had requested. He pulled out the scrap of paper that he had hurriedly noted the details on when she had called him last Saturday dinner time; she always had a fantastic sense of timing. He could barely read his own scrawl. He could just make out *search for old and ma*

and Hacca spelled with cc and then something else illegible. *Oh well here goes nothing* he said to himself as he keyed in the term and hit enter.

There was a single hit, a reference to the archives of the Hop Growers Association. It never ceased to amaze him the obscure kinds of things you could find in the historical records. He clicked on the link and waited as the archived document loaded, the network speed via the university server seemed to be painfully slow recently. Meanwhile, he did a quick search about hop growing in Oxfordshire using his phone. *Hmm, that is interesting*, he murmured. It seemed that in the 1800s hop growing had been a thriving industry in the region of the Berkshire downs just south of the Thames, the area that today made up the District of South Oxfordshire.

Glancing back at the screen he noticed that the document had loaded. It was the transcript of a letter from the wife of a leading local hop grower to a friend in Kent. He read on.

Excerpt of a letter from Mrs Helena Wild to her friend Mary Gates

East Hagbourne, July 5ᵗʰ 1889

Dearest Mary,

We have all but completed our preparations for the impending move. To be frank I will be glad when the carts are finally loaded, and we can depart for Kent and the prospect of better times. The hop harvest is looking like it will be poor again this year and I am quite glad that Henry has finally seen sense and decided to sell the farm.

Young Agnes has been the most trying of the three children during these past few weeks. I suppose it is to be expected given her age and the fact that nanny dotes on her so. I have quite given up trying to instil discipline into her. She cannot seem to learn that young ladies do not run barefoot through the hop gardens in pursuit of squirrels.

Last Sunday, after Henry had informed the children of our plans for the move, I had cause to become quite vexed by her behaviour. She was quite upset that we will be leaving and out of spite she ruined her best Sunday dress by romping around in the garden with her brothers. As a punishment I locked her in the old oast house until she could learn some manners. It was only when nanny came to me that evening, clearly quite distraught, that I realised I had perhaps taken things too far. It seems that Agnes, having spent the afternoon in the oast house, had fallen asleep upon a stack of new kiln liners and become all but hysterical. She claimed that the old oast house was haunted by a ghost called "old ma Hacca". I have never heard such a fuss; she could not be consoled, and I had to resort to fetching the local physician to administer a sleeping draught. In the days that followed, Agnes gave the oast house a wide berth and would not settle down to sleep unless I went to her personally and promised that this "old ma Hacca" would not be able to get into the house. To be honest, I am quite done with this business and can only hope that once we have relocated to our new abode Agnes will be restored to her normal cheery self...

... I will be most glad to be joining you and the rest of the family for tea upon our arrival at the end of the month. Until then I wish you the best of health.

With much love and affection,

Helena

"Well, I never!" he exclaimed, "This will get Margaret excited". It seemed to fit with the other cases and was from East Hagbourne of all places, a clear geographical link. "What on earth can be the relationship between all of these?" he pondered as he saved the document and started drafting an email to Margaret. *I shall have to call her as well*, he thought, knowing full well that Margaret was not very good at checking her email.

Later that evening he managed to get through to Margaret.

"Oh, Andrew it's you," replied Margaret as she picked up the phone. "I have been wondering when you might call."

"Hello to you too Prof. Did you read the email I sent you this afternoon?"

"No, sorry. I've not got round to checking that yet today. Give me a moment and I'll pop into the study. Just starting up, might take a minute or two. So, did you find anything?" she asked hopeful that he hadn't just called to check up on her.

"Yes, I did. I ran the search for *old ma Hacca* spelled with *cc* which you asked me to do, and I found another example…"

"What about the other search?" she asked. Suddenly, Andrew realised that the rest of the note he had scribbled down and couldn't read must have referred to a further search. Just as he was about to humbly excuse himself, she interrupted again; evidently, she had managed to open the email.

"Well, I never. Another example from East Hagbourne, that is interesting. Hmm, yes hop growing used to be very common in this area. In fact, I think the very farm where Lilly lives now used to be a hop farm, she will be excited."

"Indeed, I thought you would be pleased," beamed Andrew. "I'd love to know what it is that links them all together, there must be something."

"I do hope so. It will take a bit more detective work I expect. There are quite a few background references which I haven't had a chance to look at yet. Anyway, as I was saying, the other search term, did that not result in anything?" she enquired again. It seemed Andrew was not going to be let off the hook that easily.

"Er, sorry. I didn't run it. I have to confess I couldn't read the last part of the note I scribbled down when we last spoke. What was the other term you wanted me to look for?"

"Oh Andrew," sighed Margaret. "The other search was for *Hacca and dream* again spelled with *cc*. I thought it would be best to be thorough in case a different combination of words had been used. I don't expect we'll find anything new, but I would like to check for peace of mind."

"Yes, of course. I will try to do it as soon as I can. I'm really sorry Prof." He felt quite foolish and was doubly frustrated with himself as he probably wouldn't get a chance to go into the college until the following week.

"That's okay. I've got plenty to be getting on with so waiting a few more days won't hurt," she replied, her tone softening a little. "I'm grateful that you can find the time to help, you must be rather busy with all the faffing about switching to home teaching again and what not. Just give me a tinkle when you get a chance."

"Will do, Prof. Hopefully I will find something else exciting. Speak soon," he said hanging up. He breathed a sigh of relief; the old Prof could still make him feel like a naïve student at times.

Having read through the copy of the transcript that Andrew had sent her, Margaret was feeling in a much brighter mood. Clearly the hint from the local history book, that older references tended to use the *cc* spelling of *Hacca*, was correct. This letter was from the late 1800s, they seemed to be going on a journey back through time. It was a little curious though, it didn't seem quite like the others. The young girl thought she had seen a ghost rather than experiencing a dream. Although thinking about it, Hannah said she'd thought her *old ma Hakka* was a ghost. Asides from the geographical link she was still non-plussed as to what the connection could be. At any rate she thought it would be best to give Lilly a call and tell her about it. She knew Lilly could only pick up email on the veg shop computer so she probably would want to know before the weekend.

In the event, it seemed that talking to Lilly would have to wait. Margaret tried to call several times and couldn't get through. The phone was permanently engaged for the rest of Thursday evening. She sent Lilly an email anyway and just hoped that she would get it. *Maybe I'll try again on Saturday afternoon* she thought.

Saturday afternoon proved to be quite eventful for Lilly. Right at the end of her morning shift she had managed to grab a chance to check her email and had hurriedly printed out the document that Margaret had sent her. Her mind was all of a buzz as she read snippets of it out loud to Oma on their drive home.

"Oh, and listen to this bit… *It seems that Agnes, having spent the afternoon in the oast house sleeping upon a stack of new kiln liners had become all but hysterical. She claimed that the old oast house was haunted by a ghost called "old ma Hacca"…*" she jabbered excitedly. "What's an oast house?"

"A kind of kiln where they used to dry the hops. We used to have one here at the farm many years ago, but it was in a very poor state of repair, they knocked it down and replaced it with a barn, I think. It was before my time; Gramps would be able to tell you more about it," Oma replied as they turned into the farm lane.

"But Oma. It's so exciting, another old ma Hakka story and you were right about the spelling! What would I do without you?" she planted a big kiss on Oma's cheek and bounced out of the car dashing towards the house in search of Gramps. As she rounded the corner, she nearly walked straight into a ladder that was propped against the wall.

"Mind out!" called Robbie from above, clutching on for dear life.

She looked up sheepishly, "Sorry, are you okay?"

"Yes, I'm fine. Nearly done in fact. Could you tell William that I need a hand with passing down some tools."

"Will do," she replied and made her way inside. The shock of seeing Robbie and nearly causing an accident had completely eclipsed her earlier excitement.

Gramps was just heading outside with two steaming mugs of tea. "Robbie said he's finished and asked if you can help with the tools," Lilly told him as she made her way to the cloak room.

"Oh, don't forget to ask him round for Sunday lunch," Oma called after him.

"Isn't that against the rules?" enquired Lilly. "I thought the latest lockdown restrictions meant you couldn't have guests round even if they sit outside?"

"Well, I decided that since he lives on his own, he might like to join our household bubble. That way he can enjoy some human company and a good meal from time to time," replied Oma smiling.

Lilly was quietly pleased about this but tried not to show it. She didn't want Oma to know her attempts at match making were paying off. Just as she was trying to think of an alternative topic of conversation the phone rang. "I'll get it," she said and slipped out into the lounge before Oma could say anything.

About ten minutes later Lilly returned to the kitchen with a smile on her face. "That was Margaret, she wanted to check that I had seen the email. She is as excited as I am about this latest dream example. She thinks that there may even be a link to our farm! She checked some local Parish records, and it looks like the Wild family sold their hop gardens to us in 1889, just as it said in the letter. Isn't that amazing!"

"Yes, that is interesting. Don't you think so Gramps?" prompted Oma trying to draw him into the conversation although right then he seemed more interested in his doorstep of a cheese and pickle sandwich.

Lilly filled him in on the exciting news while he ate. "Yes, that sounds right. Our family has owned most of the land in this valley since the early 1800s and I know we acquired various other bits and pieces over the years. I remember there was an oast house out the back of my uncle Ted's place; I used to play in it as a boy. I was rather disappointed when they knocked it down, the tractor shed they replaced it with was nowhere near as exciting," he mumbled through a mouth full of food.

The rich smell of roast chicken came wafting in from the kitchen as Oma ushered Robbie into the dining room to help Lilly finish laying the table.

"Lunch will be ready in about 20 minutes. Could you keep Robbie entertained while I finish off the vegetables and gravy," she said returning quickly to the stove to tackle a pan that was just about to boil over.

"Sorry I'm a bit early. I overestimated how long it would take me to walk here, I usually come by car," he stammered.

"That's okay, you can help me with the cutlery. The canteen is in the left-hand drawer of the dresser."

"Right oh," he replied.

There was a moment of awkward silence. Lilly decided to break the ice. "Oma, sorry Breda. Breda tells me you're an arborialist. Is that the right word?"

"Yes, well technically it's arboriculture but really it's just growing and looking after trees. I work for a local tree charity and manage the woodland on the other side of the Astons."

"Tree charity, interesting. I don't think I knew that there were charities for trees," replied Lilly with a hint of sarcasm.

Robbie didn't seem to notice and pressed on with an anecdote. "Trees are fascinating beings. They have many secret ways. Did you know that they can defend themselves?"

This conjured a strange image in Lilly's head of a tree creature sitting on a horse with a jousting lance. She had rather an overactive imagination. "No, I didn't," she replied, barely managing not to laugh.

"Yes, as soon as an animal starts to nibble their leaves, they produce a chemical which makes them taste bitter, so the animal leaves them alone," he continued brightly, feeling pleased that Lilly seemed to be taking an interest. Often people seemed bored by his stories about trees. "You know even more intriguing is that trees can talk to each other. Not in the sense that we do of course but they do have ways of sending messages," he paused as he saw Lilly smiling at him. In former days Lilly would have thought he was being a bit of a nerd but now she was captivated by his passion and the breadth of his knowledge. She found his child-like enthusiasm almost endearing.

"Fancy a spot of the old sherry before we get stuck in to lunch?" chipped in Gramps appearing with a bottle and some glasses.

"Well, I'm not driving for a change so why not," replied Robbie enthusiastically. He was starting to feel a bit more relaxed.

As they sat down to lunch the conversation shifted to talk about the recent storm and the roof repairs. Robbie commented that he had been quite busy clearing debris from trees which had lost branches and blocked paths. As they paused while Oma cleared the dishes and made some custard to go with the apple pie Gramps took the chance to discuss the findings from Lilly's latest Hakka dream example.

"So, I was thinking about that Hakka dream you

mentioned yesterday. The one where the young girl fell asleep in the oast house on some kiln liners."

"Yes, what about it?" replied Lilly a little embarrassed. She wasn't sure she wanted Robbie to know about her crazy dreams.

"Not sure I've heard of Hakka dreams," said Robbie looking puzzled.

"It's a project I'm working on with a local historian. I won't bore you with the details. Anyway, we have found a few accounts of people who have had strange dreams about, or think they have seen ghosts of, an *old ma Hakka*. We are trying to find a link between them," she said trying to move the conversation on quickly.

"Well, I was wondering what hop kiln liners might have been made of. Probably some sort of wood I would think. Do you know, Robbie?" continued Gramps.

"Hmm, well it could be a number of things. Something pretty fire resistant; I know glass blowers use pear wood, but I doubt if it's that, you would need too much of it. Willow maybe? I've probably got a book at home which will tell me, I can take a look if you like," offered Robbie.

"Oh, that would be really kind, thank you. The more background information we can find the better," beamed Lilly.

Just then Oma reappeared. "Who wants custard with their apple pie?" All hints of conversation were quickly banished as they tucked in to steaming bowls of dessert.

CHAPTER 13
GEORGE

The November lockdown had proved to be even more tedious than the first one. Andrew had been cooped up at home trying to work from the dining room table while his wife held endless online coaching sessions in the study. Even though the kids were at school it felt as if there were only one or two hours in the day when he could do productive work. Most of that was spent preparing and recording lectures or tutorials for his students. He had very little time in which to do any meaningful research and when he did his efforts were often stymied by lack of access to the materials he needed. Getting to the college library was difficult; they were running a strict timetable, so he didn't get to visit more than once a week and then for only two hours at a time. The search he had promised to do for Margaret languished at the bottom of his to do list. He was grateful that she was being patient, or at least, she was not sharing any frustration she might be feeling directly with him.

Finally, in the last week of November his luck looked like it was about to change. He had managed to secure a double session at the library due to a late cancellation by one of his colleagues. He spent most of Sunday afternoon compiling a list of searches he wanted to do; he was determined not to waste a minute of the precious four hours he had booked for the following day. As he packed up his bag making sure not to forget any essential item, he was feeling pretty pleased with himself. A whole morning in the library, it felt like winning the lottery, he was almost giddy with excitement. Then it happened, his phone pinged as he received a new message. The dreaded curse of unpredictability that the Covid pandemic had brought to everybody's lives was upon him. The NHS track and trace service were notifying him that he had been in close contact with a person who had tested positive, and he would have to self-isolate for the next ten days. "Fuck!" he shouted, screwing up his neatly written list and hurling it at the study door. "Bloody typical," he groaned as he stormed into the dining room and poured himself a large brandy. He was glad his wife had taken the children out to play in the park, it was going to take a while for him to calm down.

Two and a half weeks later Lilly was in the loading bay of the veg shop checking off the contents of the latest set of deliveries. "There is a customer out front asking for you, lady called Margaret. Have you got a minute to spare?" called a voice through the screen door.

Margaret, that's unusual. I wonder what she can want, thought Lilly as she brushed the dust from her knees and made her way into the shop. "Hello Margaret, it's lovely to see you. I hope there hasn't been a problem with your order," she said feeling concerned, it was not often that Margaret braved the slippery streets to venture out and about.

"Lilly dear, how lovely!" she exclaimed beaming. "No problems with my order, don't worry. Actually, I have a delivery for you." She thrust an envelope into Lilly's hand. "Andrew finally managed to come through with that final search. It's all in there; I thought it best to bring it over in case you didn't get a chance to read your email. You look run off your feet poor thing."

"Lilly, Lilly, sorry but we need you out back," called one of the drivers from the warehouse doorway.

"Oh, thank you Margaret. I shall take a look and give you a call. Sorry, I don't have time now. Thank you for taking the trouble to come in…" Lilly dashed off. She just had time to stuff the envelope in her bag before a clipboard was thrust into her hands.

As the December evening started drawing in, Lilly made her way home through the gloomy lanes shrouded in a mist that was just beginning to freeze. She was thinking of the steaming bath that she planned to lounge in for as long as possible before dinner time. Every muscle in her body ached, she had been on her feet all day and had quite forgotten about the package that Margaret had given her. Dumping her bag on her bed she hurried to start running the bath, only when she returned did she notice the contents had spilled out onto the floor. *Ooh, I'd forgotten all about you*, she thought easing the envelope open and peeking inside to find a thin sheaf of papers with a note clipped to the front. Penned in Margaret's elegant hand was a cryptic message, *I think I've found the link, it's the wood!* it read. *What on earth?* she thought to herself. Not wanting to let her bath get cold and too excited to wait until afterwards she decided to read the papers whilst soaking in the warm bubbles.

Excerpt from the diary of Father Thomas – Reverend at Hagbourne Church – Local History Archives

12th March 1865

Today has been a rather troubling day and I feel somewhat compelled to make a written account of it. Never in my years as a man of the cloth have I heard a tale of such misfortune. It concerns young George, a former labourer from the village paper mill that has recently been forced to close. The poor young lad, having nowhere else to go has been sleeping in the hayloft adjoining the mill's upper barn. Until a month ago he claims it was a safe and comfortable place to sleep despite the winter cold. But since the February storms when the roof was damaged, he has been quite troubled. The branch of a nearby poplar tree had come clean through the roof and shattered one of the rafters above the spot where George had made his bed. He was lucky not to have been in the loft at the time. By way of earning his keep he had aided the mill owner with some urgent repairs using some of the very timber from the offending branch.

When George came to me after morning service today, he was in a very sorry state. The mill owner's wife all but dragged him by the scruff of his coat into the vestry where I was removing my robes. He was quite dishevelled even in his Sunday best, his hair wild and matted, his eyes dark pools beneath a creased and grubby brow.

Stammering he told me in halting words that he thought he was possessed by a spirit. "She won't let me rest. Night after night she comes to me in a whirl of thrashing noise, her voice whispering to me like the wind," he said. I asked him to whom he was referring, and he broke down, quite bereft with tears welling up in his eyes. "I never seen her, she's just a voice in the rafters. She comes to me in my dreams. It's like she's callin me to her, oold ma, oold ma Hacca she's sayin," he sobbed.

"Yes, it's always the same, he wakes up shouting and frightens the other boys. Yelling about this "oold ma Hacca" as he calls her," the mill owner's wife added. "He's possessed father, is there nothing you can do?" By this point George had descended into such a state of angst that he was unable to say more. As to where he had got the notion about an "oold ma Hacca" from I cannot tell. There is a stream that runs through the village which bears the name of Hacca's Brook, but I cannot see how that would relate to his dreams or the evil spirit that he refers to.

I eventually managed to calm both George and the mill owner's wife by assuring them that I would seek guidance from the Lord and that they should return tomorrow to hear my council. I hope that the Lord will provide me with some sign in my evening prayers tonight for I have little idea of what to do to help this boy.

13th March 1865

I must share my concern for George, alas, did not return today. I cannot think on what may have happened to him. I shall take a trip to the mill tomorrow to seek him out; I feel that it is most urgent…

14th March 1865

A most curious things has occurred; one might even say that it is something of a miracle. I travelled to the mill this afternoon to seek out young George. On entering the farm gate, I was greeted enthusiastically by the mill owner's wife. "It's a miracle!" she proclaimed. "Your words of faith that the Lord would provide an answer have rid young George of his evil spirit." She barely paused for breath before launching into an explanation that George had spent the night in a new spot in the lower barn and had slept like the proverbial log, as she put it. "He didn't dream of this evil oold ma Hacca, not once."

I was quite taken aback by her praise. All I had done was to promise to pray for an answer and had felt

quite lost thinking that I had not yet received one. Our
Lord truly does work in mysterious ways...

Lilly had quite forgotten where she was and, in her excitement, she nearly slopped water over the papers. "Oh, my word, I see what Margaret meant," she said as she skimmed back over the first passage. There did seem to be a link between George's dream and the branch of the tree that had almost fallen on him. She was a little sceptical about the divine intervention that Father Thomas had alluded to. Lilly was not really a spiritual being and preferred a more rational explanation. *I wonder where the paper mill was and whether the barn is still there? I bet Gramps will know*, she thought as slipping and slithering she extricated herself from the bath, dipping the tail ends of the sheets of paper in the water and leaving a trail of footprints across the floor.

As she reached the kitchen, a little out of breath and still dripping, a dressing gown hastily drawn around her, she gave Gramps a bit of a start.

"Are you okay there?" he asked, looking her up and down and wondering if she'd had some sort of accident.

"Yes fine," she replied. Suddenly realising she was creating a small puddle on the floor, and she must look a bit of a sight.

"What have you got there?" he asked, eying the crumpled and slightly damp papers in her hand. "Must be important."

"Er, yes. Margaret gave them to me today at the shop. I only just had the chance to read them. She found another example of a Hakka dream. A man called George from the Paper Mill at Hagbourne. I was wondering if you knew where it was?"

"Hmm, the Paper Mill you say. Well, there was a mill

not far from here but that was closed down in the 1800s," he replied scratching his chin thoughtfully.

"The account mentions a barn where George slept. Do you think it is still there?" Lilly asked.

"No, all of the old buildings were pulled down years ago. They kept getting flooded and most of the wood was rotten by all accounts."

Lilly felt suddenly deflated. If the barn was no longer there, then it would be harder to piece the puzzle together. "Are there still poplar trees growing nearby?" she asked.

"Poplar trees, hmm." Gramps paused and closed his eyes.

"Well, maybe. There are a few dotted about along the edges of fields and brooks. There used to be a lot more of them."

Lilly's eyes brightened. "Do you think we could go and look tomorrow?" she asked hopefully.

"We could, although…" he paused and scratched his chin again. Lilly was starting to get impatient.

"You might need to ask Robbie to help you. This time of year, without their leaves, I'm not sure I could tell you whether you were looking at a poplar or a willow."

Just then they were interrupted by Oma as she came bustling into the kitchen with a bag of potatoes from the pantry. "You might need to wait to talk to Robbie. I just got off the phone to him, he has gone down with a cold and won't be able to come round for lunch tomorrow."

Lilly had a sudden sinking feeling. "It's not Covid is it?" she asked, all thoughts about poplar trees seemed trivial in comparison.

"No, no, don't worry. He had a test, not Covid thankfully. Just a cold," reassured Oma.

"Oh, thank goodness. Is he ok though, he must be poorly if he can't make it round for lunch?"

"I think he was more concerned about giving it to us than anything else. Such a considerate lad." Oma's eyes sparkled as an idea popped into her head. "What if I make him some nice chicken soup and you can take it round to him for his lunch. What do you think Lilly?"

"Ooh, yes I could. I think he'd like that. He always loves your cooking," she beamed. Of course, it would give her an opportunity to ask him about poplar trees as well. Maybe she would get the answers she wanted after all. "I had best go and get dressed," she said feeling much brighter again.

"You best had, don't want you getting a chill," replied Oma eying Lilly's state of undress disapprovingly. "Go on, dinner will be about half an hour."

Robbie's house was not at all what she had expected. A small farmhouse annexe tucked away at the end of a lane on the other side of the village, she almost mistook it for an outbuilding. Every spare centimetre of the little front garden was crammed with pots containing tree seedlings of all shapes and sizes. She picked a path carefully to the front door. *I hope the inside is not as cluttered as this*, she thought as she rang the bell.

"Hi Lilly!" came a voice from above. "The door is open. I'll be down in a minute," said Robbie from the upstairs window.

As she stepped inside, she felt like she had been transported to another world. The hallway was very neat with just a pair of shoes on the boot-rack and a single coat hanging on the back of the door. Along the walls were several paintings, the most captivating of which was a floor to ceiling rendering of a tree. It was stunning. At first, she thought it was a photograph but as she moved closer, she realised it was a painting. Tiny brush strokes captured the intricate veins in the leaves and the patterns in the bark were exquisite. "Wow!" she breathed.

"You've met my Elm tree I see," said Robbie stepping up behind her.

"It's, it's… it's beautiful," she said, almost lost for words. "Did you paint it?" she asked.

"Me, no!" he laughed. "My aunt, she was an amazing painter. She did all of these," he replied with a hint of melancholy. "Shall we go through?" he said ushering her into the kitchen.

"I brought soup," she said, setting the still warm pot down on the table. "Oma thought you needed feeding up and she wanted me to check that you are looking after yourself properly. Actually, she told me not to say that," she grinned.

Robbie chuckled, a laugh which quickly turned into a fit of coughing. Lilly looked on quite concerned, her feelings for Robbie running much deeper than she had realised. She rubbed his back gently.

"I'll be okay in a minute," he croaked, his eyes watering.

"I'll get you some water," she said. Letting him rest a while and get his breath back she set about heating up the soup. The kitchen was as immaculate as the hallway. Just the bare essentials, neat and tidy, everything in its place. For a moment she wondered whether there would be more than one bowl and set of cutlery.

"This is a lovely place," she commented as they sat down to eat.

"It belonged to my aunt. I used to come here after school to do my homework. I would sit where you are now and watch her paint. It was always really peaceful. She said painting filled her up and made her feel whole. I envied her."

"How come?"

"Oh, it's a long story…" he replied, looking up with a slight frown.

"I'm not in a hurry," Lilly added, curious to know more about this shy and gentle man.

"Okay. I guess I'll end up telling you sooner or later so it might as well be now," he sighed. "I wasn't always destined to be a tree man. My parents wanted me to follow in the family tradition, to become a doctor like them. Insisted I focused on academic subjects and none of the *wishy-washy nonsense* that they claimed my aunt filled my head with. They were happy for her to give up her time to look after me when they were too busy jetting off to conferences, but they didn't want her meddling and distracting me from my studies," he sighed. "I did as I was told of course. They were delighted when I got into Oxford to study medicine, they liked the prestige. I hated it. After a year I dropped out and went to do a course in arboriculture at a local college. Well, you can imagine their response, they pretty much disowned me. Wrote me out of their will, said they didn't want to see me or my aunt again. She stuck by me, gave me a roof over my head, helped me find a job. After she passed away, she left this place to me and all of her paintings. When I look at them it's as though she is still here with me." He took a deep breath and wiped a tear from the corner of his eye. "Your soup will get cold," he said and started to steadily spoon his into his mouth staring at the table, not wanting to catch her eye. She reached forward and put her hand on his, they ate on in silence.

"You look tired," he commented, breaking into her reverie. "How was the veg shop yesterday? Oma not working you too hard, is she?"

Lilly was pleased that he said *Oma* rather than *Breda*, he was starting to feel more like one of the family. "It was a bit manic but not Oma's fault. We are just getting so many orders at the moment. Not just for veg but for all the other Christmassy things that people want as well. I didn't stop all day."

She helped Robbie clear the table and insisted he sit down while she washed up. He was still looking a little pale despite the soup.

"Oh, there was one thing I was going to tell you," he said getting up and fetching something from a shelf by the fireplace. "I found out what wood kiln liners are made from. It's not willow but Black Poplar."

"You're kidding!" she said almost dropping the bowl she was drying.

"No, it has a section on it here in this book about Black Poplar trees. The wood is quite fire retardant and it's also very flexible and shock absorbent, so they used to use it for things like suspension in carts and for floorboards. A whole range of things really." He looked up. Lilly was about to burst with excitement.

"Poplar trees, yes, it's definitely poplar trees. That's the link! I was going to tell you; Margaret found another example of a dream. This one was a young lad who was sleeping in a barn where a branch from a poplar tree fell on the roof.

They used some of it to make repairs and after that he started having strange dreams like the other ones, about old ma Hakka." She quickly dried her hands and reached into her bag. "Here, I'll show you," she said passing him the papers that Margaret had given her. "I was going to ask if you could help me see if the tree is still there. Gramps said the barn is gone but the trees might still be there. He said you would be able to identify them even without their leaves."

"Slow down," he said smiling. "You'll burst a blood vessel. Why don't you finish up there and give me a moment to read through this?"

Lilly blushed. "Sorry, just excited. We've been trying to piece things together for a while. This is the break we have been looking for," she grinned and kissed the top of his head before turning away quickly to finish the washing up.

"What's this scribbled in the margin?" he asked. "Something about there being two barns and a change in sleeping location being George's magic cure."

"Let me see," said Lilly looking over his shoulder and re-reading the passage from Father Thomas's diary. "Oh, clever Margaret. I hadn't noticed that before. See here, the first reference is to the upper barn where the tree fell. This later section refers to the lower barn. George only had the dream when he was in the upper barn with the poplar wood repair." She looked up, her eyes shining with excitement. "All of the dreamers have their dreams when they are sleeping near to something made from poplar wood. The chest, the attic gable, the carts, the kiln liners, the barn roof… oh my goodness… my bed too!" She gasped. "Gramps told me that my bed had been repaired using some poplar wood. A strut had been broken when my uncle slept on it. I had completely forgotten about it!" She was almost jumping up and down with excitement.

Robbie just sat there staring at her in amazement. He had never seen Lilly quite so animated before. Her excitement was intoxicating, it had lifted his mood considerably. "When I'm better we can go and look for poplar trees together." *Maybe Christmas is not going to be so bad after all*, he thought as he helped Lilly put away the last of the lunch things.

Later that evening after telling Gramps and Oma all about her discussion with Robbie, Lilly was still feeling excited. Gramps had confirmed that he had indeed repaired her bed with a piece of poplar wood although he couldn't recall where he had got it from. Initially she was frustrated but then she remembered that the tree from George's story might still be there. It was even possible it was the same tree. Robbie had told her that poplars typically lived for two hundred years or more so it was feasible; she couldn't wait until he was well enough to help her find it.

As she paced up and down her room, thoughts churning through her mind, she suddenly realised she hadn't shared the news with Margaret. *I must give her a call, she'll be so excited*, she thought as she headed downstairs to the phone. Even after all this time the fact that she couldn't get a decent mobile signal grated on her a little.

"Hi Margaret, its Lilly. Is now a good time for a chat?"

"Oh, hello dear. Yes, in fact I was just thinking about you and wondering what you had made of George's story."

"You were absolutely right about trees being the link. In fact, I have some further news for you on that front. I spoke to Robbie today and he told me he had found a book about Black Poplar trees which suggested that the kiln liners and maybe parts of the carts from some of the other dreams were also made from poplar. As is part of the bed in my room; I confirmed that with Gramps this evening. It all seems to make sense, thinking about it now it's obvious really, I mean I only have my dream when I sleep in my bed…" Lilly wittered on barely pausing for breath.

"Oh, that is good to know. I thought I was on to something. So, your Sir Galahad knows more than just how to wield a chainsaw then," replied Margaret teasing.

"He doesn't cut down trees Margaret. He's an arboriculturist, not a tree surgeon," responded Lilly indignantly. "We also deciphered your cryptic note about George's magic cure."

"Oh good. It's an interesting pattern isn't it, and now that you have further evidence of the link between the dreamers and poplar wood for more of the cases things seem to be falling into place quite nicely."

"Yes, but there are still some things I don't understand. Not everyone who slept near the poplar wood had those dreams. What is special about them? About me?"

"That my dear, is an excellent question. Something to mull over, I think. I shall spend some time during the Christmas hols going through all my notes to see if I can find some more clues."

"Yes, I will try to do the same. I'm hoping Robbie will be able to take me out to find the tree mentioned in George's account. Gramps thinks he knows where it would have been, hopefully it's still there," replied Lilly. "You're not going to be on your own over Christmas, are you?" she added, suddenly feeling guilty that she hadn't thought to ask before.

"No, more is the pity. I will be spending a couple of days with my eldest daughter and her family. I am in their *bubble* apparently. I just hope I can stay off the booze; her husband is enough to drive anyone to drink."

"Oh well, you make sure you put your feet up and let them look after you," admonished Lilly knowing full well that Margaret would not be able to resist interfering in the kitchen.

"You sound just like Andrew!" huffed Margaret but secretly she was pleased that Lilly cared about her.

"Oh, yes. Please do thank Andrew for helping with the searches. We couldn't have got this far without him."

"I will do of course. From the email he sent it sounded like he had a thoroughly dreadful time of it over the past few weeks. I shall be sure to pass on your regards."

"Okay, well I'll let you go then. Have a good Christmas!" Lilly hung up. *My Sir Galahad*, she mused thinking about what Margaret had said. She had a vision of Robbie in shining armour wielding a chainsaw instead of sword. It made her chuckle, only Margaret would come up with something like that.

CHAPTER 14

DREAM OF DREAMS

Christmas morning had finally arrived; Lilly was seated at the kitchen table peeling sprouts when she heard the rattle of Robbie's Land Rover pulling into the yard. A couple of minutes later there came a scuffing and scraping as he struggled through the back door, his arms laden. Lilly jumped to her feet.

"Let me help you with those," she said. She could never quite fathom why men chose to carry so much at once rather than making a second trip. Just in time she rescued a biscuit tin before it toppled to the floor.

"Oops!" said Robbie looking a little flushed.

Oma came in from the dining room where she had been preparing the place settings ready for lunch time. "Ah, Robbie it's you. I wondered what all the commotion was about."

Spying the box of produce and the tins on the table she looked pleased. "Thank you so much for bringing these over. I quite ran out of time to do last minute shopping yesterday."

"That's okay Breda. I am happy to provide my share. It's so kind of you to invite me, I couldn't possibly have turned up empty handed," he winked at Lilly. He had certainly not been empty handed a moment ago.

"Anyone fancy a sherry?" offered Gramps through the open doorway.

"Ooh, it's a bit early for me William," replied Robbie. "I wouldn't mind a coffee though," he said glancing at Lilly hopefully.

"Good idea, I'll make a pot," offered Oma. "Lilly why don't you show Robbie to his room so he can find a place for the rest of his things," she continued, narrowly avoiding tripping over his bag on the floor.

As they passed through the hallway Robbie took in the Christmas atmosphere. The subtle scents permeating from carefully placed boughs of pine and holly adorning the stairwell. The soft glow of lights twining round the tree by the front path that he could just make out through the warped panes of the old front door. Hand crafted winter scenes dotting the shelves around the fireplace where a log fire was gently smouldering in the grate. All of this was topped with the smell of brandy and spices emanating from the kitchen where the Christmas pudding was steaming on the range. He couldn't remember a time that had felt this much like Christmas; the kind of Christmas you read about in books.

"Penny for them?" he heard Lilly ask.

"Hmm, what?"

"You looked lost in a daydream. I was wondering what

you were thinking about," she replied as she made her way up the stairs.

"Oh, sorry. Yes. I was just taking in the festive feel of the place. It's a long time since I had a proper Christmas," he smiled.

After lunch, according to Oma's long established Christmas tradition it was time to exchange gifts. Robbie nervously handed Lilly a neat little package. She carefully unwrapped it taking pains not to tear the paper. It was the book about Black Poplar trees that he had shown her the other day. She beamed at him.

"Oh, Robbie thank you! That is absolutely perfect."

"Look inside," he replied.

As she opened the cover a slip of card fell out onto the table. It was a small and very detailed painting of Black Poplar flowers and leaves. "Oh, Robbie. It's beautiful," she gulped, her voice cracking slightly. "Did your aunt paint it?"

"Yes. I found it the other day. It's part of a set of illustrations she did for a book."

"Oh, my that is lovely," said Oma as she peered over Lilly's shoulder. "Don't forget to give Robbie his present."

Lilly hesitantly offered him a box decorated with Christmas paper and ribbons. Suddenly she felt that it was a less than equitable exchange.

"Ooh, Lebkuchen! My favourite," he exclaimed and couldn't resist popping one of the chocolate coated heart shaped biscuits into his mouth." He grinned at Lilly. She laughed. How on earth he could manage another mouthful of food after a huge Christmas lunch was beyond her.

"Shall we go for a walk?" he suggested. He was keen to stretch his legs and enjoy the remains of the afternoon sun.

"We could go and see if we can find that tree of yours. If you bring the book, I can show you how to identify poplar trees at any time of the year."

※

Their walk had proven to be only a partial success. The place where she was hoping to locate *her tree*, as Robbie put it, was a disappointment. They found the old mill, described in the account of George's dream, quite easily but there was no sign of any poplar trees in the vicinity. Undeterred Robbie had suggested that they extend their walk a little to take in a spot where he knew there was a large old poplar tree. As they approached it, he had pointed out the characteristic shape of the branches and how the bark was rough and pitted. Looking through his binoculars she was able to see the pattern of buds at the tips of the branches which Robbie assured her would become beautiful crimson flowers in the spring. They took a photo of the tree, and he showed her how to record the location as a grid reference using an app on his phone.

When they returned to the farmhouse, they found Oma and Gramps dosing by the fire. It was four o'clock and just getting dark. "Whaah," yawned Lilly. "I could do with a snooze myself." They made their way up to her room and lay down for what she told herself would be a brief nap.

An hour later she was woken by Gramps calling up the stairs. "Anyone fancy a cup of tea?"

"Yes please. We'll be down in a moment," replied Lilly turning to look at Robbie who was just stirring beside her.

"Did you dream?" she asked him. Curious to know whether sleeping on her poplar bed had any effect on him.

"No, I don't think so. How about you?"

She thought for a moment. "No, actually I didn't. How weird. Maybe you have cured me of my dreams," she replied brightly with a giggle.

"Maybe I just cured you of your sadness," he mumbled as he nuzzled the hair at the back of her neck and breathed in her warm chocolatey scent. *You have certainly cured me*, he thought as he fought the urge to go back to sleep.

They were just a week into the new year; Christmas felt like it had been a million years ago. The weather had been persistently wet, and Lilly had not been able to get out to continue her search for the poplar trees. She was slightly distracted as she joined Janet in the park.

"Hello Lilly. Thank you so much for agreeing to come out for a chat. I thought it would be good to continue with our weekly talks especially as the days have been so gloomy."

"Thank you for suggesting it, Janet. I think a walk is just what I need to blow the cobwebs away."

"Yes, and it's so much nicer to talk in person, I find the conversation tends to flow more freely. So, tell me how have you been over the past couple of weeks; have you been keeping your dream diary?"

"Yes, mostly. I have found there are times when I don't have my dream, or at least I don't remember having it. I am fairly sure there is a link to my bed. I was also wondering whether there was a link to how I am feeling." She paused, unsure how to phrase things.

"Go on," encouraged Janet with a smile.

"Well, the other day Robbie and I fell asleep on my bed." She felt her face starting to colour but seeing that Janet was not bothered she continued. "He didn't dream and neither did I. I joked that he had cured me of my dreams and his reply got me wondering."

"What did he say?"

"He said that maybe he had cured my sadness. So, is it possible that there is a link between the dreams and my mental state?"

Janet paused a moment to take in what Lilly had just said.

"I think it is possible, yes. There is good evidence of a link between what is called REM disorder and dreaming that many people with anxiety and depression suffer from. In fact, they dream too much, it exhausts their brains, so they tend to wake in the early hours often with vivid memories of their dreams."

"Oh, that is interesting. One of the historical accounts of dreamers that Margaret found refers to a link between REM state and Schizophrenia. Could they be related?"

"Ah, well I'm not sure about that. Schizophrenia is not really my specialty," replied Janet looking a little sceptical.

"So, you also mentioned your bed being important?"

"Yes. I only have the dream when I sleep there. What is more there seems to be a similar link in all of the Hakka dream accounts we have found so far. All of the dreamers sleep near to something which is made from poplar wood," replied Lilly with such enthusiasm it made Janet laugh.

"Well, it's good to see you in such good spirits. If you don't mind indulging me, I would like you to keep up with the dream diary for a little while longer. It will be good to see if the relationship between your mood and the dreams continues to be evident."

"Yes, of course. I actually quite like writing about my dream. It is nearly always the same but occasionally I pick up on subtleties I had not noticed before. It's also a good basis for comparison with the other dream accounts. Margaret and I will have to show you what we have found when we get a chance."

"I would love to. Hopefully we won't have to wait too long for this current lockdown to be lifted. Until then let's keep up with our weekly phone calls."

"Okay, sounds good," responded Lilly as she contemplated the sky. It had just started to drizzle again and foolishly she had forgotten her umbrella. Walking home was going to be a soggy affair.

It was a cold, crisp day in late January. The kind of day when the blueness of the sky hurts your eyes, the air is so clear you can almost taste the frost. Even in the early afternoon when the sun was at its highest the ground was frozen hard. The footpaths rutted and bumpy where the mud from recent rains had set solid.

Lilly had been waiting for the opportunity to get out and continue her quest, searching for *her tree* had become something of an obsession. Robbie had shown her how to identify the Black Poplar tree even in its state of winter undress, the characteristic bark with the deep fissures and the unmistakable tracery of the branches so unlike its close relative the willow. When she woke up that morning, she had been excited by the prospect of getting out to explore new paths at the back of the farm which until now had been swamped with flood water and slick with mud. Having finished her morning shift at the veg shop and bolted down a quick lunch she was glad to be out in the fresh air.

As she set off down the lane at the edge of the farm, she consulted her map. It was decorated with the locations of Black Poplar trees that she had found already, there were more than she had imagined. Robbie had given her the impression that they were rare, but her experience seemed different; the search for *her tree* was taking much longer than she had anticipated. *It's a pity that Gramps couldn't remember where he had got the branch that he had used to repair my bed*, she thought to herself for the hundredth time. Anyway, it was good to be outside, the weather had been so poor for the past few weeks, she had been going stir crazy being cooped up inside.

Lilly wound her way through densely packed blackthorn still adorned with last season's sloes. Past thickets of hawthorn carpeted in red and pulsing with the call of redwings sampling the winter fare. The air was so still, she felt the illusion that she had been transported to another place entirely, a place far away from any human intervention. The sun was warm on her back, and she was starting to sweat despite the chill air. As she rounded a bend in the path, she felt an odd sense of familiarity even though she knew she had never been there before. In front of her, on the other side of a rickety wooden bridge stood an enormous Black Poplar tree. Anchored to the banks of the brook it took pride of place at the corner of a wheat field. The air around it seemed to shimmer in the bright sunshine.

"Hello, and who are you?" she said out loud. She felt drawn to the tree even though it was on the other side of the stream. As she went to tuck her map securely in a pocket, she remembered Robbie's rule to always take a picture of the tree and note down the grid reference. *Best do that now before I forget*, she murmured to herself recalling the occasions when she had forgotten and had to retrace her steps. Using her phone, she took a couple of pictures of the tree, it was so large she could barely get it all in shot. She noted the position on her map and then tucked it away safely. As she drew near, she felt her pulse rise in anticipation. If she stretched across the stream, she would just be able to reach its main trunk. Taking off her glove she gingerly reached forward; the air around her felt charged. As she rested her palm on the bark a wave of recognition pulsed through her. It was almost like an electric shock, but she didn't want to pull away. "Hello tree," she said smiling with a surge of overwhelming joy. She had to remind herself to breathe. "I have found you at last," she whispered softly. As the bank started to give way beneath her boots, she realised she would have to sever her connection and find a better spot. Either that or risk a dunking in the ice-cold water.

Casting around for an alternative she spied an old branch which straddled the brook and would allow her to cross into the field. She had a momentary doubt, maybe she would be trespassing. She quickly dismissed the idea, technically Gramps owned these fields even if he rented them out to other farmers. The other side of the tree was bathed in sunlight and there was a convenient crook in one of the branches which provided an ideal place to sit. As she snuggled into it and rested her cheek on the bark, she felt like it could have been tailor made, just for her. She was drawn into a hazy dream as the tree rushed up to greet her.

It was so like the beginning of her usual dream yet richer and more vibrant. She felt suffused with a golden glow, energy coursing through her veins as though it was passing down from the leaves as they gathered the sun's rays. She felt the gentle swoosh of her body flexing in the wind and a subtle low vibration humming in the background. The tickling prickle of pecking and nibbling, a million tiny feet swarming over her limbs. A sweetness in her mouth drawn from the roots of the tree as it dipped into the surrounding brook. Over time, the air became more cloying and took on an acrid note almost burnt. She felt hoarse and stifled, working slightly harder to breathe. She started to feel thirsty, her skin hot and dry becoming shrivelled; when a flush of moisture came again it was bland, slightly bitter. The tickling and prickling slowly diminishing. The gentle undercurrent of humming in the background beginning to fade replaced with a growing sense of loneliness. She felt herself sniffing the air but smelling nothing sweet, stretching out her fingers and toes searching, searching but finding few connections. Over time the world seemed more muted and slowly, slowly the lullaby "ool ma, ool ma, oold ma Hakka" was building and building, louder and louder until she could feel it reverberating through her skull. It was as though the tree was signalling with all its senses, calling, calling, trying to be heard.

She woke with a sudden jolt. A dog was barking and splashing in the brook, its owner calling it frantically. The sun had gone behind a cloud and Lilly started to feel the chill. She looked at her watch, it was nearly four o'clock. She checked her phone; it said the same. She had been sitting there for over an hour. She should have felt chilled to the core and yet she felt warm and alive like never before. In a daze she started back on the path home.

"We were just about to send out a search party," said Robbie. Lilly was confused, why was Robbie there? He usually only came for tea on Sunday.

"I was worried about you; thought you might have gone over to Robbie's," said Oma. "You must be frozen, let me take your coat and then you can have a spot of tea by the fire," she continued, fussing Lilly and ushering her to the sofa in the lounge. Gramps handed her a mug of tea and placed a large slab of fruit cake on the side table next to her. Lilly suddenly realised she was gasping for a drink and totally famished. She said nothing until half the cake was gone and she had drained her mug. Oma, Gramps and Robbie looked on expectantly. Her head swam with the hangover of emotions from the dream. *The dream of dreams* she thought to herself.

"Found my tree. I had no idea…" she tailed off.

"No idea about what?" asked Oma gently, seeing that Lilly was completely washed out.

"I think I understand now but I'm not sure I know how to put it into words. It's as though the tree has been calling out to us, hoping that we will hear and understand. Although I'm not at all sure whether it's a message for us or for other trees. It's all a bit confusing, I'm not sure I can find the words to explain it," she started repeating herself. Suddenly she felt very tired, that swimming feeling you get with jet lag when your body tells you it needs sleep and starts shutting down. "I think I'll just lie down for a bit," she said as she snuggled down onto the sofa and the world closed in around her. She drifted into the deepest and most restful sleep she had experienced in over a year.

Oma pulled a rug over her and switched off the light. They would leave her be for now.

PART 3
RE-CONNECTING

In the corner of a field stands a tree. It is the Signal Tree, waiting patiently to be found, to be seen. Not seen with just the eyes but seen with all the senses. Waiting to be known in ways long forgotten, to be known and understood. Waiting to share the burden of its secrets, the millennia of memories passed from ancestor to clone, the patterns in their wood.

CHAPTER 15

DECODING THE SIGNAL

"**H**ey sleepy head." Lilly felt her shoulder being nudged gently as Robbie's voice slowly permeated her senses. Carefully she eased herself up, her mind all fuzzy with sleep.

"What time is it?" she asked.

"Just gone nine thirty."

"Oh, so I've slept for a while then. What's for dinner?"

"A while yes. You may be better off thinking about breakfast. Here have some coffee to get you started," replied Robbie grinning at the confusion on Lilly's face as she eventually realised that it was morning.

She pulled her knees up to her chest and slowly sipped the warm sweet coffee. It felt good. She felt good, more rested than she had in months. She yawned. "You mentioned breakfast?" she said eyeing him hopefully.

"Yes, we saved you some bacon and eggs. I can bring it in if you want."

"I'll come to the kitchen. I need to stretch my legs."

As she polished off a plate of breakfast followed by toast and more coffee Robbie waited patiently enjoying the warmth of the kitchen range and the sight of Lilly glowing with pleasure.

"Mmmm, I think that must be the best food I ever tasted." She pushed the plate away and sat back patting her slightly distended stomach.

Robbie couldn't wait any longer, his curiosity was too great. "So, you found your tree then?" he asked.

"Ooh yes. Wow! It was amazing. It was like I knew it was her even before I got there."

"Her?" he asked quizzically.

"Uhuh, can't really explain why but it felt like a she. It was electric and so rich like, well it's hard to describe. Like looking through a kaleidoscope but not."

Robbie frowned. "A kaleidoscope but not?"

"Well, I didn't really see things as such. It was more an explosion of sensations; I was overwhelmed with joy in a way I have never felt before. It changed over time too. It left me with an aching, a sense of yearning. I am not sure I experienced it all. A dog barked and brought me back to reality a bit abruptly. I think I need to go back." Her breathing was quick and excited, her eyes had taken on a brightness he had never seen before.

"Are you sure? It might be too much for you. You were in quite a state when you got home yesterday evening."

"I think it will be different next time. If you are with me, I am sure I will be okay. I want you to see the tree, my Signal Tree. She is so beautiful," her voice cracked; tears of joy trickled down her cheeks.

"Okay. Maybe this afternoon when it's a little warmer. In the meantime, why don't you show me the pictures you took and where it is on the map. You remembered to make a note, I assume?" She nodded enthusiastically as she retrieved her phone and map from the pocket in her coat. He snuggled up next to her feeling suddenly protective.

That afternoon they ventured back to the tree. It was a dull and chilly day, they walked quickly to keep warm. The tree did not seem as far away as she remembered but it still took her breath away when she saw it nestled by the brook, *Hakka's brook* according to the map.

"Isn't she magnificent?" exclaimed Lilly as she did a little dance and twirled her way across the bridge. "How old do you think she is?"

"Well, we can measure her girth to get an estimate, but we would have to take a core sample to be sure."

"Oh, I don't want to hurt her," replied Lilly. A core sample sounded very brutal.

"Here, hold the other end of this," puffed Robbie as he struggled to stretch a rope around the trunk of the tree at shoulder height. He looked at the marking on the rope. "Probably about two hundred years give or take a few," he said, making a note in his pocketbook. "That is pretty old for a Black Poplar. She has a few war wounds," he remarked, pointing out scars on the trunk where branches had been ripped away in winter storms. "There is also a whole dead section at the back. She must be fighting off some kind of fungus which is slowly eating away at her." *Why am I calling it a her*, he thought to himself? He wasn't usually sentimental about the trees. Looking at the excited glow on Lilly's face he knew why.

"She won't die yet, though will she?" asked Lilly suddenly concerned by his last remark.

"Oh, probably not. Trees like this can live with fungal damage for many, many years. There is plenty of good growth at the front. See there are lots of buds waiting to burst open when the warmer weather comes." He pointed to the upper branches and offered Lilly his binoculars for a better look.

"How can we tell if it's a she or a he?" asked Lilly. She had read in her book that Black Poplars were single sex trees.

"We can't right now. We will have to wait until they flower. The male and female flowers are quite different. We should know in early April I expect."

"Will we have to wait that long?" Lilly said rather despondently.

"You can't rush nature," he replied smiling. He knew Lilly was not a patient being, she had spent far too much of her life in the busy, bustling urban world of instant gratification. Waiting was something that would take her time to learn.

They had spent a while at the tree, Robbie standing watch as Lilly settled into the crook in the branches and gave herself up to the dream state that she had experienced the previous day. After about half an hour Lilly had resurfaced, her face aglow with joy. She had experienced it all again, it was just as before, nothing missing, nothing more. She had been anxious to get back and write it all down. Robbie was relieved both because she seemed okay and also because he was starting to get very cold. Now sitting by the fire sipping tea and eating cake it was almost like they had experienced a time warp. Robbie drifted into a doze as Lilly scribbled fervently in her notebook keen to capture every aspect of the dream before it faded in her mind.

A couple of days later, after supper, Lilly found time to sit down and start trying to make sense of her latest dream. She had cleared a space on the large dining room table and set about reviewing her notes on the Hakka dreams. Methodically transcribing key information from each dream, including her own, onto index cards. The name of each person, the date of the dream, the location, the poplar artefact and so on. She also created a card for the *Signal Tree*, as she had decided to call it. She noted the location and approximate age but wasn't sure what else to include.

Laying out the cards in the chronological order of the dreams she was hoping to see that the timelines matched up with the tree. *If it's two hundred years old then it would have started growing in about 1820, let me see,* she thought as she shuffled through the cards to find the oldest account. "Hmm, George in 1865, forty-five years difference and his branch was not from Signal, we know that. Hmm…" she mumbled. Looking again at the cards and re-reading the notes she had written about the Signal Tree dream, *the dream of dreams,* she was struggling to see how things were related. "There must be some way in which the contents of the dreams match up with one another, I just can't see the pattern. What are you trying to tell me tree?" she sighed and started sifting through the accounts again, there must be something she was missing, but what?

Maybe it's the poplar artefacts, she thought trying a different tack, but this didn't seem to lead anywhere either. The poplar artefacts in the dreams were all muddled up in terms of chronology and for some of them she couldn't be sure of the source, they were clearly not all from the same tree. Hannah's dream was quite recent, but the poplar chest dated back to Tudor times which was much earlier than the Signal Tree. She didn't even know where the wood from the carts or kiln liners came from. "This is hopeless!" she huffed throwing the cards onto the table in frustration.

She was staring at her notes willing them to make sense when Oma came in with some crockery to put away in the dresser.

"What are you trying to do there?" she asked as she stole a glance over Lilly's shoulder.

Lilly talked her through the notes and the cards and tried to explain her thinking. "The problem is nothing seems to tie together no matter which way I look at it. There must be something missing."

Oma said nothing for a while. She was looking intently at the cards laid out on the table. "That's interesting," she said eventually.

Lilly looked at her expectantly. "What's interesting?" she prompted as Oma paused again.

"Well, you think the Signal Tree, as you have called it, is two hundred years old."

"Give or take. At least that is what Robbie estimated based on its size," interrupted Lilly.

"Okay, well I don't know if it's relevant but that would cover seven generations in human terms. There are seven Hakka dreamers, if you include yourself, spanning seven generations."

"So, what you're saying is one tree generation is equivalent to seven human ones," blurted Lilly, suddenly excited. "But how can the dreams tell me about what has happened over the past two hundred years?" she continued feeling despondent again.

"Maybe they don't have to," commented Oma. "Maybe it's only important to understand what has happened over that time period and relate it to the Signal Tree dream."

Lilly re-read her account of the dream of dreams hoping to find a clue. "But the dream doesn't relate to specific events, there are no dates in tree time!" she replied feeling quite exasperated.

Meanwhile Oma was rearranging things on the table. She didn't seem to have heard what Lilly was saying. She placed a pot plant next to the Signal Tree card and put a place mat down near to it with Lilly's card adjacent. Then she took a pepper pot and placed it at a further location with Michael's card next to it.

"What are you doing Oma?" asked Lilly feeling intrigued but also a little impatient. Oma seemed to think in strange and random ways sometimes.

"I'm making a map," explained Oma. "The pot plant is the Signal Tree; the pepper pot is Didcot power station which opened in 1970."

She scanned the remaining cards and picked out Albert's card. Taking a fork from the drawer she put it at another location on the table. "Upton Railway Station," she said as she put Albert's card next to it.

Lilly joined in. She placed a spoon near to the fork with Will's card next to it. "The cart," she said.

Oma took a wooden ornament from the shelf and placed it close to the pot plant along with Agnes's card to represent the hop kiln. Finally, she placed a folded paper napkin next to Lilly's mat and put George's card down. "There, the paper mill," she announced looking up proudly.

Lilly suddenly remembered they hadn't added anything for Hannah, so she put a further placemat near to Albert's fork. "To represent the chest," she said smiling.

They had made a map of sorts. Lilly rifled through her box of papers and took out her map of the local area which she had been using to chart current tree locations. Comparing their table map with it she had a sudden realisation.

"All of the dream locations fall close to a network of small streams and brooks; the Signal Tree is at the point where they meet up. Oma you are a genius!" she exclaimed kissing the top of her head and hugging her fiercely. "The Signal Tree will have witnessed changes to the environment around all of these locations."

She looked again at the power station, this didn't quite fit in as it wasn't on a stream. Then it came to her. "The power station burned coal, right? So, what if the tree was aware of the change in air quality after it opened?" she gabbled, barely pausing for breath.

"Yes, and it would have been affected by the trains too as they were powered by steam and later diesel. The air in the local area was probably quite sooty once the railway arrived. I am not quite sure when that would have been, but we can check," added Oma, getting caught up in the excitement.

Lilly looked at her Signal dream document. "Maybe when I felt the sensation of finding it hard to breath that was because of poor air quality," she mused. "I think one of the other dream accounts mentioned something about that too," she said rummaging through the documents that were now strewn across the table. "Yes, here it is," she pointed to a passage in the account from Albert's dream which referred to rasping and wheezing and the air tasting burnt. "The feeling

I had in the Signal dream was similar to that," she looked up at Oma feeling very pleased with their progress.

"It's not what I had expected at all, but it certainly seems to make sense." Lilly realised it was going to take a bit of work to map out the changes in the local environment over the past two hundred years. Changes that humans with shorter lifespans would not be aware of but that the tree would have noticed. "We are going to need some help with deciphering this. Help from Gramps, Robbie and Margaret with her knowledge of local history and from you of course," she added turning to Oma.

"Oh, don't do that yet!" she blurted. Oma was starting to tidy up the things on the table. "I want to make a copy of the map so we can share it with other people." She paused closing her eyes, trying to think what the best way would be to capture the map, she would need something quite big. "Do we have any of that brown paper we use in the veg shop for packaging; that could do as a canvas couldn't it?" she asked.

"I think there's a roll in the storeroom out back. I'll go and check," replied Oma as she headed out the door.

CHAPTER 16

BUILDING A PICTURE

Lilly's map was a masterpiece. She had enjoyed taking the time to carefully embellish each of the dream locations with a detailed, hand-drawn rendering of the dream artefacts as well as adding the paths of the brooks and streams, the route the railway would have taken and many other aspects of the local area. She had re-discovered her love of art.

She was busy working on a sketch of the Signal Tree when Robbie poked his head round the door.

"Gramps is making tea and wondered if you would like a cup," he asked.

"Ooh yes please," she replied without looking up.

A few minutes later he appeared again with a couple of

mugs. "Wow. I didn't know you could draw like that. My aunt would have been impressed," he said kissing her cheek and placing her tea down next to her.

"I always liked art at school until we had to choose between vocational and academic subjects. My dad made me choose the academic ones, wanted me to become a lawyer like him," she sighed. "I would really like to paint some of these, but I don't have the stuff and probably wouldn't find the time anyway," she added picking up her pencil and continuing with her drawing.

"So, this is the map then. The one you were telling me about," added Robbie trying to get Lilly's attention again. She seemed totally absorbed in what she was doing. He was quite taken by her obvious skill; he made a mental note to discuss it with Oma. They had been scratching around for ideas of things to get Lilly for her birthday which was fast approaching. Art materials could be just the thing.

Lilly looked up. "Oh sorry. Yes, I should probably explain so you can get a sense of things. I am going to need your help with deciphering some of the parts of the dream." She gave him one of her winning smiles which he found hard to resist.

He chuckled. "Come on then Rembrandt, show me what's what."

She spent the next few minutes explaining the map and describing the thought process behind it. He stepped back and took a few moments to take it all in. "I think I get it. That is really smart; your Oma certainly has a way of bringing things to life. I never would have seen all that from just looking at the written transcripts," he paused again leaving Lilly hanging on expectantly. She was just about to jump in when he added, "So you want help with creating a timeline spanning the lifetime of the tree. Capturing changes in the local environment, weather, air quality, water, farming, industry that sort of thing?"

"Yes exactly!" she responded, relieved that he seemed to understand.

"Right. Well, I can certainly help you with some of that. What have you got so far?"

"Not that much yet," reflected Lilly as she looked down at the very sparse timeline she had sketched out below the map.

"We are here in 2021. The power station was built in 1970. The Upton railway line was expanded during the war in 1943 and originally built in about 1880. The main railway at Didcot was expanded in 1918 and originally opened in 1840. And we think the Signal Tree started growing in around 1820. That's all so far," she said looking up. "I still need to look through Oma's book to find some dates relating to hop farming and the paper mill. I could really do with some help from Margaret, but I can't seem to get hold of her, she isn't answering her phone," she added.

"Well, it's a good start," replied Robbie as he scanned the timeline. "What about these?" he asked referring to the colourful sticky notes that Lilly had added beneath the timeline sketch.

"Oh, yes. Those are the changes I noticed in the dream. I know which order they go in but I'm not sure what dates they relate to so I thought if we put them on sticky notes, we can move them around."

"Clever idea," he murmured as he leaned in to study them more closely. "Difficulty breathing equals air quality; feeling thirsty equals lack of water or drought; water tasting bitter equals pollution; reduction in tickles and nibbles equals fewer insects?" he looked up.

"Well, I wasn't quite sure on that. It kind of feels right based on both my dreams; the tickling and nibbling on my skin could be insects or birds or something like that on the bark of the tree."

"Mmm, makes sense." Robbie looked back at the remainder of the notes. "Feeling lonely equals fewer trees from clearing hedges? Feeling hotter and shrivelled up equals warmer weather or drought?" Robbie nodded. "Very interesting," he added.

"So, you think you can help?" asked Lilly a little hesitantly. She felt like some of the ideas were a bit of a leap in the dark but then they had to start somewhere.

"Absolutely! I can take a look at the local temperature and rainfall records that kind of thing. A friend of mine works for the environment agency so she should be able to help," he paused to skim over the list again. "I wonder about the sense of loneliness bit. I think you are right about that. Trees do communicate through their roots and through chemicals in the air so fewer neighbours would disrupt that. I can look at local tree survey records to see whether there were any points when poplars were felled."

"Oh, could you. That would be great," Lilly jumped up to give him a hug narrowly missing the half-drunk mug of tea perched at the edge of the table. "Oops, that was close," she giggled and proceeded to do an excited little jig. "I can't wait to tell Margaret all about it. I think I'll try to call her again this evening."

"Oh, hello Janet," said Lilly as she answered the phone. She had quite forgotten that they were due to have one of their therapy chats.

"Hello, Lilly. Is now still a good time for us to have our call?" replied Janet picking up on the hesitant note in Lilly's voice.

"Now is fine. Sorry, I thought perhaps it might be Margaret, I have been trying to get hold of her for a few days now."

"Oh gosh, you probably haven't heard. Margaret's in hospital, she's got Covid."

"Is she okay? I mean obviously she's not okay or she wouldn't be in hospital, but well do you know how bad it is?" responded Lilly feeling quite flustered by the news.

"I think she is over the worst of it. She's been in for a couple of weeks but is off the ventilator now and seems to be on the road to recovery. I spoke to her eldest daughter yesterday and she seemed optimistic. We shall just have to wait and see."

"Oh, thank goodness," croaked Lilly, hot tears welling up in her eyes. She felt very guilty; she had been quite frustrated that Margaret had not answered her calls. The whole Hakka dreams projects seemed quite trivial all of a sudden.

"It's okay dear. I realise it must be a bit of a shock. I know you are quite fond of Margaret. I'm sure she will be all right. You know how stubborn she is," soothed Janet, trying to make her feel a little better. "Perhaps we should leave our chat for another time, maybe next week?"

"Er, yes maybe that would be a good idea," sniffed Lilly. "Could you let me know if you hear any news, though, in the meantime?"

"Yes of course I will. Now you're sure you're okay?"

"Uhuh, yes. I'll be fine. Just a bit of a shock. I've got so used to lockdown and things, I had kind of forgotten that Covid was still real. Thank you, Janet."

"Okay, bye for now then." Janet hung up leaving Lilly to absorb the news. With tears still rolling down her cheeks she made her way into the kitchen where Oma was peeling the potatoes for dinner.

"Whatever is the matter?" gasped Oma quickly putting down her knife and rushing to give Lilly a hug.

"I feel so ashamed," blurted Lilly. "There I was feeling cross with Margaret for not answering my calls and all the time she's been in hospital…" her sobs muffled the rest of her words.

"Oh, my love it's okay," soothed Oma, slowly stroking her hair and letting her cry out her tears. After a few minutes Lilly was able to regain some semblance of control. Drying her eyes and wiping the snot from her chin she took a few deep breaths.

"That's better. Now why don't you tell me all about it while I finish these," said Oma as she picked up a potato and continued to peel.

It had taken a day or two for Lilly to get over the initial shock of hearing the news about Margaret. She had rolled up her brown paper map and thrust it into the corner of the dining room feeling quite disgusted with herself. The hours at work had dragged by and she had slept fitfully, the Hakka dream returning to taunt her in the early hours leaving her feeling tired and even more guilty. She had resorted to sleeping in a spare room but even then her sleep was fragmented, her anxiety taking hold again. Finally, Oma had intervened and phoned Janet to see if there was any news.

"There you are. I spoke to Janet earlier," she said spotting Lilly sitting gazing out of the dining room window.

"Oh, what did she say?" replied Lilly turning towards her expectantly.

"You will be pleased to know that Margaret is doing much better. She will need to be in hospital a while longer, but they are pleased with her progress."

"Oh, that is good news," said Lilly breathing a sigh of relief. She suddenly felt much brighter.

"Yes, it is isn't it. Now don't spend too long daydreaming. You should probably get dressed soon. You don't want to still be in your pyjamas when Robbie gets here."

"Okay," replied Lilly rolling her eyes. Oma seemed to be quite averse to the idea of taking things slowly on a Sunday morning. She turned back to gazing out the window at the hedge. It was alive with chirruping noises and flitting motions. Occasionally a little bird would pop out and fly off returning a few moments later with a tasty morsel that it had scavenged from the nearby bird table.

"A penny for them," said Gramps as he set down a cup of coffee next to her chair.

"Hmm? Oh, I was just watching the birds. Gramps, you know about birds, don't you?"

"Some, yes although your Oma is better than me and my eyesight is not what it was. Why do you ask?"

"Well, twice now I have seen this little family of birds that flit along the hedge as though they are on their way somewhere, just passing through, never sitting still."

"Can you describe them?"

"It's tricky, as I said they never sit still long enough to get a good look. They are smaller than those," she replied pointing at a sparrow in the hedge. "And they have long tails."

"Ahh, probably long-tailed tits. Might be best to look in a book," said Gramps as he ambled off.

Lilly turned back to the window wondering if her little, long-tailed friends would grace the scene yet again.

"Here we go," said Gramps reappearing with a battered old book in his hand. He showed her the page entitled *Titmouse Family* and halfway down was a picture of the very bird she had kept seeing. Indeed, it was a long-tailed tit.

"Yes, that it!" she said excited; "Oh and I've seen some of those too," she added pointing at the blue tit.

Gramps smiled. "You can keep hold of the book for now if you want." It was good to see Lilly taking an interest again. As a little girl she had often come to him to show him the latest snail or insect she had found in the garden; a passion which seemed to be resurfacing now.

Setting the book on the windowsill she returned to gazing out of the window, sipping her coffee, and savouring the moment. It started to become a regular habit for Lilly, she began to look forward to her daily episode of "Hedge TV" as Gramps called it. Oma was quite relieved as Lilly's mood slowly improved and she was more her normal self again.

Lilly's familiarity with the birds that frequented their hedge slowly grew; she began to recognise them from their calls as much as by sight which was just as well because some of them could prove quite elusive. Hardly a day went by when she didn't notice something new. *Better than regular*

TV any day, she thought to herself. There was just as much drama, birds fighting over scraps of food, two males coming to blows over the nearby female, infants squawking by their parent's side constantly demanding attention. A regular little soap opera in miniature form playing out right there in her garden.

She gradually improved on her repertoire of bird recognition adding Dunnocks, Goldfinches and even a Black cap to her list. Most days it was too cold to sit outside so she watched from the comfort of the sitting room window as the birds went about their business. On one occasion she was simultaneously excited and perplexed as a bird of prey swooped past the window and snatched a sparrow from the hedge. She balked at the apparent cruelty feeling sorry for the sweet fluffy little sparrow but later when she recounted the tale to Gramps, he reminded her that it was nature's way. Everything had its place in the food chain, Sparrow Hawks, for that is what the bird had been, had to eat too.

Lilly was just hanging up her coat and sloughing off her shoes on her way in from work when she noticed Gramps in the dining room. He was so absorbed in studying the brown paper map that he didn't notice she was there.

"Evening Gramps," she said as she moved to stand next to him.

"Oh, Lilly! I wish you wouldn't creep up on me like that," he gasped. He looked at her somewhat sheepishly. "I hope you don't mind; I saw it stashed in the corner and I was curious. We never did get round to talking about it." Sweeping his hand across the surface of the map he gestured at the note marked *Dig for Victory*.

"Go on."

"Well, I was only a young lad during the war, but I remember them digging up every available space to plant vegetables and the like. Pastures, lawns even the village green were all ploughed up and put to seed. I got quite upset because we no longer had anywhere to play football."

"But it was necessary right? I mean from what I've read we were terribly short of food and people were starving."

"Oh, yes it was absolutely essential at the time. I don't think we could have won the war without it. It's what happened afterwards that I have never been quite so sure about."

"How so?"

"Well things didn't go back to the way they had been before. Not the farms around here at least. I recall my father and uncles having many heated discussions about it around this very table." He paused and rubbed his back which was sore from bending over. "I tell you what, why don't we put the kettle on, and I can tell you all about it over a nice brew?"

"Good idea," replied Lilly. She was very interested in what Gramps had to say but had been somewhat distracted by a growing need to go to the loo. "I'll just nip upstairs and get changed."

When she came back down Gramps was just settling into a seat at the table, a couple of steaming mugs of tea beside him. "Now, where was I?"

"Heated discussions," prompted Lilly.

"Oh yes. Well, the main topic of debate was whether we should return most of the land to pasture, which it was most suited to, given the poor drainage, or whether to take advantage of the Ministry of Agriculture subsidies and continue growing grain. In the end they decided they couldn't afford to go back to the old ways. Although I don't think my father was ever totally comfortable with it."

"I guess change is always hard to get used to," commented Lilly.

"Oh, it wasn't change per se that was the issue, it was the kinds of change and the pace of it. There were new machines which, although they saved a lot of time, required bigger fields so we ended up grubbing up hedges and felling trees left right and centre. He was a great lover of trees, bit like your Robbie, so that never sat well with him." Gramps paused to wipe his glasses and take a sip of tea. "The trees were the biggest challenge. Thinking back a lot of them were poplars, they created too much shade and the seeds would carpet the fields and smother the young plants. They had to go. Our fields were especially prone to flooding too, so we spent countless hours digging and clearing drainage ditches. In just a few years the landscape changed completely."

Lilly was touched by how upset Gramps seemed about this and patted his arm gently.

"Oh, it's OK love. Just getting old and sentimental I suppose. There was always something new to get to grips with. The new varieties of wheat which gave higher yields and the fertilisers we were encouraged to use to increase productivity even further. My father didn't like that one bit. Costs went up and up. Money for seed, money for fertiliser, money for machines to sow the seed and spread the fertiliser. Even though he was able to share some things with my uncles we became more and more dependent on the subsidies to make ends meet. He even ended up selling a bit of land, which I know he regretted as it was quickly sold on to developers to build houses."

"How big was the farm in those days?" asked Lilly

"Well, between my father and uncles we owned all of this," he said gesturing at a substantial area of the valley which took in all the local brooks and streams. "My uncles sold up years ago, but I tried to keep as much of our land as possible. I rent most of it out these days, but I was determined not to let the money grabbing developers get a hold of it." He looked up at her glassy eyed, colour building in his cheeks. "Our family have been custodians of this land since my grandfather's grandfather acquired it in the early 1800s, I'm not about to let that change, not if I can help it!"

As he paused to drink more tea Lilly took a further look at the map. She had a sudden realisation. "If the farm has been in our family's hands as long as you say, then that would make me the seventh-generation farmer. The Signal Tree has been watching over us all that time!"

"Yes, and it looks like we haven't done a very good job of taking care of the place," he sighed. "I just hope that we can work out how to put things right again." He looked into her eyes, hopeful that she would understand.

"Thank you, Gramps," she said tenderly patting his arm. "This is all really valuable information. It will help me a lot with filling in some of the gaps in the timeline. Maybe when we have the full picture, we will be able to see what to do," she added hopefully. "You don't perhaps remember when some of these changes came about?"

He chuckled. "You don't ask much, do you?" Grinning he continued, "It's okay. I know it means a lot to you, this project. It means a lot to me too. So much of this information has got lost. If we are not careful people will think that the land around here has always been like this. Just like we look at a faded photograph and don't realise how much of the original colour is missing," he sighed. "My memory for dates has never been much good but I expect we can find out most of what you need. My father kept meticulous notes. I have all his ledgers and diaries stored out in the old barn; I'll dig them out for you tomorrow if you like."

"Oh Gramps, that will be fantastic. Thank you!" beamed Lilly. If she could pin down when the hedges were cleared and when they started using fertilisers that might help to make more sense of the tree timeline.

"You mentioned using fertilisers. Would your father also have used pesticides maybe?"

"He might have done. I certainly had to resort to that to keep the crop yields up. Some years were terrible for pests. It will all be in the records…" Gramps took off his glasses and rubbed his temples.

"Thanks Gramps," repeated Lilly feeling a little guilty for pushing him. He was clearly quite overwhelmed by it all. "I'll fetch you a fresh tea, you've hardly touched that one."

Gramps had been good to his word and over the course of the next few evenings Lilly was able to find dates for most of the things they had discussed. The details of the human timelines were beginning to crystallise nicely. The match with the chronology from the dream wasn't perfect but Lilly felt that it was probably good enough. She had to keep reminding herself that tree time was fuzzy and the sensations in the dream blurred from one into the next. There was a lot of overlap, the poor tree had probably not known what to make of it all, everything seemed to have changed so fast.

Oma had been a great help too. Whilst Lilly was absorbed in Gramps's files, she had been trawling through local history books to find out information about the hop farms. She had carefully marked on the map the locations of the hop gardens and added some dates to the sticky note charting when most of them were abandoned in the late 1800s. One thing remained unexplained; the source of the poplar wood that was used for the kiln liners. Oma had not been able to find any mention of that. She had added a further sticky note saying *Robbie* as a reminder to Lilly to ask him about it when she next had the chance.

The chance to ask Robbie came round quicker than expected. Lilly was sitting outside one of the greenhouses taking the chance to soak up a rare moment of sunshine during her lunch break when a shadow fell across her face.

"Working on your tan I see," said Robbie as he planted a kiss on her cheek and squeezed in next to her on the bench.

"Fat chance of that," she replied. "What brings you here on a weekday?"

"Am I not allowed to visit my beloved during my lunch break?" he asked, grinning. "I was passing this way and thought it might be nice."

"It is nice. Of course, it is," she smiled and snuggled into his shoulder for warmth. It was chilly despite the sunshine. "Actually, I had something I wanted to ask you."

"I have some news for you too, but I'll let you go first."

"Oh, okay," Lilly hesitated, suddenly curious about what Robbie had to tell her. "I was working on the timeline with Oma and although we have been able to find some dates for the hop farms, we couldn't find out anything about where they got the poplar wood for the kiln liners. She thought you might know."

"Oh, right. So, you're sure it was poplar wood then?"

"Yes, there was some mention of that in one of the books. They used other wood as well, but it seems that it was mainly poplar."

"Well, I expect there aren't any exact records, but they would have pollarded the local trees quite frequently and remember there were lots more poplar back then so there would have been a regular supply of it. I noticed that most of the trees we have found have been pollarded at some point, you can tell by the way they are growing now."

"Good. Well, I expect that will be enough information for now. I don't think it's critical for building up the picture of the Signal Tree timeline anyway," added Lilly.

"You're probably right. Speaking of the Signal Tree timeline what I have found out is likely to be much more relevant," he paused for effect, grinning broadly.

"Oh, don't keep me in suspense. You are such a tease!" huffed Lilly slapping him gently on the arm.

Robbie did a mock drum roll on the arm of the bench. "I had a chance to look into the local records from the environment agency. There were a couple of things which really stood out. There was a big change to the drainage systems throughout the area in the early 1900s to try and tackle the problems with flooding. That would have meant that the water table in the area would have slowly dropped, and the tree would have experienced drought more often. Poplars are very moisture loving and sensitive to drying out."

"Oh, wow. Yes, that would fit perfectly with the feeling thirsty part of the dream," added Lilly as she fidgeted with excitement.

"And there's more. I looked at the temperature record too. They have some records for Oxford which cover the last two hundred years. There is a lot of variation, but average annual temperatures have been slowly rising and there is a very notable increase since the 1970s."

"What since the power station at Didcot was built you mean?"

"Well, I doubt that the power station was the direct cause but globally the increasing number of coal and gas fuelled power stations has been linked to a rise in temperatures."

"Global warming you mean?"

"Yes exactly. So, when you say that you feel hotter and more shrivelled up towards the end of the Signal Tree dream that is probably why."

"Oh my, poor tree! First, we cut off its water supply and then we put it in an oven. No wonder it's not happy," sighed Lilly. "That all seems to fit together really well. Thank you!" she said giving Robbie a squeeze.

"I didn't get a chance to look at the local tree records yet, but I can do that by the weekend if you like."

"Oh, right yes. Maybe you won't need to. Gramps had loads of records from the farm. Ledgers and diaries that his father had kept. There are quite a lot of entries in there about when the hedges were cleared, and trees were felled."

"Oh, that sounds great. I bet they are a fascinating read; I would love to take a look."

"Sure, of course although be prepared for lots and lots of detail. Great Gramps was a very meticulous man," she grinned and rolled her eyes. "You know, it's quite exciting really, being a part of all this," she added.

He looked at her quizzically. "Go on," he said.

"Well according to Gramps, the farm has been in the family since the 1800s, which makes me the seventh-generation farmer. It's amazing how much has changed in that time, we seem to have lost so much. If it wasn't for the Signal Tree, I don't think we would have a clue. It's almost like things were destined to happen this way, with my dreams and things…" her voice drifted off as she became lost in thought.

He wasn't sure what to say, there was so much to take in. He was just about to speak when his phone pinged, "Oh, blast it! I had best scoot off or I'll be late for my next appointment. See you Saturday afternoon." He kissed Lilly and dashed off leaving her to mull over the new information while she finished her lunch in the fading sunshine. She was so deep in thought she barely noticed him go.

CHAPTER 17

FULL FOCUS

Lilly was quite worn out when she arrived home from work. The emerging spring meant that plants in the greenhouses were growing at a frenetic pace. There were seemingly endless rows of seedlings to re-pot and thin out. She had lost count of the number of lettuces, radishes, cabbages that she had carefully nursed over the past few days. It was mundane yet satisfying work and it had given her plenty of head space for organising her thoughts and ideas about the emerging chronology of the Signal Tree dream. The latest information from Robbie was particularly exciting as it would finally allow her to fill in the missing links which had been bugging her for a while.

At dinner she had said very little to Oma and Gramps, such was her pre-occupation, her mind buzzing to bursting point. She hastily bolted down her pie and mash barely registering the flavour. She was determined not to delay a moment longer; anxious to get it all down on paper before she forgot some essential detail. She mumbled to herself as she wrote. *Okay so we start with the railway and the impact it had on air quality and the difficulty breathing. Then the drainage that Robbie mentioned leading to being thirsty. What next? Oh yes, the use of fertilisers causing the water to taste bitter. Hmm where does the hedge removal fit in? Oh yes, the starting to feel lonely and then that overlaps with the loss of tickling feeling because of the pesticides. Then what was it Robbie said about temperature increasing and the feeling hot and shrivelled up. Yes, yes that was it...*

Having written the details out in order she compared her latest notes to the account of the Signal Tree dream. She was saddened by the emerging picture which no one generation would have noticed. From a human perspective each of the changes would have seemed like a step up the ladder of human progress, each one a step away from our connection with the wider natural system, which was changing much more slowly, locked in the memories of the trees that have witnessed them. And yet she still felt dissatisfied. The words on the page didn't seem to be enough to capture the full intensity of the message that she held in her head. They were too monochrome and one dimensional, it didn't seem to do the depth of the knowledge justice. She had to find a way to make it more tangible, more textured, to somehow capture the emerging layers of meaning. The village clock striking midnight brought her out of her trance-like state. Whatever more needed to be added would have to wait. She was exhausted and she had work in the morning.

She slept fitfully. Images and words swirling in her mind. Her usual Hakka dream played out in the same way it always did but after she had been jolted awake, she found further sleep elusive. It was nearly five o'clock and still quite dark. She felt the sudden urge to draw. She made her way downstairs, shrugging on her dressing gown as she went. The original brown paper map was spread out on the table where she had left it partially covered with the notes she had frantically scribbled the evening before. Pushing them aside she realised that every scrap of available space was taken up with notes and sketches. *This is no good*, she thought to herself as she rummaged in a pile of paper searching for a clean sheet.

As she settled down to draw, she found her hand moved effortlessly across the paper. A complex translation of the timeline image that she held in her head slowly emerging. Growing in detail illuminated by the pale dawn light as it began to tinge the world in purples, reds, then glorious orange. The birds began to sing, their chorus building and building adding notes to a complex symphony of deeper knowing that was flowing from Lilly's mind onto the page. And yet, even now the edges of her perception were slightly blurred. She couldn't quite bring things into full focus; an element was still missing. Scanning the crumpled brown paper map one annotation seemed to stand out in bold, Hannah's chest. It was still just a square box marked with the word *Chest*. It lacked structure. She closed her eyes and tried to imagine what it looked like. She knew she had seen a photo of it somewhere, but it wouldn't come, her sense of it was vague as if she was seeing it in low resolution. Somehow, she knew that until she had seen the chest, touched it, absorbed it then she would not be able to complete the picture. There was something that she did not yet fully appreciate.

Lilly had decided to take a walk to clear her head. The hectic week topped with the lack of sleep had left her feeling dull and slow. The crisp morning air was a perfect tonic for the soul. She felt the full force of Spring awakening around her. A sea of blackthorn blossom cloaking the hedgerows in white, their intoxicating scent wafting towards her. Intertwined melodies of birdsong a cannon of little voices celebrating the emergence of fresh shoots and other delicacies to be sampled from nature's table. Despite her fatigue Lilly felt strangely at peace with the world.

Leaving her muddy boots at the door she was welcomed by the warm kitchen aromas of brewing coffee and baking bread.

"Oh Lilly. There you are. There was a phone call for you while you were out," said Gramps looking up from his morning paper.

"Ooh who was it?" replied Lilly as she quickly helped herself to a hot roll and some coffee.

"I think Oma said it was Margaret," he replied through a mouthful of toast.

"Margaret. Are you sure? I thought she was in hospital still."

Gramps just shrugged. "You'll have to ask her."

"Ask me what?" said Oma bustling into the kitchen with an armful of laundry.

"There was a call for me?"

"Oh, yes. It was Margaret. Such a lovely surprise to hear from her. She's back at home now and wondered if you could give her a ring."

"That's fantastic news!" beamed Lilly as she rushed towards the lounge. "I'll call her right now."

On the second ring Margaret picked up. "Hi Margaret! I got the message that you called," said Lilly.

"Oh, hello there my lovely. It's so good to hear your voice. I have thought a lot about you these past few weeks."

"Me too. About you that is. I heard from Janet that you were in hospital. I was terribly worried about you."

"Indeed, but I'm on the mend now and raring to go. What doesn't kill you makes you stronger and all that." Margaret sounded remarkably upbeat.

"I'm so glad to hear it. I had been trying to get in touch with you to discuss the Hakka dreams but when I heard from Janet, I felt quite selfish. It all seemed so trivial compared to what you must have been going through."

"On the contrary. It's what kept me going through the long days and dark nights. I was determined to get better and get on with my research. I figured there must be at least one last book left in me yet," she laughed.

Lilly felt most relieved although she couldn't shake off the idea that Margaret was putting on a brave face. "Great, there is so much news I want to tell you. Although I don't want to tax you too much."

"Lovely. I can't wait to hear more about it but before we get into that I have some news for you." Margaret ploughed on in her usual fashion just pausing occasionally to catch her breath. "As soon as I got out of the wretched hospital I got in touch with Andrew. Asked him if he could get hold of a copy of that book on Tudor architecture, the one that referred to the cottage in Upton. Anyhow he worked his usual wonders and came up trumps. Managed to borrow a copy from the Bodleian library. They hold pretty much every book that was ever printed you know, quite remarkable. Well, it confirmed the information we knew already about the gable end being poplar wood and dating to around 1500 or so. It's such a pity the cottage burned down…"

Finally, Lilly managed to get a word in. "That's great to know. Be sure to thank Andrew for me. Now there was one thing I wanted to ask you. It's about the chest from Hannah's dream."

"Hold your horses. I was coming to that dear. Just give me a moment," Lilly could hear Margaret coughing at the other end of the line. "Now the chest. Yes, well I think we are in luck there. It turns out the curator of that museum is a good friend of mine from university days. She confirmed the chest is still there although it's not kept on regular display. She mentioned something quite exciting about it. When they got it, they checked into the provenance of it a bit more and they did some carbon dating. It turns out it is much older than we thought. It had been re-worked in early Tudor time around 1480 but the lid, which is made of poplar wood, came from a tree which was growing in the early 1100s."

"What? So, that must mean it's around a thousand years old. Well, I never that's amazing!" yelped Lilly with excitement. "Based on what I have found out I think the chest is something of a missing link. Hannah's dream must be different somehow although I can't quite put my finger on it. I would really love to see the chest. I get the feeling if I see it then everything will fall into place."

"Well, I can ask if it would be possible for you to visit the museum. Now that they are lifting some of the restrictions it might be easier."

"Oh, could you? That would be amazing!"

"I shall put it on the list. Now Lilly my love. I would dearly like to hear more about what you have found out but maybe we should leave that for another day. All this talking has quite worn me out."

"Of course. Perhaps I could come over to your place for another socially distanced cup of tea in the conservatory and I can show you the timeline I have been constructing. It will probably make more sense if you can see it for yourself."

"Jolly good. I'll give you a tinkle when I feel up to it and we can arrange something then. Speak soon my dear." Margaret rang off leaving Lilly standing there trying to grapple with what she had revealed about the chest.

"All okay love?" asked Oma from the open doorway.

"What? Oh yes. Yes, Margaret is fine, remarkably well actually."

"Oh good. You looked a bit worried, so I wasn't sure."

"Hmm. Oh no, not worried as such just a bit intrigued. Margaret told me she had found out a bit about the chest. You know, the one from Hannah's dream. It turns out its not Tudor after all but much older. Perhaps a thousand years old. I find that quite staggering. She's going to try to arrange for me to see it," continued Lilly hopefully as they both returned to the kitchen. Lilly felt she could do with another cup of coffee.

The chill March winds had finally abated and for one day at least it looked like spring was finally on its way. Lilly was lounging on the sofa toasting her feet in a patch of sunshine which was slowly charting the passage of the afternoon. The book she was reading was beginning to blur before her eyes and she was at the point of tumbling into sleep when a knock at the door jolted her back to reality.

"Knock, knock," came Robbie's voice from the back door. "Anyone home?"

"In here," called Lilly sliding off the sofa to great him. He gave her an enormous bear hug and stood there grinning at her. "You're in a good mood," a quizzical tone creeping into her voice.

"I am," he replied rather unhelpfully. He loved to tease Lilly and keep her guessing whenever he had something exciting to tell her.

"And…" she replied in mock indignation stepping back and pretending to glower at him.

"Okay, I give in," he beamed. "We need to go on a little journey," he continued, he was not quite prepared to give in, not yet.

"And pray where do we need to go?"

"All in good time my lady," was his only response as he grabbed her shoes from the rack and presented them to her with a ceremonial bow.

"Oh, give over!" she replied, trying not to laugh. "Do you think I need a coat?"

"Knowing you. Yes," he said over his shoulder as he made his way out the door. She had to run to catch up with him as he proceeded along the lane. "Oh, we're going on foot then are we," she called.

"Yes, come on! It's not far."

After a few minutes he stopped and turned towards her. "Okay, nearly there. Now I want you to close your eyes and let me guide you."

"Okay, if I must!" she replied. "Just take it slowly, I don't want to trip over." They progressed together slowly round a bend in the path and then stopped again. She was desperately trying to think what it might be.

"Now open your eyes!"

She opened them and followed his gaze. "Wow! That is amazing, stunning. When did that happen?" she gasped.

"I noticed it yesterday on my way home from work. All the poplars have suddenly burst into bloom, it must be the warm weather that's triggered it."

The tree in front of her was clothed in a blanket of claret red flowers. As they walked closer, she could see the detail of hundreds of little red catkins which had burst forth from the buds at the tips of each shoot.

"The male trees have red flowers, right?" queried Lilly as she turned to him with a grin.

"Correct."

"And the other trees?"

"Pretty much all males. The only one I haven't checked yet is the Signal Tree. I thought we should go and see that one together."

"Ooh, okay. Do we have time to go and see now?"

"Yes of course. It shouldn't take more than twenty minutes from here and we can take a look at some of the other trees on the way."

A few minutes later as they rounded the final bend in the path Lilly found herself holding her breath. She so desperately wanted the Signal Tree to be female. "What colour are the female flowers again?" she asked hesitantly.

"Sort of yellowy green. I've only really seen them once or twice; female trees are much less common." Robbie was also hoping that Lilly wasn't about to be disappointed. He crossed his fingers as the Signal Tree came into view, peeking out from behind a willow.

"Not Red!" beamed Lilly. "But not yellow either. In fact, I can't see any flowers," she said starting to feel a little uncertain.

Robbie took out his binoculars. After a minute or two of careful searching he was able to spot a few yellow catkins just starting to protrude from the buds. "Here, look through these. Just up there on the left. You can see a couple of yellow flowers."

Lilly grabbed the binoculars and after frustrating seconds twiddling with the focus, she was able to spot the flowers and confirm for herself that the Signal Tree, her tree, was indeed a female." She started to do her trademark jig and giggled with excitement. Nearly knocking Robbie off his feet, she hugged him fiercely. "I knew my tree was a *she*," she whispered as she leaned in to kiss him.

The sun was low in the sky and the evening chill was beginning to creep from the fringes of the brook. "We should probably head back now," said Lilly reluctantly. "I knew I should have worn a coat." She laced her arm through Robbie's hoping to steal some of his warmth.

"It's a pity she's on her own out here. It's possible that none of the pollen from the males will reach her," said Robbie wistfully. "It's such a shame that when they cleared the hedgerows, they singled out the females to be felled. They were the ones that caused the most problems, their seeds blanketing the crops in downy drifts. Anyway, we'll have to wait until May to find out. If she does set seed, I'd like to keep some and see if we can get them to grow. I've never tried to do poplars before," he continued with an excited gleam in his eye. "Maybe you can help me. It can be our little project."

Lilly squeezed his arm. She liked the idea of having a project to share with Robbie.

A few days later Lilly was presented with a whole new project of her own. As she set down her plate having polished off her second slice of birthday cake Robbie eagerly thrust a large package into her hands.

"It's from all three of us," he said, smiling enthusiastically.

"I hope you like it," added Oma.

"If it's as good as that cake then I am sure I will love it," replied Lilly as she carefully teased apart the wrapping paper. Inside was an ornate wooden box with her name carved across the top.

"That's my contribution," beamed Gramps proudly.

"Oh, it's beautiful," gasped Lilly.

"Look inside," prompted Robbie fidgeting beside her. He was clearly excited to see her reaction.

Prising open the lid she was confronted with row upon row of colourful tubes neatly arranged in a hand crafted tray. She lifted the delicate handle in the middle to reveal a palette, a set of brushes and knives.

"We thought you would prefer acrylic to watercolours given the way you draw. I hope I got that right," said Robbie.

"I've got you a bunch of canvasses and an easel as well, but they were too big to wrap. Some of them belonged to my aunt; I'm sure she would have wanted you to have them," he continued a little embarrassed at feeling so emotional.

"It's perfect. Just perfect." Lilly looked up, tears streaming down her cheeks. "I don't know why I'm crying. This is the best present I've ever had. Thank you. How on earth did you know; this is exactly what I wanted?"

"Oh, silly!" replied Oma handing her a tissue. "It's obvious you love drawing!"

"You did mention wanting to paint a couple of times too, so I thought it was about time you got the chance," added Robbie reaching over to give her a hug.

"Now who wants another cup of tea?" asked Gramps as he headed to the kitchen in the hope that no one would notice the tears welling up in his eyes. Lilly looked so much like Caroline had at that age. He had made her a box for one of her birthdays too. He still kept it in his workshop; it was full of the little things they had collected together over the years.

Later that evening they sat around the table, the remains of a good dinner strewn before them; Lilly was updating Oma and Gramps on the flowering of the poplar trees when the phone rang.

"I wonder who that could be at this late hour?" said Oma.

"It's hardly late, its only half past eight," countered Gramps as he reached out to answer it. After a moment he turned to Lilly. "It's for you love. Margaret wants to wish you a Happy Birthday."

"Hi Margaret!"

"Hello there my dear. A little bird at the shop told me it

was your birthday today so I thought I would call. I have a little gift for you."

"Ooh what?" replied Lilly. "I mean, thank you. That is really kind of you," she added suddenly remembering her manners.

"Well, I've been in touch with my friend, the one who's the curator of the museum. I have managed to arrange for you to visit tomorrow if you're free. She can spare an hour in the afternoon to show you the chest."

"Really! That would be amazing. Yes, I think I am free tomorrow afternoon. What time?" She looked at Robbie hopefully. He nodded; he was free too.

"She suggested four o'clock. Would that work for you?"

"Yes, I think so. Hang on a minute while I check with Robbie." Lilly turned to him, "Will you be able to take me to the museum at around four o'clock? Margaret has arranged for me to see the chest." He nodded back at her. "Yes, it looks like he can take me so that would work."

"Jolly good. Now I guess I should give you the address, so Sir Galahad knows where to go."

"Cheeky!" admonished Lilly with a chuckle suddenly recalling the mental image of Robbie in a suit of armour wielding a chainsaw. "I'll just get a pen, hang on a moment."

Having taken down the address and phone number and thanked Margaret again for making the arrangements, Lilly spent a few minutes updating her on the news about the flowering of the trees. She ended the call with a promise to get in touch again early next week, Margaret was very keen to know all about the museum trip as soon as possible.

"Ooh, I'm so excited! Today really has been the best birthday ever," squeaked Lilly. *And the first one in years that won't be blurred by the haze of a hangover*, she thought as she finished her glass of elderflower cordial. "Is there any chance of some coffee?" she asked.

"I'm sure we can rustle some up for the birthday princess," joked Gramps as he eased himself out of his armchair and made his way to the kitchen. "We might even be able to manage some truffles as well. I think you deserve them," he grinned.

The storeroom of the museum smelled musty; a fine film of dust coated the surfaces.

"I'm sorry it's a bit of a state in here. We had to furlough most of our staff over the past year so only the bare minimum has been done to keep the place ticking over." Kathleen the curator was a little embarrassed at having to clear cobwebs away to get to the chest at the back of the room.

Lilly looked on in keen anticipation. She could already sense the power emanating from the chest where it sat nestling between two cardboard boxes.

"I expect Margaret told you that its much older than the Tudor period; well, the lid at least could be from the early 1100s. As you can see it is made from a single piece of poplar wood," explained Kathleen as she pushed the chest towards them on a small trolley.

"Probably a branch that was pollarded given its girth," added Robbie as he bent forward to open the lid and examine the construction. He looked round at Lilly who was standing beside him totally transfixed, a strange expression of total awe upon her face. "Are you okay?" he asked.

"Mmm, yes, I think so. Can you feel it?" she replied.

"Feel what?"

To Lilly it felt like the air around the chest was pulsing with energy. It was drawing her towards it just as the Signal Tree had done. "Can I touch it?" she asked looking up at Kathleen.

"Yes, you will need to put on these cotton gloves. The old wood is very sensitive to moisture."

Having donned the gloves Lilly reached forward, her hand trembling slightly in anticipation; she realised she was holding her breath. Relaxing into the moment she grazed the surface of the chest lightly with her fingers and then placed her palm firmly on the lid.

She felt herself sinking softly into a gentle swaying motion, feeling warm and bright. She couldn't see anything clearly; there was just a vague sense of green all around. Her other senses felt like they were on overload. The exquisite taste of sweet, fresh water as though it had come straight from a cool spring. The air rich with the sickly scent of flowers, so fresh it was like being on a mountainside. There was so much sound, layer upon layer of notes unlike anything she had ever heard before. Buzzes, whirring, tick-ticks, whistling and chirring, knocking and thudding all on top of a background whooshing and moaning. Her skin felt tingles and prickles all over it. All around her the gentle soothing rhythm of the lullaby "ool haa, ool hakka, ool ma, ool ma hakka" on and on.

It was all quite familiar and yet so much richer, deeper. She felt a pulsing through her fingers and toes reaching out, probing, searching, finding. Making connections; thousands of tiny golden threads of energy linking her to others. Sniffing intently, she became aware of a complex vibrant scent in the air a mixture of notes some warm and bold, others gentle and light; two distinct characteristics, one male, one female. It was wafting all around her, a form of greeting. She felt herself responding, releasing a scent of her own from every pore of her being, a rich and wholesome scent, the scent of mother.

Then she felt a jolting, thudding, jarring sensation an awful cracking sound followed by a lurching, falling…

Suddenly she was awake and back in the museum. She could hear Robbie's voice.

"Lilly, Lilly, are you okay?" he was shaking her shoulder gently.

She looked up at him confused. "Yes, I think so," she stammered. She realised she was lying on the floor next to the chest, her gloved hand still outstretched. "What happened?"

"One moment you were reaching out to touch the chest and the next you just collapsed in a heap. I thought you'd fainted or something."

"How long was I out?"

"Just a couple of seconds, thankfully."

"Oh, it felt like I was gone for much longer. I had a kind of dream…" The essence of the dream came drifting back into her consciousness. She realised that there had been something profoundly missing from her earlier dreams. The overwhelming sense of connection had been lost; the Signal Tree's world had been silent in comparison. She finally understood the feeling of longing, searching and searching that she had felt before. Over the course of the last millennium the number of poplar trees had been so dramatically reduced and they were so sparsely distributed that their golden threads were broken, they couldn't find each other anymore. The extent of the disconnection came to her like a jolt. "Have you got a pen? I need to write things down, while they are still fresh in my mind," she asked Kathleen as she allowed Robbie to help her to her feet.

"Yes of course. I'll get you some water too. You look dreadfully pale," she replied hurrying off in the direction of her office. Robbie decided it was probably best if they followed; gently he took Lilly's arm and guided her towards the door.

As they walked Lilly pictured her timeline map in her mind. The image of Hannah's chest now brought into full focus entwined in the branches of old Ma Hakka, glowing threads of gold spooling out in all directions but not quite reaching the Signal Tree which had no threads of its own. *Or maybe just one thin thread*, she thought to herself gripping Robbie's arm tightly and silently hoping that some pollen will have reached her tree and enabled it to set seed.

CHAPTER 18

BEYOND THE MIRROR

As they crawled through the Sunday evening traffic Robbie tried to relax and not grip the steering wheel too tightly. He stole the occasional glance at Lilly who had been lost in contemplation ever since they left the museum. He tried not to worry but it was hard not to be concerned about her fainting episode. Just as he was about to ask for the umpteenth time if she was okay, she turned to him and asked him if he believed in the supernatural.

"Well, I've never really thought about it. I get this sense of inclusion and belonging sometimes when I am alone in the woods, but I wouldn't say it was a supernatural experience or anything like that. Why do you ask?"

"When I touched the chest, it was as if I had moved into another plane of existence, I experienced this sense of deeper knowing that I can't explain. Almost spiritual as though I was communicating with the Universe. Now, sitting here, everything feels different somehow. As if I can see the world properly for the first time." She frowned at him, "I've always thought of that kind of thing as new age nonsense but now I'm not so sure."

"My aunt always used to say that you should use your heart as much as your mind when trying to make sense of the world. She used to get really frustrated with people who asked her to explain the meaning behind her art. To her it was how it made you feel that was important. I think she was right; logic can't explain everything." He gave her leg a reassuring squeeze. "If you feel that the chest was communicating something to you then I think it's important that you pay attention."

She smiled and let out a sigh of relief. "I'm glad you don't think I'm crazy."

"Not at all. Now fill me in on things. What has changed?"

Lilly ran through some of the differences that she had sensed between the Hakka dream, as she referred to it, and the earlier Signal Tree dream.

"So much has changed in what, a thousand years or so…"

"That would be about seven generations of poplars," added Robbie.

"Really? Seven tree generations, I hadn't thought of it like that. So that means whilst Signal is telling us about just seven generations of humans, Hakka is telling us a far longer story…" Lilly paused. "Seven tree generations that would be what, forty-nine human generations! That's incredible…" she looked at Robbie, her eyes gleaming with excitement. "Everything felt richer, purer, lighter and the level of connection that Hakka had to other trees. Well, it was almost overwhelming. I think I understand what was missing, that sense of disconnection that the Signal Tree now experiences. Over the space of those seven tree generations, she has lost touch almost completely." Lilly looked over at him hesitating for a moment.

"Go on," he encouraged.

"Well, it's just occurred to me. Apart from the increasing sense of disconnection, the two dreams start off being quite similar. It's really only during the latter part of the Signal dream that everything begins to feel really different. In Signal's lifetime, just two hundred years, the level of change that she has experienced is so dramatic and yet we humans don't seem to have noticed, not really…" She fell silent letting the enormity of what she had experienced in the dreams sink in.

"You know, before I moved to live with Oma and Gramps, I hadn't had any real experience of nature for years. I never really thought about it. What is worse, whenever I heard someone banging on about the environment and climate change, I used to tune out, it was all blah blah blah. I feel so ashamed, how could I have been so blind?" Her chest felt tight with emotion as tears welled up and thwarted any attempt to say more.

"It's okay. You are not the first one to feel this way and you certainly won't be the last. You don't need to feel ashamed. It's so easy to get lost in our everyday lives," replied Robbie.

"But it's not okay. Not for the Black Poplars. If things don't change then soon there won't be any left. If we're not careful there won't be any of us left either!"

Robbie reached out and took her hand. "Well then, we will just have to start doing something about it won't we."

That evening as she sat in front of her dresser and combed out her wet hair Lilly remained in a reflective mood. She had got over the original emotional shock but still couldn't shake the sense of disappointment in herself. *How could I have been so blind?* she kept saying to herself over and over as she battled with a knot in her hair. Looking in the mirror a realisation suddenly came to her. She only had a limited view of the world based on what was reflected back and most of the time she was only really focused on herself not even paying attention to the other things she could see. It was a perfect metaphor for the egocentric view of the world she used to hold. *We need to learn to look beyond the mirror to see how things really are!* she thought, realising that the dreams had helped her to do just that. *How can I help others to see that too?* she pondered. *I'll have to ask Oma what she thinks and while I'm at it I should probably take her up on the offer to cut my hair*, she thought as she scrutinised the many split ends which were playing havoc with the brush.

The following morning Lilly was just tucking into a nice slice of cake when her mobile rang. It was Fi again. Lilly had noticed a missed call earlier in the morning but had dismissed it as a misdial. She had a few minutes of her coffee break left so she decided to pick up.

"Hello."

"Oh, hi babes, wow it's so good to hear your voice. Haven't spoken in ages! I was wondering if you wanted to go out for some drinks this evening now that we are allowed out to play again?"

"That might be a bit tricky as I don't live in London anymore. I am in Oxfordshire now on my grandparents' farm."

"Ooh, all that mud and stinky animal poo, yuck. You must hate it living with the old fogies. I don't suppose there is much to do in the back of beyondshire you must be going loopy out there. Surely you can get a train or something. A night out on the town would do you good. What do you say?"

"I quite like living here actually and if it wasn't for my grandparents, I would probably be living rough on the streets right now. It's been over a year Fi. Where were you when I needed help? No don't answer, you were shacked up with Ralf and too busy to answer my calls," Lilly spat, her blood pressure starting to rise.

"Oh babes, I'm so sorry. I didn't realise things were so bad. I just assumed you would go to your dad's or something. I had a tough time too you know. Ralf dumped me and I was transferred to working at the freight terminal. It was awful," replied Fi defensively. "Luckily, I wasn't there too long. I got in with Neil, you remember him, we started having a bit of a thing. He got me a spot working on the executive flights. Let me move into his flat in Soho," she added trying to divert Lilly's attention.

"Sounds lovely, I am so pleased for you," replied Lilly with more than a hint of sarcasm.

"Well, the work is okay, but Neil has turned out to be a bit of a bastard. We had a spat and he has gone back to his wife in New York. He wants me to move out of the flat."

Here it comes, thought Lilly, Fi wouldn't have called unless she wanted something.

"I've found this lovely little flat, and I was wondering if you wanted to come in with me. We could split the rent. It would be just like old times…"

"I'm actually quite happy where I am Fi. I have a good job; I'm making new friends and I'm beginning to realise that there is more to life than bars and shopping. You are always welcome to visit, you never know you might like it."

"No ta Lils, the country air must have addled your brains. Are you sure I can't change your mind babes?" pleaded Fi, she was starting to sound quite desperate.

"Really, no thank you Fi. Now I'm sorry but I have to get back to work. It was nice talking to you."

"Oh babe, don't go…" whined Fi.

"Sorry Fi but I have to." Lilly hung up.

She felt stunned, how could she ever have been friends with Fi, she was so shallow and self-centred. To make a call like that after a whole year, it was quite staggering. Lilly couldn't help feeling a tiny bit sorry for her though; having been in that situation before she knew how lonely it could feel. *Perhaps it will do her good, Fi could do with learning to live within her means, at least she has a job*, thought Lilly as she brushed the cake crumbs from her lap and headed back into the shop.

Later that afternoon Lilly was sitting out on the patio letting her tea go cold. It was as though the garden was breathing a sigh of relief after an unseasonably cool spell of weather. A pair of sparrows were gathering materials for their nest. Tufts of pampas grass acting like sails in their beaks making their flight haphazard as they battled against the stiff breeze. As she turned to take a sip of tea, she realised that Oma was watching her.

"You know, I only realised recently how much I missed

being around nature. Sitting here with the birds is so relaxing." She turned back to look at the garden and the field beyond. "Most of the people I knew at school and work dismissed nature as being messy and dirty. They couldn't wait to get back to the cleanliness and sterility of their city homes. I don't think any of them had ever had the chance to see the beauty in it, to breath in the complex aromas in the air, to feel the freedom of it. It's quite sad when you think about it." Lilly's chest was bursting with emotion, overflowing with the joy of seeing and a sense of loss for others who looked but did not see. She was still reeling a little from her conversation with Fi earlier that morning. Fi was exactly the same, she had never known the beauty of the countryside and was not even willing to give it a try.

"It's not so uncommon, I suppose," replied Oma. "We generally don't miss what we never knew. I think that is why I went into teaching. Young minds are so inquisitive when you give them a chance." A frown crossed her brow. Lilly looked at her a little puzzled.

"Do you miss teaching? I thought you said it was not your true path?"

"To start with I loved it but over time it got to be a bit mechanical. All grades and rankings, even for the younger children. It felt like we were in a factory turning out automatons that could do exams rather than helping children to develop and grow," she sighed and patted Lilly's hand. "Sorry to sound so gloomy. Thinking about it brings back difficult memories. I'll bring you another tea, I think that one has gone cold." She left Lilly to enjoy the birds.

Closing her eyes and breathing deeply Lilly conjured the image of the Hakka tree entwining the ancient chest, its golden filaments streaming out in all directions probing the air, connecting with the trees which once stood all around it. She reached for her brush and started to paint, her hand moving across the canvas making strokes she was barely conscious of, the image of Hakka dancing forth from her subconscious. She shivered slightly as a draft crept beneath the barn door behind her.

Gramps had not quite put the finishing touches to her painting studio. He had insisted on making a space that she could call her own, where she could work undisturbed by his carpentry; a space not permeated by the ubiquitous wood dust he created. On Robbie's recommendation he had fitted a huge skylight in the north facing side of the barn roof to provide the ideal lighting. Together they had found some old shelves and a workbench which was the only furniture she needed. The easel that Robbie had given her took pride of place in the centre of the studio. As she worked the rickety old bar stool creaked beneath her.

On the wall beside her she had placed the small picture of the Black Poplar leaf, twig and flowers that Robbie's aunt had painted. It was her talisman, a constant source of inspiration for her work. She could get lost in the detail of it, always seeing something more than she had noticed before. Next to it were some of her sketches and practice pieces. Renderings of the Signal Tree and the intricate patterns in its bark, samples of poplar wood which Gramps had sanded and polished to reveal the delicate patterns in their grain. Along the far wall was hung the version of the timeline map which Lilly had carefully re-drawn and embellished with detailed pictures of each of the Hakka dream artefacts. It was helping her to look beyond the mirror of the everyday, that brief snapshot in time and to take a longer view, a view rooted in tree time. She felt drawn to use her art to try to make sense of it so she could share the wonder she felt with others.

"Margaret has just arrived," called a voice from the door.

Lilly was shaken from her reverie; she had quite forgotten the time. Today was a special day. The first day when the weather was warm enough to contemplate having a barbecue outside. She had invited Margaret to join them; they were going to celebrate the completion of the tree timeline together. She hadn't felt so excited in a long time. "Okay, I'm coming," she called in reply. Looking down at her paint-stained hands and overalls she realised she should probably make herself presentable before lunch.

"There you are!" called Margaret as Lilly headed for the farmhouse. "Look at you all covered in paint. It's just as well I'm not allowed to give you a hug," she joked.

Lilly grinned. "Sorry, I lost track of time. I'll just go and freshen up and then I'll be right out."

Returning to the courtyard Lilly was greeted by the delicious aromas of meat and corn sizzling on the barbecue. Robbie was standing there, tongs in one hand, beer in the other, feeling rather sheepish in the frilly apron that Oma had insisted he should wear. Lilly planted a big kiss on his cheek. "You look fetching dear," she chuckled.

As she took a seat opposite Margaret, she noticed her glancing furtively at the studio door. "Not yet Margaret, you will have to wait until we have eaten," chided Lilly.

"So Robbie keeps reminding me," replied Margaret giving him a fierce look before bursting into laughter. She was feeling quite mischievous, and she hadn't even had anything to drink. *Who needs alcohol anyway, I'll take good company any day!* she thought to herself.

The garden was soon filled with the sound of chatter and laughter punctuated with the odd clink of cutlery as they all settled down to eat.

"Lilly tells me you are writing a book about the Hakka dreams," said Oma.

"Oh, yes. I think it's going to be my best. I've not enjoyed anything so much in ages. Working with Lilly has been such a pleasure. She would make a fantastic historian you know," beamed Margaret.

"Thanks, but no thanks," replied Lilly. "I think I'll stick to painting rather than writing, it's more my thing."

"Talking of painting. Robbie here says you are rather good. So, I was wondering if you would consider doing the illustrations for my book?"

Lilly didn't know what to say. She suddenly felt terribly embarrassed. "I'm not sure my work would be worthy of that," she stammered her face flushing hot.

"Well, I think I'll be the judge of that," replied Margaret smiling. "Now shall we go and take a look?" she continued as she rose slowly to her feet and made a move towards the barn.

Robbie looked over at Lilly and Oma. "Why don't you show Margaret the way and Gramps and I will follow on with the Elderflower Champagne and glasses."

Standing in front of the tree timeline Margaret was almost lost for words. She turned to Lilly and gently squeezed her hand. "Blow the social distancing rules," she muttered. They stood there together, absorbing the raw beauty of the story that Lilly had captured in her art. "More than worthy," she whispered.

"A toast to the Hakka dreams!" pronounced Gramps, thrusting glasses into everyone's hand.

"And to the Signal Tree. May she guide our way!" added Robbie, his voice cracking with the emotion of the moment.

"You know, I am really rather humbled," stated Margaret. "I have to confess that initially I was rather sceptical about believing that a tree was trying to communicate with us but seeing it all together like this…" she paused and looked at Lilly in admiration, "…well I have to say it really does seem to make sense; I have learned something that books could never have taught me…" she chuckled. "I think this old dog might finally have learned some new tricks," she added grinning.

Oma was staring at the emerging image of the Hakka tree which Lilly had started to create that morning. It was quite captivating, the golden threads picked out by the afternoon sun playing across the canvas as it streamed in through the open door. "Oh my," was all she managed to say as she felt a surge of enormous pride well up inside her. "Your mother would have been so proud of you!"

Lilly felt quite overwhelmed by it all. She looked over at Robbie in a silent plea for help.

"Shall we go back outside and have some dessert?" he suggested.

Oma had created a beautiful flan from the remaining supply of last season's canned apples. "Custard or ice cream?" she enquired as she placed a slice in front of Margaret.

"Ooh, would it be naughty to have both?" she replied in excitement. "I haven't had pudding this good in ages," she added picking up her spoon in anticipation. Between mouthfuls of food, she continued their conversation.

"You know, until I saw the whole thing laid out in front of me, I had not really appreciated the story that the dreams are trying to tell. What an awfully human centric view of the world I have."

"It had the same effect on me. I felt like I was seeing things through a different lens, finally able to view the world in full focus," agreed Lilly "I noticed how disconnected I was, how we all are really. I think I want to use my art to help people see the connections that are broken, help them to re-make the links," she added.

"Go on," responded Robbie with a look of encouragement. He knew she had something more to say but, despite the friendly company, she would be hesitant.

"Well, I haven't really got any firm ideas yet. Perhaps something like a bottle of milk merging with a cow in its pasture. Or maybe a bag of frozen peas blending into the pea plants in a field and the farmer sowing the peas. Something like that anyway," she looked around the table hoping that what she was saying made some kind of sense.

"Interesting," replied Oma. "Maybe you could link it to some of the things we sell in the shop."

"Mmm yes, and some of the things on the farm too," added Gramps looking across to the apple trees at the end of the garden and noticing the murmuring of the bees going about their business. "Like honey. You could have something with honey and bees and blossom," he suggested, smiling enthusiastically.

"You could maybe even extend it beyond that," said Robbie, continuing the emerging train of thought. "Maybe capturing a link to the wild spaces around us and not just the farms?" he added glancing at Lilly.

"What, like wildflowers you mean? Maybe I could do more than one version of a picture. I could do the honey, and bees and wildflowers too. Perhaps link that to mowing grass compared to letting things go wild. That sort of thing."

"Exactly! Trying to get people to understand the importance of natural spaces in their lives. Maybe link it to rewilding somehow," he added. Rewilding was one of his life passions and he was always quite frustrated when people he spoke to had little appreciation of the crucial role that natural meadows and woodlands had to play. They seemed to think his work was just about manging tree plantations.

"I'm going to have to make some notes on this," said Lilly jumping up and heading to the studio to grab her notebook. "I'll be back in a minute!" she added looking at Margaret and suddenly feeling guilty about abandoning her guest.

"You go ahead dear. I'm quite happy here. Is there any chance of seconds?" she replied, eying up the remaining slice of flan.

By Tuesday afternoon the joy of the barbecue felt like a distant memory. The veg shop was short staffed again and Lilly had been called away from her usual work in the greenhouse to help with re-stocking the shelves. She was busy sorting through the array of new pet supplies that they had started stocking during the pandemic. Rabbit food, dog food, cat food, wild bird seed, the list seemed endless.

"I'm surprised you have started selling this," came a voice from behind her. Feeling a little startled Lilly turned round to find Betty standing next to the sacks of chicken food and wagging a disapproving finger at her.

"Hello Betty. Yes well, we thought we would branch out a little. Other customers seem to appreciate being able to get their petfood here as well as their weekly veg." Lilly smiled a little sheepishly, Betty was quite a formidable character. She owned a large orchard nearby and kept a flock of free-range chickens. The eggs she supplied to the shop were always very popular.

"It's not the pet food per se dear but this chicken food that I object to," replied Betty sternly. Seeing that Lilly seemed a little confused she decided to elaborate. "It's made from soya, and I know for a fact that particular brand imports the stuff from South America. By selling that you are endorsing the cutting down of the Amazon rainforest!" said Betty, her tone becoming increasingly harsh.

"Oh, gosh. I had no idea," replied Lilly desperately trying to diffuse the situation. Betty looked like she was about to blow a gasket.

"Sadly, not many people have a clue about where their food comes from and what environmental impact it has. If I were you, I would get rid of the stuff and if you are going to sell chicken food then at least make sure it's sustainable!" Betty was coming up to full steam now.

"Thank you, Betty. I will certainly look into it. What do you feed your chickens on? Is there something you could recommend?" continued Lilly trying to stay calm and apply the pragmatic approach she had been taught at the airline.

"Corn dear. I feed them corn. I get it from a local organic farm. Here, I'll write the details down for you." Betty rummaged in her bag for some paper and a pen. She thrust the scribbled note into Lilly's hand. "Be sure to discuss it with Breda won't you," she said and hurried off before Lilly could reply.

Lilly just stood there. She felt like she had been hit by a mini tornado. Looking down at the sacks of chicken food she felt very unsure of herself. *Could we really be contributing to deforestation?* she thought to herself. She sincerely hoped not, Robbie would be appalled. Leaning over she took a picture of one of the sacks. *I'll do a search on that later*, she thought.

As they were closing up for the day Lilly took the chance to use the office computer. The conversation she'd had with Betty was still very much on her mind. She typed in the name of the chicken food brand and hit search. The first hit was from the official company website; it didn't help much. Scrolling through she managed to confirm that the chicken food was made from soya and that it was imported but there was no mention of the exact country of origin. She went back to the original hit list and found a series of articles with rather sensational headlines claiming that the supplier had been forced to *come clean* about *the dirty truth* etcetera. On further inspection most of them didn't refer to a reliable source of information. Lilly wasn't sure what to believe. Then, slightly lower down the list of hits, she spied something more promising. A much more measured article written by a reputable environmental charity which referred to official reports and published scientific data. Just then, Oma put her head around the door.

"There you are. It's gone six. Gramps will be wondering where we've got to."

"Oh sorry! I just need to print this," replied Lilly as she made her way to the printer. Oma gave a her a curious look. "I'll tell you all about it in the car."

As Lilly gathered up the printout an idea crept into her mind. Maybe she could make a painting about this, linking eggs to chickens to soya pellets to deforestation. The image slowly came together in her mind's eye. Grabbing some scrap paper, she started to make a sketch. *Beep beep!* Came the sound of the car horn. "Oops, I'm coming!" she called realising that she was keeping Oma waiting.

It wasn't until after dinner that Lilly had the chance to talk to Oma about her rather unnerving conversation with Betty. She had mentioned it in the car, but Oma had been quite dismissive about it all and was not in the best of moods given that Lilly had made them late. Now, as she dried the dishes, Oma glanced at the sketch and papers that Lilly had left on the kitchen table.

"This sketch looks interesting dear. Tell me again, what was it that Betty was going on about earlier?"

"She was upset about the chicken food we have started selling. She said it was made from imported soya and was linked to deforestation in the Amazon. She gave me the name of a supplier of organic corn, suggested we should stock that instead." Oma raised an eyebrow. Lilly ploughed on before she could interrupt. "So, I looked it up online and I found the article you see there. It turns out Betty is right. I have to say I'm a bit shocked," she paused as Oma scanned through the article.

"It got me thinking," she continued as Oma looked up. "The other things we stock in the veg shop, where do they come from, how much of it is imported, how is it grown, how much of it is organic?"

"Well…" Oma paused and put down the plate she had been drying. "So many questions. Where to begin? I guess you could call the veg we grow ourselves organic although I never got round to getting it officially accredited, too much paperwork and our customers have never really asked about it…" she tailed off again.

Lilly continued scrubbing her pan and waited patiently for Oma to continue. She was clearly feeling quite uncomfortable.

"As for the veg from the wholesalers. We do take care to ensure we know what the country of origin is, but I have never really looked into the exact sources and farming methods used. I'm not even sure it's very easy to find out. The labels and invoices certainly don't mention anything about it. I suppose you can find that out online, but I've never been very good at that sort of thing." She looked over at Lilly in dismay. "I'm sorry dear."

"Oh, Oma," Lilly moved to give her a slightly soggy hug. "It's okay. I didn't know either. Maybe we can learn about this stuff together?" she smiled and gave Oma another squeeze.

"This sketch is interesting. I can see now what you are trying to show. Very clever," added Oma.

"We'll have to see," replied Lilly bashfully. "I want to try to paint it, I hope I can do it justice."

Oma smiled. "If it's anything like the pictures you have done so far, I'm sure it will."

"Maybe I could do another one about other aspects of farming. Not sure how I would do that though. How could I capture organic farming, seasonal, local that kind of thing…" Lilly tailed off deep in thought as she scrubbed at the pan oblivious to the fact that it was already spotlessly clean.

"I wish you would sit still!" muttered Lilly. The chicken she was trying to sketch had not been a very obliging model. She had started out trying to paint her *amazon to eggs* work based on some photographs but had been finding the rendering of the feathers difficult. She wanted to capture the play of the sunlight on the intricate patterns of the wings in more detail. There was no substitute for the real thing even if her subject insisted on rooting through the scrub at the edges of the hedge while she tried to work.

"Gramps said I would find you here," chuckled Robbie amused at the site of Lilly lying on her stomach berating the chickens.

Lilly stood up and brushed herself off. "Now I realise why your aunt chose to paint plants. At least they don't wander off," she commented directing the last rebuke at the bird which had now entirely disappeared into the hedge.

Robbie planted himself down on the bench and started sifting through Lilly's sketches. "These are really good! Is this the one about deforestation that you were telling me about?"

Lilly looked over his shoulder. "No that's for something else. I was trying to think of a way to show different farming methods and link that to the food people buy in the shop. I'm not quite sure how to get it across."

Robbie placed two of the sketches side by side. One had a large expanse of field with a tractor spraying crops linking to a supermarket and a microwave oven. Lilly had written *dull green, brown and grey tones* across the corner. The other was of smaller field with smiling people picking crops by hand linking to a market stall and then a family cooking together in the kitchen. The words *bright and colourful* were scribbled down the side.

"Interesting..." he looked up at Lilly.

"They're OK but they don't quite work. I know..." she said frustrated. "I'm not sure people will see the contrast between them and make the link..."

"Well..." he paused a moment. "What if you combined the two scenes into one picture? That way the colour schemes you have chosen could really work..."

"Oh, you are a genius! Of course, that's it." She jumped up and started gathering her things together. "Could you bring those?" she said striding off up the garden towards the barn.

By the time Robbie arrived in the studio Lilly was already fully absorbed in creating a new sketch. He quietly set things down on the bench and went off to make tea. He knew it would be useless to talk to her until she'd finished decluttering her mind of the images which had come bursting forth from their conversation.

Half an hour later he took her out a cup of freshly brewed tea.

"How's it going?" he asked.

"Good!" she replied looking up beaming. "Thank you."

"You are most welcome," he said offering her the tea.

"Oh. I meant thank you for helping with the inspiration for the painting. But the tea is nice too!" she grinned as she placed the cup on the now very cluttered bench.

He looked around at the canvasses she had stacked up along the walls of the barn. She had made a start on a good many of the ideas that they had discussed over the past few weeks. It was an impressive collection. Like his aunt she had the curious habit of working on several pieces at once, slowly developing a consistent style across the collection.

Standing next to him she nuzzled his shoulder. "I know some of them aren't quite finished but what do you think?"

"Powerful, beautiful. Just like the artist," he said placing his arm around her waist and pulling her in close.

Suddenly she realised that Robbie must have dropped by for a reason. She had been so distracted by her art that she had completely forgotten to ask him. "Sorry my love. I have done my usual trick of forgetting to ask how you are. Have you had a good week?"

"Yes, in fact I have, and I have a little surprise for you," he grinned and produced a small brown paper bag from his pocket. "Take a look."

Inside the bag was a mass of white fluffy cotton-like material. She looked up at him a little confused.

"Black Poplar seeds," he announced proudly. "I was passing by the Signal Tree this morning and noticed that she was shedding seed. I know we had discussed collecting it together, but I wanted to make sure I got some before it all blew off in the wind and got mixed up with the willow fluff."

"Fantastic!" squeaked Lilly as she jigged up and down with excitement.

"Yes, hopefully they will germinate. I thought maybe you could help me pot them up tomorrow. I have been doing some research and have a few ideas to try out."

"Oooh, I can't wait. Let's go and show Gramps," replied Lilly as she dashed out towards the kitchen leaving yet another cup of tea to go cold on her workbench.

Robbie laughed to himself as he set off in pursuit. *What have I let myself in for?* he wondered.

CHAPTER 19

TESTING THE FOUNDATIONS

Lilly was in the shower when the phone rang. Moments later Gramps was knocking at her door.

"Robbie's on the phone, he wants to speak to you."

"I'm in the shower Gramps. Can you take a message please?"

Conscious that she was already running late, Lilly hurried to rinse off and dashed out of the shower leaving a trail of wet footprints across the bedroom floor. Just as she was battling with trying to pull on her jeans over barely dry legs Gramps came puffing up the stairs again to give her the message.

"He wanted to know if you have a pair of high heeled shoes you can bring with you when you come over later?" He called through the door.

Lilly was confused, *what on earth has Robbie got planned?* she thought to herself as she wrestled with her top. They were supposed to be planting poplar seeds and then Robbie had promised to make dinner for her. She was planning to stay over at his place for the first time. *If I need shoes, do I need a dress?* she wondered.

"Did he say what the shoes were for?" she asked.

Gramps was no help. "I didn't ask that; I would have thought you are expected to wear them!" he replied a little non-plussed by the illogical question.

Lilly decided it would be best to call Robbie back.

He was amused by her confusion. "The shoes are to help with planting the seeds, to mimic being trodden in by animal hooves. Do you have any that you don't mind getting dirty?" he asked.

Lilly giggled at this; it conjured a mental image of her doing animal impersonations while stomping in the earth in her best shoes.

"I do have some old shoes that should be suitable. I will dig them out. Anything else you want me to bring? A sheep costume or maybe a cow bell?" she joked.

"No, that's all. Besides your lovely self of course."

"Okay, I'm almost ready. I'll be over soon." she replied.

She hung up and set about packing the last of her things. She found the shoes at the bottom of her wardrobe along with a newer pair of sandals. Deciding that it might be nice to dress up a bit for dinner she shoved those into her bag along with a pretty summer dress that she had barely worn; there hadn't been much call for party clothes over the past few months.

She arrived at Robbie's just in time for lunch. Cycling with her overnight bag and a picnic lunch balanced on the handlebars had proved to be quite a challenge. She had managed not to fall off despite a close encounter with the hedge at the corner of the driveway. It was a glorious sunny day, so they decided to sit out in the back garden in the shade of an apple tree which was heavily laden with fruit.

Lilly closed her eyes and took in the sounds and scents that were swirling all around her. The garden was thick with summer flowers and the sound of bees and hover flies busily gathering nectar. The dappled sunlight threw patches of warmth on her arms and legs as she sat back against the trunk of the tree.

"Mmm, this is nice," she murmured.

"Don't get too comfy," replied Robbie patting her arm gently. "We've got work to do."

"Ever the task master," she replied pretending to be put out but secretly excited at the prospect of planting the Black Poplar seeds from the Signal Tree. She was still curious about what Robbie had in mind concerning her shoes. "So, what is it that you have planned?" she asked.

Robbie got out a folder and talked her through his ideas for different ways in which they could sow the seeds. "I have never planted tree seeds like this before, so I did a bit of reading round. No-one talks much about poplars, but I found some references to willow, which are similar, they are both from the same class of cotton woods with fluffy seed coatings."

"Okay, but this all looks rather complicated. Surely if you just put the seeds in a pot, they will grow, won't they?" asked Lilly.

"Well. that's just it. The fluff makes the seeds good for being dispersed by the wind. Poplars are what you call pioneer trees. They seek out new locations to colonise which can be quite a long distance from the parent tree.

The problem comes when the seeds land. The fluff forms a hydrophobic layer around the seed which can stop them from germinating."

"A hydro what?" asked Lilly, unfamiliar with the term.

"Hydrophobic, it means water repellent. It can be difficult to make the seed wet and that needs to happen before it can germinate." Robbie looked up to check that he was making sense.

"Ah okay, now I get it." replied Lilly. "But why aren't we going to put them in pots?" she asked as she reviewed the details again.

"Trees don't generally like being in pots, particularly if they are moisture loving like poplars. It's hard to keep their roots wet enough. So, I've prepared a nursery bed at the end of the garden where it's shady and the soil should remain damp. Let me show you."

They set off down the garden. Lilly remembering, at the last minute, to bring her old high heeled shoes with her.

"It's a bit muddy," she commented as she sank into the turf at the edge of the path.

"I think you are going to have to accept that we are going to get a bit muddy my dear," grinned Robbie.

He had set out a grid on the soil marking areas to be planted in different ways. On the first they spread out some seed and pressed it down onto the soil with the palms of their hands. In the second square they did the same but then scattered soil over the seed to cover it. Planting the final square proved to be the most fun. Once they had spread out the seed, Lilly donned her old high heels and stomped all over the square mimicking the way cows or sheep might crush the seed into the soil with their hooves.

"Moo!" she said as she stamped up and down and then bending over, she made to butt Robbie with her pretend horns.

"Steady there, Ermintrude!" he laughed. Then as one of the shoes came off, she lost her footing and they both tumbled over in the mud. They just lay there both crying with laughter until they felt like they were going to burst.

"I don't think I've had so much fun in years!" she grinned and smeared mud across his cheek.

"That does it! I'm going to get you for that," he replied wiping his muddy hand across the back of her shirt and proceeding to tickle her.

Writhing in the mud she descended into another fit of giggles. "I think I'm going to need a bath," she managed to gasp between bouts of laughter.

Refreshed after a luxurious half hour soaking in a sea of bubbles, Lilly emerged from the bathroom to the tantalising scent of garlic and rosemary. Robbie was making Lyonnaise potatoes with chargrilled chicken and homegrown salad for dinner. She suddenly realised that she was starving and had to force herself to take time over getting ready. She wanted to look presentable and having misaligned buttons up the front of her dress and straggly hair was not really the look she was going for.

As she entered the living room Robbie looked up from where he was setting the table.

"Wow! You look amazing," he said smiling.

"Why thank you," she replied doing a little twirl in her dress and blushing. "I'm glad you like it."

Robbie helped her into her seat and poured a glass of

sparkling apple juice. "Dinner won't be long. I just have to finish the dressing for the salad."

"I can't believe you've made all this. I had no idea you were such a good cook," said Lilly as she nibbled at some bread and olives.

"Like most useful things, I learned it from my aunt. She loved to cook, and we used to spend hours gathering food from the garden and preparing dinner together," he sighed.

"I never really learned to cook before I came to live with Oma. She's very patient with me but I feel I still have a lot to learn. I guess my main problem is that I tend to get distracted and then I burn things. I'm glad you are cooking and not me," added Lilly.

"I'm sure you'll get the hang of it with practice," said Robbie as he placed a plate of steaming chicken and potatoes in front of her. "Help yourself to salad."

Dinner was followed by a dessert of fresh peaches and ice cream. Feeling comfortably full and more than a little bit dozy she accepted an offer of coffee. "I need something to keep me awake," she joked as she cleared the table and made a start with the washing up.

"Oh, leave those. We can do them later," suggested Robbie.

"No. You cooked. I wash," she insisted.

"Okay. I'll put on some music and when you're done maybe we can dance."

Melodic tones of jazz filled the warm evening air. Lilly and Robbie hummed quietly as they snuggled up close to each other and swayed gently in time with the beat. It was a perfect end to a magical day.

❧

The weekend she had spent with Robbie felt like a distant memory. It had a bittersweet quality, at once intensely delightful and yet full of yearning. It had marked the beginning of a new phase in their relationship but also a moment of parting. Robbie had been seconded onto a project in Scotland and would be away for a few weeks. In his absence Lilly spent her time on her art whenever possible; making the most of the warm evenings after work to complete many of the canvasses she had started as part of what she was calling her *re-connection collection*. There was one aspect from the Signal Tree timeline that still eluded her; the sense of thirst and shrivelling that she had attributed to changes in water level and warming which had become increasingly apparent over the past fifty years. How was she to capture that through her art; linking to things we can see in the everyday? Time and again she circled back to it, but no inspiration came. She had made a multitude of rough sketches of withered trees and smoke belching from the coal fired power station, but they lacked the cohesion of the other canvasses. *How is the observer going to know what the painting is trying to convey?* was the question that kept bubbling up in her mind and, as yet, remained unanswered.

Work at the veg shop had settled into a new routine over the summer months. Now that many of the Covid restrictions had been lifted there was no need to offer such an extensive delivery service, so Lilly was spending much of her time working in the greenhouses maintaining the supply of fresh salad leaves and herbs. It was calm, methodical work which came as a welcome change allowing her to recuperate and take things at a slower pace. It was not without the occasional challenge though; the greenhouses were old and some of the equipment was proving to be increasingly unreliable. One sunny morning as Lilly cycled into the yard she was confronted by the sight of Jack, one of the warehouse staff, frantically sweeping water from the one of the greenhouses.

"Oh, thank goodness you're here!" he shouted as he saw her dismount. "I've been here since seven dealing with this. The irrigation system sprang a massive leak. I had to shut the mains water off to stop it. There was water everywhere!" he moaned, gesturing at the pool of water that still remained and looking down at his totally sodden shoes.

Lilly didn't know quite what to say. *Shit what a mess!* came to mind but she managed to stop herself from saying it out loud.

"Blimey Jack, thank you! You have done an amazing job. Why don't you go and get yourself cleaned up? I can take things from here," she said with an air of confidence that she did not feel inside. *Trust this to be the day when Oma is away at the wholesalers*, she thought as she made her way towards the office. It was still early and most of the staff had not arrived yet, she would have to tackle this on her own.

Just then Jack popped his head around the door. "I forgot to say, when I told you I had to shut the water off I meant to the whole site so we can't flush the loos or anything..."

"Ah, okay. I'll get straight on it then. Do you happen to know of any local plumbers?"

"Nope, sorry," shrugged Jack making a swift exit before she could ask him anything else.

She dialled Oma's mobile but, as expected got no response. *Shit*, she thought to herself. "Shit, shit, shit, ow!" she said as she kicked the side of the desk in frustration. "I know, I'll call Gramps, he's bound to know someone."

Thankfully, Gramps had not yet headed out to his workshop and the phone was answered on the second ring. She hastily explained the situation and then found herself holding her breath in anticipation as he paused to think.

"Hmm, well your best bet is probably Brian's lad, now what is his name? Nope won't come to me. Anyway, he has a plumbing business and lives locally."

"Great, thank you Gramps. Do you maybe have a number for Brian that I could call?" Lilly replied her patience beginning to wane.

"I expect so. I'll have to look it up in my book. Just give me a mo…"

Seconds ticked by slowly. She could hear Gramps shuffling about and muttering to himself.

"Here you go," he said finally and read out a number.

Having repeated it back to him twice to be sure she had it right she thanked him and hung up quickly before she got drawn into any further conversation.

As it turned out Brian's son, Gareth, lived just up the road and was able to drop by to take a quick look before he headed out on another job.

Lilly greeted him with much relief as he pulled up in his van. Together they went to survey the damage.

"Tsk, tsk. I haven't seen anything quite this ancient in quite a while," he muttered shaking his head.

"Do you think you can fix it?"

"Not quickly. I don't have the parts with me. This is all imperial gauge stuff, so I'll have to root around to find something."

Lilly frowned. "It's just that we had to shut the water off to the whole site. If we can't get it back on, I'll probably have to close the shop. The staff can't be without toilet facilities," she added starting to feel a bit desperate.

"Ah, now there I can help. I expect there is an isolation valve which will shut off just this part of the system. Can you show me where the main stop cock is?"

"Hmm, I'm not sure but I can find out. If you wait here, I'll send Jack out to you. He's the one who shut the system off this morning," replied Lilly as she headed back to the office hoping that Jack was still around.

Ten minutes later Gareth reappeared with a smile on his face. "Okay. I managed to isolate the sprinkler system and the rest of the water is back on. I should be able to come by later this afternoon to do some repairs."

"Thank you!" beamed Lilly. "You're an angel."

It was not until nearly four o'clock that Gareth returned. Lilly had been on her own all day in the office fretting, she hated the uncertainty of waiting and had struggled to concentrate on anything. In the end it proved to be a fairly straight-forward repair.

"Just one of your valves that had totally corroded away," commented Gareth as he proudly presented her with the evidence. "I managed to jerry rig a replacement which will see you good for now, but you really need to consider an overhaul of the whole system. The new ones are much more water efficient and most of them use rainwater rather than the mains supply. Your water bill must be huge!" he added.

Lilly felt a little embarrassed. She hadn't really taken much note of it before but looking around her she realised that the system was probably the original one that had been installed sometime after the second world war.

"Your heating system is out of the ark too," continued Gareth gesturing at the oil fuelled boiler at the back of the greenhouse. I bet you get through a ton of oil keeping these greenhouses warm in winter. A mate of mine specialises in new heat pump systems which warm the soil beneath the plants rather than the air. Much more efficient and they can run off renewable energy too. You've got plenty of space for some solar panels on the shop roof. I can get him to give you a quote for a whole system if you like," he added getting more and more enthusiastic by the minute.

Lilly's mind was spinning. She was not at all familiar with the new technologies that Gareth was suggesting but upgrading to a more efficient system seemed like an obvious thing to consider.

"Thank you, Gareth. I'll have to discuss it with Oma, I mean Breda, but if you could let me have some information that would be really useful."

"Of course. In fact, if I give you one of my cards you can take a look at my website. You'll find loads of useful stuff there," he said handing her a card. "Oh, and I can send you a quote for the irrigation system along with the invoice for today's work if that would help."

"Err. Okay. Thank you," replied Lilly blushing. She had quite forgotten to ask him about payment.

"My pleasure. Oh, and give my regards to William and Breda," he added as he turned to go.

On the cycle ride home Lilly's brain was awash with ideas. She was getting the sense of a picture, actually two, that she wanted to paint. She finally knew how to create a link between the tree's sensation of thirst and water wastage. The comments made by Gareth had brought home the fact that she took access to a seemingly limitless amount of water for granted in her everyday life. What he had said about the boiler system had hit home too. There must be so many ways in which we waste precious energy thinking little of where it comes from and the impact that has on the world around us. That image was a little less distinct in her mind, but she knew now where to begin and was hopeful that Gareth's website would point her in the right direction. She couldn't wait to tell Oma and Gramps all about it. Not only could she share her ideas through her art, but she might also be able to make real changes to the veg business which would have a positive impact. With her legs pumping almost as fast as her brain was churning, she made short work of the journey.

She arrived at the farm to find Oma and Gramps sitting together at the kitchen table.

"You won't believe the day I've had…" she blurted and then stopped. Oma was staring at a sheet of paper which lay crumpled on the table before her. She looked up at Lilly with tears in her eyes.

Gramps patted her shoulder and said, "I'll put the kettle on while you tell Lilly all about it."

Oma gestured for Lilly to sit down beside her. Glancing at the paper Lilly could see that it was a letter addressed to Oma.

"I didn't go to the wholesalers today love. I went to see the landlord, the one who owns the land where the veg shop is. Well, in fact it wasn't him I saw but his solicitor. He was too cowardly to face me himself." Oma paused. She was clearly very angry.

Squeezing Lilly's hand, she continued. "He wants to sell the land and has given me three months' notice on the lease."

"But he can't do that," protested Lilly. "Can he?" she added feeling suddenly unsure.

"According to his solicitor he can. The terms of the lease are very complicated so I can't be certain. I will have to ask for a second legal opinion."

"Couldn't we find a way to buy him out?"

Gramps laughed. "Even if we could find the money it wouldn't help. He's already been made an offer by a local developer and they're the kind of people with very deep pockets."

Lilly suddenly felt outraged. "You mean they want to build houses on it!" she spluttered.

"I know it sounds outrageous but there is little we can do. It's happening all over the area. It's not just us."

"But three months Oma. That's so soon, we'd need to be out by Christmas…" Lilly added her voice suddenly failing her.

"I know love and that's the one thing I think we can fight. The way the lease is written it's quite ambiguous. Hopefully we can have longer although I'm not sure what we can do. Even if we can find a new location, I doubt we'll be able to afford it."

Lilly felt utterly deflated. All her ideas for new improved greenhouses seemed totally irrelevant now. She sat in silence and drank her tea.

Oma patted her hand gently and decided it was time to change the subject. "So, you had an eventful day I hear. Gramps told me about the leak in the greenhouse…"

"Yes, all sorted now. One of the valves in the sprinkler system had gone and it created quite a flood. Fortunately, Jack was able to shut off the water before any real damage was done and Gareth was able to fix it this afternoon. He suggested we should upgrade the system, but I guess that won't be necessary now," replied Lilly.

"Gareth, that's the name of Brian's son," said Gramps suddenly as if he had been trying to recall it all day.

"Yes, that's right. He sends you both his regards."

The rest of the week had been hard for Lilly. Robbie wasn't going to be back until the end of the month, still ten days away. She had spoken to him on the phone, they had talked into the small hours of the morning, but it was not the same as having him there beside her.

Going to work felt strange. Oma had insisted that no-one at the veg shop should be told anything until they had heard back from her solicitor about the legality of the three months' notice. Lilly found it very hard to pretend that everything was fine especially at break times when they would gather for a brew and a chat. The talk was inevitably about plans for Christmas, even though it was still September, or saving for a holiday next year, something special since they had missed out this year due to Covid. She would just sit there in silence staring into her cup, desperately hoping that the news, when it came, would go in their favour. Oma was arguing for a year's notice, that would give everyone much more time to get things in order and allow for the possibility to relocate to another site.

All thought of completing her paintings had deserted her. She couldn't even face going into her studio, knowing that if she did so she would either spend hours just staring at a blank canvas or in her frustration hurl paint at it in a haphazard fashion creating a mess that she would later regret. In the end she decided to visit the Signal Tree. She always felt a sense of tranquillity and grounding when she was near it. Stretching her arms wide to embrace the trunk and placing her cheek against the roughened bark she closed her eyes and allowed herself to feel the slow rhythm of the tree. The gentle murmur *ool ha, ool ma, ool ma hakka* intertwined with the swish of the leaves rustling in the breeze. The tap, tap, tap of a bird way up in the branches searching for grubs. The faint musty scent of leaf mould mixed with a hint of balsam. Being with *her* tree helped Lilly to regain a sense of perspective. The issue at the veg shop was like a blink of the eye compared to what *Signal* had seen in *her* lifetime. Tiny in relation to the scale of change that *she* had endured. As she stood there in the warm evening sunshine, her feet dusty in the dried-up brook, Lilly felt a sudden desperate thirst which could not be quenched by the water in her flask. Resting her forehead on the tree she drew from its inner strength and felt a renewed sense of purpose. *I will not give up on you now*, she promised.

The following Sunday afternoon had passed in an instant, or so it felt to Lilly. She had sketched out the main features of the two remaining pictures depicting re-connection to sources of water and energy and was experimenting with a colour scheme for the latter. How to capture the darkness of coal relative to the vibrance of the sun. It was more complex than simple use of black and yellow, she needed to somehow convey a sense of dimension. Completely lost in her own world of creation she did not notice Robbie until he wrapped his arms around her waist.

"Hello," he whispered, grazing her cheek with a gentle kiss and nuzzling into her neck. "I've missed you," he murmured.

She turned to embrace him; all thoughts of painting instantly evaporated. Her heart felt full to bursting as tears came unbidden to her eyes.

"I'm sorry," she said looking up from his tear-soaked shoulder. "I don't know why I am crying. I've never felt so happy," she laughed.

She stood there wrapped in his arms, head resting on his shoulder, eyes closed, swaying gently, feeling his warmth, listening to the rushing of his heart. "I could stay here with you forever."

"Not quite forever," he replied. "I think dinner is ready." They could hear Gramps calling from the kitchen door. "You can tell me all about this later," he continued gesturing at the canvasses.

"They can wait. I want to hear all about Scotland first," she said, grabbing his hand and leading him towards the door.

The sky was descending into blackness and a rush of warm air engulfed Lilly as she stepped outside the shop and locked up. She felt the instant prickle of sweat on her lip and was transported back in time to a moment when she had opened the cabin door on arrival at Shanghai during a tropical storm. This was not at all what you would expect on an early October evening in Oxfordshire. The hot wind whipped the hair across her face as she battled with her keys. A moment of respite as she sat in the car was soon replaced by anguish. Rain lashed at the windscreen mixed with a debris of leaves and twigs ripped from nearby trees. She picked her way slowly through the gloom desperately hoping that she would not encounter anything larger in her path. *Relax and breathe* she murmured to herself; *you can do this*. Finally, she spied the entrance to the farm, *almost there*. As she battled to make the turn, the air was rent by a massive boom which shook the car around her, replaced momentarily by an eerie silence before the wind came rushing back, hurling foliage in her path. Spurred on by the fear of getting trapped, Lilly made a desperate dash for the back door. Soaked to the skin, she stood at the threshold taking a moment to adjust to the brightness of the kitchen interior. Just then the lights flickered and went out.

"Don't panic. Stay there a moment while I light a candle," came Oma's voice from across the room. Robbie's face suddenly loomed towards her in the glow of a head torch. Smiling, he handed her a towel.

"I was wondering where you had got to," he said as he embraced her and started to rub her down. Her teeth were chattering, and she was shaking all over; not from cold, it was stifling hot, but from shock.

"Here, sit down and I'll fetch you some tea," said Gramps. She smiled; tea was his cure for everything.

"I am so glad to see you," she whispered to Robbie.

"You know me, never one to miss out on Friday supper," he replied with a reassuring grin. "Now let's get you into some dry clothes."

The storm raged for most of the night. Lilly had found shelter in Robbie's strong arms and at some point, drifted off to sleep, *old ma hakka* infiltrating her dreams for the first time in weeks. As she woke with a jolt in the early dawn, she couldn't help feeling that something dramatic had happened. She was overwhelmed with a sense of foreboding.

"You okay?" came Robbie's sleepy voice from under the covers.

"Not sure," she replied. "It's like I heard *Signal* calling but then everything went silent." She nuzzled down into his arms, and he stroked her hair to calm her. Sleep proved elusive, she just stared at the chink of slowly brightening sky beneath the edge of the curtain and waited for the day to arrive.

The power was still out but luckily the old kitchen range was still alight and Oma had made coffee and porridge for breakfast. Gramps came in through the back door huffing and puffing, shaking his head.

"I hope you have a chainsaw in your Land Rover," he said looking across at Robbie." There's a tree down across the lane, we're blocked in."

"Yes, I do but if it's a big one we might have trouble shifting it even if I can cut it up."

"It is quite big, but I was hoping you would be able to winch it out of the way. Maybe I should call Mike and see if he can lend a hand with his tractor." Gramps wandered off into the lounge leaving Lilly and Robbie staring at each other. She had gone quite pale.

"Are you alright?" he asked.

"I just realised what the boom was that shook my car last night. I think it was the tree falling behind me," she stammered.

"It's okay, you're here now and you're safe. That is all that matters."

"The phone is out. Someone will need to walk over to Mike's to see if he can help," sighed Gramps as he slumped down in his chair.

"Let's take a look at the tree before we do that. We might not need a tractor," commented Robbie. He was not certain it was safe to be wandering about, the wind was still blowing strongly enough to rip a branch from a tree, and he didn't want anyone to risk getting injured. *Never go into the woods in a storm* he recalled one of his instructors from college telling him. It was good advice.

In the end they found that the winch on the Land Rover was adequate to the task, and they spent the morning trimming branches and hauling logs until the lane was clear. Watching Robbie dressed up in his protective clothing and wielding the chainsaw Lilly was reminded of the nickname that Margaret had given him. *My very own Sir Galahad* she mused. She desperately hoped that Margaret was okay, it can't have been fun sitting out the storm alone. It was so frustrating not to be able to call her.

As the morning passed the wind began to ease and Lilly felt increasingly anxious about the Signal Tree. She couldn't shake the feeling that something was terribly wrong. In the end, after a well-earned lunch break, she persuaded Robbie to accompany her. It was obvious even from a distance that all was not as it should be; the shape of the treeline had altered dramatically. As they turned the final corner she stopped abruptly in her tracks. Rotten along its length the Signal Tree's trunk had split in two and now straddled the brook, the old bridge crumpled beneath it. The path was completely blocked with debris, tangles of branches suspended in the arms of neighbouring trees. The exposed root structure steadily shedding clods of soil into the rushing waters. A gaping hole in the now vacant canopy let in a steady drizzle of rain. The Signal Tree was down.

Lilly was beside herself with anguish. Utterly distraught she fell to her knees clutching the nearest branch, holding it close, sensing the terrible pain of the dying tree as its life blood ebbed away. Looking up she let out a primordial wail, which ululated across the valley. With her chest constricting in despair, she buried her head in her arms and sobbed uncontrollably. "No, no, no," she repeated over and over. "You can't leave us, not now, not like this," she whispered to the tree.

Robbie placed a re-assuring hand on her shoulder. "There is nothing we can do to bring her back; we have to accept that." He paused unsure of how to console her. "We can try to make sure she is honoured in the best possible way. We can find her a final resting place, here beside the stream, where she can slowly age and return to the soil in dignity like the ancestors before her."

"Thank you," whispered Lilly through a veil of tears. "I think she would like that."

"Now, we should probably get back before this rain gets any heavier," he added, helping her to her feet and wrapping a protective arm around her. She was soaked to the skin and shivering with cold.

Dinner that evening was a muted affair. Oma had managed to cook up a decent stew on the range and as they sat around the kitchen table, they shared their news from the day. Gramps had been visiting other farms and managed to piece together fragments of information. The power was out across the whole county along with several mobile phone towers. People were having to rely on word of mouth. It looked like tens if not hundreds of trees had been blown down.

"It was definitely the worst storm in living memory," he concluded with a sigh.

Oma coughed gently and drew a crumpled envelope from the pocket in her apron. She had received it the previous day, it was a letter from her solicitor. "It seems we have no legal case to extend the notice period of the lease. The veg shop will have to close by Christmas," she mumbled, almost lost for words.

As they sat together, staring quietly at the flames flickering and dancing in the hearth, it felt as if their world was on the brink of collapse like the spent ashes sinking through the grate. Just then, a log flared and crackled sending forth a shower of sparks as if to say *we are not done, not yet.*

PART 4
GROWING TOGETHER

In the corner of a field stood a tree. It was the last of a long family line, each generation somehow casting forth a path into the future. Spread not just by seed, but by clone, sucker, windthrow. It was the daughter of an ancient tree; not two hundred years alive, as we perceive, but one thousand years or more, springing forth from the mother of her kind Old Hakka herself. And yet, though all may feel lost, we should not lament the passing of this tree. When in the darkness we stand, seemingly alone, we should open our minds, our hearts, our senses to all the wisdoms of our pasts, to the faintest whispers in the wood, *do not give up; our hope is strong.*

CHAPTER 20

TUMBUH BERSAMA

On the morning after the storm had finally blown itself out, Lilly awoke with a strange feeling of calm determination. She had been cloaked in a dream so vivid and inspiring that she was reluctant to leave it behind. It was not at all what she had expected to dream about. With all the trauma of losing the Signal Tree she had half dreaded falling asleep and being plagued by the worst feelings from her usual Hakka dream.

Instead, she had found herself sitting in a room full of people, all with indistinct features yet strangely familiar. They had been speaking in a language she could not understand. Beside her sat a woman, very old, who looked a little like Oma. The woman would occasionally look round to her and whisper something in translation.

"They all agree," she had said and then sometime later she had added, "we will work together to transform this place, to help it thrive again, the way it should be."

Frowning, Lilly had asked, "how should it be?"

The answer came back, "as it always was before." Lilly was confused but before she could say anything the old woman had added, "we will grow together the things to which our land is most suited."

After that, things had started to fade, faces and voices all blurring together. Yet as they receded Lilly's understanding seemed to grow. She arose with the thought, *we need to keep growing veg we just need to do it in a different place, here on the farm. We need to let the land return to how it was before. Before all the hedges were grubbed up and the pastures ploughed…* She sat up rubbing her eyes and stretching. The pillow beside her was empty, Robbie must have risen early. Scrabbling to find a pen and some paper she started to write down as much as she could remember. *What were those words they were saying?* she asked herself. All she could recall was something that began with *moop* when the old woman mentioned that they all agreed and later on something like *tumba bersma* which they had kept repeating and must have had something to do with growing. *Who was that strange old woman anyway?* she thought as she pulled on some clothes. She had been so much like Oma both in the way she looked and in the way she spoke, the same kind of accent. It was really quite strange, but Lilly had never felt so sure of anything in her life, *I must tell Oma all about it, we can save the veg shop after all!*

Nearly tripping over herself in her excitement she leapt down the stairs two at a time and burst into the kitchen. It was empty. She eyed the dirty plates in the sink and the half full pot of coffee on the stove. Her enthusiasm ebbed away like a spent wave. *Oh well, I might as well have some of that coffee* she thought as she hunted for a clean cup. Lilly gravitated towards her favourite morning spot in the lounge, her *Hedge TV spot*, as Gramps called it. Sipping at the scalding coffee she took in the scene. The garden was a total mess. Debris from nearby trees strewn across the lawn. The shrubs and fruit bushes seemed to have survived but had taken on a strange sideways tilt as had the garden shed which looked to be collapsing in on itself. Odd items, buckets, sacks, a garden chair were all piled up against the hedge, itself denuded, stripped bare of its remaining leaves. She felt her resolve slowly slipping further from her grasp. *It was just a silly dream, how can we possibly set up the veg shop here?* everything felt so hopeless.

Just as she was about to turn away to refill her cup Lilly noticed a bedraggled bird sitting on a nearby branch. A blackbird, steadily preening its matted feathers trying to dry off in the gentle breeze, it looked unphased by the altered landscape. Now and then it would pause to sing a few notes. Lilly recognised it as the signature greeting call of the blackbirds which she often heard at dawn and dusk. Until now she had not thought much about its meaning. Perhaps it was, *how are you?* or maybe *all is well*. Whatever the meaning she could hear a steady chorus of answers from neighbouring birds. The community of blackbirds sharing their news, they had survived the storm and they were getting on with their daily routines. They couldn't afford to sit about and feel sorry for themselves, there were worms to catch. *Thank you, mister blackbird*, whispered Lilly. His intervention had stopped her thoughts from sliding downwards into the abyss of self-pity and lost hope. It made her think about her own flock. Oma, Gramps and Robbie were all safe, even though they were strangely absent this morning, *no doubt getting on with useful things,* she mused, *but what about Margaret?* She picked up the phone, but the line was still dead. Just as Lilly had decided to go over to see her in person, she heard a movement in the kitchen.

Oma was off-loading an armful of eggs into a dish on the counter. She smiled as she saw Lilly. A smile that belied her true feelings. Lilly had never seen her look so tired and fragile, and old. It was the first time that Lilly had realised Oma was getting old, she wasn't even sure of her age. In her mind she was just Oma and would be that way for ever.

"Is everything okay?" she asked.

"Pretty much," sighed Oma. "The roof of the hen house has been blown off. It took me a while to find the silly birds. They have taken up residence in the hedge behind the barn. I found them all apart from one, but I expect she'll turn up at some point. These eggs are all I could find but there are probably more dotted about the place. We will have to keep an eye out." Then in her usual stalwart fashion Oma continued, "have you had breakfast love? I can make you some eggs if you like."

"I can do that. You just put your feet up. I'll bring you a cup of coffee," Lilly replied as she set about preparing scrambled eggs on toast for the two of them. Oma looked like she could do with a bit of feeding up.

"Have you seen Robbie and Gramps at all?" she asked.

"Oh, yes. They were up at dawn. Wanted to make the most of the day. There is still so much debris to clear. I think they will be back for lunch."

"I was thinking of going over to check on Margaret later. I guess I should probably walk. Maybe I'll wait until this afternoon so I can get an update on the state of the roads before I go," Lilly said, half to herself as she concentrated on not burning the eggs. She was itching to tell Oma about her dream, but she wasn't sure if now was a good time. Oma looked so tired.

"Here we go," she set down a steaming plate in front of Oma. "Do you want any sauce?"

"This looks lovely. No sauce thank you. Who puts sauce on scrambled eggs?" asked Oma with a wry smile. She knew the answer. Only a bachelor like Robbie would do such a thing.

"I didn't ask. Did you sleep okay my love? I was a bit worried that those awful dreams might come back, given what's happened," said Oma as she paused between mouthfuls.

"I slept quite well. Thank you," Lilly hesitated and then decided she might as well take the plunge. "Actually, I did have a dream but not the one I was expecting. Something altogether new and quite intriguing. I was wondering if you might help me to understand it."

"Oh, and why do you think I can help?" replied Oma warily.

"Well, where to begin…" Lilly took a moment to gather her thoughts and then described what she could recall of the dream. She decided not to mention her idea about the veg shop yet; it might prove to be too much for Oma to take in all at once.

Oma looked bemused, "the old woman, you say she looked and sounded a bit like me?"

"Yes, but I feel certain she wasn't you. I'm sorry that probably doesn't make a whole lot of sense." Lilly looked up at Oma feeling quite foolish. She held her breath half expecting Oma to tell her it was all nonsense, just a silly dream. In fact, Oma had a really odd expression on her face. One of almost shocked realisation.

"It can't be," Oma whispered, almost to herself. She looked across at Lilly, her mouth set firm, as if she was trying to reach some sort of decision.

"Come with me," she said and headed out of the kitchen and up the stairs.

Lilly followed, "where are we going?"

"You'll see, all in good time, you'll see."

They passed through Lilly's bedroom to a door set in the wall behind her bed. Lilly had been in there once before. It was just a storeroom full of old boxes, cobwebs and dust. From the shelf which was set against the partition wall Oma pulled down a small suitcase; very old, made of leather with heavy brass buckles. She carried it back into the bedroom and placed it on the bed.

They both stood there looking down at it. Lilly's mind was spinning, she looked across at Oma standing there, a tear running down her cheek.

"This belonged to my Oma, we called her *Nenek*," she whispered trying to stifle a sob. "She meant the world to me, my *Nenek*."

Carefully Oma opened the case and began to set the contents out on the bed, one by one. A set of notebooks, a bundle of photographs held together by a ribbon, a picture in a tarnished silver frame. When Lilly saw the picture, she let out a little gasp.

"That was her! That was the old woman in my dream. But how can that be? How can I dream about someone I have never met before? How can I have a dream about your *Nenek*?"

"I think what is perhaps more remarkable is how you could have a conversation with someone who could only speak Indonesian and Dutch," replied Oma.

Lilly didn't know whether to laugh or cry. She wrapped her arms around Oma and together they gazed at the picture, deep into the eyes of the old woman, a woman with a message from their past.

"Tell me about *Nenek*," whispered Lilly.

"I think I may have already told you that before she came to the Netherlands, where I grew up, she had lived in Suriname. Well, her family hadn't always lived there, originally, they had been from a small Indonesian island, I forget the name of it. She used to tell me stories about the old ways, the traditional ways in which her people had lived with the land for thousands of years before being ripped from their homes and forced to live as farmers in a strange country on the other side of the world. She was always remarkably calm and positive. She used to tell me it was important for us not to lose touch with who we are and where we belong. We need to tell the stories of our ancestors so that we keep the deep knowledge of the land alive for future generations. Perhaps your dream is a reminder that we need to make sure the chain is not broken now."

"You mean that somehow, *Nenek* was trying to reach out to me in my dream in the same way that the trees were reaching out. To make sure we don't lose their knowledge?" Lilly was stunned.

"Yes, I think I do. Although I can't understand how," said Oma looking at her quizzically. "Some of the words you mentioned from your dream. They seem somehow familiar to me; I think they might be Indonesian words. We might be able to find out more from these," Oma gestured at the notebooks. "Those were *Nenek's* diaries. They are mainly written in Dutch, I'm a bit rusty but I am sure I should be able to figure some of it out."

"Wow!" replied Lilly as she took up the book from the top of the pile and carefully opened it. The pages were packed with a dense, delicate script. She couldn't make sense of any of it.

"Do you want to help me take these downstairs. I think I will need to find my Dutch dictionary."

Unearthing *Nenek's* diaries seemed to have given Oma an injection of energy; her eyes had regained their usual sparkle and there was a spring in her step. She was humming a little tune to herself as she set the table for lunch.

"The boys should be home soon," she commented to Lilly who was busy slicing bread to go with the soup that Oma seemed to have magicked up from nowhere.

Sure enough they heard the crunch of gravel on the drive and moments later the heavy clomp of boots in the hall.

"I hope you're not bringing mud into the house," called out Oma, although she knew full well that Robbie and Gramps wouldn't dare commit such a crime.

"Food smells good," called out Robbie. "Just going up to grab a change of clothes…" his voice trailed off as he headed up the stairs.

A few minutes later they were all gathered round the kitchen table, steam rising from the freshly prepared bowls of soup.

"How was your morning?" asked Oma eager to hear the news about the storm damage and the state of the roads.

Gramps was busy shovelling a hunk of bread into his mouth so Robbie decided it would be best if he answered.

"Busy and a bit challenging if I'm honest."

"Oh, how so?" Oma replied frowning.

"The road into the village is pretty much clear. Between us and the other farmers we have managed to move all the fallen trees. The lads from the electricity board have got their work cut out replacing the fallen power lines, but they have made a good start. Said we might get some power back by tomorrow if we're lucky."

"And the challenging bit?" queried Oma. She could tell that Robbie was skirting round something.

"Hmm, well that's the bad news. The road to the south is in a really bad state. The bridge just before you get to the Aston turning is gone, along with a big stretch of the road. Completely swept away by flood water. There are several trees down, but we can't get to them. We bumped into a surveyor from the highways agency and he said there are several roads across the county that have been damaged and this one is a low priority. He wasn't optimistic about getting it re-opened any time soon. They'll have to do a full survey and see how much it's going to cost."

"So that means we'll have to go the long way round if we want to head out Reading way at all," added Gramps. "Still at least we can get up to town and the veg shop easily enough so that's something."

"Oh dear, that is going to make things tricky for some people. Did you manage to check on the veg shop? Is everything okay there?"

"Yes, all fine. A few branches here and there in the carpark but nothing too serious. I can take you over there later if you like," offered Gramps.

"Oh no, that's okay love, I'll take your word for it. I think I'll stay at home and sort through some things here…" her voice tailed off as her gaze shifted towards the dining room where she had started sifting through *Nenek's* diaries. She was keen to get back to them.

"Is the road clear up through the village past the church?" asked Lilly.

"Not quite. There is a power line down which still needs to be sorted. Why do you ask?" said Robbie.

"I wanted to go and check on Margaret. She lives over that way. Would it be safe to walk over?"

"Yes, I expect so. I'm heading out that way after lunch to help clear some of the debris at the school. I can drop you by the church if you like."

As they drove through the village Lilly took in the scene. Much of the storm debris was already being cleared away. People of all ages, friends, neighbours, strangers all helping each other with gathering up branches and clearing mounds of detritus from the gutters and drains. It was a veritable hive of activity. Most properties seemed to have avoided damage although one lane was partly blocked by a fallen chimney stack and a couple of garages had been flattened by falling trees, the remains of crumpled cars just visible beneath a sea of branches.

Robbie dropped Lilly off next to the church yard. The route she would normally take was cordoned off for safety; the pathway strewn with a jumble of power cables, engineers working feverishly to restore the electricity supply. She gave them a wide berth and headed up a gravel pathway circumnavigating the church yard and ducking under the remains of an ash tree before reaching the lane that led to Margaret's house. She was relieved to see that the place looked relatively untouched by the storm. She rang the bell but got no answer. *Please be okay* she whispered to herself as she pulled the handle again, still no answer. Lilly peered through a couple of windows but couldn't see anything. She called out but got no reply. *I'll have to go round the side*, she said to herself.

The scene that greeted her was one of utter destruction. What had been a beautiful garden and orchard was now a lake of muddy water punctuated here and there with floating branches, plastic bags, garden chairs. The tide mark of flotsam at the edge of the terrace gave an indication of just how close the house had come to being flooded. Lilly could hear the steady rhythm of a broom sweeping away at what sounded like gravel. As she rounded the corner, she saw Margaret trying to clear a path through shards of glass; the conservatory now a mere skeleton of metal framework behind her.

"Hi Margaret!" she called out.

"Oh, Lilly my love. What a wonderful surprise!" Margaret set down her broom and picked her way through the glass to great her. "We had best go in the side door," she advised in her usual matter of fact tone.

"I'm so glad you are okay," said Lilly hugging Margaret fiercely.

"Steady on, don't want to break me now do we. How about a drink? I think I've earned one and you look like you could do with something to pep you up dear. Will have to be coffee though, no point in falling off the wagon, no telling where that would lead us both eh?" she chortled, grinning at the look of concern on Lilly's face.

"Yes, a coffee will be really nice," laughed Lilly realising that despite everything, Margaret was still able to see the funny side of things.

Margaret set about boiling some water over a small camping stove.

"How have you been managing without power? Have you been able to cook okay?" asked Lilly.

"Yes, yes. All fine. Janet has been a marvellous help. They have a gas stove over at the rectory and she has been keeping me supplied with hot soup and what not. Knowing Janet, I expect she has been keeping half the village supplied," she chuckled.

"How about you dear? How are things at the farm and the veg shop?"

Lilly took a moment to sip her coffee. She couldn't quite face talking about the Signal Tree, not yet, so she decided to tell Margaret the news about the veg shop instead. Margaret seemed to take great offence at the idea of building houses on the veg shop site.

"Unbelievable! The little swine. His father would never have dreamed of selling up that land. We went to school together you know; me and Lawrence. He was a gentle soul, always had time for everyone in the village. Passed away earlier in the year, one of the many victims of that dreadful virus. To think his son could do such a thing..." Margaret almost spilled her coffee she was shaking so much with indignation.

"It's hit Oma hard too. She puts a brave face on it, but I know she is really worried. She hasn't been able to tell the other employees yet; we only heard back from her solicitor on the day of the storm. We'll need to clear out by Christmas."

"Oh dear, that's awful timing. Do you have any idea what you are going to do?"

"Not really. To be honest we haven't had time to discuss it. Everyone has been so busy the last couple of days," Lilly paused; she wasn't sure whether to mention her idea about moving everything over to the farm which had come to her after her strange dream. "I did have one thought but it's probably crazy..."

"Go on," encouraged Margaret.

"I had this strange dream and it made me wonder if we could start over at the farm. We have the space, an old barn that could be converted to a shop, room for greenhouses and the fields don't flood so we could maybe grow some of our own veg too." Lilly's tone grew more and more excited but then doubt crept into her mind. "I've no idea how much it would cost though..." she trailed off with a sigh.

Before Margaret could respond they were interrupted by the doorbell. "I wonder who that could be?" she muttered, slowly easing herself up out of her chair. The bell rang again. "Hold your horses, just coming, just coming!" she called.

It was Robbie. "Hi Margaret! Is Lilly here with you? I am just heading back to the farm and wondered if she wanted a lift."

"Ah Robbie. Lovely to see you dear. Yes, she's here. Why don't you come in a minute?"

"Oh, best not. I don't want to trail mud all over your floor."

Having gathered up her things Lilly appeared beside Margaret.

"Oh, there you are dear. Your Sir Galahad has come to rescue you. Lovely to see you dear. You must come over again soon, once things have calmed down a bit." Margaret seemed a little deflated now that she was going.

"Why don't you come over to the farm once the power is back on? You can enjoy one of Oma's feasts and I can tell you more about my dream and ideas for the farm."

"Oh, that would be lovely dear, thank you," replied Margaret her eyes brightening.

"Your dream?" asked Robbie quizzically as they set off together down the drive.

"I'll tell you about it later once I've had a chance to talk to Oma," replied Lilly with an impish grin. "How was the school? Was there much damage?"

Robbie sighed. He knew better than to probe further. Lilly did love her secrets.

It was not until the next morning that Lilly had a chance to discuss things further with Oma. The power was still out, and they had resigned themselves to another day of clearing up after the storm. Oma had decided that there was no point in rushing to try to re-open the shop. She told herself that everyone would be too distracted sorting out their domestic concerns to bother about buying vegetables that they probably wouldn't be able to cook. In reality she just couldn't face the idea of having to break the news to her staff and customers. It was all just too much to contemplate. Instead, she had found a distraction in going through *Nenek's* diaries; she was quite pleased by what she had found.

"I have discovered the meaning of some of the words you mentioned from your dream," she said to Lilly as they were washing up the breakfast dishes.

"Oh really!"

"Yes, you had them partly right. I think the first word you mentioned, when they all seemed to agree, was actually *mupakat*, which is Indonesian for *consensus*. *Nenek* describes it in her diary as a form of council of elders where they discussed important things relating to the community such as the use of land, crop rotation, sharing out the harvest that kind of thing. They had to gain agreement from everyone before they could proceed with a plan."

"Well, I guess that makes kind of sense. *Mupakat, mupakat*, it sounds like the word I heard."

"The second phrase is even more intriguing. You had it almost right, *tumbuh bersama*. It means *growing together*. *Nenek* mentions this in the context of the community farming together a bit like a modern cooperative I guess." Oma looked across at Lilly who was brimming with excitement, "were there any other words you can remember?"

"I'm not sure. The one thing which really struck me was what *Nenek* said at the end about *working together to transform this place, to help it thrive again, the way it should be. As it always was before, growing together the things to which, our land is most suited*. It made me wonder whether she was telling us what to do about the veg shop." Lilly looked up, hopeful that Oma would understand what she was getting at.

"Oh, and what do you think she was suggesting?" asked Oma. She looked a little uncertain.

Lilly decided to take the plunge. "What if she was telling us to move the veg shop here to the farm. To start growing some of our own veg here as well. To return our land, the farm, to how it was before. Before all the changes that were made since the war. I seem so sure that's what she meant. It feels so right, I can't explain why. Call it a gut instinct," she fidgeted in anticipation; unsure what Oma would think.

"Oh, I see," was all she said and then she seemed to become lost in thought. "Well, it is a bold idea, I'll give you that. I'm not sure what Gramps will think. Then there's the cost of course. I've no idea how we would afford such a thing…"

"But you think it could work, right? I mean what other option do we have?"

"Calm yourself dear," Oma patted Lilly's arm. "I think it is worth discussing further. Let's talk about it some more later on when Gramps and Robbie are back. See what they think." Oma gave her an encouraging smile. "Now let's go and see if we can find that missing chicken, shall we? I think I heard it clucking about by the shed earlier."

CHAPTER 21

IMAGINED REALITIES

Oma and Lilly had spent a good hour securing the last of the rogue chickens and hunting down the eggs which had been laid in all manner of places.

"I think I'll make us all omelettes for lunch. That will be a good way to make the onions and mushrooms that we have a little more appetising." Oma thought it was rather ironic that they were running short of fresh vegetables; another reminder that she needed to get on with sorting things out at the shop.

In spite of everything she was able to put on a good lunchtime spread. Freshly made sourdough bread, pickles, and some local goats cheese complemented the omelettes nicely. Robbie and Gramps made short work of their portions before moving on to tea and cake.

"Mmm, I was ready for that. Thanks Oma," said Robbie with a satisfied sigh. "I've never been so busy," he added stretching and working at a knot in his shoulder muscle which was sore from wielding his chainsaw. "You've done a grand job sorting out the garden, it almost looks normal, whatever that is," he added.

"Well, it wasn't all me. Lilly has been a great help; she has developed a keen set of chicken whispering skills in the process," chuckled Oma. "Still, we probably need to think about getting back to the shop soon. If only the power would come back on, we won't be able to do much without that. I have to say I'm not really looking forward to it. I have no idea what I'm going to say to everyone."

"You'll think of something love," said Gramps patting her on the shoulder. "You're always good with words," he added hopefully.

"Maybe it would be easier to tell them if you have a plan to share at the same time. Maybe something like we discussed earlier. The idea I had from my dream…" Lilly paused, chewing her lip and hoping that Oma didn't mind her bringing this up now.

Oma sighed. "Okay dear, you might as well explain and see what they think."

Lilly started by telling Robbie and Gramps about the strange dream that she had the night after the storm and what she and Oma had discovered in *Nenek's* diaries. Then she introduced her ideas for moving the veg shop to the farm, growing some of their own veg and returning the farm to the way it was before.

"I know it sounds a bit pie in the sky, but I think it's what the dream was trying to tell me to do," she concluded, looking at them both waiting for some sign of agreement and reassurance.

"Hmm, well I suppose we could convert the other barn into a shop of sorts. At least as a temporary start. I think the upper fields would work well for growing veg, they don't tend to flood in winter and the soil's not too stony," offered Gramps.

"What about the greenhouses?" asked Robbie "Do you think we could move them? We could maybe make some space at the back of the yard if we demolished the remains of the old sheds. The light is good there," he added.

"Great!" enthused Lilly. She smiled at Oma hoping for some sign of encouragement from her too.

"I suppose we could do it. It would be a lot of work but with some help from the shop staff we could probably manage it. Perhaps you could call in some favours from the other farmers for some of the heavy lifting?" she added looking at Gramps who nodded enthusiastically. "The only thing that bothers me is the cost. We have been barely making a profit on the shop this past year due to the pandemic and we don't have much saved up."

Seeing the deflated look on Lilly's face, Robbie decided to step in with a suggestion of his own. "I wouldn't let money put you off. Once we have a plan, we can determine how much it's likely to cost and then set about raising the funds. That's the way charities do it; if you can hook people into believing in your idea it's surprising how generous they are prepared to be."

"There was one part of your suggestion that I wasn't clear on," said Gramps. "The bit about returning the farm to the way it was before. Before what exactly?"

"Oh, yes, sorry. I probably should have been more specific on that. In the dream I clearly remember *Nenek* saying that we should transform the place to the way it should be, the way it was before. It made me think of my Signal Tree dream and the fact that since the war we have significantly changed the way we farm the land, felling trees, clearing hedges, that sort of thing. So, I think she meant that we should reverse some of that by planting some new hedges and trees, re-creating some pasture. Perhaps we can take a look at the old maps and records that your father kept to help us see what we could do?" explained Lilly.

"Ah okay, well it's worth a look I suppose. Although we shouldn't get ahead of ourselves. Doing that sort of thing on top of what we have already discussed would be an awful lot to take on in one season."

"Okay, okay. I get it. I'm just excited about the idea that we have a chance to do something really different. Imagine what a great place it could be. It would be like a phoenix rising from the ashes!" Lilly was almost fizzing with emotion.

Oma couldn't help chuckling. Lilly's overwhelming excitement had given her a renewed sense of optimism. "Well, I think we are all agreed that we should start making a plan and take things step by step. So, let's begin by going out to take a look at the barn and seeing how much room we would have."

By mid-afternoon they were making good progress with imagining how a future veg shop could look and assessing what changes to the barn would need to be made to accommodate it. Lilly had just finished sticking a rough sketch onto the sheet of brown paper that they had adopted as their design board when they heard a series of whirs and beeps; the power was back on.

"Hurray! At last," said Robbie with a sigh of relief. He and Lilly had decided that if they got electricity back before dark then they would venture over to his cottage to check on things. As his house was on the far side of the stretch of damaged road, they would have to take the long way round; so far, they hadn't found the time during the day and hadn't fancied stumbling about in the dark with a torch. He looked at Lilly, "we should probably get going."

"Let me make you up a flask and something to eat," suggested Oma. "Just in case," she added.

Robbie agreed, there was no saying no to Oma. He went out to check on the Land Rover to make sure he had enough fuel and some emergency tools in case they encountered any fallen trees or floods. A few minutes later Lilly came out with a basket full of food and an overnight bag. "All set?" she asked.

"Yep, let's go."

In the end the journey had proved to be remarkably straight forward. The only thing they had encountered were some escaped sheep that must have taken advantage of some broken fencing. Robbie had decided to leave them to someone else to deal with; he had done plenty of helping out over the past few days, now it was time to look after himself. Much to their relief his cottage was undamaged, and his tree nursery seemed to have come through the storm unscathed. They both hurried to the bottom of the garden to check on the patch where they had sown the seeds from the Signal

Tree. The ground was very soggy, but the tiny seedlings were still there just about clinging on. "Thank goodness," whispered Lilly, "I'd had visions of coming back to a pond or a mud slick." She squeezed Robbie's arm, "shall we go in, I'm getting chilly."

As Robbie went about setting a fire in the stove, Lilly unpacked the food and checked the fridge. There wasn't much food in there but at least it seemed to have kept OK; the only thing that was off was the milk.

"I'm glad Oma gave us a hamper otherwise we would have had to survive on beans on toast for dinner."

"And what is wrong with beans on toast?" challenged Robbie in mock indignation which set them both off laughing. Lilly laughed until her sides ached. It was good to be able to relax, the slightly sombre mood at the farm had got to her more than she had realised.

"Do you mind sorting out some food while I go and check everything is okay upstairs?" asked Robbie.

"Sure, no problem. How long do you think it will take for the stove to be hot enough?"

"Oh, I wouldn't bother trying to use that for now. It will take ages. Just heat the pie and spuds up in the microwave, it might go a bit soggy but at least it will be hot."

A few minutes later Robbie returned with bundles of bedding. "We shall have to try to set this out by the fire to dry, it's got really damp upstairs. I think the gutter got damaged and some water has seeped into the wall. Might be best to sleep down here tonight."

"Ooh, that will be nice and cosy. A bit like an indoor camping adventure. Do you want to sit up at the table or shall we go the whole hog and have a picnic in front of the fire?"

"Picnic sounds good. I'll grab some cushions."

Replete after what felt like the best meal she'd had in ages Lilly sat back and rested her head in Robbie's lap. She closed her eyes and almost dozed off as he slowly stroked her hair. "It's good to have some time to ourselves," she murmured gently nuzzling his arm.

"You know, I've been thinking."

"Uhuh."

"Well, I was thinking about what you said earlier when you were telling us about your dream."

"Go on," replied Lilly turning her head to look up at him.

"You mentioned about returning things to the way they were before. I was just wondering if there was an alternative interpretation. What if we think more like a tree; think longer term. Maybe *how it was before* doesn't mean what you thought it meant; maybe it means in a state of balance with the world not some fixed and rigid snapshot in time."

"I'm not sure I follow quite what you mean?"

Robbie took a breath and tried to compose his thoughts. It was difficult to find the right words to describe such an abstract concept. "Okay, well let's think about it like this. How do we know exactly what the conditions were like so long ago and whether they were actually the best they could be? Also, we need to remember that the environment has changed a lot in the past seventy-five years, trying to artificially turn the clocks back might not be the best option for us or nature."

Seeing Lilly nod as if she was starting to get his point, he plunged on with a growing depth of passion. "What if we let nature decide what is best suited to the land and just let some of it go wild again rather than actively changing anything. If there is one thing I have learned over the past few years it's that we understand a lot less about the environment that we are a part of than we think we do."

Lilly sat up and grinned at him as he sat there breathless with excitement. Kissing him on the forehead she said, "Robbie, you are a genius! That is exactly it. Wow I've still got a lot to learn master tree guru."

"Oh, so now I'm a tree guru as well as a knight in shining armour. You'll have to be careful, or all of this grandeur will go to my head!"

"But seriously. I think it's a great idea. You have all that experience from the wilding project you worked on in Scotland, and it will mean we can get started quicker because we won't have to do as much if we are leaving it to nature to do all the work," jabbered Lilly her enthusiasm building again like a kid in sweet shop.

"It will mean less physical work, but we will need to plan things carefully and get a lot of expert advice…"

"But just imagine Robbie; a little piece of wilderness right on our doorstep!" she hugged him tightly.

"Yes, it could be pretty amazing couldn't it," he replied yawning.

Lying there wrapped in each other's arms beneath the slightly damp covers they both dozed off with dreams in their heads, dreams in their hearts, dreams of hope for a brighter future.

The return of power also marked a return to the veg shop. Lilly and Robbie joined Oma to take a look around and assess the situation. There was no significant damage to any of the buildings although it was difficult to navigate the carpark due to fallen branches and a collection of random debris which has been blown there from neighbouring properties. What they found inside presented more of an issue.

"This is no good. No good at all," sighed Oma as she covered her nose with her sleeve. "Half of the stock seems to have gone bad. I expected that for the perishables but even these greens have gone over."

"Some of it will be salvageable, I'm sure," replied Lilly trying to be optimistic. The stench of rotting cabbages was really quite unpleasant. "Let's go to the office and try to come up with a plan," she suggested, keen to get away from the smell.

Oma checked the phone but there was no dial tone. "Have you got any mobile signal?" she asked Lilly although she already knew what the answer would be. Lilly shook her head; although power was back it seemed that restoring lines of communication was going to take a bit longer.

"Oh, well I guess we are going to have to do things the old-fashioned way," continued Oma. "We are going to need help from the shop staff to go through the stock and see what can be salvaged. Can you both take care of that for me? The addresses are in the top drawer of the filing cabinet. I'll take a trip over to the wholesalers and see what they have available." In some ways she was glad of the distraction. She still had no idea how she was going to broach the subject of the lease being terminated and the imminent move. Maybe a drive over to Abingdon would give her time to think.

"Okay, sounds like a plan," agreed Robbie. "Shall we try to get everyone back here after lunch then?"

"Yes please. As many as you can find. If there are other

volunteers that would be good too. I have a feeling this is going to take while," said Oma as she headed out the door.

The list of employees was quite short and thankfully most of them lived in the village. "How shall we do this?" asked Lilly.

"Well, it's probably quicker if we split up. If I drop you over by the church, I'll head over to the far end of the village then we can make our way back here. Make sense?"

"Sure. As good a plan as any," agreed Lilly, giving his hand a squeeze. She always liked the feeling of certainty that Robbie conveyed. It helped her to stay calm and focused.

There were three employees to visit in her half of the village. The first two houses were quiet, and it appeared that no-one was home. Just as she was rounding the corner and heading towards the third house she bumped into Janet.

"Oh, Lilly. Hello. It's really nice to see you. How are things?" she asked.

"Oh, hi Janet. Not so bad, thank you," she replied trying to be optimistic, but Janet instantly saw through her. "Well actually things look a little tricky at the veg shop, a lot of the stock has been spoiled. We need to get in touch with the staff to see if they can come in to help out and agree a plan for getting things running again. It's all a bit of a mess and so far, I'm not having much luck tracking people down. Hopefully Matthew will be in," she added looking across at his house on the other side of the lane.

"Oh, that is a pity. I am sure I can gather you a few helping hands. We have some people helping out at the church community kitchen. I'm sure I'll be able to persuade them to come over to you after we are done with lunch."

"Thank you, Janet. You are a star!" Lilly beamed.

"Maybe we will be able to take some of the spoiled stock off your hands too. I'm sure some of it will be okay to use even if you wouldn't be allowed to sell it. It would be a shame to see usable produce go to waste especially now when supplies are short," added Janet. She was always one to make the best of a situation.

When Lilly got back to the shop, she was relieved to see that Robbie had been a little more successful than her in rousing some support. Matthew had promised he would be over later after he had finished patching up a leak in his roof. He'd told Lilly that the others on her list were probably busy helping Janet; Lilly really hoped that they could be persuaded to join them later. In the meantime, they set about dividing up the tasks of assessing the stock and setting stuff aside for disposal. At least now that the warehouse doors had all been opened the awful smell was starting to fade.

Janet was true to her word, and they were soon joined by more helpers. They had pretty much a full complement of the shop staff plus a few others from the church who were eager to spot items to rescue from the waste pile which was rapidly growing into a mountain far larger than they had anticipated. *We are going to need a bigger skip*, thought Lilly as she wheeled over yet another barrow load of slimy tomatoes.

It was mid-afternoon before Oma returned. Lilly and Robbie were just finishing a well-earned cup of tea when she drove up. The look on her face was anything but encouraging.

"Lilly dear. Can I borrow you for a few minutes please? Let's go to the office."

"Err. Okay yes of course." She turned and shrugged at Robbie who offered her an encouraging smile.

"I'll get on with checking the remains of the stock," he said as she turned to go.

When they reached the office, Oma let out a big sigh. "As you might have guessed it's not good news," she said slumping into her chair. "The wholesaler has very little stock and is not expecting much in the near future. It seems that the supply chains for the whole of Northern Europe are messed up. The storm was bigger than we realised. We could be in for a bit of a food shortage and prices are starting to rocket up already. Anyway, I have until tomorrow morning to decide whether I want the stuff I have reserved; mostly root veg and less perishable things. After that it's hard to tell what we will be able to get hold of..." her voice faded, and she put her head in her hands.

Lilly placed a hand on her shoulder to comfort her. "It will be okay. We'll find a way."

"I hope so Lilly. I hope so," Oma looked up at her with a glassy look in her eyes. "It's just so hard to know what the best things is to do. It feels like trying to pick your way across a muddy field. You think you know where you are going and then suddenly you are knee deep in mud with only one shoe."

"I do have some good news," offered Lilly. "We have managed to salvage about half the stock. Mostly the less perishable stuff like spuds and carrots. The staff have been great, and Janet managed to find us some extra helpers. We've nearly finished checking through everything so there's not too much left to do today. Robbie has been keeping track of it all and Janet will gladly take some of the less damaged stuff off our hands so we can reduce the cost of disposal by quite a bit."

"Oh, thank you Lilly. That will be a great help," Oma paused for a moment and then seemed to come to a decision.

"Can you get everyone together in about fifteen minutes? I was originally planning to tell everyone about the issue with the lease and our plans to move the shop, but I think it will be best to wait until next Monday; give ourselves some time to think a bit more over the weekend."

"Right, yes of course. I'll go and round up the troops." Lilly stopped at the door, "let's make it half an hour. I'll bring you a bite to eat and some tea in the meantime. You look like you need it."

"Thank you dear. Oh, and could you ask Robbie to pop in and show me the inventory please?"

"Yes of course." Lilly hurried off to find Robbie and grab a slice of cake for Oma before it was all gone.

"Oh, there you are," said Robbie poking his head round the kitchen door. I was wondering where you had got to. Is Oma, okay?"

"Yes and no. I'll let her explain it to you. She wants you to take her the inventory you've pulled together. I thought you could take these in as well while you're at it," replied Lilly as she handed him a tray with tea and cake. "I need to go and round everyone up for a meeting at half past," she added as he turned and headed over to the office.

The minutes seemed to tick by more and more slowly as Lilly waited for Oma to appear. It was gone half past and Robbie hadn't returned either.

"I thought I might find you here," came a voice from behind her. It was Margaret.

Lilly smiled for the first time that day. "Oh, Margaret, what a sight for sore eyes. How are you? I didn't expect to see you here."

"Oh, I'm fine dear. I was helping out at the kitchens this

morning, returning a favour to Janet. When I heard about the shop, I thought I would drop in and do my bit. I'm not sure I've been much help but, many hands make light work as they say," she smiled and patted Lilly's arm. "You look worried dear."

"Well, a little I suppose. Oma has had a hell of a time of it. I just hope she's okay. We agreed to have a meeting at half past but now it's nearly quarter to," Lilly felt the panic rising up inside her.

"Calm yourself dear. Robbie's with her, I'm sure she's okay. I expect she has just lost track of time."

Just then Oma and Robbie emerged from the office.

"Thank you." said Oma trying to get everyone's attention. "Thank you all for coming. I am so grateful for your help. It is much appreciated." She paused to look around the room and tried to smile. "These are challenging times for us all and we need to try to keep things going as best we can. My top priority at the moment is to ensure that we provide a service to our community and keep up the supply of fruit and vegetables, as far as we are able for as long as we are able." She paused again as the whole room let out a collective sigh. "We have some stock which we can sell, and I have managed to secure some more from the wholesalers which can be delivered on Monday so we should be able to open the shop then. After that it is not clear what the situation will be, so I suggest we feel our way along a day at a time." Everyone started to murmur, and Oma had to raise her voice to be heard. "I would like to ask the shop employees to stay behind for a moment as I have some other matters to discuss with you. Thank you."

The murmuring built in volume, transforming into a barrage of questions. Robbie decided to step in. "Please,

please! Everyone please calm yourselves. I am sure you have many questions, but it has been a long day for all of us and you will appreciate that we need more time to think and plan. We will do our best to keep you updated. Now as Breda has requested, if the shop employees can stay behind for a moment, it is probably best for everyone else to make their way home now. Thank you." He started to shepherd people out of the room.

Lilly noticed Margaret hovering at the door trying to get her attention. "Sorry love, I just wanted to grab you before I go. I have some news and some ideas which might be useful to share. Do you want to pop over at some point on Sunday?"

"Oh, well yes. Er what about if you come over to ours for lunch? I'm sure Oma won't mind, and we'd be glad to have your input. There is a lot to think about…"

"Okay, if, you're sure. I don't want to put you to any trouble dear."

"It will be a pleasure," Lilly smiled warmly. "I'll get Robbie to pick you up at midday on Sunday…" She was interrupted by Oma calling her over. As she turned to join the others, she couldn't help wondering what news Margaret had to share. They could all do with something good right now.

CHAPTER 22

MUPAKAT

S aturday had been a subdued affair. They all felt numbed by the events of recent days. Oma had taken to her bed; she had been so exhausted. The final conversation with the veg shop staff had left her feeling broken. Yet again she had felt unable to reveal the full picture to them, deferring the discussion to a later meeting which was now planned for Monday evening. She had used the excuse that she wanted everyone to be there. She hated herself for the white lie, honesty was core to who she was.

Lilly and Robbie were also feeling the after-effects of living on adrenaline since the storm had hit. Unlike Robbie, it was a familiar state of being for Lilly. Her years of learning to cope with the intense shifts on long haul flights had taught her that on the first day you just needed to accept the fatigue and rest. If you tried to fight it, you would end up feeling even more tired. Robbie had been disconcerted by the idea of doing nothing when there was so much to be done. He had tried to get on with planning for the shop move but had made little headway and the enticement of coffee, cake and a warm spot on the sofa next to Lilly had soon got the better of him.

Gramps had spent the day fretting, riling against imagined foes that cloaked him in despair. Repeatedly cursing them under his breath, "damned landlord, blasted weather, silly wholesaler," he muttered, begging them to leave his poor Breda alone. No amount of tea could bring him out of his black mood, and he was only placated when Oma finally made an appearance on Sunday morning.

She seemed remarkably well and greeted them with a smile as they sat around the kitchen table discussing plans for the day. Robbie was due to pick Margaret up late morning in time for lunch and was surprised when Oma suggested that he fetch her early. "No point in discussing everything twice," she commented, before setting about pouring more coffee. "Now who is going to help me prepare lunch?"

Gramps sat there gaping. Oma would never cease to amaze him. Even after all their years of marriage he could not fathom where she got her energy from. "No need to look like a frog catching flies," she said as she kissed him on the cheek. "Now why don't you make yourself useful and fetch me some potatoes from the pantry?"

"Right oh," he replied and shuffled off.

"Are you sure you're up to cooking Oma?" asked Lilly. "You should probably take things easy; you've had a hard few days…"

"It's okay dear. I like cooking, it helps me to relax, get my head straight. If I had to just sit there watching others, I think I would explode!" she smiled and patted Lilly's arm to re-assure her. "We can do it together. I'll let you and Gramps do the fetching and carrying. How's that?"

"Alright then," sighed Lilly. She knew there was no point in arguing and maybe Oma had a point, being busy would be a good distraction.

Margaret and Robbie arrived just as they were putting the pie in the oven. "Perfect timing," said Oma. "The pie will be ready in about forty minutes which gives us just enough time for a cup of tea and a chat."

"I'll put the kettle on," said Gramps. Making tea was the one thing he felt he could do better than anyone else. "You lot go through to the dining room; I'll bring the tea when its ready."

As they settled around the table Oma decided to get straight down to business. She could see that Margaret was curiously eyeing the notes and sketches stuck all over the brown paper planning board and she was keen to pre-empt any questions.

"I have done a lot of thinking over the past few days and there is one last thing I would like to share with everyone which I think will help us to consolidate our plan." She paused as Gramps came in and offered round cups of tea. "You all know we need to close the veg shop and we have started to make a plan to move it here. There are some near-term priorities which we will need to iron out and there are also some longer-term things which need more thought. It is one of these that I want to discuss now as it will put the rest of what we do into a certain context."

She paused again and looked at Lilly with a smile. "I have been reading more in *Nenek's* diaries…"

"*Nenek* was Oma's grandmother. She was the old lady in my dream," whispered Lilly to Margaret.

"…she talked a lot about working together as a community where everything is done on the basis of consensus. I would like to re-make the veg business into a cooperative and to name it *Mupakat* to celebrate my *Nenek* and the continuation of our ancestral relationship with the land albeit in a very different place. I believe the fundamental principles would be the same, agreeing what to grow, how to share out the harvest and employing some of the traditional regenerative farming methods such as inter cropping which we don't really use today. In addition to the current staff, I want to invite others from the community and neighbouring farmers to join." Oma took a sip of her tea, her hand shaking slightly with nervous anticipation.

Lilly's eyes were bright, and she reached out to squeeze Oma's hand. "That will be perfect. Just what *Nenek* wanted." Robbie and Gramps nodded enthusiastically. "Count me in!" they both said almost simultaneously which caused everyone to laugh.

"I think it is a marvellous idea," added Margaret. "Just the kind of shot in the arm that the village needs to bring everyone together after all the challenges we have faced this past year. Bravo to you!" She raised her teacup in a mock toast. "I have a little something to add into the mix, if I may?" she added looking to Oma.

"Please go on. Lilly mentioned you had some good news to share."

"Yes, yes, I do. Really rather exciting actually. I heard back from my publishers; they have agreed to give me an advance payment for the *Hakka Dreams* book. It's not a huge amount, just five thousand pounds but it's a start."

"That's fantastic news!" Lilly almost bounced out of her seat.

"I've decided that I want to invest my half in the veg shop, in *Mupakat*. If you'll let me of course."

"Well, that would be… that would be most generous. Are you sure?" asked Oma.

"Yes, absolutely. I'll let Lilly decide what she wants to do with her half," she said with a wink, amused that Lilly had only just remembered that they had agreed to split any royalty payments from the book between them.

"You mean I get a couple of thousand pounds?" gasped Lilly.

"Yes dear," chuckled Margaret.

Lilly turned to Robbie, "We could put it towards the rewilding project," she beamed.

"Well, we could. Perhaps it's best to decide which things are top priority and make sure they get investment first," he replied a little shyly. He wasn't sure what the others would make of the rewilding idea.

"Rewilding?" asked Gramps. "That sounds interesting…" He was interrupted by the cooker alarm which was loudly announcing that the pie would be ready.

"Let's discuss that over lunch," suggested Oma as she bustled back to the kitchen to see to the final preparations. Margaret went with her.

"I am happy to help with setting up the co-op. I can probably pull some strings with the local council and I'm sure I can rope in Janet to help too. She always has such good ideas of ways to raise funds…" wittered Margaret, her voice fading as the door close behind them.

"She loves to get stuck into organising things, this will be right up her street," observed Lilly, "I hope Oma knows what she is letting herself in for." She couldn't help chuckling as she and Robbie set about laying the table.

It was not until they had pretty much cleared their plates and Gramps was busy mopping up the last of his gravy that the topic of rewilding came up again. Robbie was a little hesitant.

"I don't really want to distract from the main business of moving the shop and setting up *Mupakat*. I see the rewilding idea as more of a side project really…" he looked at Lilly unsure of where to begin. She nodded encouragement. "Well, it comes from something Lilly said about the dream she had where *Nenek* spoke to her. There was a phrase she used which got me thinking. *Nenek* told us we should return the land to how it was before. Initially Lilly thought that meant to how it was before the war, but I have a different interpretation. I think *Nenek* was suggesting we return it to a state of balance with the world not to something fixed. That would have been the way it was when it was left to nature. So, the idea would be to let some of the land return to being wild. I don't have any detailed plans yet, but I have some experience from my time in Scotland and I know quite a lot of people who have been doing rewilding for a few years…" he trailed off. "As I say it's probably just a side project."

"I disagree," said Gramps.

Robbie looked shocked and was just about to launch into a defence when Gramps put his hand up and smiled. "I disagree that it's a side project. I think it's a fundamental part of what we are planning to do. If I have learned anything from listening to the teachings from *Nenek's* diaries, it's that we need to think longer term and think about how things are interconnected. We will need to make some choices which will reach far into the future, beyond our current generation. Choices about which land to use for growing, which to set aside for rewilding, as you call it, how to manage the irrigation, many, many things. I'm all for putting every idea on the table now and making sure we reach a consensus about what will be best for the land and the community."

Lilly was stunned, she had never seen Gramps speak with such passion about anything before. Oma smiled and patted her hand, "Now that is the William that I married," she said as she turned to Robbie. "I agree too. We should make the rewilding a part of the plan. It's about time we put nature back in charge!"

Robbie sat there beaming. "Anyone know the Indonesian word for rewilding?" he asked, half joking.

Business at the shop had been frantic all day. They had been confronted by a long queue snaking round the side of the building as they arrived to open up early on Monday morning. By lunch time pretty much all the existing stock had been sold and they were starting to make a significant dent in the new supplies from the wholesaler. As the day drew to a close Oma had started to realise that they would probably run out completely by the middle of Tuesday. She had never in all her years at the shop experienced such a deluge of customers. Despite many attempts she had been unable to reach the wholesaler by phone and had got tired of being put on hold for what seemed like an eternity each time.

Well, I guess that makes planning easier, she muttered as she sipped the last of her tea and got ready for the long awaited and much dreaded meeting.

"All set?" asked Lilly looking up from her desk.

"As ready as I will ever be, I suppose," she sighed. "Lets' get on with it."

The staff had all gathered in the now rather sparsely stocked storeroom. The vibrant chatter faded to a low whisper as Oma entered the room.

"Thank you all for staying. I know it has been an exceptionally busy day so I will try not to keep you long."

"The past week has been one of the strangest and most challenging that I think any of us have ever experienced. In addition to dealing with the aftermath of the storm I have also been burdened with a difficult decision. A decision which affects us all." Pausing for a moment Oma surveyed the room. "A little while ago I received notice from our landlord of his intention to sell the land on which our shop is sited. I delayed communicating this to you because I wanted to check the legality of the terms of notice. On the day the storm hit I received word that we will have to vacate the site by the end of December. I am sure you will appreciate..." Oma's words were drowned out by a rising murmur of discontent.

"Please let me finish, there will be plenty of time for discussion!" she glowered fiercely around the room waiting for silence. "Until now I have not felt able to share this with you. I thought it best to wait until I had a plan to share, and I am sure you will appreciate the many distractions we have had to deal with. So, what I would like to propose is that we relocate the shop to the farm and set it up as a new business, as a cooperative that you will all have a chance to join. Some of you will be able to help us with the move, others will not. What I can promise you is that I will support you all in the best way that I can during the interim period and will offer you all employment in the new business when we re-open in the new year."

Oma paused again, surprised at the stunned silence which greeted her announcement. "I realise this is a lot to take in and you will all have questions. Some I will be able to answer now others we will have to defer to later when we have had time to develop a more detailed plan. A plan which I hope you will all feel able to contribute to. I ask you please to raise your hand if you have something to say and I will take comments and questions one by one."

Much to Lilly's surprise the rest of the meeting proceeded in an orderly fashion with people taking their turn to speak and listening intently to the answers.

"She's rather good at this isn't she. Must me the schoolteacher in her," whispered Robbie, in quiet amazement.

"I'm just relieved that they all seem to be taking the news so well. I'm glad we waited; I think if Oma hadn't had a plan to share, we would have had a riot on our hands," sighed Lilly, suddenly feeling very tired. "Can we go now?"

Janet was in a pensive mood as she finished her discussion with Oma about some of the shop's now redundant chillers. She was pleased that they would be able to find them a new home at her community kitchen which was desperately in need of some cold storage. On her way across the carpark, she spotted Lilly perched on an old pallet at the entrance to one of the greenhouses, paused with a cup of coffee halfway to her mouth, staring into the distance.

"Hello Lilly," she said as she took a seat beside her.

"Oh, hello Janet," Lilly replied, a little surprised to see her there.

"I was just visiting Breda to talk about the chillers. Thought I'd join you for a moment. You look like you have been busy here," she added as she surveyed the sparse interior of the greenhouse. "How are the plans for moving the greenhouses shaping up?"

"Well, not so good actually."

"Oh, you looked like you were having a good chat with the engineer earlier. What's wrong?"

"What's right? Might be a better way of asking. He said that due to corrosion on most of the frames it won't be practical to dismantle them. The best we can do is save the glass and send the rest for recycling. I hadn't budgeted for buying new frames, so it looks like the plan for having greenhouses at the new site is dead in the water. We just don't have the money, Janet," she sobbed, suddenly overwhelmed by tears.

Janet rubbed her back gently, helping the tears to flow freely. She knew full well that letting all the emotions out was exactly what Lilly needed right now.

"When was the last time you had a break?" she asked after a few minutes.

Lilly looked at her blankly. "I don't remember but there is so much to do Janet. I don't think I can afford to. I want to keep finding the strength for Oma's sake, but I feel so empty right now…"

"Oh Lilly. Everyone needs a break sometimes. Its far better to take small breaks to keep your resilience topped up than to run yourself down to empty and then have to pick up the pieces." Janet patted Lilly's hand to reassure her. "You are no use to Oma if you can't think straight."

"I know you're right Janet but it's hard not to feel guilty when everyone else is so busy. I don't think it's fair on them if I take a whole day off."

"Well, what about your usual routine? What are the normal things you used to do every day, every week that you enjoyed? Are you still finding time to do those?"

"Not really. I usually go for a walk but, well with the weather as it has been I kind of got out of the habit. I used to go to visit my tree to help me get my thoughts straight but with everything that has happened, well I don't think I can face seeing her like that, all broken with her branches strewn across the path. We still haven't had the time to put her properly to rest..." Lilly's voice started to crack, and she had to fight back fresh tears.

"What about your painting? Have you been in the studio at all?" asked Janet trying to divert Lilly's attention away from the tender topic of the Signal Tree.

"Well, no. I'm not sure I could paint right now. I am supposed to be working on the illustrations for Margaret, for the Hakka Dreams book but..." she paused and looked up at Janet with a frown.

"But what?"

"I'm not sure where to begin I guess."

"Maybe there is something else you could start with instead. Are there any other things happening which you are excited about?"

"Hmm, I'm not sure. Robbie is super excited about the rewilding project. We spend hours discussing ideas." Lilly's eyes brightened a little.

"Okay, perhaps you can try to find a bit of time each day to paint about that then. Why not have a go tomorrow," suggested Janet. "I think it will do you the world of good," she added.

"I will try," Lilly promised. A spark of an idea for a rewilding picture was already starting to form in her mind. "Thank you, Janet!" she added giving her a big hug. "I feel much better already."

As Janet made her way home, she felt pleased about how the conversation with Lilly had gone and was hopeful that by starting to paint again Lilly would be able to recoup a little. The trauma of the Signal Tree was a little more troubling; it had the potential to do long term damage if not addressed soon. She was so proud of Lilly and the progress she had made over the past year; she didn't want it all to unravel again. *I shall have to speak to Robbie about the tree*, she thought.

A day or two later Lilly decided to take Janet's advice and spend some time in her studio. Shaking off a mild feeling of guilt she told herself it was perfectly allowed, after all it was Saturday. *But where to begin?* she thought to herself as she flitted restlessly from one spot to another like a butterfly in search of its favourite flower. She fiddled with trays of paints and rummaged through old canvasses, but nothing seemed to quite click. She flopped down on the stool feeling a little despondent. "It's all very well making time for my art, Janet, but I have no idea what to paint!" she muttered to herself. As her eyes settled on the tiny picture of poplar leaves and flowers, her lucky talisman that Robbie's aunt had painted, something else that Janet had said filtered back into her mind. She recalled that little spark of interest that had been ignited, "The rewilding project," she whispered to herself knowing immediately what she wanted to paint.

Lilly had become so wrapped up in her new project she could barely think of anything else. The rest of Saturday had disappeared in the blink of an eye and come Sunday morning she was itching to return to the studio. As soon as it was light enough, she dragged on warm clothes and headed out, coffee in hand, eager to pick up where she had left off. Sometime later she was roused from her thoughts by the sound of hooves clopping across the yard. Hooves belonging to several horses by the sound of it. "What on earth?" she muttered, but curiosity got the better of her and sliding off her stool she went to take a peek.

"Ah, there you are," said Robbie grinning from ear to ear. "Awesome, aren't they?" he added patting a huge cart horse and gesturing at the other three. "This one is called Robbie too," he chuckled. "Makes things a bit confusing."

"What are you doing with cart horses?" asked Lilly, thoroughly bemused.

"Ned here is helping us to move something heavy. You might want to come and watch," he replied as they started to make their way out onto the lane.

Lilly suddenly realised where they were headed and dashed inside to grab her coat and boots. Robbie had been talking about finding a way to move the fallen Signal Tree with Gramps last night at dinner. The problem was they couldn't get a tractor down the path and would need a considerable amount of manpower to move it in one piece even if they were able to use hand winches. The alternative was to cut it into small chunks, a solution which totally horrified Lilly. Gramps had suddenly started grinning and suggested that Robbie talk to his friend Ned who might be able to find a way of providing the necessary horsepower. At the time Lilly had not realised he literally meant *horse power*!

By the time Lilly caught up with the others she had worked herself into a frantic state. Allowing her imagination to get the better of her she had envisaged a scene of total destruction in which the Signal Tree, her tree, was being chopped into tiny pieces for use as firewood. She knew this to be irrational, Robbie had promised her that they would just clear away enough to restore the pathway; moving any cut branches into the undergrowth where they could rot away as nature intended. As she neared the stream, she saw that he had been true to his word. Much of the overstory still hung suspended in the arms of neighbouring trees. Just a small section had been cut away to allow access and they were now well on the way to fixing chains around the largest piece of the trunk which lay across the shattered remains of the bridge. Lilly slipped her arm into Robbie's as he stood watching.

"Fantastic, aren't they?" he said. "Nothing like good old-fashioned horsepower. They used to use horses all the time to help with forestry work. Still do in some places. I don't know why I didn't think of it before."

"So where do you want us to drag this magnificent specimen to?" asked Ned.

Robbie turned to Lilly, "where would be best do you think?"

Until now Lilly had not given it much thought. Where would be a fitting final resting place for this tree? In her heart she wanted it to be some kind of permanent memorial, a place to come to remember and to celebrate the unique connection she had made. She knew that in reality things never last for ever, and it would be far better to place it somewhere to rot down slowly, where it could return precious nutrients to the soil and nurture future generations of trees to come. She pointed to a shady spot beside the stream where it could slowly sink into the mud and become draped in tumbling weeds and blanketed with moss. "Over there will be just perfect."

Feeling a glow of emotion emanating from her heart and radiating towards the surrounding trees, Lilly knew this was a really special moment. She watched as the horses took up the slack, straining, snorting, steam rising from their backs. Between them they made short work of laying the Signal Tree to rest; nestled in the mossy bank, peaceful at last. Lilly laid a hand on the torn and twisted trunk, its wounds still raw from the storm, she closed her eyes. Although the feeling of surging energy was gone, she still felt a sense of connection to the past, to ancient memories passed on from old ma Hakka. There was something new as well. An altogether different quality, a gentle pulsing through the wood and the soil giving a feeling of deeper power and connection. Pausing for a moment she realised that it had been there all along hidden beneath the other layers of sensation, subtle, gentle like the beating of a mother's heart, as though the very earth beneath her feet was alive. She felt strangely content as Robbie roused her gently, placing his hand on her shoulder. "Thank you," she whispered, kissing him softly on the cheek, "I feel like I can move on now."

As they turned to leave, she stole one last look at the gaping hole in the bank of the brook where the tangle of roots lay exposed beneath the yawning gap in the now vacant canopy. She knew she would probably not return until the spring and things would no doubt be starting to look very different by then.

Walking arm in arm they followed the horses back towards the farm. "Do you think we should have some working horses on the farm?" she asked. Lilly didn't need to wait for an answer. Of course, Robbie wanted some, she could tell just by the look on his face. He was still grinning from ear to ear.

The days were becoming shorter as the slow march towards the winter solstice continued. The rough notes and sketches which had populated the brown paper planning board gradually transformed into new realities. Progress at the farm shop had maintained a steady pace and they were confident in being ready for the grand re-opening in early January. Oma had tried her best to keep the old site functioning for as long as possible and had been able to continue providing the local villagers with a sporadic supply of root vegetables and potatoes. It was a far cry from the luxury fare that they usually had on offer in the run up to Christmas, but it was greatly appreciated none the less.

Plans had been drawn up for the formation of the *Mupakat* Cooperative. Oma and Gramps had been pleasantly surprised by the level of interest in the village with Janet and other local councillors quickly lending their support. Winning over the neighbouring farmers would take longer but Gramps was confident in his powers of persuasion. The biggest challenge that they faced was raising the money. They had enough to get the new shop off the ground thanks to the generous donation from Margaret but the broader plans for the veg farm and greenhouses would need considerably more investment, not to mention Robbie's rewilding project.

So, it was to this end that one morning in early December Lilly found herself up to her neck in boxes. Boxes of books, boxes of ornaments, trinkets and nick-nacks of all descriptions. When she had volunteered to help Janet and Margaret sort through donations for the upcoming *Mupakat* fundraiser that they were organising she had not quite realised what she was getting into. *Oh, my word this is going to take for ever*, she thought, her back was already beginning to ache from bending over so much. She decided to focus on the books and found herself a little spot in the corner of the village hall where she could lay them out on the floor and try to arrange them into some kind of categorical order.

Her mind kept drifting back to her art studio, somewhere she would much rather be she decided. Having finished the piece inspired by rewilding she had, at last, felt able to contemplate the book illustrations. Margaret wanted more than just a cover, she also wanted title sheets to introduce each of the chapters; something relating to each of the key artefacts and characters from the chronicle of Hakka Dreams. She had quickly decided that her usual preferred medium of acrylic was not going to be suitable. Her early pen and ink sketches were good but didn't quite work, they didn't bring enough colour. As she sat there like an automaton sifting through nursery rhymes and children's books, not quite paying attention, musing over her sketches in her mind she suddenly came to a halt. In her hand was an old and tatty collection of *Winnie the Pooh* stories, the torn dust sheet sporting one of the original E. H. Shepard illustrations. She felt a knot of excitement in her stomach, the image she had held in her mind's eye, the one of Albert, was transformed from the drab pen and ink sketch to a simple rendering in watercolour with spots of green for his tunic and red for the blanket on his wooden cot. She realised that she could use watercolours to add primary accent colours to give warmth and depth to all of her pictures. *I think there are some watercolours in the box of his aunt's stuff that Robbie gave me, ooh I can't wait to try them out*, she whispered to herself. Setting aside the copy of Winnie the Pooh she hurried to complete the sorting of the remaining books, eager to get back to her art.

Lilly pretended that she had forgotten it was Robbie's birthday until the end of the day. He had been finishing the construction of the new shelving in the part of the barn which would be used as a storeroom and was just packing up for the evening. Having finished experimenting with watercolours in her studio Lilly decided to sneak in and surprise him.

"Happy Birthday!" she announced with a twinkling smile, and she presented him with a small parcel wrapped in brown paper. "You thought I had forgotten," she teased.

He unwrapped the package to find half a dozen muddy and slightly wrinkled potatoes. "Wonderful!" he said pretending to be pleased.

"I thought we could make some chips. You keep saying how much you have been missing good home-made chips so when I saw these, I set them aside for you."

Robbie didn't know quite what to say. She was right but it still wasn't quite the birthday treat he'd had in mind. Lilly started to laugh as she pulled out another slightly larger package from behind her back. "I also made you this," she grinned.

Inside the wrapping was a beautiful painting. Lilly had captured an early morning scene in which a couple stood hand in hand looking over a farm gate. The path ahead was bathed in rays of golden sunlight picking out the tumble of grasses and waist high foliage, small flecks of orange, yellow and pink petals peeking out between the leaves. At the bottom she had written an inscription *Wild Beginnings*. Robbie looked up, speechless.

Smiling, Lilly kissed him on the cheek and said, "shall we go and make those chips? I'm starving." All he could do was laugh.

CHAPTER 23
WILD BEGINNINGS

The New year greeted them all with a very wild beginning. The so-called *Beast from the East* had returned and with it came weeks of sub-zero temperatures and bitter Easterly winds. Physical progress with the *Mupakat* farm and rewilding projects had come to a halt, it was too cold to be outside for long and the ground was as hard as iron.

The shop had re-opened as planned, Oma was able to secure enough supplies of root vegetables and winter greens to keep up with demand although salad crops, which were normally imported from Southern Europe, were hard to come by. The unprecedented snows in Spain coupled with the storm damage to the hot houses of Holland meant that fresh tomatoes were now considered a luxury item. The question of setting up their own greenhouses on the farm became a pressing one and despite her earlier enthusiasm Lilly was a little hesitant about the idea of installing heating. She certainly didn't want to go back to the old oil-powered system that they had before, and heat pumps would be no better unless they could secure a supply of renewable electricity. No matter which way she looked at it the cost seemed prohibitive and despite several lengthy conversations with Gareth and his friend Alan, who installed low carbon heating systems, they had been unable to find a solution which she could afford. So, it came as quite a surprise when Gareth came charging into the shop one afternoon waving an envelope enthusiastically.

"Lilly, Lilly. There you are. I have some great news. I think we have found a way round the greenhouse problem!" he said thrusting the letter under her nose and continuing to explain with much excitement.

"Ooh, slow down Gareth," she replied. "I'm not following. Maybe start from the beginning?"

"Oh, right. Yes sorry," he paused and took a deep breath. "Okay so my mate Alan, well he got a call from some folks up at the university. They are working on a new experimental heat pump system for greenhouses and are looking for a site to test it out. They have a grant and everything so we wouldn't need to find much money, we'd just need to cover the cost of maintenance once it had been installed. It would be for a couple of years trial period and then we'd get to keep the system afterwards. It sounds amazing don't you think?" he said grinning from ear to ear.

"Almost sounds too good to be true," said Oma who had been listening in from where she was sitting in the back office.

"I'm sure it's kosher. Alan has worked with them before and not had any problems," added Gareth a little defensively.

"Okay. Sorry. I didn't mean to be rude love," replied Oma.

"As you say it does sound really promising. Why don't you let us have a look at the paperwork and then we can discuss it with the other *Mupakat* members as well?" suggested Lilly with barely disguised excitement.

"I agree, very sensible dear, maybe we should also run it past our solicitor," added Oma as she took the envelope from Gareth. "Thank you for this," she said smiling warmly and squeezing his elbow. "Forgive an old lady for being cynical."

"Of course," said Gareth blushing slightly. Oma had been his teacher once and still had the habit of making him feel like a little boy even though he now ran a successful plumbing business and was one of the *Mupakat* investors. "What would you like me to say to Alan?"

Oma and Lilly looked at each other. "Well, we have a *Mupakat* meeting next week. So, if we can get consensus and our solicitor does not raise any major concerns then I think we should arrange a meeting with him and his university colleagues to discuss next steps; maybe some time in early February?" suggested Oma.

"Right, okay then. I'll suggest that to him. Fab, really fab," beamed Gareth turning on his heel and whistling as he left the shop.

"I do hope it's as good as Gareth made out. We could do with a bit of good fortune for a change," said Lilly as she returned to re-stocking the shelves.

As it transpired, they very quickly gained consensus for moving forward with the plan. One of the other cooperative members had secured a potential collaboration with a community energy organisation that wanted to install solar panels on the farm buildings but would only be able to do so if *Mupakat's* energy demand was sufficiently high and able to justify the expense of installing the cabling and battery storage system. The heat pump project would certainly do that, so it was really a win-win from everyone's point of view. Lilly had been delighted that they were finally making some progress, at least with moving the veg farm forward.

For Robbie things had been proving to be far more challenging; very few people it seemed were willing to make a commitment to invest in the rewilding project and he was left with the daunting task of applying for government funding for the scheme. Late one evening after a long day discussing plans for the greenhouses with Alan and Gareth, Lilly returned home to find Robbie slumped over the dining room table with his head in his hands.

"You okay there love?" she asked, gently rubbing his back.

"Not really," he groaned. As he looked up at her she could see he had been crying. "I've been trying for hours to make sense of this bloody form. I've never been much good at this kind of thing. All the words just seem to merge together and dance on the page. I can't make sense of any of it. Why do they have to make things so complicated?" He rubbed his face in frustration.

Lilly looked down at the pages strewn across the table and was about to try to say something positive but thought better of it. Robbie probably needed to get it off his chest.

"I mean, look at this section here," he gestured and started reading aloud. "*Provide details of the Natural Capital Potential of the project*, what even is *Natural Capital Potential*?

I mean really! Why is the system so obsessed with having to put a financial value on everything? It disgusts me, how can I put a price on nature?" He started sobbing again and buried his face in Lilly's arms. "I'm not cut out for this Lilly; I'd far rather be in the woods any day; I know where I am in the woods."

Lilly stroked his hair gently. "It's okay love. You don't have to do this on your own. Remember we've got your rewilding friends and experts coming in a few days' time. They will be able to help us. They must have filled in loads of forms like this before."

"I guess you're right," he sighed.

"Now let's leave these for now. I'll fix us both a hot chocolate and we can snuggle up in front of the fire."

"Mmm, that will be nice. You can tell me all about your day," said Robbie trying to smile through exhausted eyes.

By the time Lilly returned from the kitchen he had dozed off on the sofa. She snuggled up next to him and sipped her chocolate. "I'm sorry I've not been here for you, my love. We'll do things together from now on, I promise," she whispered gently.

True to their ancestral legacy they had decided to convene the first meeting of the *Mupakat Council of Elders*, as Oma called it. Although it was more a *Council of Advisors* as they had no elders with the knowledge and experience that would be required to make informed judgements and decisions. In addition to the regular members of the *Mupakat* cooperative Lilly had invited a couple of representatives from farming organisations which supported nature friendly approaches and Robbie had invited some friends and colleagues from the various woodland and rewilding charities that he had worked with as well as some respected experts in areas such as water management, soil ecology and biodiversity. In the end there were so many people who wanted to get involved in the project that they had been forced to hire out the village hall to accommodate everyone.

The hall looked like a military campaign headquarters with a large, annotated map adorning one of the walls and a rough three-dimensional model of the farm site and neighbouring fields, which Gramps had taken great delight in constructing, taking pride of place in the centre of the room. True to the tradition of ancient councils, as described in *Nenek's* diaries, everyone was seated in a large circle. After a brief welcome from Oma, they each took it in turns to introduce themselves and explain what they hoped to contribute to the meeting. Then it was Robbie's turn to open the dialogue with a short summary of the project and what they were hoping to achieve. Lilly squeezed his hand as he got nervously to his feet.

"Huhum, welcome everyone." He paused a moment and scanned the room before taking a deep breath and unconsciously rubbing his damp palms down the seams of his trousers. "Okay, so err, so what I would like to do this morning is introduce the scope of the project in terms of the land and resources which we have at our disposal and then get your input on the initial ideas that we have in terms of their practicality and natural potential. I would like to note that we have a number of ongoing discussions with neighbouring landowners and farmers but for the time being

I want to focus on the land we have already secured. To help you with this we have prepared a map which is colour coded accordingly and a model which provides some additional details. Once I have concluded with my brief introduction, I suggest we have a break so you can familiarise yourselves with the map and model. Any questions?"

After a few murmurs and shakes of the head Robbie decide it was safe to continue. "Okay, good. So, currently we have around 500 acres of land which is owned directly by the *Mupakat* cooperative. This is highlighted in green on the map and is mainly pasture with brooks and a few copses of trees including a handful of Black Poplars. The fields directly around the farm are currently on lease to neighbouring farmers and committed for growing one final season of grain crops. The plan for at least two of these is to be converted for vegetable growing. The remaining land will be considered for rewilding or conversion to silvo-pasture with a small number of grazing animals, potentially deer, wild ponies or cattle, and perhaps some wild pigs. We also plan to plant a small grove of Black Poplar trees as part of a tree conservation project."

Again, Robbie paused to make sure everyone was following. "Right, so err, beyond the land owned by *Mupakat* there are a number of farms which could potentially contribute land to the rewilding scheme. Most of this is pasture and prone to flooding. This area is highlighted in orange on the map; beyond it you will see a red zone which is part of the neighbouring farms but only on a lease-hold basis as it has been sold to development companies." Robbie couldn't help but sigh and raise his eyebrows at this point. "So, if we include the green and amber land, we will have a total of 1800 acres available." This was met with a murmur of excitement around the circle.

"Okay, right, so finally, I would like to mention an aspect which provides us with a unique opportunity." Robbie paused to gesture at a thick red line which was drawn across the middle of the map. "This represents a road. A road which used to link two of the local villages but has been closed since the storm due to significant damage caused by flooding and is unlikely to be re-opened in the near future. I would like us to consider the possibility of converting the road to a path for active travel, either walking, cycling or horse riding with a much smaller bridge over the brook than would be required for cars. That way we could remove much of the fencing which currently divides the land and allow free roaming for the wildlife and grazing animals. I realise that this is quite an ambitious proposal, which will probably require a lot of negotiation with the local authorities but, I wanted to include it here so that we have the opportunity to discuss it now before we have firmed up on any of the plans as it would be harder to add in later." He held his breath waiting for a muttering of dissent but all he got was silence.

"Okay, well, err, I guess that completes the introduction then. Err, I suggest we break for coffee and let you familiarise yourselves with the map and model before we continue the discussion." As he sat down, he was greeted by an enthusiastic round of applause. "Well done!" whispered Lilly as she squeezed his knee.

After the break Oma explained how the remainder of the council session would work according to the rules for open dialogue as set out in *Nenek's* diary. Each person in turn would have the opportunity to provide their first impression of what they had heard from Robbie and make any suggestions they thought would be useful. She asked them to refrain from commenting on anything said by other members until everyone'd had the opportunity to contribute. After this first round Robbie would then have an opportunity to reflect on what had been said, answer any questions which had been raised and make some adjustments to the proposal for further consideration. The process would then be repeated with another round of comments from those who still felt they had something to contribute. Once no further ideas were forthcoming the council would be asked if they all agreed to move forward with what had been suggested, thus establishing consensus for the plan.

She looked across at Robbie and desperately hoped that his nerves would not get the better of him. In the end she need not have worried as the charity members and other experts were quite used to this kind of co-creation approach and quickly set a good example for others to follow. By the end of the morning, they had concluded several rounds of dialogue and Robbie was able to take advantage of the lunch break to pull together a summary of the revised plan based on all the notes that he and Lilly had scribbled down during the discussion. He was in awe of the way in which she was able to capture the essence of the suggestions so concisely.

"How do you do that?" he asked Lilly.

"Do what?"

"Your notes are so neat and to the point, whereas mine are rambling barely legible scribbles."

"Oh, practice, I guess. We used to have lots of briefings on rules and regulations at the airline, so I got used to taking notes. Without them I would have been hopeless."

"Well right now, without you, I would be hopeless," he replied, smiling gratefully.

"We're a team, remember. You did a great job out there; you are much better at thinking on your feet than I am," she grinned. "Now why don't you let me get this lot into some sort of order while you get us something to eat," she suggested.

Once everyone had eaten and had moved on to coffee Oma decided it was time to reconvene.

"Thank you everyone. If you could please take your seats, we will get going again," she boomed in true schoolteacher style.

"Good. Now, I will call on Robbie to present a brief summary of the revised plan."

Robbie stood again. This time feeling much more comfortable and certain of a good reception; after all, the plan he was now presenting belonged to the whole group not just to him.

"Thank you for your invaluable contributions this morning. We now have an outline plan which is split into three broad phases." He paused and smiled at Lilly, grateful for the excellent notes which she had crafted for him.

"Phase one will start this year, funding permitting, and will include planting of the Black Poplar grove and letting the pastures in the green area on the map go wild. We will also embark on a series of assessments of the green and amber areas including aspects such as soil quality; water management and drainage; the wild deer population and biodiversity in general." He paused to let everyone absorb what he had said.

"Phase two will start the following year and will be influenced by the outcome of the assessments carried out in phase one. Two of the remaining *Mupakat* owned fields, which are currently leased to other farms, will be set aside for veg growing and the remainder will be sown as wild meadow. A water management strategy for the whole land area including green and amber sections will be developed."

"And finally, in phase three, the fencing of the area will be adjusted to allow for the introduction of further livestock in addition to the native deer population. This may include wild pigs, ponies and potentially some cattle depending on what is considered appropriate based on the area of land available and whether the proposed road conversion has been approved."

"Alongside all of this we will develop a plan for public outreach and education to ensure that local people are informed and made to feel a part of the project." Robbie paused and then nodded at Oma.

"Thank you, Robbie. Now, before we continue, does anyone have any final comments or questions?" Clasping her hands tightly behind her back Oma desperately hoped that no-one would say anything to de-rail the process at this late stage. She gazed around the circle making eye contact with each member in turn, but her glance was only met with smiles and slight nods. "Right well, in that case then I will ask one final question. Based on this plan, are we all agreed?" Each council member took it in turns to stand and state their agreement. "We have consensus then," added Oma smiling with delight as a flutter of applause rippled around the room.

Later that afternoon Lilly found herself having a fascinating discussion about soil with Veronique who was a professor in soil ecology at a local research centre. The weather had turned warmer, and it felt like spring might finally make an appearance. Robbie had headed off with his colleagues from the tree charity and one of the experts on water management to review his planned site for the Black Poplar grove and Lilly had been left to entertain Veronique whom she initially found quite intimidating but quickly warmed to once she realised that they both shared a passion for painting. After showing Veronique her studio Lilly decided that it was nice enough to sit out and have tea in the garden.

"So, Lilly, have you decided which fields you would like to use for the vegetable growing?" asked Veronique as she gazed over the hedge at the vista of brown furrows which made up the surrounding arable land.

"Well, I am hoping that this neighbouring field will be suitable. It doesn't flood and it's nice and convenient."

"Have you had a chance to test the soil yet?"

"Yes, I did that the other week as soon as it thawed enough. Gramps helped me. We used one of those soil-test kits for pH and other elements. The nitrogen levels were really low, which is not surprising I suppose. I was thinking we should add some manure to help with that." Lilly paused to look at Veronique, but she couldn't tell from her expression what she was thinking. "Do you think that would make sense?" she asked.

Veronique smiled. "It is probably a good start. I would maybe suggest growing a green manure crop and maybe legumes such as peas or beans to boost the soil carbon and the nitrogen levels; adding too much manure can lead to nitrogen overload which may cause problems with water pollution," she replied but it was clear to Lilly that there was something more she wanted to say.

"Go on. Don't worry, I know I'm a total novice when it comes to farming. There is nothing you can say that would offend me."

"Okay. Thank you, Lilly. Well, you know, there is so much more to soil quality than just the chemical composition. That is something that most modern farmers seem to have forgotten. It's also about the level of organic matter and the soil ecology. The worms and other micro fauna that you can't see with the naked eye as well as all the fungi and micro-flora. Good quality, healthy soil is literally teeming with life. You will probably find that this soil is far from healthy and will take some time to regenerate fully."

"Oh, I see. Well perhaps I don't. I've never really looked if I'm honest."

"If you like I can take some soil samples and analyse them in my lab. You are welcome to come and visit to see for yourself. Once we know more, we can develop a plan for improving your soil as quickly as possible."

"Really, that would be amazing. Thank you!" Lilly beamed with excitement. "Are there any books you could recommend. I mean something simple that I would be able to understand. I would love to learn more."

Veronique chuckled, "Of course. Although I think you underestimate yourself. Now, shall we go and take a look?" she suggested.

It was not until late spring that Lilly found the time to sit down with Margaret and talk about the Hakka Dreams manuscript. As Margaret poured them both some tea Lilly couldn't help noticing the sad remains of the once grand conservatory now just a denuded skeleton of timber framework, the shattered glass long since disposed of.

"Will you get round to replacing the glass do you think?" she asked.

"What's that? Oh, the conservatory. Well maybe I'll get round to it at some point. To be honest I have been so busy with the book I've barely had time to give it any thought."

"You seem to have made lots of progress with it. I'm really sorry I've not had more time to run through it with you."

"Nonsense my dear. You've been busy with other things. I must say I was super impressed with the *Mupakat* meeting the other week. Your Sir Galahad is full of surprises isn't he. I would never have imagined he could have such a commanding presence. My experience of such meetings is that they are usually like trying to herd cats, everyone going off in their own direction. Yes, very impressive."

"Thank you, Margaret. I will be sure to tell him. He was absolutely petrified you know," beamed Lilly.

"Well, it didn't show, not from where I was sitting. And what a plan, so exciting. I can't wait to see how it all unfolds," grinned Margaret, her eyes bright with enthusiasm. "Now let's get down to it. What do you think of the Agnes chapter?"

Lilly flicked through the pages of the manuscript relating to Agnes and the hop farm whilst drinking her tea.

"Good. I like that you have added some context around the hop farming in the area and included this map that you found. You know it's fascinating really when you think about it. The evidence of those farms is still there even after more than a hundred years."

"Oh really. I had no idea."

"Yes, some of the walks I did last year were along the paths marked on your map and you could clearly see hop plants growing, cloaking the hedge rows which would have bordered the old hop gardens."

"Well, I never. You know I'm not sure I know what a hop plant looks like."

"Hmm, maybe I should add some details to my title picture for the Agnes chapter. A picture of a hop vine and flower perhaps."

"Good idea. I shall make a note of it," replied Margaret.

"It's interesting isn't it…" Lilly paused suddenly lost in thought.

"What is interesting?" prompted Margaret after a couple of minutes of silence.

"Oh, sorry. Yes, well I was thinking about what you said, not knowing what a hop plant looks like. Until last year I wouldn't have known either, but now somehow, I feel transformed. I see things, I mean really notice them and if I see something new, I am curious to find out what it is and how it fits in with everything else. I was never like that before. In the past if I had been dragged out for a walk, I would have been sullen and stubbornly immersed myself in music through my headphones, my eyes glued to the ground fearful of what I might step in. Occasionally I notice people doing similar things, either walking their dog or lagging behind a family group. I want to shake them, tell them to wake up look around, listen, see what they are missing, understand where they belong. I find it so frustrating you know. Now I have woken up I want everyone to do the same." She looked at Margaret her face glowing with passion. "You probably think I'm quite naïve," she added suddenly feeling rather embarrassed by her outburst.

"Not at all. It's wonderful to see you so fired up. You remind me of my former self, so much energy and conviction. So, what are you going to do about it?"

Lilly was a little thrown. She hadn't expected such a question. She had rather hoped Margaret would suggest something.

"Well, gosh. I'm not sure," she stammered. "I mean, I don't think just talking about it is enough. If I think about my old friend Fi or my former self for that matter. If someone had tried to lecture me on taking a greater interest in nature and why it was so important, I would have thought they were old fashioned, out of touch, some sort of tree-hugging hippy," she laughed. "Ironic really, now I am a tree-hugging hippy."

They both fell about laughing. "Okay, okay," said Margaret trying to regain her composure. "So just telling people probably won't work so what else could you do?"

"Hmm, well I guess showing them might work but then you run into the same problem. Getting city people to come out to the countryside would be really tough. They would have to want to come, how do you make them want to come?"

"How indeed?" said Margaret. She had a little twinkle in her eye, as though she had an answer, but she wanted Lilly to find it for herself. Lilly looked at her in frustration and was about to mutter something rude when something popped into her head.

"Oh!" she said and started laughing all over again. She remembered that she'd had this kind of conversation with Margaret before, when she had first started her painting. "A picture is worth a thousand words," she stammered as she tried to supress another fit of giggles. Breathing deeply, she managed to calm herself. "My art," she said. "My re-connection collection. I finished it ages ago and you keep nagging me about exhibiting it. I think now might be the right time to do that. We can link it in to the *Mupakat* project as part of the public outreach."

"Finally!" said Margaret. "You know for someone so smart you can be awfully dim sometimes," she added with a kind smile. "No offence intended of course."

"None taken," replied Lilly as she gave Margaret's hand a reassuring squeeze.

"So, if you will allow it, I can make arrangements with a friend of mine who works at the art centre. We should be able to get an exhibition slot in the next month or so. What do you say?"

"Wow, so soon. Er yes, gosh. Well, er, that would be amazing," replied Lilly feeling slightly abashed. She was not at all confident in her ability as an artist despite the favourable comments she had received from friends and family.

"Good, well that's settled then. More tea?" added Margaret as she shuffled off towards the kitchen.

CHAPTER 24

SHARED PERSPECTIVES

As the plan agreed at the *Mupakat* Council of Elders slowly unfolded, Lilly naturally fell into a new role of coordinating the public outreach and communications. Watching the neighbouring fields slowly transition from brown to green as they sported their final coats of barley and wheat, she resigned herself to the fact that the evolution of the veg farm depended on the results of the various soil and drainage surveys that Robbie was busily coordinating alongside his work with the tree charity. It would take time, many months of time, as they slowed the pace of their efforts to match the seasons and learned to think and act more like trees. So, she filled her days instead with preparations for the upcoming art exhibition that Margaret had arranged. Although her canvasses were complete there was still much to do in terms of setting the work into the context of the *Mupakat* project and providing some perspective on what she was trying to communicate with her paintings.

On the day before her exhibit was due to open, Lilly was busily putting the finishing touches to the display. It was getting late, and the art centre had long since closed to visitors, so she was taken by surprise when a voice piped up behind her.

"This yo work?"

"Er yes, yes, it is," replied Lilly as she turned to see a young woman standing there admiring her paintings.

"Mupakat, what is that?"

"It's er, it's Indonesian, it means consensus."

"Hmm, interesting. How you come to name it that?"

"It's a long story," sighed Lilly. "My mother's side of the family is from Indonesia originally, a long time ago."

"I'm originally from Ghana myself, well on my mama's side, my dad he from Essex originally," the young woman chuckled. She had a warm and friendly smile. "I'm Amelia by the way. Storyteller. I'm doing some sessions here this week," she added gesturing to the theatre entrance behind her.

"Lilly. I'm, well I'm not sure what I am exactly. As I said it's a long story," replied Lilly as they bumped fists. She still found it odd that no-one shook hands anymore.

"I like a good story. Yo got time for a drink? I think the café's still open."

Lilly surveyed the gallery. She had done all she could for now, the rest could wait until morning. "Sure, why not," she replied.

Over a cup of hot chocolate Lilly shared her story of the past year and half. From the shock of losing her job, her slow recovery at the farm, her painting and how that helped her to see things clearly and re-connect with the world around her, through to meeting Robbie and their plans for *Mupakat* and rewilding. She left out the details about her dreams as she felt that was way too personal to share with someone she had only just met. Amelia struggled to believe that Lilly had once been an airline steward.

"I can't believe you was a trolley dolly for an airline, lady with your talent, you well shot of that girl!" she exclaimed, chuckling.

Lilly would normally have been offended by the term *trolley dolly*, an airline stewards' job was way more involved than just pushing a drinks trolley up and down, but she liked Amelia and realised she meant no harm, it was just her way of speaking. "So, what about you. How did you come to be a storyteller?" she asked.

Amelia told her all about growing up in London. How her aunt was a drama teacher and had encouraged her to get into acting. How her mum and her nana had been keen on growing things; finding space in every nook, on every shelf for a pot of flowers or tub of herbs. Even growing tomatoes in window boxes suspended ten storeys up from her nana's flat.

"So, when I finished theatre school, I started helping Auntie with drama classes. She was into what she called *urban street theatre*. We used to go to all sorts of places and get the pupils to imagine stories about how the place came to be like that and what it might be like to live there. That sort of thing. A lot of it was based on the history of the buildings or the community but sometimes we would add in something about the plants or wildlife. Those were the bits I liked the most. Anyway, now I do that kind of story telling all over, specially with kids and youngsters trying to help them explore and understand the nature in the world around them even if it's in the middle of a city, there's always something." She looked up at Lilly and smiled. "I guess we is like two peas in a pod really, you with your art me with my stories, both trying to share the same thing from different perspectives, like."

"Yes, when you put it like that, I guess we are," replied Lilly. "If I get some time tomorrow maybe I could sit in on one of your story sessions, I'd love to find out more about it. If that's okay of course?"

"Yea, right, cool. Yea of course. An maybe I could visit your Mupakat farm, or whatever you call it. Not tomorrow obviously but maybe sometime soon? Shall I give you my mobile number so we can arrange something?"

"Sure. Great, that would be great. We would love to show you around."

"Cool. Well, I'll see you tomorrow then. Good luck with yo exhibition; I'm sure the punters will love it."

Much to Lilly's relief the exhibition had been a great success. Sitting round the kitchen table the following Sunday she recounted some of the highlights as they all tucked into a leisurely breakfast of bacon and scrambled eggs.

"The gallery was packed for pretty much the whole time. I couldn't believe it. Everyone was so complimentary, it was amazing," Lilly beamed. "And did you see the reviews in the local papers? When I spoke to the reporter from The Herald, I was so terrified I could hardly get my words out, he must have thought I was a right idiot, but he obviously liked my art so that's something," she continued between mouthfuls. "Oh, and did I tell you the most amazing bit? Just as I was packing up, this lady from a museum in Oxford came up to me. She wants me to give her a call about arranging to show some of my work at an exhibition they are doing on climate change and sustainability later in the year. How amazing is that!"

Oma chuckled. "Slow down dear. You'll give yourself indigestion!" she patted Lilly's hand. "I'm so pleased it went well. I knew it would."

"Thanks Oma. Yeah, I'm so relieved." Lilly turned to Robbie who was grinning at her with pride. "We had a lot of interest in the rewilding project too. Loads of people were asking about it, quite a few wanted to come and visit, and everyone kept asking whether we have a website. That's something I need to sort out asap I think."

"So, what did you say about visiting?" asked Gramps. "We're not set up for that yet and the last thing I want is for people to be tramping all over the farm," he added, looking worried.

"Oh, it's okay. I said we weren't accepting visitors yet," replied Lilly.

"That won't stop them," he muttered. It was clear that Gramps was not entirely comfortable with the public outreach side of things. He would be much happier if they could just get on with looking after the farm without any *outside interference* as he called it.

"Well now is probably a good time to discuss our options regarding visits. The sooner we can start offering something the easier it will be to avoid unwanted intrusions," suggested Robbie pragmatically.

Lilly nodded. They had been talking a bit about it over the past few weeks and she knew Robbie had some ideas to share.

"Okay, well I had some thoughts based on what I have seen at other rewilding projects. A lot of them offer guided tours of various types showcasing the farming methods and the local wildlife, that sort of thing. One thing which seems to be very popular is what they call intergenerational tours where they take families, children, parents, grandparents around together on a tractor-drawn wagon. Apparently, it's a real eye opener for the kids when their grandparents share stories of what nature was like back in their childhood days." He paused to see what Gramps and Oma made of the suggestion.

"Go on," said Oma, nodding with interest.

"Well, I thought we could do something like that but rather than using a tractor we could have a horse-drawn wagon. It would fit better with our sustainability goal and kids in particular love horses." He grinned at Lilly knowing that she would be amused; he loved the idea of using horses on the farm wherever possible.

"Well, that sounds very sensible," offered Gramps who slowly seemed to be warming to the idea of guided tours.

"I wonder…" said Lilly, an exciting idea had just popped into her head. "Did I tell you about Amelia, the lady I met at the art centre?"

"Yes, briefly. She does some sort of theatre, right?" replied Oma.

"That's right. She describes herself as a storyteller; she does what she called urban street theatre with young kids. Encouraging them to explore their surroundings and make up stories based on what they see. I watched one of her sessions it looked like a lot of fun. Anyway, she is really keen on getting kids from urban environments to take more of an interest in nature. She asked if she could visit us and maybe set up some sort of joint project. We could add something like that in alongside the other tours. What do you think?"

"Sounds like a brilliant idea," said Robbie.

"Okay. Well, I'll get started with drawing up a list of possible tours we could offer and then we can sit down and flesh out some of the details later. Everyone happy with that?" suggested Lilly, looking to Oma and Gramps for confirmation. They both smiled and nodded.

"Now, who wants more tea?" asked Gramps.

By the time Amelia had the chance to visit, summer was in full swing. Lilly had decided to take her out on a walk to enjoy the afternoon sunshine; after a day or so of rain she was glad to be outside. They were wading through grass which was now waist high at the edge of one of the fields that had been left to go wild.

"It is so different to last year when it had been heavily grazed by cattle. I can't believe how quickly everything has grown," commented Lilly. She was quite overwhelmed by the scents of the myriad wildflowers, many of which she would struggle to name and some that she had never seen before. They paused to watch a Cinnabar moth as it fluttered around the ragwort which was slowly creeping back into favour.

Amelia let out a startled yelp as she ducked to avoid a swallow whooshing past, making a last-minute alteration of its flight path skimming down the hedge searching for insects. "Blimey, I've never seen one so up close before!" she exclaimed with glee.

They both stood for a while taking in the amazing air display as a whole flock of swallows coursed up and down, skimming by just out of reach, bright flashes of red and blue flickering in the sun as they passed.

"I've never seen so many either; not this close up. Just the odd one or two as distant blurs. I remember how Gramps helped me to distinguish a swallow from a swift during one of our Hedge TV discussions," said Lilly.

"Hedge TV?" asked Amelia with a wry smile.

"Oh yes, sorry. It's what Gramps and I call it when we sit watching the birds in the hedge outside our sitting room," chuckled Lilly.

"Close your eyes and listen," she told Amelia. They both stood there, quiet and still in the moment, tuning in to the sounds around them, becoming more and more aware of the symphony of bird calls and insect voices building in the background. The incidental music of life, always playing, seldom heard.

"Wow, now that is really something!" whispered Amelia.

As they headed back towards the farm Lilly pointed out the various features of the landscape. The fields where they were hoping to grow vegetables. The brooks and meadow where Robbie was keen to start planting the Black Poplar grove.

"It's all very much a work in progress but hopefully you get the idea of what we are working towards."

"What about those over there?" asked Amelia pointing to the half-constructed greenhouses.

"Oh yes. That's the set of hot houses we are building so we can grow some of our own salad crops and tomatoes. They will be heated by some amazing new heat pump systems that are just being developed. Everything is going to be powered by the solar panels that we've just installed on the rooves of all the farm buildings."

"Amazing. Really amazing. You have so much goin on. I can't wait to see it when it's all finished."

"Well, it will be a few years yet," replied Lilly. "Why don't you come inside, and I'll show you the master plans and what we are thinking of putting together in terms of tours."

Oma joined them bringing in a tray of tea and some freshly made scones with jam.

"Amelia this is my Oma, Breda," said Lilly by way of introduction.

"Oh, yes. Pleased to meet you. Lilly told me all about you comin from Indonesia an that."

"Well sort of. It was actually my Oma, *Nenek*, whose family were originally from Indonesia. It's a distant part of our family heritage."

"Right, wow. Long time ago then. My family is from Ghana on my mother's side. That's where I get my interest in nature from, I guess. My nana always said it was important to keep up with the old traditions."

"Indeed, it is. Although I think it's increasingly hard to do that with people leading lives which are more and more separated from the land and nature. Lilly has been telling me about some of the exciting work you have been doing to help children from urban backgrounds re-connect with nature."

"That's right. It's somethin I started doin with my auntie. Using storytelling and street theatre to highlight the presence of wildlife everywhere and how we can easily make more space to enjoy it. Makin use of imagined realities and visioning to see how we can make a depleted space better. Doesn't matter whether its rural or urban, it's up to local kids to *see* for themselves. We've done a few projects in London so far and I've just started workin with a group in Oxford. Of course, it's always easier if we can show the kids how amazin nature can be so they are not limited by their own experiences. That's why I think it would be great if we can combine some of the work we do with what you are doin here. Lilly mentioned some tours you are planning to run. I'd love to hear more about that," explained Amelia.

They spent the rest of the afternoon together working through ideas on how they could adapt the tours and combine them with Lilly visiting the urban groups and sharing some of her artwork to educate and stimulate ideas as well. Lilly was really excited by the concept of combining both the rural and urban perspectives and had a number of new seeds for paintings she wanted to create along those lines. The next few weeks were going to be very busy indeed.

Autumn was rapidly approaching and there was one thing which Robbie had repeatedly been putting off dealing with. Since the road closure after the storm, he'd spent less and less time at his cottage and it was getting to the point where he was only dropping in once a week to check for mail and water the plants. He made the excuse to himself that he needed to keep the cottage on because of the tree nursery but in reality it would have been easy enough to move the saplings. No, the bigger issue was that he felt like he would be leaving his aunt behind. Now it was nearing the time when they were due to plant out the seedling trees and his final reason for staying would be gone. It left him feeling melancholy and subdued.

"What's up my love? You seem glum. I thought you would be excited to be finally planting out our Black Poplar seedlings?" enquired Lilly as they loaded the last of the small saplings into the trailer.

"Oh, I am. I am. It's not that," he replied "It's just that now I no longer have any excuses not to sell this place. I know we could do with the money and there is plenty of space for all my stuff at the farmhouse…" he paused feeling his throat tighten. He looked at Lilly fighting through glazed eyes. "It's just that. Well, I feel like I will be leaving her behind, you know," he sobbed.

"Oh sweetie. I know. Shhh. I know," she replied as she folded him into her arms and let him cry out his hot tears. In some ways he had never quite finished grieving for his aunt. "We'll have all of her pictures with us. They are where her memory lies," she whispered trying to console him.

He looked up sniffing and dried his eyes on his sleeve. "You're right I know, but it still feels hard. I guess it will just take time to adjust. I can't put it off for ever can I so it might as well be now as any other time," he said firmly, talking more to himself than to Lilly.

She smiled and smoothed his unruly hair. "That's better. Now we should probably get going with these or we'll run out of time to plant them before it gets dark."

The planting of the Black Poplar grove marked a significant point in their rewilding journey. In the end they had decided that the best location was in the field neighbouring the site where the Signal Tree had stood. They planted around a hundred trees all told, twenty of which were the saplings grown from the seeds that Robbie had gathered the previous year. They had carried out DNA analysis to ensure that they had a good mix of male and female trees and were hopeful that this would mark the start of a larger re-introduction project.

Several of Robbie's tree charity colleagues had gathered along with members of the *Mupakat* Council of Elders to celebrate the planting. Lilly had been sure to take lots of photos to include in a press release to add to the website which she was developing. The party continued late into the evening with much champagne being consumed both of the alcoholic and elderflower varieties. By the end, Robbie had been able to set aside his sadness and share in the joy of creating an important legacy. He knew his aunt would have approved.

Margaret had not been able to make it to the tree planting as her arthritis had flared up owing to the colder, damper weather. She had telephoned to congratulate Robbie and had asked Lilly if she wouldn't mind dropping by at the weekend as she had something she wanted to give her.

"So, what is all the mystery then?" she asked as Margaret ushered her in through the front door.

"All in good time my dear. All in good time. Now why don't you take a perch there and I'll finish making the coffee," said Margaret pointing to a seat by the kitchen counter.

Lilly sat and fidgeted as Margaret shuffled slowly about the kitchen. She was desperate to jump up and help but knowing how stubbornly independent Margaret was, she decided to stay put.

"Right then," said Margaret as she slid into the chair next to Lilly and proceeded to pour the coffee. "If you look under that box next to you, you'll find a little something special."

Lilly half expected to find a plate of biscuits but instead there was a carefully wrapped package about the size of a book. Picking it up she realised it was a book.

"Well go on then. Unwrap it." It was Margaret's turn to be impatient.

Lilly carefully prized off the tape at one end and slid the book out. It was a hardback book with a cover of black, green and gold. The title read *The Hakka Dreams – the great acceleration, an alternative perspective*. Her name in gold letters next to Margaret's.

She gasped. Running her fingers over the embossed image on the dust cover she couldn't help grinning; she was rather proud of the way she had managed to weave a golden thread entwining the dreamer and the chest within *old ma Hakkas* branches. The spine crackled as she opened the book and imbibed the heady smell of fresh print. Eyeing the slightly grainy off-white texture of the paper, she was pleased to see that the publisher had been true to their word and used recycled materials.

Quickly turning the pages, she scanned through to find her illustrations beautifully rendered in colour. Albert's bed with its red blanket, Agnes in her blue dress next to the oast house swathed in yellow-green hop flowers. Taking a moment to read a few words she realised what a fantastic job Margaret had done to create such a readily flowing and engaging narrative that captured the essence of the dreams so perfectly. "It's beautiful Margaret. Just beautiful. Thank you."

"No, thank you my dear. It has been such a pleasure. You know this book could not have happened without you," replied Margaret as she gently squeezed Lilly's hand. "It has changed me in so many ways. It has given me a much better sense of place and connection to my community than I ever had before. I have spent my life buried in books, telling other people's stories. I am glad to be a part of this unfolding story. Seeing you and Robbie grow and do new and amazing things, bringing everyone along with you…" She paused looking deep into Lilly's eyes. "I have to confess though, that I really struggled with the idea that the trees could be communicating with people, with you, through the medium of dreams. You seem to be able to tap into a deeper source of knowledge somehow. To be honest it still baffles me a bit…" she tailed off, completely lost for words.

"Thank you, thank you for believing in me. It felt really weird to me too, but deep-down in my gut I knew I had to listen, it felt so right; I couldn't have made sense of it all without your help. It has ended up being about so much more than I could have ever imagined. Who knows what future dreams will unfold, what stories will be told about the things we are doing now, together? All of us, you included, not just me and Robbie." Lilly beamed, tears of joy and gratitude streaming down her cheeks.

"Look at us. Such a pair of silly sausages," sniffed Margaret. "Now drink up. Your coffee's getting cold."

They took a few moments to sip their drinks and compose themselves.

"I gather the tree planting was a big success. Janet phoned me this morning to tell me all about it."

"Yes, it was. It felt so good to be planting those new little trees alongside their mother." Lilly paused suddenly feeling a little sad.

"You miss the Signal Tree don't you," said Margaret "Do you still go and visit her?"

"Not often. When we laid her to rest I kind of made my peace with her. I stop by now and again to say hello. I guess I'll have more of a reason to go now that we have the new saplings to look after. Robbie and I plan to go again next week to commemorate the anniversary of the storm. I can't believe that it's almost a year since she blew down."

"Yes, and what a year it has been," added Margaret.

The chill of an early frost still lingered in the shadows as Robbie and Lilly made their way across the stream to the place where the Signal Tree had played her enduring role as nature's sentinel. One year on from the storm it felt so different, so tranquil. Their clouded breath drifted gently on the faintest breeze, footsteps crunching on a crisp carpet of fallen leaves.

Lilly stood with her back to Robbie, her hand resting gently on the twisted log that once formed part of the Signal Tree's massive trunk. She could still just feel it, the gentle pulse of energy and if she closed her eyes and concentrated, she could hear the faint murmuring, *ool ma, ool ma hakka* as the ancient tree sighed in her sleep. She felt Robbie's hand pressing softly on her shoulder.

"At least she's not alone now," he said pointing to the newly planted grove of trees nestling in the corner of the field.

As Lilly looked across the brook something else caught her eye. It was a small shoot sprouting up from where the roots of the Signal Tree used to be, from a piece of windthrow that must have been shed during the storm. She gasped and pointed excitedly, "look, look there at that shoot. Signal hasn't left us after all!" She felt an overwhelming sense of gratitude to the tree, her tree and the longer-term tree's perspective that it had given her. "Let's hope that this new shoot and the saplings beside it will live to witness a better, kinder future than their mother had to bear," she whispered.

"To generation 8, may they all thrive!" said Robbie as if proposing a toast.

Lilly wrapped her arms around him and nuzzled in close to his neck, enjoying his musky warm scent. "Do you think perhaps we are ready to bring our own generation 8 into the world?" she asked coyly, smiling up at him.

His face broke into a broad grin. "Mmm hmm, perhaps," he whispered, gently resting his head on hers.

For now, at least, they were content to savour the moment. Safe in the knowledge that they were not alone, that the whole family of life would be there to share the journey with them, and maybe, if they learned to listen carefully, it would help to guide the way.

END NOTES

How did I come to write this book? I certainly didn't wake up one morning with the idea in my head.

It stems from a point in the first Covid-19 lockdown. I started taking daily walks for exercise and to stop myself from going crazy. I am fortunate to live in a rural village so there were plenty of nature filled routes to explore. Over time I realised that there were many different trees on my routes that I didn't recognise. I knew the common ones such as Birch, Sycamore, Rowan, Hazel, Oak, Cherry, Hawthorn etc. but others were new to me. I set myself the challenge of learning more trees and over a period of weeks I taught myself to identify most of those that I came across such as Whitebeam, Hornbeam, Field Maple. For some reason there was one particular tree that caught my eye. A huge, majestic

Black Poplar which, in winter, I would have probably mistaken for its close relative the Willow. When I read more about this tree, I found that it was quite rare. According to records there are probably only around 7000 such trees in the UK and less than a third of those are female trees. The fact that trees can be a single sex was new to me too; I had always thought that all trees bore both male and female flowers but in fact nature is far more complex than that. Searching locally, I was able to find eight Black Poplars along the paths that I walked and could see quite a few more along the edges of neighbouring fields. The tree I had found first was perhaps the largest and according to the book "The Black Poplar" by Fiona Cooper, it could be around 200 years old. One afternoon as I stood beneath this tree and surveyed the world around me, I got to wondering what changes the tree had seen over those 200 years, if only it could tell me somehow.

That got me to thinking – how could you write an account from the perspective of a tree? Had anyone done that before? One notable example was the comparatively recent novel "The Overstory" by Richard Powers. A powerful exploration of trees, their ecology and our relationship with them. The novel was built upon emerging scientific understanding of how trees propagate, communicate and survive in a wide variety of environments. Their symbiotic relationships and the way they nurture or compete with each other. It was influenced in part by an intriguing book "The Hidden Life of Trees" by Peter Wohlleben which gives a personal account of the author's lifelong learning about trees in his neighbouring forest in Bavaria.

My interest in trees coincided with a journey of re-discovery and re-connection that I had embarked upon. For much of my adult life I have used my intellect to study and rationalise the world around me. There is nothing wrong with that, but I had come to realise I was incomplete, something was missing. I had forgotten how I felt about things. If we are in the habit of breaking things down and reductively analysing them, we lose the beauty of the whole and we can miss the interconnected nature of things.

I was on a journey to re-learn how to feel, to really see things as they are, to get a full sense of them. So, when I thought about "my tree" I tried to imagine how it might sense the world around it. I have tried to capture this in the dream accounts. Although of course the dreams are an imperfect medium as humans always relate what they experience to similar previous experiences, we pattern match, and thus we anthropomorphise. If we think about pain, we relate it to a pain we felt before, if we think about joy, we do the same. Because different people have different patterns to match to, they interpret things in different ways. So even if two of us have the same experience, we will take different ideas about that experience away with us.

So why dreams? Most, if not all, of us dream. There are many ideas about why we dream and how we can interpret them. One I came across a few years ago was outlined in the book "Human Givens" by Joe Griffin and Ivan Tyrell. I had the misfortune to suffer a traumatic experience and had developed a high level of anxiety which eventually led to a break down. As part of my therapy, I was introduced to the idea that when we are anxious our "inner security guard" is on high alert, particularly at night when we are asleep. In this situation we tend to spend too much time in REM sleep dreaming, trying to make sense of things with an overactive mind and our brain becomes exhausted so we frequently wake in the early hours, and we often remember our dreams, at least momentarily. So, dreams felt like a suitable medium to use to "communicate" memories, in the case of our story, from the tree to our dreamers who have all suffered some form of trauma or anxiety and hence are susceptible to dreaming and likely to remember the dreams.

Okay so we have a tree, the story of which we want to tell, and we have dreams as a medium. But what is the story? My journey of re-connection was about learning to see/ feel better how we fit into the natural world around us, to understand how we can do that (or used to do that) in a more harmonious way with respect to all the life on our planet. So, it is a story about re-connection, but to understand how to re-connect we have to see first the disconnection. That is what the tree is telling us. How over the past 200 years (and more) humanity has become disconnected from the living planetary system. The tree can't tell us this directly, but we can get hints. This is what I have tried to portray in the "dream of dreams". Making sense of these "hints" is not a trivial exercise. It takes understanding of nature, geography, history, climate science etc., many disciplines which we traditionally choose to keep separate need to be combined to build the picture. It requires contributions from many people, people who see things in different ways, pattern match to different experiences, are capable of imagining things in words, pictures, shapes. A rich tapestry of imagining building the whole. When they each view it, just like when dreaming, they take different things from it. They build a rich, community view of the world and the possibilities that it holds.

So, if the story is about trees and dreams, about re-connection, why call it Generation 8? Again, this is a perspective thing. What is a generation? To humans a generation spans roughly 20-30 years, to a poplar tree it spans maybe 150-200 years. One generation of a tree spans approximately seven generations of humans so one tree experiences what seven sets of people might experience. That is the essence of the problem we face, our human centric view/experience is too myopic to see slow changes, the gradual erosion of baselines. The world around us has deteriorated so slowly that a single generation does not notice it and easily dismisses the recollections of our elders as faulty memory. Surely, we are making progress – look at all the new things we have done and how much they have improved our lives. This is what we tell ourselves. The tree has a different view and if we take time to pull together the pieces of the puzzle, we can see that a lot has changed in the past 200 hundred years and not all of it is good.

So why a Black Poplar tree and not another even longer-lived tree, the old English favourite the Oak perhaps? Well, there are two reasons. Firstly, time frame, the critical period of "most change" has been over the past 200 years since the industrial revolution, sometimes referred to as "the great acceleration". So, the lifespan of a single generation of poplar is a good fit. Secondly the Black Poplar is at risk of extinction. The male/female nature of these trees means that they rely on proximity to maintain a gene pool that is diverse enough to provide them with sufficient resilience to survive. Whilst they can propagate by shedding branches (so called windthrow that I allude to in the book), branches which can sometimes take root and grow into another, genetically identical, tree; this erodes their resilience over time so if they are too dependent on this, they will not survive longer term especially in such a changing environment as we see today. This is similar, in some ways, to the current situation for humans. If we don't change our path soon, we may force such a dramatic change to the environment that we don't have time to adapt despite having a large population and rich gene pool. The tree and human situations are perhaps a yin-yang view of extinction potential.

Why an airline steward as my main character? I don't know an enormous amount about working in the airline industry save what I have gleaned from my travels. In the past I travelled quite a lot on business; I have observed the crew going about their routine tasks, overheard some of their conversations, glimpsed what their lives might be like. If you asked me, did I set out with such a character as Lilly in mind when I had the idea for the book, I would say no. Somehow, she just evolved in my mind. Ideas fuelled by news stories about airline employees being laid off due to the pandemic, intertwined with my understanding of the impact that our modern jet set lifestyle is having on the environment. Flying is something that we take for granted, something we almost feel entitled to. We forget that package holidays and annual trips abroad are an invention of our generation, part of the great post war acceleration. Also, using an airline steward felt like a good metaphor for the scale and immediacy of the level of change that we need to make. For Lilly on her own it feels like an impossible task but with help from her family, friends and the community around her she is able to find a better way to be and a place where she belongs. She is a metaphor for hope and possibility.

Towards the end of the book, I focus more on community, a sense of place, of belonging. We often look to indigenous cultures to understand how to truly belong in the place that we live; something we seem to have forgotten somehow. We need to relearn how to live in cooperation with our community and our land – perhaps I should take more care with my words here and adjust this sentence – neither the community nor the land belong to us, we belong to them so rephrasing to "live in cooperation with the community to which we belong and the land in which it is placed" is probably a better way of saying it.

Many people refer to indigenous cultures, or first peoples, from North America or Australia as sources of inspiration. I think it is important to remember that we all stem from similar ancient cultures wherever we live, unfortunately most of them have become lost to us. So why did I choose the ancient Indonesian culture as my example? Not because it is more significant than others or has anything particularly different to tell us but more from a whimsical sense of connection that I gained from a good friend of mine who is descended from that culture and told me stories from her past.

It is maybe easier to imagine how to translate indigenous ways (as a surrogate for our lost ancestral ways) into modern life within small rural communities but how can we do that on a larger scale in a more urban environment where the disconnect from nature is even greater? Perhaps it is not so different, if the Covid pandemic has taught us one thing it is that we can cope better with challenges when we come together as a community, share our common skills and resources, look out for each other. Not forgetting that we are each, at the same time, powerful and vulnerable in our own ways.

So, this story is one of hope, hope in the face of enormous challenges, a shared hope stemming from renewed understanding. Regaining the deep knowledge of how to grow together, a knowledge that stretches beyond a human centric sphere to encompass all life, the whole planet and the intricate web of interactions that has been woven throughout time. We have a lot to learn but the answers are there if we dare to look and share what we see.

I chose rural Oxfordshire as the setting for the story because it is where I live, a place to which I am slowly learning how to belong. I will leave it to you to imagine the transformation of your place and how you can grow within it together with your community, creating a gentler, kinder place in which future generations can thrive.

In our story we cover all of these aspects, and we learn that humans need to re-connect with nature and they need to extend their world view not just to see better what surrounds them but to see and think longer term. To learn to think more like a tree and get that longer time perspective; to ask themselves, how might the things we are doing today affect the next generation, generation 8, and beyond to another seven generations hence (future generations of all things not just humans)? I am indebted to the authors of the books "The Good Ancestor" (Roman Krznaric), "#FutureGen" (Jane Davidson) and "Wilding" (Isabella Tree) for sharing their ideas on how we can go about putting this into practice.

ACKNOWLEDGEMENTS

Writing a novel presented me with a new and exciting challenge. Being able to break free from the rigid constraints of scientific writing and let my imagination run wild was at once refreshing and daunting. Without the help and encouragement from my family and friends I think the project would have stalled completely.

In particular, I am indebted to my husband Paul whose patience and enthusiasm have been boundless. To my daughter Katherine for her helpful suggestions and insight into the younger generation's perspective which have proved invaluable. To my daughter Lauren for her artistic inspiration. To my friends Jenny, Helen and Steve for kindly agreeing to read early versions of the manuscript and provide many useful suggestions for improvements. To

Fran for generously offering to copy-edit the manuscript and correct the many inconsistencies in grammar and punctuation. Thank you!

ABOUT THE AUTHOR

Heather Comina was born in 01971 (at 326ppm atmospheric CO_2). Her lifelong exploration of the world started with a childhood immersed in the science of the everyday, her formal education culminating in a doctorate in chemistry. She has spent much of her career engaged in the study of human disease seeking to develop new medicines. In 02018 (at 407ppm atmospheric CO_2) she woke up to the reality that our home is in peril and founded *Climate Concepts UK* with the aim of untangling complex ideas about the climate and biodiversity crisis and making them accessible to anyone. She is passionate about exploring ways of seeing the world through different lenses. *Generation 8* is her first novel.